Someone Like You

Other titles by this author

SOMEWHERE AND FOREVER

How was it, Robyn Thompson wondered, as she tentatively touched the back of her head where a very large lump was slowly rising, that a day out at Tombstone, Arizona on the anniversary of the gunfight at the OK corral had landed her in jail being given the third degree by a non-too-friendly marshal? Who, just as an aside, was absolutely drop-dead gorgeous—if it weren't for his damned fake moustache.

* * *

AND THEN I FOUND YOU

Being wet through and covered with mud was not a problem, Julia Wentworth decided, and neither was her inability to trace a long-dead relative, but the fact that she was dangling upside down, suspended by the back of her green Holofil jacket and in the process of being abducted by a lunatic wearing eighteenth-century fancy dress was definitely cause for concern.

Someone Like You

Kathryn A. Saynor

To order additional copies of this book, contact:
Xlibris Corporation
1-888-795-4274
www.Xlibris.com
Orders@Xlibris.com
37466

In memory of Karron Mazur, a dear friend who is sorely missed by those who knew her.

A big thank you to my pal Lydia who described her ideal hero perfectly and without reservation, and to her mother for gramatical correction and editing suggestions. Finally and not least, I am most grateful to Janet Burns, a long time and very much appreciated friend; without her knowledge of eighteenth century history I likely would have flunked.

ONE

Lydia McKenzie sucked a lungful of air, and with a final heave shoved her mountain bike to the top of the embankment. Far below, Thurston Reservoir gleamed like liquid bronze in the remaining soft red glow of an autumn sunset. It was beautiful.

Beautiful and lonely.

With a grunt, she wiped a sleeve across her eyes, determined not to cry. What was the point? It was over and done. The best thing to do was to get on with life—at least her sister said so. Lydia looked at her left hand and twisted the sparkling stone around her third finger. Had it really been two years? Two years of trust and intimacy all dashed so horribly. Had she really been so blind? The truth was yes, and, she told herself, bloody stupid. Sticking her finger in her mouth, she sucked hard and tugged, but the ring stuck fast. Grumbling, she climbed on her bike and glanced again at the body of water below. Perhaps if she were to dunk her hand in cold water, her finger would shrink and the ring would come off. Then she would fling it, just as far as it would go—out of sight and hopefully very soon out of mind.

Holding up a hand to shade her eyes, she considered the sun, now low in the sky. Darkness fell quickly at this time of year, and it would take a good twenty minutes to reach the water by way of the bike trail; straight down would be quicker. Assessing the almost vertical bank, Lydia geared herself up for a bumpy ride, noting the loose shale and jagged rocks that ran through a bank of prickly gorse. One foot still on the ground, she paused remembering for a moment the helmet and kneepads sitting in her sister's garage, then with a final doubtful glance at the precarious descent eased the bike over the edge. It was tedious and the going rough, but content in the knowledge that soon she'd make it down to the water's edge, remove the rather large diamond she wore, cast it as many miles as she was able and be back home in time for dinner, Lydia persevered. A patch of loose shale appeared unexpectedly. She braked hard to control the ensuing skid, and would have succeeded had it not been for a small rock, which flew exceedingly straight and fast—and hit her squarely between the eyes.

"Shit!"

She let go of the handlebars and flung a hand to her head as the bike careered wildly and began to slip. Hands tightly against her face, she hit the dirt somehow missing most of the sharp rocks, and started on a crazy downhill tumble, her bike bouncing along behind like a faithful hound.

How long she lay in the shrubbery without moving or without opening her eyes, Lydia didn't know, but she was cold and pretty well soaked through from the damp grass by the time she regained her senses. When at last she opened her eyes there was an unrelenting pain behind them, and her vision was far from clear. With a groan, she made three attempts before struggling to her feet.

"Bloody hell." She pressed a hand firmly against her head, and was grateful to encounter no bleeding. The rest of her hadn't been so lucky, and all four limbs bore an abundance of scratches and abrasions. She shuddered. Damn, but it was cold. Wrapping her arms about her body in an effort to insulate her skimpy spandex shirt, she dared a glance around, blinking at the pain as she opened her eyes wider. Something was different. Something had changed. She had reached the bottom of the hill but could neither see nor hear water, and there were an awful lot of trees in the vicinity. So many in fact that if she hadn't known better, Lydia would have sworn she was in a forest, but apart from recently planted conifers around the perimeter of the reservoir, all was open land, the deciduous trees having been cut back some years ago. She looked at her hands, first at her broken fingernails, then at her bloody, gravel encrusted palms, and then at the glittering rock still languishing on her finger. Was it a sign? Should she recant her decision to break with the dreadful Darwin? She looked at the ring again. "Well out of it, girl," she mumbled.

With a sigh, she studied the tangled heap of metal nearby. It was an expensive piece of machinery, more of an expense than it need have been, and one she'd fought hard with both her conscience, because of the cost, and her ex-fiancé because he most certainly wasn't going mountain biking and didn't see why she should either. The extravagance had obviously paid off, and upon closer inspection, there was very little real damage; the wheels were still round and the brakes worked. Lydia climbed painfully astride, then noting the crazy angle of the handlebars dismounted, fixed the front wheel between her knees and prepared to give the stem a good hefty twist. She stopped and cocked her head to a faint but audible sound.

Breathing—heavy breathing.

Without much thought, she dragged the bike over a slight grassy mound into a hollow, thick with dead leaves and providing a fair hiding place. She crouched low. It seemed like the sensible thing to do, after all, it was nearly dark, and if someone were skulking around and breathing like *that*, they were definitely up to no good. She held her breath and peered over the edge of the ditch.

A figure staggered into her still-hazy vision, stumbled, tried to rise then fell to the ground not ten feet from where she knelt. Lydia gasped and almost gagged as the man, suddenly aware of her presence, lifted his face and looked directly at her. Only one eye remained clearly visible amidst his blackened and swollen flesh, and he stared wildly as he tried to speak, spitting shreds of broken teeth amidst bloody pink foam. He stood, swayed once, and then dropped to his knees on an outstretched arm. Lydia knew there was no choice but to offer help, whatever the man's reasons for wandering around, he was obviously in need of it.

"Wait," she called and started from the pile of leaves. "Stay where you are and I'll go for an ambulance." Prevented from further discourse, as the man summoned all his remaining strength and heaved himself to his feet grasping at a nearby tree for support, she listened incredulously to his words.

"Get out of here," he gasped. "Go . . . whoever you are. No, wait!"

Lydia hesitated, finding his speech difficult to comprehend.

"Here . . . take this . . . quickly." He dug deep into the lining of his large heavy coat and pulled out a piece of paper. "Take this," he repeated and clutched at his throat. "I ain't about to make it."

She stepped forwards, reached towards the man, and took the paper then quickly stepped back as he lurched and fell once more to his knees. "Look, I'm going for help. Stay here, lie down, and stay quiet." There was little she could do except find the nearest telephone. "Just wait. I'll be back."

"No! Don't come back. Find Jack. That letter . . ." The man sucked in a short breath, accompanied by an ominous gurgle deep in his lungs. "Jack . . . Jack Palmer."

A shout rent the air, and another.

The man on the ground squinted as best he could through his one eye. "Get out . . . of here . . . now. They'll kill you. Hide . . ." He clutched his throat again and wheezed, "Jack Palmer."

Lydia needed no further bidding, and without more ado she scrambled back into the ditch just as three men appeared from the trees. Two carried large wooden clubs; the third swung a coil of thick rope in his hand.

She watched silently from her nest and froze when one of the men turned and looked in her direction. She waited, convinced he must have seen her, and released the breath she had been holding only when he returned his attention to his two companions. Horrified, she watched a merciless beating take place before her eyes. The man on the ground stood no chance against the men with clubs, and certain she was about to throw up, she turned away.

The man carrying the rope called the proceedings to a halt. "Take his coat. It has to be there," he snapped.

Lydia recovered herself, took a deep breath, and peeked again.

The men bearing clubs duly laid down their weapons and ripped the man's coat from him. They examined it thoroughly and threw it to the ground in disgust.

"Nuthin'," one of the men grumbled and kicked the helpless victim.

A malicious smile broadened the face of the man with the rope. "Just give us what we want, and we'll leave you be," he said with a sneer.

"Ain't . . . got . . . nothing," was the barely audible response.

The man began to twist the rope into knots until it formed a noose. Lydia gripped her hands tightly to her mouth knowing there was little she could do. She was no match for these men. But to let them kill a man in cold blood, how could she?

"One last chance. Tell us what you done with the letter an' we'll leave you be," the self-appointed hangman said, slipping the noose around his victim's neck.

"Aye, an' . . . kill me . . . anyway," the man whispered hoarsely.

From her vantage point, Lydia heard reference to the letter, the letter she had stuffed unceremoniously into a pocket inside her shorts. Perhaps if she were to give it to the men, they would go away. It might not be too late to save the man out there lying on the ground even severely injured as he already was.

A loud curse prevented her from deliberating the point further. The man on the ground, lifted by the noose around his neck, made no sound and fell back to the damp earth with a sickening thud.

"Dead, 'e is. Dead as a doornail," one of the men affirmed.

Dropping his rope, the would-be hangman uttered a vile oath and kicked the body hard. "Waste of time that were," he snarled. "His Lordship won't be happy we didn't get that letter. Best hide this." He kicked the body again. "See to it." He turned and swaggered off, leaving the other two to grouse and argue about how best they should dispose of the corpse.

Lydia began to tremble violently in the realisation that she had just witnessed a murder and was in possession of a letter that a number of people would likely kill to get their hands on. The fact she might die of hypothermia if she didn't find somewhere warm soon was equally alarming. She waited, and watched as the two men did a poor job of concealing the body. They seemed anxious to be on their way.

Darkness fell, and when a short while later she emerged from the leaves, a bare sliver of moonlight, partially obscured by a bank of clouds, cast an unearthly glow through the trees and was the only light to guide her. Quickly pulling her bike upright, she set about straightening the handlebars. That accomplished, Lydia looked around and began to push the machine through the trees.

"This isn't right," she mumbled, coming to a halt a short distance later. Hard as she might listen, there was no sound of water, and where an open landscape planted sparsely with pine trees should have met her blurry gaze, there grew thick deciduous forest.

A track appeared before her straining eyes, and as it looked well used, she climbed aboard and pedalled along it. The moonlight was becoming a little stronger, and Lydia felt a surge of relief at the obviously well-used trail stretching out before her, confident it would lead to civilization. Concluding she had suffered a concussion and wandered somewhere strange in a state of half consciousness, she began to feel better and had no doubt that everything else was just a bad dream. That man hadn't been murdered, and when she delved into her pocket for the letter, it wouldn't be there.

It had never happened.

She rode on for a couple of miles. Not a sound broke the silence save the squish of bike tyres in damp earth and the occasional screech of an owl from somewhere above. A sensation that all was not well grew with every revolution of the pedals, and Lydia stared into the darkness, thankful she had not come across anything else to add to the nightmare. Some way off in the distance, a faint light appeared.

A pub.

Thoughts of a blazing fire filled her mind. And if the thirty quid she had in her shorts would run to a room, she would stay the night and have a good long soak in a hot bath to ease the stinging wounds on her arms and legs. She pedalled faster spurred on by thoughts of warmth and comfort.

The lights came closer—much closer. In fact, they were moving towards her at an alarming rate accompanied by a great rumbling. Sensing unknown danger, she leapt from her bike and ran for the ditch. She would have made it if her knee hadn't given out, but suddenly she was helpless on the ground and staring upwards as a crazily swaying coach, pulled by four horses, bore down upon her.

"Whoa! Hold up, there," the driver shouted and hauled frantically on the reins.

The horses plunged to a snorting halt not four feet from where Lydia lay too amazed even to cry out.

"What the devil's the matter?" a man's angry voice demanded.

"Somebody in the road, Your Lordship."

"Well, drive around, man. Or over 'em if you have to. Just get me home."

"Aye, Your Lordship, just as soon as I can calm the horses," the man replied testily and continued to struggle with the team.

Lydia scrambled to her feet and addressed the coach driver. "Can you help me, please? If you could point me in the way of a pub, or a main road, or a telephone . . ." She waited, and when no reply seemed forthcoming said, "Or if you could give me a lift, I'd be grateful. I really need to get somewhere warm." She beamed hopefully at the driver who peered down at her in an unfriendly manner, his face barely lit by the pale flicker of a pair of coach lamps.

"Outa the way," he snarled and set his whip across the horses' backs.

"I . . . I really need some help, couldn't you . . ." Lydia staggered back as the lead horse responded and leapt forwards. "Well, thanks for nothing," she yelled above the din of clattering hooves and watched the coach draw past. A pale faced man stared out at her, and then they were gone.

She swore a couple of times and hobbled to where her bike lay, having no doubt that hypothermia was setting in, and she was experiencing hallucinations—very real ones. Slowly she climbed astride and continued along the darkened track. Barely able to coordinate hands and feet or think straight, she couldn't quite bring herself to believe there was another light ahead, and this one appeared to be stationary. As she approached, she became aware of a high stone wall rising up beside her. The light belonged to a gatehouse where all appeared to be locked and barred. Dismounting, she laid the bike on a grassy bank and walked to the gates. Only to find them also locked and bearing sharp spikes along their tops. In her feeble and befuddled state attempting to climb over was not an option.

"Hello, is anyone here? Hello." She walked to the small gatehouse and called again. "Anyone at home?" She rapped as smartly on the door as her damaged knuckles would allow. "I, I'm sorry to bother you, but I'm lost," she concluded, feeling helpless and a bit of a twit.

After what seemed like an age, a door creaked open a crack to partly reveal a man swinging a lantern above his head. "Who be ye?" he demanded. "Shoutin' about all hours o' the night?"

"Oh, thank goodness."

"I asks again, who be ye?" He thrust the lantern at Lydia.

"You . . . don't know me," she stuttered, "but I really need some help." The old man, his leathery face furrowed in puzzlement, said nothing but held the lantern higher and continued to stare. "I hurt myself when I fell, and . . . I . . . I'm freezing. Please," she finished, her final words barely a whisper. She stumbled forwards as her knee gave out.

"Steady then." The man placed the lantern on the ground. "Ye be in a right ol' state. Get ye self inside then."

"Th . . . thank you." She took the arm he offered and leaned heavily as he led her through the small door and into a dimly lit room where the remains of a fire glowed weakly in the grate.

The man looked her up and down a couple of times then released her arm. "Sit ye down over there." He nodded. "By the fire. I'll make it up a bit. Weren't expectin' visitors," he added before collecting his lantern and closing the door. Without another word, he disappeared from the room.

Lydia sank down on a hard wooden chair and dropped her head back against the wall with a great sigh. Something was well out of order. The strange clothing, the speech—and then there was the matter of a coach and four, not to mention a murder she had thought to be only a nightmare. She groaned and squeezed her pounding temples; it didn't alleviate her headache and seemed to make her teeth chatter more. She hoped her host had some painkillers.

The old man returned and built up the fire. Soon it was blazing in the grate, and he turned his attentions to Lydia. "So, what ye be doin' out there, dressed as ye are? I ain't never seen clothes like them afore," he said, eyeing her spandex shorts and shirt suspiciously. "Barely clothes at all if ye asks me."

Self-consciously she wrapped her arms around her body. "If you have a blanket, I'd appreciate it."

"Oh, aye." He moved to leave the room, turned and said, "Like summat to eat would ye?"

Lydia managed a smile. "Something hot to drink, perhaps?"

Some time later, warmed and less weary, Lydia faced the man in the strange clothing, and determined to have her answers. It seemed he was having similar thoughts.

"I ain't never seen nowt like it," he said, finally shaking his head. "Foreign are ye?"

"I'm not from around these parts, if that's what you mean," she replied carefully, hugging the blanket, scratchy as it was, around her and holding a pewter mug tightly in both hands, grateful for the warmth. "Thank you for the drink. What is it?"

The old man suppressed a smile. "Some 'erb stuff me wife shown me. Healin' tea she calls it, an' I adds a little drop o'summat." He winked.

Lydia offered a slight smile and looked around the room. "Where is your wife?"

"'Er sister be sick with another bairn. My wife be a bit o' a mother hen an' she be takin' care o' them."

"Oh, I'm sorry."

He shrugged. "Ah, she be 'avin' too many bairns, that one. This'll make her fourteenth an' four dead already." He shook his head.

"That's a lot of children," Lydia agreed.

"Aye, an' that bloody 'usband don' take no care neither."

Lydia said nothing, sensing the man didn't care for his brother-in-law. She sipped some more of the herbal brew and realised just how tired she was. "I'm sorry, I didn't introduce myself." She freed up a hand and held it out. "Lydia."

"Umm, well . . . I be right pleased to meet ye, Miss Lydia."
He didn't offer his own hand or his name.

Uncertain what to say next, Lydia sipped more of her drink.
Her bones were warming through nicely, but she ached all over;
what she wouldn't give to fall into a nice hot bath. Without
warning, she yawned, holding a hand firmly against her mouth
for a few seconds. "Well, I'm warmer now thank you, er Mr.?"

"I be Judd Sparks."

"Well, Mr. Sparks, if you could let me use your telephone,
I'd like to call my sister. She'll be worrying about me by now."
She offered a short laugh. "Probably called the police."

He looked puzzled. "Don't rightly understand what it be
ye needs, miss."

"I need to call my sister, please."

"Needs to write 'er a letter?"

"Look, I'll tell you what." Lydia thought carefully. A change
of tack was obviously called for. Some of the older population
in these Yorkshire villages were a little behind the times. "If
you'll point me in the direction of the nearest town or pub,
I'll be on my way." She made as though to move.

"Village be five mile away yonder. There be the Blue Bell,
but it ain't no place for ye."

"That's not so far." Inwardly she grimaced at the thoughts
of another five miles of cycling. Her scraped and bruised limbs
were beginning to complain loudly, and the pounding in her
head was relentless.

"Aye, I suppose it ain't, but like I says, it not be the place
for a . . . someone . . . like yeself, ye understands. But I can't
rightly offer ye a bed 'ere." He scratched his head thoughtfully.
"Aye, well, I can sleep out by the fire. Ye can have the bed.
No sense in goin' out there more tonight. All sorts o' ruffians
roamin' around."

Lydia was busy assessing the merits of a five-mile ride versus
spending the night with an aging stranger, who dressed funnily
and spoke even funnier, when there was an urgent banging
on the door. She looked up sharply, the blanket slipping from

her shoulders, and watched as Judd Sparks jumped to his feet as though expelled from a cannon.

"Who be ye?" He sidled close to the door and pressed his ear against the wood but didn't draw the bolt.

"Judd, man, open the door," a highly agitated male voice responded from the other side. "Damn it all, let me in."

Judd flashed a brief glance at his visitor and then flung back the bolts and threw the door wide. A tall, youngish man—his dark cloak wrapped around him, and wearing boots so long they came over his knees—staggered into the room and made as though to seat himself by the fire. He stopped short upon seeing the unfamiliar figure sitting there.

He stared.

Lydia stared right back—she just couldn't avoid it. He was the most incredible looking man she had ever set eyes on, and he was glaring at her as though she had two heads.

"Who the hell are you?" he demanded without preamble and spun on a booted heel. "Judd! What's going on?" He held a hand to his ribs as he spoke.

"Found 'er, sir, wandering around outside in the dark. Froze to the bone she were. An' she be all scratched up an' all, sir." He bobbed his head a couple of times.

The man in the long boots turned to face Lydia. "I'm not surprised dressed like that. Do you always wander around in your undergarments?"

"I . . . I . . ." She found all words deserted her, confronted as she was by this tall, dark-haired stranger, dressed like something from an old movie and being quite unaccountably unpleasant.

He studied her for a moment longer. "Well?" He continued to glare then groaned and again grasped his side. "Bring me a seat, Judd, man," he said through gritted teeth.

"Aye, sir." The man was away and back in a trice with a sturdy chair.

"Brandy. Do you have any?" The younger man dropped the hat he was carrying and kicked it to one side.

"Hmm . . . well, sir, I . . ."

"Come on, Judd, I know 'tis smuggled; just get me a drink. Rum will do if you've a mind for it." He leaned back in the chair and loosened his cloak, allowing it to drop to the floor. He seemed to have forgotten Lydia's presence and began to struggle out of his coat.

She watched as he struggled, certain he would snap her head off if she so much as offered to help.

"Help me with this," he said suddenly.

Lydia moved slowly from her side of the fire, dropping the blanket behind her.

He appeared to consider her for a moment then held out his arm. "Aye, help me off with this coat."

She felt his eyes sweep her appraisingly and was suddenly acutely aware of her scant garments.

"Ouch, careful."

"Sorry, but you need to keep still. This coat is so bloody stiff," Lydia complained, realising it was also wet.

"Aye, fashion demands it," he stated matter-of-factly, finally slipping his arm free of the deep red and gold embroidery.

Lydia gasped. His sleeve, his very baggy white linen shirt sleeve was soaked with blood. "You're bleeding!"

He looked directly into her face and for a second appeared to smile slightly. "Aye, 'tis usual after a piece of lead has travelled through the flesh."

"You were shot?" Her mind whirled, this was getting worse by the minute, and it was all too real.

"Can you bind it? Here." He ripped part of the sleeve away. "Judd," he called, "bring a knife and some water."

"Does it hurt a lot?" Lydia asked, unable to desist from staring at the blood-soaked sleeve.

He grinned. "I've had worse. I think I shall live. But come, tell me your name. I won't enquire into your business here—not yet"

"Lydia," she said hesitantly.

He nodded. "Pleased to make your acquaintance, Lydia."

She waited. It seemed the men around here accepted her introduction easily enough but were loath to admit their own identity. "And your name?"

He considered the question. "Luke. My name is Luke."

She nodded and tried not to stare at his slightly arrogant expression, his marvellously angled face, and his disarmingly light blue eyes.

At that moment, Judd entered carrying a bottle and a glass. "Found some brandy, an' a glass for ye, sir," he stated. "Ball still in?"

"Nay, straight through, thank the Lord. A good washing out will suffice."

Lydia took her seat again, pulled the blanket back around her shoulders, and watched Judd Sparks clean and bind the wound. She couldn't help but take stock of the adequate shoulders and well-formed biceps as the man called Luke extended his bare arm. She glanced at the cloak and at the three-cornered hat lying by the fireplace, and then at the man's long dark hair restrained behind his head and tied with a wide black bow.

"Needs to give over chasin' wenches, ye does," the old man grumbled. "Get ye into some right trouble one o' these days." He received nothing but a grunted response to his comment.

Lydia sensed her eyes widening. Suddenly the blue eyes weren't so attractive. Men, they were all the same.

Finally sinking back in his seat, glass of brandy in hand, Luke said, "So, to what do we owe the pleasure, mistress Lydia?"

"I got lost after I fell off my . . ."

"Your horse," he finished for her.

"Yes," she agreed vaguely.

He nodded. "It happens to us all from time to time."

"I was just about to be on my way when you arrived."

"I did offer for 'er to stay here, sir, but like there not be much room," Judd put in.

"It's all right, really, I'll just go." Thank you anyway." Lydia rose from her seat, dropping the blanket as she did so.

"Wait."

She halted as a strong hand closed around her wrist. "I really . . ."

"You shall not leave. 'Tis not safe for a woman to be abroad by herself at night. And where is your horse?" He released her wrist and held up a hand. "No matter, 'tis of little import." He stood. "Come, you shall stay up at the house tonight. You'll be safe there."

She looked from one man to the other. "The house?"

"My house." He turned to Judd. "They'll have given up the chase by now. You may go to your bed. I'll trouble you no more." He pulled on his hat and cloak then took up his coat and slung it carelessly over his arm.

Judd shook his head. "When'll 'e learn? Someone'll do for 'im one day."

Lydia saw Luke grin as though the whole thing were a huge joke. Someone had been chasing him, had shot him, and he was being blasé about the whole episode. And she was agreeing to go off to some house somewhere with him. Notwithstanding he was the most devastatingly handsome man she had ever occasioned to meet, she had little doubt he would be married with five kids and a soccer freak to boot—not to mention his womanizing habits.

"Well?" He stood by a door at the back of the room.

She nodded. "If you're sure it's all right." Doubt cast its shadow across her face, and she knew it.

"Don't trust me?" His blue eyes mocked her. "Fear not, mistress. I'll do you no harm."

"I didn't think for one minute you would," she lied and turned to address the old man. "Thank you."

Judd accepted her thanks and thrust the blanket at her. "It be raw out there."

"Aye, you'll need something." Luke took the blanket, and before Lydia could make any comment placed it around her person.

She was instantly immobilized by two strong hands and the humorous light blue gaze of a stranger. Try as she might, indignation wouldn't come, and she found instead that she wanted to laugh. She turned away. In the morning, she could find out more about her current situation, and everything would no doubt become clear.

"Take my arm," Luke instructed. "'Tis nigh on two miles."

Seemingly without thought, Lydia looped her arm through his and stepped out into the cold dark night. She was glad of the blanket as they walked, and of the arm that held her own securely. She had held other men's arms, but this time she felt unusually secure, and delightful warm ripples tingled through her flesh. Glancing up once, she found him looking at her, and unable to summon the audacity to stare into his light eyes, she cast her glance into the darkness and allowed him to propel her along through the night towards what she hoped would be a hot bath and a warm bed—wherever she happened to be.

TWO

The house turned out to be much grander than Lydia had imagined it would be, and she was still staring, open mouthed, as Luke led her around to a side door.

"No need to wake the servants."

"No," she said and shook her head then nodded it in some fashion of agreement quite befuddled by the turn of events and the stranger by her side.

"You really are frozen. You're shivering." Luke frowned and pushed open the heavy door allowing her to pass in front of him. "A guest room is always prepared. I'll get a fire going for you, don't worry."

"You don't have to go to all this trouble, you know," Lydia whispered through chattering teeth, and sensing vaguely that her hand was again, held by her companion.

"I know," he replied. "And I also know that if I want to find out just what you're doing here and who you really are, I need to keep you alive. At least 'til the morning."

"I . . ." She pulled from his grasp.

"I was merely jesting. Follow me." He turned and led the way along several dim hallways, lit only by flickering candles that burned weakly in their sconces, before turning and ascending a great flight of stairs, which spiralled once before opening into a wide corridor.

Lydia knew she had to be dreaming and desperately hoped she would wake up soon, even though it would mean leaving this super-handsome man behind in the realms of the nonexistent. But wasn't that what dreams were all about—perfection, the product of one's own mind—things that were too good to be true?

"Are you all right?"

"Y . . . yes." She shivered violently. "Really, I'm fine."

"No, you're not. In you go." He opened a door and pushed her inside. "Climb into bed as you are." He walked to a corner of the room and tugged on a bellpull several times. "You need more than just a fire," he said, beginning to pile coal and woodchips into the grate.

"W . . . what do you mean?" She sat down on the bed and slipped off her cycling shoes.

"I mean," he said, not turning to face her, "that you need some hot food inside you, and a soak in hot water likely wouldn't go amiss either. What say you?"

"I . . . I," she chattered, "would like a bath, thank you."

"I shall see to it, and then as the hour is late, I'll not trouble you again until morning."

Lydia took a good look at him—at the way he dressed. "You dress funny."

"I might say the same about you," he countered. "Not many women go running around in their under garments—at least not respectable women." He waited, fully expecting an indignant response. He was disappointed.

"I'm too tired right now to defend the issue of my virtue." She yawned. "I'd much rather get warm and go to sleep so I can wake up from this crazy dream." She looked one more time at the cloak he wore, the leather breeches, the thigh boots, and at the embroidered coat that he flung unceremoniously over a chair back. Her eyes fixed once more on the man. He was in good shape by the looks of it, and she had already seen the lean muscles of at least one arm and shoulder exposed. Trim, definitely a bit of an athlete. That he wore his dark hair long and tied back was unusual but not too out of the ordinary, and she had no opinion of it, except for envy. Her own fair locks seemed barely to reach beyond shoulder length before becoming so unruly that she tired of the daily maintenance and had them cropped. She had longed for silken tresses all through her teens but had developed a busy outdoor lifestyle that left little time for the niceties of the beauty parlour. "Just one question before you go."

"What is it?" He turned and gasped slightly at the movement. Sensing she was about to comment he said, "My ribs. Fell off my horse. Blasted animal reared."

"Oh, I hope you'll be okay. But anyway, I wanted to ask why you wear those clothes, I mean really."

"I prefer to wear a cloak instead of a surtout for riding," he said and frowned slightly.

"But I mean the breeches and the long boots." She realised he was frowning more.

Luke shrugged. "Your clothing is, in my humble opinion, far stranger than mine." He walked over to where she sat curled in the thick covers of the bed. "With your permission." He reached out a hand and pulled away a corner of the bed covers then rolled the short sleeve of her shirt between his thumb and forefinger. "Nay, never have I seen or felt anything of the like of this stuff. What is it, and where do you have it made?"

She wished he hadn't touched her; it almost made her forget what he was like—all that chasing women or whatever reason he'd been shot. She shivered. "It's called spandex, and you needn't pretend you don't know anything about it. All this has to stop sometime you know. I will wake up. I know I will."

He began to smile and then slowly shook his head. "From what, may I ask, do you wish to awake?"

"You, all this. Murder—everything."

"Murder?" He looked at her with renewed interest.

Lydia hesitated. What if this guy had something to do with it? What if she didn't wake up? "Oh, I meant you were nearly murdered. That's what I meant."

"I see. Well, you need rest."

There was a tap at the door.

"Come."

"Milord?"

"This lady is frozen to the bone. She needs hot broth, a glass of brandy, likely a clean shift, and have a tub brought in with plenty of hot water. That's all."

The man bobbed his head and left.

Lydia watched, amazed at the ease with which Luke issued orders, and at the other man's total acceptance of them. "Milord?" she said quietly.

"I need to get rid of this damnable cloak," he muttered and turned his blue eyes on her. "Wait a moment; I'll fetch brandy from my bedchamber." He strode from the room without another word.

He returned holding a decanter and two glasses even before Lydia had time to consider what he had said. She watched, with ill-condealed admiration, as he moved across the room; his stride was long, unhurried.

"Come and sit nearer the fire there's a good blaze. Bring the bedcovers with you."

Never minding he had about given her an order, Lydia found herself doing just that. She gathered the coverlet and struggled across the room to a chair by the fire.

"Here," Luke said, handing her a glass of liquor. "I'll return presently. 'Twill do little for my reputation to be seen with a gunshot wound." He looked down at the blood seeping through the dressing on his arm. "I need to re-wrap this and change my shirt and waistcoat," he added when Lydia gave him a vaguely puzzled look.

His reputation? Was he concerned about being caught in the act, or was he afraid of further consequences?

The fire blazed comfortingly. Lydia sank deep into her chair and sipped sparingly at the brandy, a drink she had never tried before, and although she wasn't overly thrilled with the taste, it was warming. She placed the glass on the hearth. Warming as the drink might be, she needed to keep a clear head. There were an awful lot of strange people around and some unnerving things going on. She returned to her earlier conclusion, that she must have suffered a concussion, and this was some part of her inner mind playing tricks. But the fire, and the warmth it afforded were real enough, as was the brandy and, of course, Luke whatever-his-name was—now he really was too good to be real.

The door opened and a well-built woman bustled in carrying a tray.

"I brought broth, miss, like the master ordered, an' some brandy, but it looks like you already got some. Still a little more won't do no harm. Just be sure an' keep your wits about you," she added with a nod of her head and a toothy grin. "Knows what I mean. Bath'll be brought up soon." She stood back after placing the tray on a small table. "I brought some nice roast bird, and some apple pie, in case you be a bit more peckish after the broth."

"Mmm, thank you," Lydia acknowledged, still wondering at the reason she was supposed to keep her wits about her. Was she about to be molested? Ravished? Quite frankly she was almost too tired to care. In any case if the worst came to the worst she would pretend it was the dreadful Darwin and just fall asleep.

"Thank you. You may leave us now." Luke strode into the room wearing a clean white shirt under a brown and gold brocade waistcoat that hung open about well defined silk-clad thighs. "Ah, good, I was hoping there would be more than broth. I could manage a bite myself—of the pie," he added noncommittally, nevertheless, allowing the faint trace of a smile to grace the corners of his mouth.

Lydia looked at him; her glass stopped at her lips. He looked better than ever. *Devastating* was a word which came to mind. Well, not only was he handsome, he had a sense of humour. She was definitely dreaming. But how long could a dream go on? "What's the date?" she asked suddenly.

"The date?" He held a small fork and prepared to attack the pie. "'Tis the tenth day of October. Why do you ask?"

Well, at least her concussion hadn't addled her brains too much. The date was correct as she remembered it. So it's . . . Tuesday."

He stopped her mid sentence. "Nay, 'tis Thursday. Seems you took a knock on the head when you fell from your horse." He grinned. "Eat, now; no need to worry what day it is."

"But I am worried," Lydia said, putting her drink down on the table. "You just told me it's Thursday, and I know it was Tuesday when I fell off my, er, my horse." She suddenly remembered her bike lying in the grass by the gatehouse; what if someone stole it?"

Luke seemed genuinely concerned. "Then it appears you have been wandering around by yourself for a day or so. No wonder you look as you do." He hesitated for a moment then asked, "Were you, begging your pardon for broaching a sensitive subject, but were you perhaps set upon?"

"What do you mean?"

"I mean were you the victim of a violation? I dislike being so blunt but I . . ."

Lydia shook her head. "No, nothing like that."

"Well, I thank God for it, but where have you sheltered since you lost your horse?"

"I don't know," she said slowly. "Like I told you, I'm sure it was Tuesday, and now you tell me we're in Thursday, so all I can conclude is that I had a knock on the head and I've got a concussion."

"I see. You say you name is Lydia, if I may say, an unusual name. 'Tis one I've not heard around these parts. Are you from this county?"

"If this is Yorkshire, then yes, I am."

"Aye, indeed it is. Your family name, what is it?"

Lydia took hold of the bowl of broth and began to spoon the tasty contents into her mouth, pausing just long enough to answer, "McKenzie."

"Ah, a Scot. 'Twould be the best thing for England to have an alliance with Scotland; 'tis long overdue."

"It was," she agreed, then added, "I mean it is?"

"Certainly it is. Ah, the idiocy of this constant warring with our neighbours when we have the whole of Spain and, of course, the French to rely on for our sport."

She looked at him goggle eyed. "What do you mean, about relying on the French?"

"War with France is ever near the surface. They have themselves forged a close relationship with the bonnie Scots. Remember, as you must, or perhaps you were a little too young . . ."

"I'm thirty," she interjected.

"Then you likely do remember, the Fifteen."

Puzzled, she swallowed a mouthful of broth and said, "What was the Fifteen for what it's worth? The only thing I can think of is the Old Pretender in 1715, and he didn't do too well, as I recall."

"That is exactly what I'm talking about," Luke said with a smile.

It was a smile that would have floored her had she been standing. So would the fact that he expected her to remember something that had happened nearly three hundred years ago. She forced a return grin and said, "I've heard of it, but of course, I don't remember it."

"I was merely citing the relationship between Scotland and France."

"But that's all long gone, and if you're talking about the Scots, I should have thought the massacre at Culloden is a more prominent episode in history," she went on, oblivious to the changing expression on the face of the man sitting across from her. "I mean everyone's heard of *that*."

"What," he said quietly, "do you mean? What massacre is this you speak of?"

"You know, 1746, the Duke of Cumberland versus Charles Edward Stuart and all that stuff. Bonnie Prince Charlie." She looked up innocently from her broth and was about to reach for her glass when he spoke.

"What are you?"

"Pardon?"

"I repeat myself. What are you? Whence come you?" His blue eyes suddenly blazed.

"I've no idea what you mean." Inside, Lydia felt rather less brave than she hoped she sounded. What was he so upset about?

"You sit there and calmly tell me of things that are yet to come and expect me not to question?"

"I'm not sure where all this is leading, but I have a lousy suspicion I'm about to find out."

"Are you a witch? Or a spy? Nay, if you were, you wouldn't admit to it." Luke wanted to look deep into her eyes to know if she were lying, but he couldn't bring himself to do it, whether because he didn't want to know if she were lying or whether he thought she might bewitch him. He had little idea and so focused on her mouth, which was pleasantly distracting.

"Am I what? Are you mad?" She plonked the bowl on the table alongside her glass. "Look, I know I'm tired, and I've likely got a concussion, but if you're a figment of my imagination or a dream, will you please just go away. I'm going to bed." She rose and tugged the bedclothes around her. "Tell whoever it is not to worry about the bath, and I'll just sleep in my underclothes, thank you."

Luke watched without saying a word as she walked across the room.

"Well, are you going to sit there and watch me undress? Need a cheap thrill do you? Fine." She made as though to pull her shirt over her head.

"Stop! I do not need to see you undress, but I will see to it that you have a clean garment to sleep in, and in the morning, you shall indeed bathe. I would have more of this conversation after we have both slept. I believe we indeed have much to talk about."

"Your womanizing, perhaps?" she said with a slight grin.

"My . . ." He paused. "Ah, my wenching. You do not approve I take it." A broad smile spread itself across his face.

"None of my business, but it seems a bit bloody silly if you're going to get yourself shot in order to get laid. I mean," she said turning to face him, "you're not bad looking. Do you really need to go to such lengths?" Damn, but he was better than anything she'd seen in years. Maybe he was a pervert and hankered after the extraordinary.

"Your words confound me, but I believe I grasp your meaning, and I have no intention of answering the question. If however"—he moved closer—"you wish to decide for yourself, I am at your disposal, any time."

He took another step, cupped her chin in his hand and had kissed her, stepped back a pace, and was looking at her with ill-disguised amusement by the time she had recovered her senses.

She stood—gobsmacked.

"Remember, I am at your disposal, any time." He walked to the door and opened it.

Lydia remained where she was, unmoving and wishing she could think of something suitably cutting to say but found nothing would come to mind. All she could do was focus on the broad shoulders and trim hips of the man who had just kissed her, and to all intents and purposes left her wits addled. Oh, dear, she was regressing to adolescence. She had the hots for a man who apparently had women here, there, and everywhere. Still, at least there was the possibility he wasn't married. That had to count for something. Didn't it?

"Anytime, remember that," he said from the doorway. "Night or day."

Open-mouthed, she watched the door close behind him. A slight grin crossed her face, and she muttered, "Don't be afraid and just call me." She touched her mouth. The contact had been fleeting but it felt so good that she knew without a trace of a doubt had the kiss continued, she wouldn't have complained. There was a knock at the door, and a young woman entered carrying a garment that Lydia guessed was to be her sleepwear for the night. She thanked the girl, who then collected the food dishes and bid Lydia goodnight.

The gown was large, very large and it occurred to Lydia that it was a man's garment. Nevertheless, she stripped off her spandex and donned the thing. It was surprisingly soft and comfortable with long sleeves that enveloped her fingertips. She crawled into bed and pulled the covers tightly around her chin then lay on her back staring up at the canopy of the bed, and at the flickering shadows cast by the fire's glow. Why wasn't she more upset by all this peculiarity? The strange people, their clothing and their speech, and a room furnished in a style she had only ever seen in stately homes. She sighed, too tired to contemplate her fate, and snuggled farther into the feather mattress, luxuriating in its comfort, and really not too worried at all. In fact, she decided, it was all rather enjoyable, and set herself the task of working out what year it could possibly be, if October tenth really were a Thursday. An impossible task, but one she was confident would take her into the realms of the Land of Nod far more swiftly than those irritating white woolly things would. Perhaps she would wake up from all this and she could go to dinner at her sister's house after all. And when she finally disposed of her engagement ring, she would get on with her life.

Who could tell? Maybe she might bump into a great guy called Luke sometime in the not too distant future.

THREE

What a marvellous dream.

Lydia blinked, yawned, and stretched, then blinked again and opened her eyes wide. She looked out from the covers and shivered. A faint haze of condensation gathered as she let out a long, slow breath followed by a barely audible gasp at the sight of her surroundings. Was she disappointed? Was she glad? She didn't know, but she wasn't surprised.

She began to crawl out of bed, pulling the bed clothes with her. "It's bloody freezing," she muttered and made her way to the fireplace where it looked as though somebody had already cleared away the large pile of last night's ashes from the grate. Bending down, she blew gently on the remains of the fire and was rewarded by a slight flicker of orange. If she could just find something to burn, something small, paper perhaps. She looked around, fearing her efforts would be in vain if she didn't find something quickly, and paused in her search long enough to call out in answer to a knock at the door.

"Ah, good, I see you are already about this morning," Luke said, entering the room and closing the door behind him. "But pray tell me why you are grovelling around on the floor like that?"

"I'm freezing, and I was hoping to find some small bits of something to get the fire going." She looked up. "That's why."

Luke was already at the door bellowing an order to some unseen person. "That fire should have been made long afore you arose," he snapped. "It seems I've been remiss in my duty as master of this house; the staff has become lazy. Come, back to bed with you. I'll get the bloody thing going myself."

He did.

"I'm still here, aren't I?" Lydia said as she watched him at work.

"There, that should make a fine blaze shortly. I apologise, what did you say?" He walked over and sat on the bed.

"I said. I'm still here."

"Reaching out a hand, he touched her cheek. "I should say so. Why do you wear your hair thus?"

"How do you mean?"

"Short, like a village urchin."

A little taken aback, Lydia bit her tongue then said, "It's quite normal in my part of the world. I keep it this way mainly because I can't be bothered to do much with it, and I like sports, so it gets sweaty a lot."

"I see." He didn't. "Your husband, he doesn't object?"

"I'm not married."

He lifted her left hand. "You wear a ring."

"Engagement, but I . . . we . . . broke it off."

"I see."

She nodded. "I'd thought about ending it for a couple of months. Things just didn't seem right. We suddenly hadn't so much in common, and I'd begun to have doubts about our feelings for each other. But every time I thought I could tell him . . . it didn't seem the right time . . . and I felt guilty. I just kept on believing everything would be okay. He convinced me that we were meant to be together and that . . . oh, well." She took a sharp breath. "And then I . . . I made the decision, went to his house, and caught him . . . well, screwing around."

She realised her words weren't quite making sense to the man sitting by her side, still holding her hand. "I mean he was with someone else—they'd been having sex." The memory of the night she'd surprised Darwin with an impromptu visit remained raw. She glanced at her companion. At last the message appeared to have got through. "I would have thrown this," she wiggled her ring finger, "back at him, but it was stuck. In fact, it still is."

Now it was Luke's turn to nod. "A man's lust is at times a sad thing."

She looked at him. This, from the man who last night had been pursued and shot, all because he couldn't keep his hands, and likely other parts of his anatomy, off someone else's wife or girlfriend.

"You've not much room to talk."

"You do me a disservice."

She laughed. "You offered your services to me as I recall. At your disposal any time night or day you said."

He stood up. "You would wish?" There was a dangerous twinkle in his light eyes.

A challenge perhaps?

"No thank you, but I could eat breakfast if it's not too much trouble."

"No trouble at all. Now, we should consider finding suitable clothing for you."

"Do you think I could have that bath you were talking about?"

"I've already spoken with the servants; you shall bathe shortly." He looked her over a couple of times then said, "It may not be the most comfortable experience as you are rather tall."

"Well, you're taller. How do you manage?" She didn't hide the indignation in her tone.

"I have my own bathing arrangements. You will simply use what is at hand."

Lydia wasn't quite sure how to respond. She'd been put in her place for certain. "I'm sure it will be just fine. Thank you."

"After you bathe join me downstairs. One of the servants will show you the way. Now, I have things to attend to." He placed a kiss on the back of her hand before releasing it. "There are a few things I would ask you."

"I wanted to ask you something."

"Yes?"

"It's a bit silly really, but . . . what year is it?"

He was almost at the door when he turned and said, "The year of Our Lord seventeen hundred and thirty four. Shall we say one hour then?"

The door closed behind him.

So, what had she been expecting? She'd known all along something was terribly amiss. People didn't ride around on horses, get shot, wear eighteenth-century clothing and live in stately homes full of real live, fully activated servants—at least not in her twenty-first-century world. Again, Lydia realised she was taking this whole thing very calmly. Just as last night, she was feeling very, very comfortable. She grinned. Why not make the most of it? After all she'd wanted to get away from her dreaded ex-fiancé, so now here she was—

About as far away as she could get.

She bathed, and as Luke had forewarned, the tub was a tight fit, but at least she was clean, and her hair had regained a little of its natural bounce after a maid dragged a brush through it several times, while commenting on its thickness and how lovely it would look if it were allowed to grow long. Donning a heavy silk robe over a clean shift, Lydia wrapped it snugly around her and secured it with a large ornamental brooch. She declined the proffered hoops, petticoat, and various sundry undergarments, including stays, much to the disgust of the two maids, whose job it appeared was to dress her. Lydia's stomach was letting her know in no uncertain terms that it was time to eat, and she had no intention of dallying further with the conventions of eighteenth-century underpinnings.

"I'll try it all later when I've eaten," she assured the two girls who seemed much put out that their services were not further required. "I promise," she added with a quick grin and received nothing but blank stares in return.

She left her bedroom assuring herself that whatever else she may see in this home it would not come as a shock. The staircase spiralled down and around and for every step she took along its course she gasped anew. The place fairly reeked with wealth: oil paintings, tapestries, gold bedecked statues and ornaments adorned each and every wall leading to the large reception hall at the bottom of the stairway, where four enormous chandeliers, set with innumerable candles hung from the heavily corniced ceiling. Lydia stood and stared, holding the banister firmly, in case she had a sudden eighteenth-century fit and decided to faint. This was almost inconceivable.

"Lydia, there you are. I'd thought I was late, but I see you are barely out of your bath." Luke came beside her and quite without intention touched her damp hair, allowing a curl or two to take possession of his fingers for a second. "It has a life of its own."

"You could say that." She wasn't quite sure whether she'd been insulted or complimented.

"Shall we?" He offered his arm.

With a grin she looped her arm into his. "We did this last night. Twice in twenty-four hours. Not bad, considering."

"Considering what?" He continued walking. Damnation but she was pleasing to look at, especially after bathing and donning a gown.

"Nothing really, just that where I come from men don't often behave as you do."

"I offend you?" He almost removed his arm but found that he wasn't allowed.

"Not at all—I like it."

"The green silk suits you; 'tis like your hair . . ." he observed idly as they entered a room where a most magnificent array of breakfast items lay before them.

"My hair's not green." She laughed and was pleasantly surprised when her companion joined in, albeit briefly.

"Soft," he said belatedly. "Come, sit down." He pulled the chair out and scooted it expertly underneath her. "Now, tell me, why did you ask me what year it was? Have you really forgotten?"

"I'm not sure I should tell you." She looked around the room at the two men standing there.

Catching her gaze, Luke waved a hand. "That will be all; we shall attend to ourselves."

Lydia frowned. Now they were alone, and he would want to know all the ins and outs of how she came to be there. "Remember last night you accused me of being a witch or a spy?"

"Aye, I remember mentioning the like, but I don't recall having accused you. You had just made a statement that intimated you had knowledge of the future."

"Well," she said, burning her fingers on the tea dish as she attempted to follow Luke's lead and cool the beverage in the deep saucer before pouring it back into the dish, "I do and I don't, have knowledge of the future, that is."

"Explain."

"Well, I do know things that are in your future, but . . . mmm, well, they're not in mine, if you see what I mean." She took a sip of tea and wished teacups with handles had been invented.

He finished chewing. "No, I do not see. If something is in my future but not in yours . . ." He shook his head. "How can that be?"

"Because it's in my past. Or at least what was my past." She filled her fork and quickly transferred some baked egg to her mouth and began chewing—very slowly.

"You like intrigue, I see. Are you about to enlighten me?" He watched as she laboured over the obviously time consuming morsel and chose his moment swiftly before Lydia had time to refuel her fork.

"Do you promise you won't have me hanged as a spy or burned as a witch?"

"We mostly hang witches these days," he remarked offhandedly then seeing a look of abject horror cross her features, he smiled and made an attempt to allay her obvious concerns. "I have no further thoughts on your being either of those things." He hoped he was right.

"Very well then. Are you ready to hear something that's unbelievable, or it would be if it hadn't happened?"

"I am." He leaned forwards intent on missing nothing.

"I told you I'm thirty years old, right?"

"That you did. 'Tis not so old, I—"

"Cheeky sod, I wasn't looking for reassurance that I'm not past it."

"I was merely making an observation that we are of an age, and you would do well to curb that tongue of yours."

"All right," she said ignoring his remark. "So then, what year was I born supposing I've already had my birthday this year?"

"Seventeen hundred and four of course," he answered, looking a little bored.

"Wrong!"

"What mean you?"

"Oh, it's not that your mathematical skills aren't up to par, but you're wrong all the same." She grinned.

He couldn't help but allow himself a half smile back at her, and he couldn't help but admire the short thick main of pale gold that fit her head like a halo, framing the frank open features where sat an entrancing pair of dark brown eyes, which he knew were laughing at him.

"I was born . . . are you ready?"

"I am."

She took a deep breath. "I was born in the year nineteen hundred and seventy-six."

"You jest, of course."

"I do not jest, of course. See, I knew you wouldn't believe me. Now you'll have me committed to some lunatic asylum like Bedlam."

Luke contemplated his next words carefully. Whatever he had been expecting to hear, this wasn't it. "So the things you told me last night have already come to pass in your, er, time?"

"That's right."

"So this"—he swept a hand around the room—"'tis all history to you."

She nodded. "But I don't know anything really of you or your family, if that's what you're going to ask me."

"You took the words from my mouth. I was indeed about to ask you the very same. But no matter. Now, I cannot state with absolute conviction that I believe your tale; however, I would caution you not to repeat it freely, as there are those who do indeed take a dim view of heresy."

She sighed. "You *do* think I'm a witch, don't you."

"I think naught of the sort, but you must realise that you cannot go around foretelling the future without incurring suspicion. My suggestion is that you tell me more about how you came here and where you lost your horse; perhaps we may yet find the beast."

"Oh, damn. The beast as you call it was last seen in a heap by your gatehouse and should still be there if no one has stolen it."

"Could you explain that?"

"My beast isn't a horse. It's a bicycle."

"A bicycle?"

"It has wheels, like a carriage, and a small seat. You sit on it and pedal around and around."

"Then what happens?"

"You move along, quite fast sometimes."

"But why would one want to do this when there are perfectly good carriages and horses at one's disposal?"

"You'd have to try it to understand." She bolted a mouthful of food. "You can try mine if it's still outside the gates."

"I believe it to be," Luke said.

"Why do you say that?" She looked at him and frowned.

He touched his ribs briefly. "I fell over the blasted thing last night while running for the gatehouse."

"You what?" She began to giggle. "And you said you'd fallen off your horse after you were shot. Isn't manly pride a wonderful thing?"

"Aye, well," he said, looking a little sheepish. "After I was shot, I leapt from my horse and sent him on his way; he would have lost them in the woods afore returning to his stable. I ran the best part of a mile and was doing fine until I reached the gates." He paused. "Then I found myself rolling on my arse over the top of some heap of metal. I didn't stop to find out what it was."

"I see," she said smugly. "Maybe I should say it serves you right for chasing women."

"And maybe you should not interfere in that which does not concern you."

Lydia scowled and turned her attentions to her food. "You shall not speak to me now, is that it?"

"There's really very little to say I should have thought, except I hope you didn't damage my bike; it was very expensive."

"I, do damage to some inanimate object of yours? Damn it, madam, I about killed myself so careless were you upon leaving it thus." He wore a look bordering on incredulity.

Lydia glared at him. "I was lost, I was freezing, and I'd almost been run over by some hooligan in a coach not five minutes before, and previous to that I saw a man murdered right in front of my eyes." She got to her feet, slammed her utensils down on the table, and yelled, "And you sit there trying to look like you care when you really don't give a damn about anyone or anything but yourself!" She stopped, alarmed by her outburst. It really wasn't his fault all these things had happened to her. "I . . . I'm sorry, I didn't mean to shout like that, but I've never had anything like this happen to me before," she finished unhappily.

Luke gritted his teeth. "Please, sit down." Never had he known the like from a woman. "'Tis true what you say, I care mainly for myself. As for my pretending I cared for your misfortune . . ." He paused, his face hard. "I have never made even the slightest intimation of such."

Lydia gasped. She'd not expected such total and brutal honesty.

"However, I should like to assist you in any way I may if you would care to tell me what your plans are." He lifted his dish of tea to his mouth. "This consignment of Ceylon is excellent, what think you?"

"It's tea," she replied sulkily. "I prefer coffee."

He nodded. "As you will. Now, what are your plans?"

What could she say? That she wanted to hang around for a while, get the dreadful Darwin out of her system—get to know Luke a little better.

"Well, my pretty, what is it to be?"

She stared. What had he called her? The man was impossible, already she could see that, and she had only known him a few hours. He obviously had little respect for women, but hadn't she already realised that? "How's your arm this morning?"

"'Twill heal well enough. You haven't answered my question."

He was waiting for some satisfactory reply. Lydia shuffled uncomfortably in her seat, unsure what to say. Changing the subject hadn't had the desired effect. "To tell the truth, I don't know. What would you do in my place?" Clever tack girl. Put the ball in his court.

"I, in your place?" He shook his head and gave a mirthless laugh. "I cannot credit it." She glared at him as he searched for something sensible to say instead of the suggestion he wished to offer—that she stay in his company, at least for a short while, and when all this mess he was involved in had been brought to a satisfactory conclusion, then perhaps he would ask leave to court her. No, it was too dangerous to have a stranger around, and damn it all, a stranger who said she had witnessed a murder. "You have mentioned murder twice now. Would you kindly explain it to me; I like to know what is happening on my own turf."

Lydia sighed. He was exasperating but at least they'd got off the subject of her plans. She told him of how she started to fix the handlebars of her bike and how she'd become aware of the gasping man, the other men, and how they'd disposed of the body.

"Do you remember where the body is? I would mark its identity." He leaned forwards, watching her intently.

"I think I could find the general location," she said hesitantly. "You intend to dig him up you mean?"

"'Tis not a pleasant task, but I fear it must be done. I have a need to know the man's identity; 'tis possible he was carrying an important piece of information."

Lydia sucked in her breath as quietly as she was able, thanking God for giving her the wisdom not to mention the letter she had stashed in her shorts and which now resided in a locked chest in her room. He wanted the letter. But the man had said Jack, she was to give it to Jack somebody. Palmer, that was it, Jack Palmer. Could Luke's nickname be Jack? "What's your last name?"

"My last name?"

"Yes, your family name, what is it?" If it were Palmer, she would give him the letter and then she'd probably find herself back home in her own century. She wasn't sure if that was a good thing or not.

"Waverly, 'tis Waverly. Why do you ask?"

"Nothing, just wondered." Well that was that. So what the hell did he want with the letter? Was he in league with the murderers? The man with the rope had mentioned some lordship or other.

"Have you finished eating?"

"Yes, thank you." She waited as he walked around the table and slid the chair from under her.

He had terribly good manners—for a womanizer and possible murderer.

FOUR

A warm cloak was found for Lydia with the promise of more substantial clothing later in the day. She joined Luke in the great hallway where he stood tapping the hilt of his sword in a bored fashion.

He was taller than she'd previously noted, and she had to tip her head back to look into his face, which she did unwillingly; she found him incredibly attractive and knew she may just blush, or worse, burst into giggles. He wore his high leather boots, a frock of dark red velvet, and a great bunch of white lace graced his throat.

Lydia gazed and gazed a bit more, her heart doing a triple backflip before she finally caught her breath and looked away. It would be all too easy to succumb to those light blue eyes. No wonder the ladies found him irresistible, which by all accounts they did. Simply put—he was hot.

"Ready?" He held out his left arm expectantly.

She took it as though she'd done it all her life and allowed herself to be led outside though the enormous front doors, held wide by two men wearing blue livery. If she'd had doubts about all this being real, she didn't have them now.

Two horses were brought out, and Lydia's heart sank at the sight of the side-saddle perched on one of them. She turned to Luke helplessly.

"I can't ride on that," she said quietly.

He appeared confused for a second. "Does not the mare please you? I assure you she is a spirited animal, yet steady. They are a good matching pair," he indicated the two chestnuts with a wave of his hand. "We'll make a fine couple, today."

Sidling around, she turned her back to the man leading the horses and whispered, "I mean the saddle. I've never ridden side-saddle before. I don't know how."

"Tell me then how do you ride? You do ride?"

"I can ride, pretty well actually, but I ride on just a normal saddle, like that one." She pointed at the other horse.

"A man's saddle?"

She nodded, doubtful he believed her.

"Nay, 'tis not proper, and nigh on impossible in that gown."

He had a point. The gown she wore wasn't really conducive to riding astride even without the abundance of underpinnings she knew those maids had in store for her when she returned. She sighed and followed the horse to the mounting block. It couldn't be too difficult could it? She'd once ridden a camel, so how different could this be? Lydia turned and deposited her backside in the saddle, shuffled a little until she'd situated her right leg around the pommel and under the curved piece that secured her. "Do I jam my leg in here like this?" she asked, allowing the groom to adjust the stirrup to her left foot. She received nothing but a bewildered look from the man.

"There, you'll be fine," Luke said confidently, riding his horse alongside.

"Easy for you to say." Lydia shuffled some more and took up the reins, determined to damn protocol and grab the saddle if she felt the need.

He laughed then reached across and patted her hand. "Ah, my pretty, what is a man to do?" Luke pushed his horse forwards before she could respond, he was mindful that the groom had placed a whip in her hands, and she may just be of a mind to use it.

Lydia bumped along, glaring at the back of the man in front of her and calling periodically for him to slow down. "Will you bloody well wait for me; I told you I wasn't used to riding on one of these things." It wasn't nearly as bad as she'd imagined, but she had no intention of admitting it.

He turned momentarily in the saddle. "Aye, you did and likely I should have believed you, judging by the pig's ear you're making of it." He laughed. "Don't look so sour. I only jest with you. In truth though," he continued, "it would have been near an impossibility to ride astride in that gown, would it not?"

"I suppose it would, but you'll have to slow down unless you want to keep picking me up off the ground."

"I'm in no severe haste, though I should like to return before dark, I have business to attend to."

"I bet you have," she muttered. "Off out gallivanting again are we?"

He turned again, for a moment unsure how to respond then said, "Aye, I have a reputation to uphold. That is unless"—he dropped back so he came alongside, moved closer, and looked deep and unrelentingly into her face—"you have need of my services this night." He raised his eyebrows and with a suggestive wink turned away, hearing the hiss of her riding whip as it cut the air not too far behind him.

"You insufferable, arrogant bastard. I wouldn't go to bed with you if you were the last man on earth."

"'Tis just as well, my pretty," he called over his shoulder, "for I have no desire to bed a woman with a tongue as vile as your own."

It never changed, did it? Men were men, whenever their birthday happened to be. A couple of hundred years hadn't altered the battle of the sexes, Lydia decided, or the outcomes of such battles—at least in her own case. She had always been a fool when it came to her heart.

"Cannot you ride any faster?" Luke called irritably.

She urged her horse into an easy canter locking her right leg firmly in place. She'd show him all right. "Yes, I can," she gasped, catching up to the other horse, and noting with disgust how easily Luke sat in his saddle—like he was stuck there with super glue.

He grinned. "I knew you could ride in a ladylike fashion—out of character though it may be."

"I'm going to ignore your smart remarks and your insults," she shouted breathlessly as their pace increased. She was sorely tempted to grab the saddle, but pride wouldn't let her, even though she wobbled precariously in the unfamiliar position. How close she came to falling off she wasn't certain, but it was a forgone conclusion that down was the direction she would soon be heading when he called for her to slack her pace. "Thank God," she muttered, pulling the mare back to a slow trot.

"Gatehouse."

She looked up realising she'd had a fixation on her horse's ears for the last few hundred yards or so. "I see it is."

"Then come, let us find this infernal machine of yours and remove it from public view."

"Good idea." He was right, no one had seen a bicycle, and not even the most rudimentary walking machines were around yet. "It's over—"

"I know where it bloody well is. Remember?"

"Moody aren't we."

Luke glared and said nothing. Irritating as his guest might be, he found her strangely pleasant company even when she was snipping at him.

They approached the gates just as Judd ran out of his house to greet them. "Mornin' sir. And to ye, miss." He doffed his old felt hat.

"And to you also, Judd. Open the gates for us."

"Sir, beggin' pardon, sir."

"What is it? Out with it. I have much to attend to."

"Well it be a contraption I found, jus' sitting it were outside the—"

"Where is it, man?" Luke dismounted and followed Judd around the side of the gatehouse; he motioned for Lydia to follow.

"There." Judd pointed to the bicycle propped against the wall.

"My bike," Lydia chirped happily. "Please," she addressed Luke, "will you help me down?" She hated to sound so helpless, but disentangling her legs unaided without falling flat on her face was highly unlikely.

"I suppose I must." He reached up and grasped her firmly by the waist. "Take your foot from the stirrup." She was lighter than he had imagined she would be, but not too skinny where his thumbs pressed upwards into the lower softness of her breasts. He brought her to earth and released her, noting how she stared at him, and indeed how rapid his breathing had become.

"I'd do it myself if I could. Don't worry, I'll learn if I have to," she said in a manner nothing short of unfriendly. She ran to the bicycle and pulled it from the wall, spinning the pedals backwards and nodding in approval. Then she scowled. "Damn. How on earth? The handlebars." She looked up accusingly.

Luke watched, amazed, as she tried to cock a leg over the machine, but was repeatedly thwarted by her gown. "You require assistance?"

Lydia gave a huge sigh. "Yes, I'll show you what to do."

Hesitantly, Judd stepped forwards.

"I meant *you*," she said testily, nodding at Luke.

Luke moved a few steps. "What should I do?"

"Just do this, like I'm trying to do, and except for this bloody gown I could. Then pull." She grunted with the effort. "And though it pains me to admit it, I'm obviously not strong enough."

"Ah, in need of a man's strength and expertise," he said with a grin. "Allow me."

She did and within a few minutes, amidst several grunts and curses, the bike was restored to something of its former self.

It was forced but she managed, "Thank-you."

"Indeed, a pleasure. Judd you may leave us now. Thank you for removing this object from the road. You will of course mention it to no one, and we shall hide it from view, from prying eyes."

"There be a cubby-hole round the back there, no one goes in," Judd suggested.

"Perfect. I'll see to it, and remember, Judd, forget that this thing exists."

"Aye, sir," the old man said, nodding dutifully before turning and disappearing around the front of the house.

Tying both horses to a convenient tree branch, Luke looked at the bike then at Lydia who stood, hovering silently. "Well, then my pretty, show me what this infernal object is capable of, though I cannot for one moment imagine its benefits."

"You wouldn't, of course. Being a man you never see what you don't want to. If you hold it by the handlebars, maybe I can hoist these skirts enough to climb on." She pushed the bike a few feet away. "Here." Luke held the bike, not hiding a bemused look, as she hoisted her skirts and mounted very carefully. "It feels okay, surprisingly so after what it's been through. Watch, and be amazed." She took off down the driveway mindful of the way her gown flapped dangerously around her ankles.

Luke did, and he was.

"Well, now what do you think?" She brought the bike to a skidding stall in front of him.

He wore a strange expression. "'Tis quite amazing. You covered an extraordinary amount of ground with seemingly little effort. Not as fast as on horseback, or by carriage, of course," he added, not wishing to sound too agreeable.

"It's not meant to replace those things, although in town it's used as a primary source of transportation by many people. Mainly it's used as a way to exercise and to see the countryside."

Luke frowned. "Exercise?"

"Staying fit and active."

"People do not work in your time?"

"A lot of the jobs are very sedentary, and people get fat from not doing hard physical work, so riding a bicycle is a pleasant way to work out."

He nodded, mystified.

"It's much easier wearing the right sort of clothing, of course."

"The garments you wore yester-eve?"

"Right," she said and clambered off the bike. "Want to try?"

"Indeed not."

"Suit yourself, but you shouldn't be so closed minded about things you know." Deliberately she avoided looking at him, knowing he'd be wearing some sort of unpleasant frown. "Now, where is it I'm to hide this?"

"Follow me," Luke said coldly.

"Thank you," she said brightly, placing the bike inside the cubby-hole and watching as Luke heaved the door on its heavily rusted hinges back into place. "I'm not sure when I'll need it again." Hopefully not very soon.

"'Tis at your disposal whenever you desire. Judd will open the door for you."

She just couldn't read him at all. Blew hot and cold, very unsettling, but interesting all the same. At least he wasn't a boring fart like Darwin.

"Now, I would have you show me the area you believe that man's body to have been buried." He untied the horses and bent to take her foot.

"Careful, *ow!*" She made it half way up into the saddled then slipped and slid, face down, back to earth. "My bloody nose—I think I broke it," Lydia wailed, holding both her hands over the front of her face, as tears welled in her eyes.

"Let me see." He made to move her hand, but she swung away and glared at him.

"I wasn't ready. You should have made sure I knew what you were going to do." Her eyes flashed accusingly. "Now, see what you did."

"What I did?" He was mortified by her outburst. "'Tis not my fault you have no idea how to mount a horse, and I object most strongly to your accusation, madam."

"Oh, you do, do you?" She removed her hands from her face. "Well, I suppose I'm all right. I'm not bleeding."

"No, you're not." He lowered his voice. "Thankfully." She was standing close, and her dark eyes were suddenly warm and inviting. She wanted him, and who was he to deny a beautiful woman? Lydia tipped her head slightly as his warm breath trickled across her throat, and his hands slipped easily behind her head and down the centre of her back. "My pretty one," he breathed, brushing his lips lightly against hers. "*Oww*, hellfire!" He leapt back and doubled over, both hands grasped at his groin. "What the—" he gasped, his eyes slightly glazed.

"Keep your bloody hands off me," she snorted. "Pretty one indeed."

"Is that all?" he croaked, staggering to a more upright position and leaning against his horse. "Just because I said that?"

"Not just," she retorted haughtily. No, she'd remembered just in time what sort of man he was, and what a fool she'd be to get tangled up with him, even though he was as hot as hell.

"Well then, what? Oh, 'tis of no import. Are you going to mount that horse or not?"

"I am and I'll do it by myself, thank you." She looked around for a few moments before leading the mare to a tree with a conveniently low branch.

Luke took a few deep breaths and recovered his composure well enough to watch in quiet amusement as she hoisted her skirts and made attempt after abortive attempt to climb onto the branch, all the while peppering the air with mild curses.

She was a woman he could admire, even though she'd kneed him squarely in the bollocks. "Would you allow me to assist you if I first explain my fullest intent?"

Lydia glowered, knowing she had little choice if she wanted to get on board the horse anytime soon. She walked the animal to where Luke stood. He was laughing at her, those blue eyes of his held a maddening twinkle, but at least he wasn't sulking and he hadn't turned moody. Perhaps she should have brought her knee up a little harder and wiped that smirk from his face.

A short while later they rode their horses into a clearing Lydia thought she recognised. A strange feeling crept over her as she remembered the previous day's events and wondered at their reality. Could she have imagined it? Now, in the daylight the woods were nothing but a pleasing backdrop to a leisurely day out on horseback, nothing insidious or malevolent seemed to be harbouring there. She gazed dreamily at the broad-leaved trees that grew tall along either side of the dirt road. In the distance, a river gently meandered through low hills on its lazy journey to the sea, and she wondered at the changes this part of the world would soon experience and at the fate of the village a few miles down the road; she had heard there were the remains of a town below the waters of Thurston reservoir.

"That will all be under water one day," she said suddenly as though needing to break the silence which had fallen between them. She pointed across the road at the distant trees.

"Why would that be?" Luke pulled his horse to a halt and stared across the low hills beyond the trees.

"A reservoir, a huge one, will be built here because of the great demand for water. The industrial revolution will happen. Cotton mills, the woollen industry, steam—you have no idea."

"Apparently not," he remarked casually, quite struck by her enthusiasm. "Now, tell me, where you remember seeing this man buried."

"I can't be certain, but it was somewhere around here. I remember the moonlight was filtering through the trees." She steered her horse off the road. "It was around here somewhere. Look, look there." She pointed excitedly at the ground. "Tyre tracks. I came onto the road only a short distance from where it happened, so it can't be far."

Luke was already off his horse and held his arms towards her. "May I assist you to dismount, or shall you do injury to my person?"

Hiding a half smile, she acquiesced and allowed him to lift her from the saddle and place her carefully on the ground. Damn the man.

He stood back, hands raised in mock surrender. "My word, I shall not touch you again as I did."

Lydia gritted her teeth, said nothing and continued to look at the ground as they walked. After a few feet of following the intermittent traces of bicycle tyres, she called a halt. "Over there is where I was hiding." She turned. "And there, by those trees is where they dragged the body. She remained where she was as Luke handed her the reins of his horse and walked in the direction she indicated.

Luke was about to curse the fact he'd not had the foresight to bring a shovel when he spotted a crude pile of stones. It took but a short while to remove enough of the stones and loose dirt so that the body, one he felt sure he would recognise, was visible. Quickly he scraped dirt and mud from the features and cursed. Then he began to scrape the man's body clear of earth. He needed to see if by any chance the letter remained on the corpse. The chances of the body not having been searched were slim, but he needed to be sure. He was suddenly aware of softly approaching footfall, which came to a halt just behind him.

"Oh God, what are you doing?" Lydia looked down in horror as Luke exposed the dead man, and she gasped as he began to rifle through his clothing. "That's sick. You know there's a name for people like you."

He ignored her words and continued his search. "I was taking no pleasure from it, if that's what ails you," he remarked eventually.

"What were you looking for?" She was certain he wouldn't tell her.

He stared directly into her eyes. "He was carrying a letter. A letter containing important information."

"Information?"

"Smugglers. It appears they are for now to remain anonymous." He watched her closely. "There is naught to be done. The letter is lost."

She looked away. Did he know she had the letter? Had he already found it in her clothing and was just pretending all this to make her confess? Should she offer him the letter? No, the man had specifically said she should give it to Jack Palmer, and the man standing here was Luke Waverly, or at least that's who he said he was. Could he be Jack Palmer incognito? Lydia shook herself back to reality and asked, "What are they smuggling? A few kegs of brandy, can't be all that serious surely."

"That it were only brandy. Indeed, I myself do not turn down the odd barrel or two. Nay, 'tis far more serious." He paused, willing to embroider his tale only a little. "Firearms; ammunition, gunpowder, mayhap gold." His face was grim. "We are speaking of high treason."

"How do you know all this?"

"An acquaintance of mine happened upon one such consignment," he replied, bending to replace a few rocks on the man's body. "I'll send someone to bring this poor wretch to the churchyard."

Lydia waited until he got to his feet then asked, "So why didn't your, umm, acquaintance just go to the police?"

"'Tis a little more complicated than it appears. My acquaintance is not in a position to report to the authorities, and in truth, unless the accusation comes from one of high rank and with sufficient proof, no charges will hold. Come, I have work to do."

Lydia's mind whirled. Was he telling the truth? Was he the good guy in all this, or was he a devilishly handsome con man with a glib tongue who knew what he was after and how to get it? There were so many variables and no way to know the truth or who was telling it. She suddenly wished it had been raining that evening when she had ridden her bike to the top of the reservoir then likely she'd have stayed at her sister's until morning. She looked at her left hand and the ring still sitting there, a solid reminder of the jerk who had caused all this.

"Lydia."

She smiled at the sound of Luke's voice. He'd not said her name like that before. Oh, please, God, don't let him be a murderer. "Yes?"

"Come, 'tis no time to daydream."

FIVE

Three days passed, Luke being conspicuous by his absence for the last forty-eight hours or so. Lydia watched from the window of her room for a few moments longer, then turned back and walked over to the fire blazing heartily in the grate. She sat down with a grunt and fingered the beginnings of an embroidery sampler, given to her by one of the housemaids who had noted her aimless wanderings around the house.

The letter was still where she'd put it, out of sight and well away from prying eyes. But what did it mean, and how was she going to find Jack Palmer? One thing was plain: she wouldn't find him just sitting around. Lydia jumped to her feet. She would find the man if it were the last thing she did before she returned to her own time. She met with no one as she walked downstairs and through the main hall. Hoisting her skirts, she made her way outside and across the yard towards the stables. Riding side-saddle was not to her liking, but she'd managed it once without falling off. She could only improve—couldn't she? A lad saddled the chestnut mare without question and led the animal out to the mounting block. Lydia climbed

aboard hugging her heavy cloak close around her shoulders
in response to a sudden nip in the air. She trotted the mare
down the driveway to the gatehouse where Judd appeared as
though on cue and swung a gate wide for her.

"Ye be careful now, miss. Ain't so safe out there. An' there
been a highwayman workin' these parts lately, so take heed o'
my words." He touched his hat as Lydia thanked him for the
warning and rode out onto the road.

Where she was going she'd no idea except that heading
to town seemed a good way to start, and it wasn't more than
a few miles, Judd had told her.

The town turned out to be little more than a village,
consisting of several clusters of houses along a main street, a
fairly well-kept green with the obligatory duck pond, a large
chestnut tree, and the blacksmith down an alley. The sound
of the anvil being struck was somehow quite comforting,
and reminded her of childhood days when she'd stood and
watched the local farrier at work. Farther on, the smell of
raw sewage drifted into her nostrils and she continued at
a trot past a barbershop and the distasteful contents of an
eighteenth-century butcher's shop, stopping at last outside
the Blue Bell. With a great intake of breath she unhooked her
leg and slipped from the horse's back. Standing a moment,
Lydia looked around trying to decide upon a suitable place
to tether her horse when a young lad ran up and solved the
problem—or at least he would have for a penny, which she
didn't have.

"I, I'm sorry. I don't have any money." How stupid could
she be? There was no point going into the inn without money;
not only couldn't she buy food or drink, but she had no way
of buying information, which she was certain she would have
to do. She was deliberating her predicament when a man,
dressed quite presentably, paused by her side and doffed his
three-cornered hat.

"Beggin' pardon, miss, but I couldn't 'elp overhear you
be a bit short o' coin?"

Lydia consciously took a step back from the man, who, although dressed well enough, stank heavily of tobacco and bad breath. "Yes . . . I, I came out without my purse."

"You got anything to sell? I give a good price you ask anyone, 'ereabouts." He thrust his smelly mouth close to Lydia. "You ask 'em."

"I don't have anything, I'm afraid." It was true everything she stood up in was borrowed; everything except the ring on her left hand. "How much will you give me for this?" She held out her hand for him to examine the diamond sitting there.

He came up with a figure that sounded like a definite undervaluation, but since it was the only alternative, she nodded in agreement. There was just one problem, the ring refused to budge, and stuck fast as it ever had.

"It won't come off," she said apologetically, tugging at her finger.

"Allow me." The man stepped forwards and began to twist and turn the ring so ferociously she was certain he'd pull her finger off, so intent was he in achieving his goal.

"No, stop it, you're hurting me. Let go!"

"My apologies," his mouth said but his eyes weren't in agreement.

"What's happening here then?" A man, wearing a light-coloured surtout rode a big bay to a standstill a few feet away. "You all right, miss?" He raised his hat briefly.

Gathering her senses, Lydia nodded in assent. "I was about to sell this gentleman my ring, but it won't come off my finger. I came out without money, you see."

The man on the horse looked at her gravely. "Do you require money so severely you would sell your wedding ring?"

"It's not a wedding ring," Lydia said quickly. "It's an engagement ring, and I'm not engaged anymore."

The man jumped from his horse and waved a hand. "Off with you, Silas Moorehead. Shame on you, preying on a poor young woman." He shooed the man away then turned and signalled to the boy, who lounged against the door of the inn. "Take these horses, lad." He flipped a coin and turned to address Lydia. "You will do me the honour of lunching with me? I have a time to while away and would wish it be in the company of a pretty miss."

Lydia growled inwardly at his words, remembering Luke's derogatory usage. "Well, thank you, that's what I wanted the money for, but I suppose it was a bit drastic to think of selling my ring."

The man held the door as she negotiated her skirts and entered the darkened interior of the Blue Bell. She looked around at the company, mostly men, mostly very loud, and mostly drinking heavily.

"Sit over here, come." Her companion led her to a far corner of the room.

She looked at the man who settled himself across from her at the roughly hewn table. He wasn't particularly good looking. Nothing like Luke Waverly and not near so tall, but he had an interesting appearance, his eyes were intelligent, and his face open. He was a solidly built man with a somewhat ruddy complexion, his skin marked with what Lydia supposed to be the result of smallpox. She found herself checking out his attire, the white lace at his throat and that which protruded from the wide cuffs of his mid-blue embroidered coat. He'd doffed his surtout and hat and sat easily in his chair appearing totally at ease with both his surroundings and his company. She watched as he beckoned to a serving wench and spoke a few words. His dark hair, although thinning on top, was of adequate length to be secured in a queue by a blue velvet bow, and he reminded Lydia of a picture she had once seen in an art gallery, except he wasn't wearing the mandatory expression of superiority.

"Now, I have ordered food and drink for us," he said, leaning back in his chair, "mayhap you would tell me your name and a little about your business here. I don't recall ever having seen you about afore."

"I'm not from around here." Well, that was the truth.

He nodded. "And your name, if I may be so bold?"

"Lydia McKenzie."

"Ah, one of our neighbours from across the border."

"That's just what Luke said." Lydia paused to thank a girl who placed a mug of ale before her.

"Luke?" He stared at her keenly.

"Yes, Luke Waverly. I'm staying at his house for a short while, a visit sort of." She felt unaccountably uncomfortable under her companion's sudden scrutiny.

"And your business there?" The man wore a thin smile that gave away none of his thoughts.

Lydia shuffled her feet. This was no kind offer of lunch—it was an interrogation. "Well, it's difficult to explain, but I don't think I'll be staying very long." She smiled and was relieved when he nodded and seemed satisfied.

"I see. Ah, our food is here."

"Excuse me, but you do realise I have no money at all, don't you?"

He nodded. "Think nothing of it."

"But I'm certain Mr. Waverly will lend me some money to pay you back, if you write down your address for me."

"Worry yourself not. There is not the slightest need for repayment, though I agree with your statement that His Lordship would likely lend you money." He picked up his mug of ale and took a long healthy swig.

"His Lordship? He really is an actual lord then?" She picked up a fork.

"Aye, Lord Beckham. You seem surprised."

"Well, he wasn't behaving much like a lord when we met," Lydia said, and took a sip of her ale."

The man opposite started to laugh, plonked his mug on the table, and wiped his eyes as he struggled to control his mirth. "You have, I take it, preconceived ideas regarding how the aristocracy ought to behave." He chuckled, his bright eyes piercing her, awaiting a response.

Embarrassed, she looked down at her plate for a moment. "I'm sorry I didn't mean to be judgmental. This is good," she nodded at her meal. "I mean he . . ."

At this the man fell into rollicking laughter yet again. "What, what pray," he sniffed, "was he doing? Oh, this is too good, come, you must tell me." He leaned forwards on the table, his chin on his hands. "Oh, yes, pretty one, tell me."

Lydia almost told him to go to hell, but gallantly swallowed her distaste for the use of diminutives and said, "I suppose it isn't that unusual in this time, I mean these days for good looking men to go out, well . . . spreading it around."

The man opposite her fairly exploded. "Still at it, is he? Well he does have a reputation to uphold."

"He said something like that himself," she grumbled. "But he was shot and that's not funny." None of this seemed very funny at all, and she had no idea why he was so amused.

Suddenly the laughter stopped. "Shot? Has he recovered?"

"He's fine, I suppose. He did say that the ball had gone right through . . . his arm," she added.

"How came he to receive this injury?"

"Well, he didn't say exactly, but I gather he was being chased, and I got the impression he may have been caught, shall we say in a compromising position, with a lady, I guess."

The man across the table shook his head. "Will he never learn? Worry not; he's not been much different for years. Though I had thought he'd forgone some of his wild ways since he came to Yorkshire. You're right about the reputation though. His family nearly disowned him and sent him north to see to the running of the estate here, out of the way of the London set. He would have gotten himself into terrible trouble had he stayed up at the capital."

"You seem to know a lot about him," Lydia said with a scowl. Quite predictably, she had the hots for a dedicated womanizer.

"I and everyone else in the county. Some things never change."

Lydia considered the man sitting opposite her. She needed an ally. Taking a deep breath she said, "Perhaps you may be able to help me Mr . . . ."

His reply was cut short by a sudden ruckus at the bar, and he waited, his hand raised until it grew reasonably quiet again. "What was it you thought I may be able to assist you with, Miss McKenzie?"

"Well, I was wondering if you by any chance, and I realise that you probably don't, that is . . ." She hesitated. What if this man were in league with the murderers? She would really be up the creek without a paddle. Deciding her companion to be an honest, trustworthy man, she lowered her voice appreciably and said, "Do you know anyone around here by the name of Jack Palmer?" The man appeared to hesitate for perhaps a second. Or was it her imagination?

"Why do you want to find him?"

Something inside told Lydia that telling all wasn't a good idea, even if she were certain of this stranger's honesty, and her mind fairly buzzed to formulate a plausible answer. "Oh, it's not important, just someone I met said I should look him up. I'm interested in buying a horse you see, and he's apparently an excellent judge of horses." She groaned at the improbability of all this. How many eighteenth-century women were interested in buying horses? It was a man's domain. And considering she'd already stated that she had no money . . .

"Well," he said, rubbing his chin thoughtfully, "I have heard of him, and it's true, he is an exceedingly good judge of horse flesh."

"You know him? That's great. Could you tell me where I can find him, please?"

"He has no permanent residence at the moment. You say you want to talk to him about buying a horse?"

"Mmm, yes." She'd never been a good liar and felt her eyes losing contact with the very bright, clear ones watching her intently.

"Very well, though I cannot say when I shall happen upon Mr. Palmer. But when I do, I shall advise him of your request."

"Thank you." He hadn't believed a word of it, she was sure. "Still, he was going to arrange for her to meet the man, wasn't he? Wasn't that what he'd said? Actually he'd not said that at all. She looked up and smiled. "I think I should be getting back now."

"Indeed, 'tis best not to keep His Lordship waiting." There was a hint of humour in his voice.

"I haven't seen him in a couple of days. He keeps late hours."

Without saying a word, the man stood, donned his outer clothing, and assisted Lydia to her feet. Together they walked out into the chill air. It was late afternoon but still good daylight, a fact Lydia was grateful for, not wishing to travel the road by moonlight or worse—no light.

"So"—her companion raised his hat—"I take my leave and hope we may meet again soon."

Lydia accepted his offer to assist her into the saddle and settled herself before wishing him a safe journey wherever he was going, and that she indeed hoped they'd meet again so she could pay back the money for her meal.

He shook his head. "Never feel you owe me anything. Your company was payment enough, my pretty one." Taking her hand swiftly, he kissed the back of it. "Make haste to Beckham House, 'twill not be long afore twilight draws in and," he lowered his voice, "there are stories of a highwayman being abroad. I should not wish that you fall prey to him."

Lydia laughed. "You mean they aren't gentlemen of the road?"

"I . . ." he began and then simply chuckled. "I see why Lord Beckham would find your company entertaining."

"He doesn't," she said dryly. "He's interested in a different sort of entertainment, if you get my drift."

"Your what?"

"If you see what I mean."

"Aye, well, I understand he has a penchant for the ladies. Nay, lass, leave him be. He is what he is."

Was she being warned off? What was it about the man who held her horse? Something wasn't quite right even though she still believed in her own assessment of his character. No, something wasn't quite right. She mulled this point as she rode back to the house. The man who said he knew Jack Palmer, she didn't know *his* name. He had skilfully avoided giving it. She groaned. If he were involved in the murder and goodness knows what else, she could be in something of a predicament. Stuck here, somewhere back in time under threat from a bunch of murderers, and all because she was trying to keep a promise to a dead man, a man who could have been anybody, maybe even a murderer himself.

The gatehouse swam into view around the next corner, and Lydia heaved a sigh of relief at the welcome sight. Judd appeared like before, as if from nowhere, and dragged open a gate at Lydia's approach.

"Aye, be good to see ye, miss. Gettin' afeared for ye I be, all them ruffians out 'n' about." He stepped close to the side of her horse. "Word 'as it that Dick Turpin be in these parts."

Lydia's eyes widened.

Mistaking her look for that of fear, he continued, "Ye needn't be afeared, miss, so long as ye don' go out travellin' alone. Chances o' comin' across 'im ain't great; 'e looks for coaches carrying the rich people, 'e does. Be a wanted man all over England. But never killed no one though," he added, as though this fact exonerated the highwayman.

"I see," Lydia responded. A thrill ran through her. Of all the people she could run across, the infamous highwayman, folk hero Dick Turpin and, of course, his famous mare, Black Bess. She was grinning like a fool. "Has he been seen around here then, or is it just gossip?" Damn, what a story to tell when she got back home, that she'd met the tall, dark, and handsome highwayman—she had always assumed he would be tall, dark, and handsome. A strange thought ran quickly though her mind.

"Well, I don't rightly know." Judd frowned, his enthusiasm for the tale waning now that he'd been asked for actual facts. "But that's what they be sayin'. Best get on in now. 'is Lordship come in 'bout an hour ago. Wore out 'e were." He touched his hat and began to close the gate.

Lydia pushed the horse into a trot. Worn-out indeed. What was she supposed to do here? What did Luke Waverly expect? After all, he had invited her to stay, so she was a guest, but he wasn't being much of a host. She didn't want to hang around if he were out bonking every night; there was just the chance she might become the willing participant in one of those bonkings—he was incredibly sexy, and she was here alone with him. An awful thought crossed her mind. What if he brought his women friends home? She couldn't bear to think about it. She told herself it was none of her business what he did, and apart from jokingly offering his services, he had made no other real advances.

She dismounted at the mounting block. "Thank you, Peter," she addressed the lad who ran to take the mare. She stuck her fingers into her hair and wished it were longer; it would be good to fashion it into a more feminine style one evening. What was she saying? When had she ever bothered about being feminine? She gazed down at the boots she'd borrowed and shook her head sadly. Since the day she was born she'd been a bit of a tomboy. That had been the dreadful Darwin's biggest gripe—and the reason he had been attracted to her in the first place.

He complained often that she only looked like a Barbie doll when they attended some important social function; the rest of the time he accused her of looking like a vagrant—or a man.

Of course, when they'd first met he had oozed enthusiasm for her freedom of lifestyle, her natural beauty, her non-adherence to fashion. Lydia snorted. *Fickle* wasn't the word for him. *Lying, cheating, hypocritical pillock* was.

She looked up, suddenly aware that someone had walked across the cobbles and now stood blocking her way. Her eyes met with long black boots, paused at the white breeches and brown velvet frock, which concealed what she knew to be a pair of very powerful thighs, then continued up to where the obligatory white lace was knotted at the throat of its wearer. *Tall, dark, and handsome . . . was it just possible?* she wondered.

"Well, you come home sometime," Luke said, barely hiding a grin. "I was fearful for your person."

Why was she speechless? Of course it couldn't possibly be because she was gazing up into the most amazing pair of light blue eyes she had ever seen and listening to the rich intoxicating tones of an eighteenth-century male voice like she'd been struck dumb.

"Well, shall you not speak to me?"

She shook herself from her trancelike state. "Sorry, I was thinking."

"Come," he said, holding out his arm, "dinner is about ready. We are eating a little earlier than normal this eve."

She looked at him. "We are?"

"Aye, I have need of sustenance." There was a twinkle in his eyes as though challenging her to respond.

"Haven't you eaten for the last two days?"

"Of course, but naught so hearty as that of my own kitchen."

Where had he been? Surely he'd not spent the whole time having sex. He didn't look quite *that* worn-out, although, when she looked more closely there were dark shadows under his eyes.

"I rode into the village today," she said. "I took the chestnut mare; I hope you don't mind."

"Had I minded, the lad would not have saddled the animal for you. I gave instructions you were to be allowed full freedom of the house and stables." He held her arm tightly and continued walking, fully aware of the foul glare she gave him.

She bit her tongue. *Arrogant* and *insufferable* were the words that sprang to mind. Also *incredibly sexy, wonderful, gorgeous*—leave him alone. "Don't you want to know where I went?"

"You just told me." He ushered her into the house, through the great front doors held wide by servants. "You went to the town. The village as you call it."

"I mean why I went there."

"Nay, your business is your own, as is mine."

"I see," she said with rising irritation. He wasn't interested in what she had done and in his own way was telling her to mind her business where his philandering was concerned.

"Lydia, my dear." He laughed suddenly and swung her around by the arms. "Come, sit by me and tell me of your day." He ran, pulling her behind him into the drawing room. "Sit you by the fire; your bones are chilled, and although I believe I could warm them for you . . ." He turned without giving her chance to answer, walking to where a decanter and glasses stood on a small cabinet. "I know." He held up a hand but didn't turn to face her. "You wouldn't touch me if I were the last man on earth." He spun on a boot heel, holding two glasses of wine; he took a sip from one. "I believe that is what you said."

Lydia hated the amusement on his face. She couldn't tell whether he was laughing at her or at his own humour.

"Damn you," she mumbled.

"What say you? Speak up, my pretty."

"Don't call me that!" She jumped to her feet. "He kept calling me that, the man in the Blue Bell, but it wasn't half as insulting as when you say it. Damn you, I don't want a bloody drink. I'm going!" She headed for the door and almost made it. Her forwards motion came to an abrupt halt, and she gasped at the strength of the hands that grasped her decisively by the shoulders and spun her around. She was looking at a firm jaw line and felt herself being directed backwards until she could go no farther, blocked by the drawing room wall. Thoughts of struggling flashed through her mind but were dashed by the full length and weight of the body pressed against her own. She couldn't have moved if she'd tried.

Could she?

"Aye, my pretty, you want my interest; then when I offer it, you shun me. What is a man to do, I wonder?"

She shook her head. Should she knee him in the groin again?

"Think not of that," he said, staring at her knowingly.

A gasp left her mouth at his perception, and she made no other sound excepting a barely audible squeak as he bent his head and kissed her. He wasn't gentle, and she had a feeling she might be in for more than she wished to handle just at the moment, as he slid a hand behind her head and began to tangle his fingers in her hair—her tomboyish short hair. His mouth was insistent, forcing her lips apart, and his body was hard—all of it. She wanted to fight him off; she wasn't into rape, but somehow her body wasn't responding with the necessary resistance for that particular situation to arise. It was responding in a very primeval manner. His breath tasted slightly of wine, and his tongue probed her mouth skilfully igniting tiny little fires that travelled all over her flesh and seemed to congregate around her thighs and belly, where his hard body was most obvious and pressed urgently against her, ever harder. For sure he wasn't lacking in quantity, and Lydia was damn sure the quality would be top notch. She didn't want her hips to move in time with his, but they did. She didn't want to respond to the depth of his kiss, but she was doing just that, and most of all she didn't want to beg him not to stop when he pulled away, but she almost did.

"Now, are you happy?" Luke turned his back and rearranged his breeches.

"I . . . I, you had no right," she whispered, leaning on the wall for support, her knees not being very cooperative.

"Don't be coy." He walked to the table and picked up the two glasses of wine before turning to look at her. "You enjoyed that as much as I did, though I should have preferred that we were horizontal; I like my comfort. Sit down, Lydia, and stop pretending you don't want me to bed you."

"I don't believe you. I just don't believe you," she said shaking her head and moving nearer to the fire where she flopped into a chair. *Arrogant* wasn't a strong enough a word for this man.

"Then what do you believe? Here." He handed her a drink. "A burgundy from my father's cellars."

She sipped at the wine. "It's good," she muttered and realised he was speaking again.

"Are you hungry? I am. Remember, I've not had much sustenance these past days." He smiled. "Come, Lydia, we may be friends. I shall not lay a finger on you again."

She didn't know what to say. She had never met anyone like him. And wasn't that the truth?

"So, you rode to the Blue Bell. What was your impression?"

"Noisy," she replied.

He walked across to the window and pulled back a drape. "You should be careful riding out alone. There are those who would rob you of more than your wealth. Ah, I see we have a good moon this eve; 'tis a good time to be abroad." He continued gazing out of the window.

"But I thought you just said it wasn't safe to be out."

"I meant a good time for a gentleman of the road to be about his business." He turned, releasing the drape.

"Well, you'd know I suppose, being as though you apparently keep nocturnal company." She gripped her glass tightly and shrank back a fraction in the chair as he walked deliberately towards her. "Yes, thank you, I'll take a refill." She thrust her glass at him and gave a smile much braver than she felt.

Luke stopped and smiled lazily. "As you will. Did you think I was about to make an unsolicited advance upon your person?"

"No, why should I?" Damn liar. She'd been certain he was about to respond to her rather ungracious comment about his nocturnal habits.

He laughed but said nothing more on the subject. "Are you ready to eat now?" He held out a hand.

Lydia maintained a silence as Luke led the way into a magnificent dining room and scooted her into a chair before taking his own. It worried him that she was so interested in what he did. There was much at stake and the interference of a stranger, albeit a very enticing stranger could not be allowed to stand in the way of his work. Neither could he suffer to think of harm coming to her, yet what could he do? If, as she said, she was not from here, not of this time, where could he send her? There was nothing to do but keep her here, but how to limit her movements and restrict her penchant for poking her nose into things? He had little idea.

Lydia was looking around the room. This was even more magnificent than any of the other rooms she'd seen. "It's a beautiful room."

"Aye, I thought we'd dine here this eve. Now, remember what I said. 'Tis not safe for you to be wandering around the countryside unescorted, even in the daytime."

"Most highwaymen hold up coaches in the day anyhow, don't they?" she stated. "This soup's good. What is it?"

"Venison. One deer that managed to find its way into my own kitchens instead of the backyard of some poacher."

"You have trouble with poachers?"

"Aye, indeed, I do." He placed his spoon on the table and wiped his mouth. "There was a time when I first came here, some three years ago, that I was reluctant to pursue a poacher. I had the romantic notion such men were but attempting to feed their starving family when things became difficult. I was losing many deer."

"So then what?"

"I'd become too lenient. The magistrate wouldn't even look at a case I brought before him because he knew I would order clemency and not allow the thief to be hanged as he should have been. Aye, the whole of the West Riding seemed to think of Beckham as an open hunting ground. I had to stop it." He allowed his eyes to rest on Lydia's, so dark, warm, aye, and inviting. "I issued a statement that forthwith all poachers apprehended on my lands would be dealt with harshly and to the fullest extent of the law. Unfortunately, the first person my keepers caught and brought before me was a young lad, nary sixteen years. I knew the family; they indeed suffered hardship."

Slowly Lydia said, "You had him hanged?"

"I had to show I was not willing to have my lands and my stock ravaged, but no, he wasn't hanged. I arranged that he have the choice to be transported to the colonies. He made that choice and was sent to the Americas."

"That was good of you." Secretly, she was pleased Luke had demonstrated a decent side to his character; she was beginning to think there wasn't one.

"Aye," he remarked blithely, "it was."

She almost spat the contents of her soup spoon and couldn't hide a smile. "So, that did the trick, did it?"

"It did, for the main part. Of course, I cannot ever hope to stamp it out completely, nor would I. There are those at times who remain in need of pursuing such follies, and my keepers are well aware of that." He took up his glass of wine. "To you, my pretty."

What could she say, apart from, "Cheers." He'd just admitted to having told his gamekeepers to turn a blind eye to those who poached out of desperate need. The man had a heart after all.

"Now," he continued, "as I was saying about the dangers of your roving the highways alone."

"Yes?"

"I feel it best that at least for a while you would serve both our interests by staying close to the house."

"You mean I can't go anywhere?"

"There are miles of parkland you may traverse without going out on the public roads, that is all I meant."

"I suppose so, and anyway, I've no idea how long I'm staying."

"You intend to leave soon?"

"You know what I told you. It's up to you whether you believe it or not. I've no way of knowing how, if, or when I'll be blasted back to my own year." She stopped talking as a servant entered the room and whispered something to Luke.

Luke nodded then waited until the man had departed before asking, "Would you go now if you had the choice?"

His question caught her unawares, and she fumbled around with her utensils whilst formulating a suitable answer. "I'm not sure. Probably I would, except . . ." she leaned forwards on her elbows. Luke watched the transformation in her face, and the way her eyes sparkled as she spoke. "I'd love to meet Dick Turpin."

He about choked. "What?"

"I said, I'd love to meet Dick Turpin, the famous, or maybe I should say infamous, highwayman, famed for—"

"Aye, I know what he's famed for. But why in heaven's name would you want to meet him, scoundrel and vagabond that he is?"

"I always wanted to be a highwayman, when I was a kid," she said. "My family thought I was insane."

"I might say I'd agree with them."

"Well anyway, I've always thought him to have been the sort I'd go for, if he'd not been a thief, of course. I mean just the tall, dark, handsome guy on a big black horse. Sweep a girl off her feet." She glanced at Luke. He had a very odd look on his face.

"Ah, so you want to be swept off your feet; I'll bear it in mind. Now as to your meeting with this highwayman fellow, though I have doubts he is in truth tall, dark, and handsome, I feel it would be improper and unsafe. Remember, these fellows don't always stay their hand at relieving a lady of her wealth." He looked at her pointedly. "There may be other things they're after."

"You mean my virtue? Oh, don't worry yourself about that," she said sweetly. "It's long gone."

If he'd nearly choked before, Luke was about to make a better job of it and found himself reaching swiftly for his glass of wine to prevent total asphyxiation. She was looking at him with mischief in her face, and he wondered for a second if she were simply making a joke. He decided not. "Of course," he coughed, "you were engaged, remiss of me." But she'd said the words as though there had been many. He wasn't about to ask. It was one thing for him to lie with anyone he fancied, but for a lady, and especially this one—it wasn't something he wished to dwell on.

"You look shocked." She sipped her wine. "Why, I don't know, you sleep around all the time, or so your reputation goes." She smiled at him.

Gathering his senses, he responded with as much dignity as he could summon. "My reputation is just that, and I neither admit to it nor do I deny it."

Pompous bugger. "Please yourself. Anyway, I heard all about you in the pub, today."

"Ah, the man you met at the Blue Bell. He told you all about me?"

"Yes, well, some things. Seems everyone knows what you do."

"Enough, I think. As I previously told you, my business is my own. Whatever it may be, you should not be concerned." There was nothing he could do but allow his eyes to rest on her face. Still, if he were looking at her face she couldn't berate him for looking at her bosom, which he found delightful and wished he could see more.

Lydia wished he wouldn't look at her like that. His hair was too dark, his eyes too blue, and his mouth far too inviting. She looked away.

"There is plenty to occupy you in and around the house. Feel free to go anywhere you wish."

"Anywhere?"

"Aye, my pretty, you'd find my room very comfortable. I assure you 'tis the finest chamber in the house. And I always give my lady friends leave to visit anytime they wish."

The arrogant bastard was at it again. "You just can't leave off, can you?" She laughed and shook her head wishing that her short locks could wave around her shoulders like a cascade of whatever it was a romantic heroine was supposed to have flowing behind her head.

"I find it entertaining, and I believe you also enjoy the banter."

"That man at the Blue Bell said something about your finding me entertaining."

"He did? I wonder why he would say that. Perhaps I should find this rascal who casts aspersions upon my character and have him horsewhipped?"

"You wouldn't."

"Likely not. Now may we eat? I have further business matters to attend to this night. You shall remain here, and tomorrow do as you will, within the boundaries of the grounds and," he added with a grin, "within the boundaries of the law. You are safe here; you may rest easily at night and dream of tall, dark, handsome highwaymen to your heart's content."

Lydia smiled. He hadn't called her his pretty, anf for that she was grateful. She could manage the dreams all right. As to staying off the roads, now that was a different kettle of fish. Somehow she had to meet with this Jack Palmer and give him the damn letter. It was the only way she knew to get back to her own time. If she went to the inn again, she might find out something more. She frowned.

"You're frowning," Luke observed, pausing mid-mouthful.

"Just a slight problem, nothing really."

"Tell me. Perhaps I may be of assistance."

"Well." She thought quickly. "I went to the inn today, as you know."

"Indeed."

"I had no money, and I er, well I had to borrow some."

"You borrowed money? I see. Who was the kindly soul?"

"The man you said you might have horse whipped," she said gloomily.

"'Tis, no problem. Money I have aplenty and see no reason you should be without whilst under my roof, although," he appeared to think for a moment, "if you remain off the public access as I have requested, you should have no need of money." Seeing she was about to baulk at this he added, "However, you are not a prisoner here, and as my guest I cannot forbid any action; I'll give you money. A loan, you understand?"

"I understand, but does whatever brought me here understand? I might just disappear, and unless you find a way to follow me, I'm afraid the debt isn't going to get paid. Sorry, but can you still make me a loan?"

"There are always ways to pay off ones debts, Lydia. Remember that."

"Bugger off."

"Perhaps curbing your tongue would do for a start. Though I don't imagine you to be of low birth, you certainly have a way with the vernacular."

It was true her mouth ran away with her at times. Lydia found herself blushing and wondering how he could be so polite yet admonish her with such ease. "I'll try to be more ladylike," she said.

"I didn't intend any insult, merely an observation should you find yourself in company not so liberal as my own."

"Thank you, I'll remember that. By the way, that man said you were Lord Somebody or other."

"Lord Beckham, at your service. As I have been since you arrived." He sighed in mock despair. "Though as yet, you haven't seen fit to avail yourself of that service." He rose from the table, walked around, and leaned over her shoulder. Lydia shuddered. He didn't allow his body to touch hers, but he was close, and she could feel his warm breath on her neck. "You wouldn't be disappointed, I assure you."

"You don't give up, do you?"

"Never, my pretty, never." He stood up. "Now, I needs must leave. I have business to attend to, if you will excuse me. If you change your mind, the servants know where to find me," he threw over his shoulder.

He walked from the room with an easy grace. Lydia watched appreciatively. Here she was, alone in the wrong century, and the only person who could offer any support, was a devastatingly handsome guy who hovered between dishing out the insults and trying to convince her to invite him inside her knickers—had she been wearing any, of course. She'd never met the like and vowed right there and then to keep him at bay for as long as it took to return home—and she would keep her own hands to herself.

SIX

Luke turned once, glanced at the closed dining room door behind him, and then strode along the hallway. With a final glance, he took the stairs two at a time and made haste to a suite of rooms adjoining his own.

A man sat in a chair, his back to the door, and rose to his feet at the sound of Luke's entry. "About time. What the devil have you been doing? Oh," he grunted, "my thanks for the dinner." He indicated several partly eaten dishes on the table in front of him. "Excellent venison."

Luke waved a hand in the air then strode forwards and gripped the man by both shoulders. "My pleasure. Damn, but 'tis good to see you again, Jack."

"Aye, and you, though I wish 'twere under better circumstances."

"Indeed." Luke pulled up a chair. "Sit down and finish your meal."

"How's that arm of yours?"

"My arm?"

"Aye, a little bird tells me you took a piece of lead a few of nights ago." He raised his eyebrows.

"The same little bird, I take it that was in the Blue Bell earlier today?"

"The same. Now how is it?"

"'Tis healing well; nothing more than a graze," Luke responded.

"You should be careful." The man held up a hand to prevent the indignant response he knew was forthcoming. "Anything for your troubles?"

"A mere pittance by your standards and naught we were after. Now to business." Luke pulled up a chair and began to recount recent events.

"'Tis a pity our man met such an untimely demise." Jack Palmer tore at a piece of meat then added, "You searched the body thoroughly, and there was no letter?"

"Aye, I'm sure enough of that. I had the body brought back and stripped before it was suitably interred. There was nothing."

Palmer rubbed his chin thoughtfully. "And you are certain of his identity?"

"I am. Will you take a brandy, my friend?"

"Indeed, I feel much in need of such. And by the way, what's this about having me horsewhipped?" He gave a half smile.

"Ah, so you heard that?" Luke turned and handed him the brandy.

"I heard some of it. Remember, I know every hallway, secret door, and peep in this house just as well as you yourself. Cheers." He held his glass high for a moment. "I still cannot believe that our informant trusted the messenger with a verbal message. There had to have been a letter, what say you?"

"I tend to agree, but it appears not, unless it was taken, and that's something we need to prepare for." Luke took his seat again and leaned back in his chair looking thoughtful. "Not only have our enemies prohibited our being privy to their plans, but they also likely know someone is on to them."

"We need be extra vigilant, Luke, my friend. Now, tell me more of the pretty one I met today. She seemed very concerned about your nocturnal habits."

"Aye, she's inquisitive." Luke smiled. "And strong willed."

"Do you have any idea why she was looking for me?"

"In truth I don't. What reason did she give?"

"Gave me some cock-and-bull story about wanting to buy a horse, and that she'd heard Jack Palmer was a good judge of horse flesh. She's a poor liar, Luke, but I could tell she's taken a fancy to you." He laughed.

"Aye, well, there's more to think on at the moment. By the way, where's that mare of yours?"

"Well hidden, as usual, with your own black beast."

"Good. We need to move quickly to prevent that information, aye, and supplies reaching their intended destination, or England will pay dearly. Damn it, Jack, we could hold up every conveyance between London and the borders and still miss the one we need. Without that information, we're shooting in the dark."

"Aye," Palmer said, shaking his head slowly, "we are indeed, but I think we'll be lucky, if we're careful." He picked up his glass and took a swig. "So, tell me what your efforts got you the other night, besides a lump of lead that is?"

"Not so much: a couple of rings, a pearl necklace, and some coin from one lady and her gentleman. The other two passengers weren't lavishly decorated, so I let them be."

"I'm glad you're not in this business to make a living." Palmer chuckled. "You know, I've laughed more this day than I have in years. Your pretty miss had me in tears so indignant was she about your conduct. Not as she expected a lord to behave, she said. Then she blushed, and most charming it was, apologised, and assured me it was none of her business what you did." He held out his glass for a refill then stretched his arms out wide and yawned. "Like I said, she's a poor liar."

Luke wasn't listening. He was tasting the lips he'd kissed earlier and feeling the body he'd pressed upon his own and wondering at the way Lydia had responded. "What? I apologise, Jack. I was thinking."

The other looked amused. "You were looking like a lovesick calf, if you want the truth."

"Damn you, Jack."

"And I probably shall be. Now, tell me, who took responsibility for your deed?"

"As usual," Luke gave a grim smile, "I lay the blame at the feet of Turpin. With a flourish of my pistol and a flamboyant wave, I left the folks in no doubt as to who had robbed them."

"Ha, good." Jack Palmer stood and dashed down his breeches. "I'm for a night's sleep. We'll speak more in the morning. One thing I would suggest is that you prevent the pretty miss wandering around by herself. There's no telling what trouble she might find, and we need to keep a close eye on her—just in case." He looked hard at Luke.

"Aye, I have to agree, there may be more to her than meets the eye. But Jack, in truth I believe she has nothing to do with this affair."

"What you mean my good friend is that you hope to God she doesn't. I understand, yet we must keep open minds."

"Perhaps she has information and was sent as a security in case, as indeed happened, our man didn't get through," Luke said doubtfully.

The other shook his head. "'Tis unlikely, and until we are certain she's not involved in the conspiracy I've no intention of admitting to my identity. Do me a favour, Luke."

"What do you ask?"

"Don't bed her. Heaven alone knows what you'd tell her then." He chuckled, adding, "Damnation, Luke, I'm in a happy mood. Take that sour look off your face."

"There are times, Jack that I cannot think why I've not shot you."

"Because we're friends and both very misunderstood men," Palmer responded with a grin.

"There's a London coach due day after tomorrow," Luke continued. "About two o' clock, north of Tadcaster. They needs must cross the ford just after the crossroads."

"Aye, and there's another carrying mail from across the Great North Road east of Bryerly. Which one shall it be?"

The two men looked at each other and grinned.

Luke spoke first. "We don't want to run the risk of missing the one we seek . . ."

"Aye, there's a distance of about twenty miles between." Jack Palmer rubbed his chin. "We could take 'em but an hour apart; I the one and you the other." He began to chuckle and said, "That would certainly boost Turpin's reputation. A capital idea my friend." He clapped Luke on the shoulder. "Just as long as you don't show off too much."

"What mean you?"

"Well, have that horse of yours rear a little too high when you say your farewells and someone might just notice that the famous Black Bess has suddenly become a gelding. Ha-ha—ha." He slapped his thigh. "Now, really I must sleep. I rode long and hard to get here. Same bedchamber? Servants still trustworthy?"

Luke nodded. "I'll have hot water sent in for you. Tomorrow we must begin our search in earnest, given that we lost that piece of the puzzle we had hoped to have. Damnation Jack! What was I thinking? Lydia saw the murder. What if she were able to identify the murderers?"

"Dangerous, for her that is. Our enemies would not hesitate to have her topped if they suspected such. We should talk to her; though, as I stated, I do not wish to make known my identity until we are certain of the side she's on. Goodnight, my friend." He slipped quietly through a door at the far end of the room.

"I should prefer not to involve her at all," Luke grumbled, wishing he had kept his mouth shut. If he asked Lydia to help identify the men who had killed the informant, he was putting her life at risk; anyone willing to commit high treason in order to bring about England's downfall wouldn't hesitate at taking the life of one woman.

He sat in a chair nearest the fire, took up a fire iron and began prodding mindlessly at the coals. He'd not expected his life to take this turn, and he would be damnably glad when the traitors had been caught and hanged. He could get on with his life, such as it was. The past three years hadn't been easy since he'd been forced to come and live in the north, compelled to see to the estate and to take on responsibilities far beyond that which he desired. His reputation with the ladies had followed him from London, and he'd done little to dispel it, for the first couple of years at least—a different woman most nights, some reputable and some not. The death of a close friend from syphilis had drawn him up quickly in his rovings, and whilst not inducing him to abstinence, it had greatly curtailed his exploits. Luke supposed there were merits to the institution of marriage. After all, bedding with only one woman had to be safer than having many of uncertain origins. He had considered it, but had been dissuded by thoughts of what often happened to a marriage when common respect died. What to do then? To be in exactly the same position of paying whores or seeking out mistresses to find one's pleasure, and in addition, a spiteful wife to appease. He prodded the fire some more then took a swig of his brandy. Maybe he would set up a very respectable mistress, provide her with fashionable apartments and expensive clothing, and she in return would treat him like a king and pander to his every whim. He could have a child by her; though a bastard might not have the easiest time claiming any of the estate. Go to bed, Luke, he told himself. The truth was, he was afraid to close his eyes and dream. Afraid to dream of the pretty miss who'd kneed him in the bollocks, showed him her marvellous riding machine, and who had answered his kiss so sweetly, as he wound his fingers into the waves of her boyish hair. The same pretty miss who had said she wouldn't bed with him even if he were the last man on earth and who would, he was certain, knock him flat on his arse if she changed her mind.

He stood and, for a moment, wondered if she were yet sleeping. He was a fool for a pretty face; it had been said many times, and he knew it to be true. But somehow, he doubted that Lydia McKenzie was just a pretty face.

SEVEN

It was a perfect autumn day. The trees hung low in glorious variations of gold and red, occasionally releasing a flurry of crispy leaves that fell to earth and formed a thick blanket that crunched under the hooves of the slowly jogging horse. Lydia relaxed in the side-saddle, allowing the animal to take its own course, having no need to rush anywhere, which in itself was a major breakthrough in her lifestyle. As a computer technician for a large company, she was forever being sent here and there to sort out somebody else's screw-up, and what free time she had was divided between her outdoor pursuits and being at the beck and call of the dreadful Darwin—who seemed to have taken precedence over everything else. If she were in the eighteenth century to discover the meaning of life, then so be it. If, indeed, there was a meaning. Perhaps she had been in the wrong place at the wrong time? Or should that be the right place at the right time? Lydia rode on, determined not to worry because she was in no position to do anything about it. She allowed the horse to continue along by the side of a small wood, not really caring where they rode, and simply enjoying the day.

The animal snatched at a juicy piece of shrubbery here and there, taking little notice of the rider on its back; the world was peaceful. Even the birds took their time going about their business, and apart from an occasional squirrel that chattered with annoyance at the mild disturbance of the horse's hooves, there was no other sound to be heard, not a motorized or technological sound anywhere.

The horse stopped abruptly and pricked up its ears.

"What's wrong? See something?" Lydia clicked her tongue, kicked with her heel, and encouraged the horse forwards. The animal continued to stand, and stared, then offered a loud whinny in response to something Lydia couldn't see or hear. Finally, with a little more encouragement from a boot heel and a mild flick of the whip, the horse moved forwards but kept up its one-sided conversation, ears pricked and desirous of a left-handed view. A little farther along they gained a small wooden gate, and the horse came once again to a standstill and refused to budge an inch. Lydia craned her neck but could see nothing beyond the thick stock of trees. She knew it wasn't a good idea to dismount, but there was something beyond the gate she couldn't see, and after all she had been given full leave to ride anywhere, so long as she stayed away from the public highway. She slipped to the ground and drew the reins over the horse's head.

"This had better be something good, horse, I'm telling you," she muttered and reached to lift the latch on the gate. "If I can't get back on again and have to walk back, I'll have your guts for garters. Come on."

The animal needed no further bidding and barely allowed Lydia through the opening before shoving its huge form past her. With a curse she pulled it back and managed to re-latch the gate. Realising the impossibility of trying to remount into a side-saddle on a horse that wouldn't stand still, she sighed, glared at the mare and allowed it to lead her into the woods.

They'd gone about a quarter of a mile with nothing but trees to see when another sound reached Lydia's ears. Another horse. Oh no, was this where Luke brought his ladies? She dreaded bumping into him in the middle of an amorous session.

"Slow down will you, please." She yanked on the reins and pushed back on the horse's shoulder. They walked on until a crude stone chimney swam into sight between the trees followed by an equally crude stone roof that manifested as a small cottage, and as the pair came closer, Lydia saw the reason for her horse's excitement. Trotting back and forth in obvious delight at their new companion, were two of the most beautiful horses Lydia had ever seen. Both black as jet, both big, strong, and in superb condition, they roved their enclosure neighing and snorting a greeting.

"Who are you?" Lydia asked as though expecting an answer. "What are you doing out here?" She held the mare with one hand and reached out to the nearest black horse, which made a nickering noise and allowed its muzzle to be stroked. "You're gorgeous, yes, you are." The horse shifted its head slightly but seemed content to remain where it was so long as it received attention. The other animal wasn't so mild and continued to prance and stomp around, tossing its long mane and holding its tail high in an attitude of arrogance. "Show off." Lydia laughed, enjoying the horse's antics for a few moments.

She looked around. There was no sign of human presence, and much as she wanted to have a nosey around the cottage, there was no way of leaving her horse by itself. It was strange that anyone should live in such a tiny home, likely one or two very small rooms, yet own two such magnificent horses. She heaved a sigh of relief at not recognizing either horse for Luke's. This then, wasn't likely to be his love nest, and on reflection, why would he need one? There was more than ample space and opportunity up at the house for him to entertain without attracting much attention. She'd ask him about the horses, and the cottage, which she was sure was on the Beckham estates, and he'd no doubt have some simple explanation—when he eventually showed his face, of course. He'd not been around that morning, and she didn't feel comfortable asking the staff where His Lordship had gone. She allowed the three animals a short time to socialize, now and again having to chastise the more boisterous black for attempting to nip the other two and almost catching her own arm a couple of times.

It took more than a little persuasion to disengage her chestnut mare from its companions, but eventually she managed to manoeuvre the beast to where a fallen tree stump looked like it might provide the means to remount.

"Stand still, will you." Lydia sprang and had her foot in the stirrup when the horse whinnied shrilly, and spun around leaving her half in and half out of the saddle with little means of control. She struggled gamely and was almost in place by the time the mare had trotted behind a shed and was heading towards the two blacks, who had come around to the fence again. "Damn it, no. You've socialized enough for one day, and I'm getting cold." She pulled her cloak around her. The horse stomped and spun until at last in response to a firm flick of Lydia's whip it turned and set off in the opposite direction to that which they'd come. Lydia pushed the animal on not caring about the direction for the time being. So long as they were travelling forwards she was in little danger of being thrown—at least in theory. She kept to a steady canter for about a mile or so, then sensing the animal to be calmer, slowed it back to a slow trot and caught her breath.

"It's your fault if we get lost now. And if we end up on the highway and His Lordship finds out, I've no doubt he'll throw a fit. Oh, well, can't be helped," she grumbled to the mare.

They came eventually to a road, and since there was no doubt in Lydia's mind that this was the only public road, she turned the mare in what she assumed was the direction of Beckham House. There was no urgency, apart from being cold, and there were still several hours of daylight left in which to discover the route back to Beckham should she have taken a wrong turn. She rode at a leisurely pace, taking in her surroundings and allowing herself the time to consider her situation, Luke's possible involvement, and the whereabouts of Jack Palmer. Strange, how it took an acute and drastic event to make one reflect on past issues, in particular her relationship with Darwin. How many times had she turned her own world around in order to placate her fiancé? And what had she received in return for all her efforts? Heartache, heartbreak, and a severe blow to her self-esteem. Of course, there was always the rock she still wore on her third finger.

She remembered the horrible evening when she had almost thrown the ring back at him. And how he had attempted to convince her that he really loved her. She had left his apartment, gone home, cried herself silly, and called her sister, who'd promptly driven around and packed Lydia's suitcase.

Lydia had begun to feel better within several days and had even declined to speak with Darwin when he called. His last call had been along the vein of suggesting to Lydia's sister that she might like to pop the ring in a registered envelope and post it to him. In fact, he had been quite insistent. He would, of course, return all of his ex fiancée's CDs. The phone had been slammed unceremoniously down on his economically inclined babblings, and Lydia's sister had assured her it was quite legal to keep the ring.

Still, it seemed things hadn't worked out so badly after all. Here she was taking it easy, not having to keep to a time schedule, no boss looking over her shoulder, no worries about money—well not really; she just didn't have any. She laughed at her predicament and pushed the mare into an easy canter. Who'd have thought she would ever be riding side-saddle and be the guest of a fully fledged lord, and one who could make her feel like no other man ever had. It was a shame he was a self-admitted philanderer.

She recognised the beginnings of a high stone wall and knew that shortly the gatehouse would appear around a corner. A cup of something hot with Judd would be just the ticket, washed down with a little gossip about His Lordship, and perhaps even a little carefully extracted information on Jack Palmer. The gatehouse came into view, and Judd appeared to pull open a gate, doffing his hat as horse and rider passed by.

"Good to see ye, miss. Bin out ridin' again, ah sees."

"I got lost if you must know," Lydia answered. "I was supposed to stay in the grounds but something went wrong, and we ended up back out here. You wouldn't happen to have a hot drink handy would you? I'm perished."

"I would that, miss. Get yeself down off that 'orse, an' I'll tether it roun' the back. Ye get indoors 'n' sit by the fire. I be there in a trice."

Lydia thanked him, dismounted and walked into the small house where a fire blazed brightly in the hearth. She looked around for a moment then taking off her cloak threw it over the back of a chair and sat down. Judd appeared and disappeared immediately into a back room.

"Ye likes a hot toddy, miss?"

"That would be great, thanks." She stretched out her legs and wiggled her toes inside her overly large borrowed boots. "I think I should get some more boots, don't you agree, Judd?" She took the tankard he offered.

"Looks fine to me, miss."

"Cheers." She took a sip and coughed. "This is good, if a little potent. What is it?"

"Aye," he grinned, "it be a bit o' best rum, sugar 'n' hot water. More rum like than water."

"Don't tell me," Lydia said laughing, "it'll put hairs on my chest."

Judd roared and slopped his drink on the floor. "Ye be a bit of a rum un, ye be, miss."

"Like His Lordship, you mean?" She raised her eyebrows.

"Oh, aye, 'e be a rum un all right, though ye be nowt like 'im." He shook his head. "Be gettin' into real trouble one o' these days 'e will. Spendin' 'is time down in that place among them what would rob 'im blind if they got half a chance, but what'll pretend they likes 'is company jus' for a few drinks. Aye, free with 'is money he is."

"Not just his money from what I gather," Lydia said quietly. "Has he been caught before like he was the other night?"

Judd appeared to think for a second or two, then taking a long swig of his toddy wiped his mouth on his sleeve and said, "Ain't never got caught an' shot as I knows."

"What else does he do, Judd? I mean, does he work? Is he involved in politics or anything?"

"Can't rightly say, miss. I suppose 'e be like the rest o' them lords what sits in that Parliament; jus' goes when they feels like it. Turned this place around tho' past couple o' years."

"He told me something of that," Lydia said, sipping her toddy. "He said that poachers were running riot over the estates and that he managed to put a stop to most of it."

"Aye, did a fair ol' job 'e did. Surprised a lot o people an' made some enemies." Judd was nodding his head in a vague kind of way.

Lydia waited, and then when it seemed Judd intended to say no more asked, "Why did he make enemies? Do you mean the poachers who risked being hanged?"

"Naw, not them. They had a good run an' they knew 'e only be doing what the law said 'e should." He cocked his head in a direction over his right shoulder. "Up there, over the way, Lord Fulford. Furious 'e were by all accounts."

"Why, what do you mean? And who is he?"

"Owns lands all over, though not so much as 'is Lordship's family, o' course. But it be my guess 'e were expectin' to lay claim to Beckham, such a state it were in, but then along comes the young gentleman an' surprises us wi' what 'e done. I be real glad o' it, I can tell ye. Real fair." He grinned. "Turns a blind eye to some goings on 'e do."

"Like those two rabbits I saw in there?" Lydia inclined her head to the back of the room.

Judd looked round over his shoulder at the door to his back room. "Aye, make a good stew wi' a few carrots."

"He knows you do it?"

He shrugged and took a swig of his drink. "Like I say, 'e be a fair man, for all 'is wild ways."

Lydia thought for a moment. "What did you mean earlier when you said that place where he goes?"

He looked at her over his tankard. "The Blue Bell that be where 'e takes himself many an eve. Stays there near all night sometimes. An' there be times 'e stays away a couple o' days at a time, least that's what they says up at the house. Dunno where 'e be then; must 'ave one 'ell of an 'angover."

Or be too busy enjoying himself other ways. Lydia felt a sickening lurch in her stomach that surprised and irritated her. She already knew what Luke Waverly was, so it was ridiculous to be shocked or even concerned, and she certainly shouldn't feel hurt by his actions. "I see." She nodded, a little more glumly than she intended.

"Needs a wife 'e does. Someone what'll keep 'im in check. Give 'im less reason . . . well, miss . . ."

"I know what you mean, Judd." She managed a smile. "I know just what you mean."

"Aye, miss, mebbe ye do."

"Well," she stood quickly, "I think I'd better be going now. The toddy was good. Thank you." Taking her cloak from the chair, she pulled it around her shoulders and made for the door. "My horse, round the back is she?"

"Aye, I'll get 'er for ye."

"No, really, it's okay. I can see to her myself." Suddenly Lydia felt very antisocial and in need of no one's company but her own. Closing the door behind her she tramped around the back to where her horse stood nibbling a small patch of short grass. It looked up only briefly and with apparent lack of interest at Lydia's approach. Impulsively she bypassed the horse and headed for the cubby-hole. She stopped a few feet from the door; it was open an inch or two. Grabbing the door she wrenched it wide. No bike!

"Bloody hell!"

Just then, Judd appeared and pulled his hat from his head. "Don't be worryin' yeself, miss. His Lordship took it jus' a while ago. I be sure 'e don't mean no harm."

"But why? Why would he want it?"

He spread his hands. "Dunno miss."

"Well, thank you for telling me, Judd. I thought it had been stolen." Somewhat relieved but intrigued as to why Luke would want her bike, Lydia untied the mare, and with the aid of a fallen log, mounted and set the horse in the direction of the house.

Something had been nagging at her since that very first day, and Judd's words had set the thought in motion again. Those men, the murderers had said His Lordship wouldn't be very pleased. Did they mean Luke? Then there was the other guy, the other lordship, but Lord Beckham appeared to be the one everyone was talking about. She couldn't credit Luke with murder, but then she didn't know the man apart from the taste of his mouth and the feel of his body, hard and demanding, willing her to move with him as he fired a desire in her that she'd never felt the like of before.

A sound, vague at first, caught her ear. She pulled the mare to a halt and cocked her head to one side. Laughter, it was the sound of laughter. A man's laughter. Disengaging herself from the saddle, she slipped to the ground.

A short distance through the trees, Lydia halted and hushed the horse with a finger to her own lips. She immediately felt stupid and tied the mare to a tree. Following the sounds, she trod carefully, cursing each crunching step she took in the blanket of fallen leaves. It didn't take long to discover the source of the disturbance.

Some way off stood two figures, one of which Lydia recognised immediately as Luke even though he had his back turned to her; the other figure wasn't familiar at first, but it was this person who sat astride her beloved bike, roaring with laughter. His words floated to her ears across the crisp autumn air.

"Luke, man, where did you find this most marvellous machine?" The man pushed the bike forwards and began to pedal, gaining momentum and speed with apparent ease. He made a large loop around a group of trees before skidding to a halt in front of Luke.

"Remember our agreement." Luke began to laugh then said, "Ask me not that question."

Lydia found she was laughing with the men and clapped a hand over her mouth to mute her giggles. The stranger was off on her bike again. He chuckled as he pedalled, and seemingly already well versed in the mechanical workings of the bike, weaved in and out of the trees with alarming accuracy.

Lydia considered the merits of walking out into the clearing and introducing herself when the stranger turned full around to face her. She gasped at the sight of the man from the Blue Bell. What was he doing here, and behaving as though he were a close friend of His Lordship? He'd made no intimation of any such thing when he'd sat eating lunch with her. Indeed it seemed he had no desire to admit any personal connection with Luke. Lydia held her step. Until she was far more certain of this man's motives and Lukes involvement in the whole affair, it would be ill advised to disclose any information regarding the letter she held. She watched for a few minutes longer then stole away and led the mare quietly around to the right and away from the two men.

Once well away and certain she couldn't be heard, there was no alternative than to burst into laughter again. The sight of those two in their thigh boots and velvet frocks howling and grinning at each other like schoolboys was just better than a fresh cream bun. She sat down beneath a large beech tree and shook until she had stomach ache followed by a tremendous attack of the hiccoughs. At last she rose to her feet and led the horse in the direction of the house; there didn't seem to be much point trying to mount again for the sake of a short walk.

Lydia regained her composure before reaching the stable yard and handed the horse over to Peter, then gathering her skirts, she ran upstairs where a fire blazed a welcome in the hearth. She shivered. What she wouldn't give for a down-filled parka and some thermal underwear. She shivered again, convinced that October wasn't this cold in her own year, and wasn't central heating a wonderful thing? A package lay by the side of her bed, and she stared at it for a few moments before putting down her glass and walking across the room. It was a fairly large parcel and quite heavy. It didn't necessitate much effort to pull the string off to reveal the contents: two pairs of boots, one brown the other black, and a sumptuous gown of forest green velvet embroidered with contrasting silks.

"Oh, my," she gasped, holding the garment aloft, "this is gorgeous." It was like nothing Lydia had ever had occasion to wear, not even out to dinner or at conferences with the dreadful Darwin. She glanced back at the wrapping and, realising there was more, pulled out an ivory-coloured flounced petticoat, which from what she'd seen in art galleries fitted under the gown to make up the front of the garment, and a pair of low-heeled shoes in matching silk damask. "Oh, my," she said again, speaking to the room in general. Laying the garments and the shoes, which she suspected might be a tad less comfortable than her tennis shoes, on the bed she removed the boots she presently wore and proceeded to try on her new ones. She stood and walked around the room a few times, wondering at the comfort and softness of the leather. This craftsman obviously knew his trade, and somebody had gone to the trouble of ascertaining her size. She smiled at the fact His Lordship had done this for her. She would thank him, of course, but she still wouldn't trust him with the letter, not yet. She walked to the window and gazed across the tops of the trees to the low hills beyond. It was beautiful and unspoiled by the progress of the industrial revolution, no low hanging clouds of pollution and blackened chimney stacks, the air as fresh and clear as it ever had been. With a sigh, she turned back to the fire and took up her glass before settling into a comfortable chair and admiring her boots.

Footfall sounded outside her door, and she turned to answer a short knock. Luke entered and paused for a moment as though appraising her.

"I see you found the boots. They will suffice?"

"Actually, they're very nice, very comfortable. And the gown, I . . . I really don't know what to say except, thank you."

"'Tis enough that they suit. Did you ride out today?" He walked to the table and poured himself a drink, then joined her by the fire, settling into a chair opposite.

"You know I did. And I'll not lie, I went out on to the public road but only because I got lost." She waited in full expectation of some form of chastisement.

"How came you to be lost? He sipped his wine.

"It was that bloody horse if you must know." She stifled a giggle as a brief vision of the man from the Blue Bell on her bike flashed through her brain.

"Something amuses you?"

"No, I was just thinking that I shouldn't blame the horse," she lied. "But I found something interesting if you must know." She waited. If, as he had previously demonstrated, he had little interest in her day, she'd not bother to advise him of any of it.

"Aye, 'tis a bad master blames his animal," Luke remarked blithely. "So what did you find today, my pretty?" He watched closely, expecting her to offer some indignation.

She smiled sweetly then said, "I came across a cottage, a bit run down really, but round the back, in a yard were two of the most beautiful black horses I have ever seen."

A flicker of unrest passed across his eyes. "And where exactly was this? I should like to see which of my tenants has such magnificent beasts." He grinned. "Perhaps I'll increase his rents."

"Oh, no." Lydia leaned forwards in her chair. "Please don't do that."

"Worry not, I shall look into the matter delicately. I am certain there is a rational explanation. Now," he said rapidly cutting off the question he knew would follow his last remark, "what of the gown? Shall you wear it this eve at dinner?"

Whatever she'd wanted to know about the horses would have to wait. A pair of light blue eyes was taking the very breath from her body, and the owner of said eyes maintained a steady gaze.

"Well?"

"If I can fathom out how to get into it all. There's a bit more to it than I'm used to."

"You shall have someone to assist you." He smiled slightly and said, "My assistance wouldn't be to your liking, I suppose?"

"Er, no. But thanks all the same." She returned a grin. He really was something else. "So, how was your day?"

"Business, I fear, and no more."

"I see. Nothing exciting then?" It appeared he wasn't going to let on about her bicycle or his knowing the man from the Blue Bell.

"Naught you need to worry your pretty head about." He stood. "Now, dinner in one hour, does that suit? I'll have a maid sent up to assist you dress, and hot water brought should you wish to bathe."

Lydia nodded. "An hour should be okay, that tub's too small to spend a long time soaking. Oh, not that I'm complaining, of course. I'm grateful for a bathtub at all."

"Are you intimating that you wish to use the one in my room?" he said with a definite glint in his light eyes.

"No," she laughed and shook her head. "I'll not say another word. I'll just curl my legs around my waist." The minute the words were out of her mouth, she felt the pinkness rise into her cheeks and immediately knew he was laughing at her, though silently.

Luke paused at the door turned and said, "An intriguing thought, indeed. I must curb my imagination." He closed the door quickly behind him.

Lydia let out the breath she realised she'd been holding. If only she could be certain he wasn't involved in this murder business, and if only he didn't have such a reputation. A faithful man was what she needed—if any at all. Better to be alone than with someone who cheated. Did men change? She doubted it, though Darwin had professed such an event would occur the minute they were married. Lydia relaxed in her chair reflecting on that marvellous institution to which she'd almost gained membership. Truthfully, she could count on one hand the really truly happy marriages she knew. Of course, there were many others, which worked exceptionally well and were tolerable, but wasn't there supposed to be something more? She had been accused of demanding too much from a relationship, or at least that's what her very-well-married and sensible, businesslike sister kept telling her. 'Stop living in a fantasy world,' she had advised each time Lydia met with disappointment, or each time she turned down an invitation for a date set up by her sister, who seemed to have her own ideas about what Lydia needed. She smiled. At least her sister had been gutsy enough to tell Darwin where to go. A tear sprang unbidden to the corner of an eye, and she found herself sniffing away further indications that she was about to bawl. What if she never saw her sister again? What would her family do when she didn't come back from her bike ride?

She stood and began to tidy the packaging that lay by the bed. Several days had passed, and supposing time passed at the same rate in her century, there would already have been a police report filed. And what had she been doing? Apart from riding around on horseback and living a life of luxury, not much, except bemoaning the fact that an incredibly sexy hunk to whom she was undeniably attracted was a philanderer and certainly not what she was looking for. It was strange that Luke had said so little on the fact that someone was keeping two very expensive horses on his land and had even admitted he knew about them. Lydia was certain he'd hesitated before answering and that he had deliberately shifted the subject of the conversation. Judd said there had been more robberies on the highway recently, and it would stand to reason that whoever was committing the robberies wouldn't use his own everyday horse. She sat down on the bed, her earlier suspicions taking a more tangible form. Luke Waverly was a highwayman. It was obvious. She shook her head. No, it was impossible; she really should restrain her imagination. Wasn't it enough that she already fancied His Lordship, without casting him in the role of a glamorous, dashing highwayman? But it would answer many of the questions surrounding his mysterious night-time outings. She looked up, answered a knock at the door, and made a mental note to take charge of her imagination.

A maid entered, followed by two men with buckets of hot water. Duly stripped, Lydia curled into the tub as comfortably as was able and determined to stay at Beckham at least long enough to find out why Luke was risking his life by hanging out with a bad crowd, and riding the highway—if, indeed, he was.

Was she perhaps making of any excuse to justify his nightly wanderings? Maybe he didn't go to the Blue Bell as often as Judd said he did. Maybe he'd been seen there once or twice. She allowed the maid to help wrap her in a warm towel, quite certain she would never become accustomed to having another woman be so intimately acquainted with her body, however long she remained in this century. A fleeting image of someone else drying her person after she'd risen from bathing crossed her mind. A tall, dark, handsome lord with light blue eyes—eyes that she knew would one day catch her so unawares that she'd likely do anything he asked, except that all she had to do was tell herself yet again just what he really was, and she would come to her senses.

Wouldn't she?

*   *   *

The green gown looked stunning. Lydia turned repeatedly in front of the mirror, hardly able to credit that the reflection was indeed her own. Even crawling into the stays hadn't been as bad as she'd imagined it would be. Getting dressed in this formal attire was finicky, but the result was worth it; she looked and felt like a princess.

Even her chest looked different. It wasn't the cleavage she was accustomed to, and her boobs, though well pushed into view at the top of the gold embroidered stomacher, were held firm and didn't bounce around like two little boys fighting under a blanket when she moved, as was often the case when she wore a flimsy underwired bra with her evening dresses. It wasn't that she minded being well endowed, but there were the tacky jokes she was often the brunt of, and the sleazy remarks made in passing by lecherous males who fancied they had the right to an eyeful and stared rudely before offering their comment and turning away with a smirk.

Well, all was firmly in place, if obvious, this evening, and she had the feeling that although His Lordship had offered his services and made it plain he was very willing, his inherent good manners would prevail, and tonight at least she would be accorded some respect.

A pair of maids offering quiet compliments held the doors as Lydia glided out into the hallway. Lifting her wide skirts, she set out for the top of the stairs, feeling a bit like a ship sailing up a channel. She reached the dining room only after a precarious descent of the staircase nearly sent her tumbling headlong down it. Luke got to his feet as she entered and walked forwards to greet her.

"'Tis as I previously observed," he said, his eyes sparkling in the candlelight. "Green suits you." He took her hand, kissed it, and then led her to a chair.

Lydia realised she'd not said a word and looked up to smile at him in a manner she hoped would compensate for her lack of speech and apparent witlessness. There was laughter in the light eyes, but he said nothing further and took his seat across the table.

"You seem subdued," he said at last. "Is something the matter?"

Shaking her head she answered a brief, "No, I'm fine."

"You don't appear to be fine. Did you take a chill while you were out riding, perhaps?"

"No, I'm tired that's all, really."

Luke raised his glass of wine, indicating that she do likewise. "To being in the company of a beautiful woman." He raised his eyebrows and leaned over the table, allowing his glass to chink against Lydia's.

What was she supposed to say? And to having the most gorgeous, sexy man sitting opposite me? "Thank you, you're very kind."

"And you are very formal, this eve, pretty miss." He was certain she'd berate him, but at least she'd speak to him.

He couldn't be a murderer, he just couldn't. "Why do you call me that?" she asked suddenly.

"Because you are." He leaned forwards. "And tonight you are astoundingly beautiful, and if I were not bound by your words, I may be suggesting a situation that is not befitting my position as a gentleman."

"What do you mean, bound by my words?"

"Did you in fact not say that you wouldn't have me if I were the last man on this earth or something to that effect?" He gave a wickedly lopsided grin and resumed sipping his wine.

Lydia fought for words, which didn't want to manifest. "Yes, I did say that and . . . and I mean it." There, she'd said it. She congratulated herself on her strength of character, and then wished she could swallow those very same words.

Luke nodded. "So it seems, and 'tis likely a good thing for I have other matters to turn my mind to. Ah, dinner, and not before time, I have urgent business this night." He spoke vaguely to the servant and anyone else who happened to be listening.

"May I enquire as to your business?" Lydia dared herself.

"Indeed, you may not."

Although this was the reply she'd half expected, Lydia felt rebuffed. "I see. Secret business, is it?"

"Your inquisitiveness does you no justice."

"I was just wondering. If you're off down to the Blue Bell, maybe I could come with you for a drink." Damn it, she'd irritate the hell out of him if she had to, but she would find out the truth of his nightly sorties.

"Did I hear you correctly? You wish to visit the Blue Bell?"

"Just for a quick drink, you know." She didn't meet his gaze and toyed with a piece of something on her plate.

"You have interest in my business there?"

"Your business? What business is it of mine what you do down there? Everybody knows anyway." She glanced up at his face. His blue eyes had taken on a cold, hard gleam. Maybe she'd shut up now. Making him angry wasn't perhaps such a good idea; he might throw her out into the street.

"Quite frankly, I am appalled at your audacity. No one speaks to me thus, and you, mistress, shall refrain from it." He spoke with quiet, deliberate calm.

"What do you mean? I'm only repeating what everyone else says," she said, feeling a little piqued at his tone.

"And what everyone else says is none of their business either. Damn it, Lydia." He stood and pushed his chair back. "I have quite lost my appetite for eating in your company."

She stared, stunned into silence as he turned from the table, called to a servant to have food brought to his chambers and walked purposefully across the room.

He paused in the doorway, turned and pointed a finger. "Do not ever feel you have any involvement in my affairs. Whatever I choose to do is my business alone. Keep to your own affairs, and I will attend to mine. My life and how I live it is nothing whatsoever," he jabbed his finger in the air, "to do with you. And if 'twill set your mind at rest, I wouldn't have you, even if you begged me. Oh, and Lydia . . ."

"Yes?" She tried not to sound hopeful and silently cursed him for the pig he was.

"You have carrot in your teeth." With that parting shot he spun on his heel and strode from the room.

Lydia sat gobsmacked, and for a moment wasn't sure whether to laugh or cry. Then she reached for a toothpick and the nearest item of polished silver—carrot indeed. If she had imagined Luke to have feelings for her, they were dashed, and if she had any sense, she wouldn't care. But common sense seemed to have deserted her, along with her resolve to stay well clear of men, particularly the one upstairs in a fuming temper.

*   *   *

Luke stomped upstairs to his rooms and threw himself into a chair. His meal was placed before him, and he dismissed the servant with a scowl.

"Was that so necessary?" Jack Palmer entered quietly and began pouring two glasses of brandy.

"What?" Luke swung to face the man.

"I said, was that really necessary, my friend? You were little short of brutal."

"There was no other way, Jack. She's too inquisitive, and it could be dangerous, for all of us." He accepted the drink he was offered.

"True, true, but—"

"Aye, I know, but what choice had I? And you yourself said . . ."

The other shook his head. "Mayhap you did the best thing. If she is safely out of the way, you've less to worry yourself about and we can attend to matters at hand. And also, your outburst may incite her to action if she is involved in this affair in any way."

"There, you see, Jack. I didn't do such a bad thing after all."

"And you can always offer an apology later."

"Damn you, Jack." He looked over the rim of his glass.

"Aye, but for now, to business," was Palmer's only response.

EIGHT

Insatiable curiosity was a character trait Lydia had never denied, and considering Luke had left the house that past night, it seemed a good idea to find out whether a robbery had been committed in the vicinity. She rode the mare steadily along the perimeter of the fences she knew bordered the Beckham estates and turned off at the little gate leading to the clearing. It was reasonable to assume that if one of the black horses had been ridden recently, it would still bear sweat marks, or at least there would be a few extra hoof prints coming and going in the dirt. Lydia's horse became agitated as they passed through the gate, and as before, she dismounted and walked at the mare's head, holding the animal in check to prevent its rushing forwards.

"I wish you'd walk more quietly," she scolded, struggling to slow their pace as they approached the clearing. The two blacks were just visible behind a corner of the barns and didn't rush out to greet the intruders; they were heavily involved in eating. Lydia's horse, somewhat quieted, allowed her to pull to a standstill some yards from the cottage and began to munch on a patch of dried but apparently tasty grass. Lydia waited and listened, not wishing to be caught snooping by whoever owned these beasts given that he might be involved in the murder she'd witnessed. There was, she was certain, a reason for her having been thrust back into this century, and she had every intention of being alive and fully active when she eventually found her way back home.

The place appeared deserted, nothing different from the day previous, except that the black horses had food. Moving warily she led the horse to where the two blacks continued to munch happily and was disappointed to note they were clean and showed little trace of having been ridden hard within the last twelve hours or so. She tied her mare to the fence and walked carefully around, noting indentations left by shod hooves in the dirt and mud. Many were obscured, she decided, by the carpet of leaves continually moving on and off the forest floor; however, on closer inspection a number of prints led in and out of the clearing on both sides. Prints she'd not noticed the day before.

She turned to look back across the clearing just as the mare pricked up her ears and sent forth a soft whinny. Lydia heard nothing, but experience told her to make herself and her horse scarce. She managed both in record time and scuttled out of sight setting the mare's attention to eating just as a rider entered the clearing. He tethered his horse and dismounted, then took a bag from the back of his saddle and with a friendly call to the two blacks walked across the yard and entered the cottage. The rider wore a light-coloured surtout and a three-cornered hat; she recognised him immediately and was doubly glad of her decision not to give the letter to Luke. It was the man from the Blue Bell, the man who had been in His Lordship's company, and the man who had been riding her bike. What the hell was going on? Just who was he, and what was his involvement in all this? Apart from the fact he was the man who said he would find Jack Palmer, Lydia realised she knew very little about him, but here he was carrying on his nefarious business under the very eyes and possible protection of Luke Waverly. An unbidden thought struck her that if he were caught Luke would be an accessory, and even being a member of the aristocracy wouldn't save him if high treason were the accusation. She shuddered at the awful idea of it. But maybe, just maybe, Luke knew nothing about any of this and was totally innocent—at least of highway robbery.

He was tried and found guilty when it came to philandering.

The man stayed in the cottage several minutes and then reappeared at the door where he stood for a moment as though listening before walking across to the two blacks and patting each one in turn and offering a few words.

Lydia strained her ears but was unable to catch what he said, and she continued to stroke the mare's neck as the animal grazed with reasonable quietness. It crossed her mind to challenge the man from the Blue Bell and ask him when he intended to introduce her to Jack Palmer, but the thoughts of confronting a possible murderer and highwayman convinced her otherwise, even though the highwayman part was intriguing. Eventually, the man remounted his bay and rode out of the clearing, apparently satisfied all was well.

Cautiously, she crept around to the front of the cottage and pushed gently on the heavy wooden door. It didn't budge an inch. She tried again, this time with a little more force and was rewarded when the door groaned and swung inwards an inch or two. Slowly edging it farther, she stepped into the dark interior and blinked a couple of times, allowing her eyes to become accustomed to the gloom. Leaving the door wide open, on the one hand for light and the other as a possible means of a swift escape, Lydia gazed around the room and its sparse contents. There wasn't much of anything, and certainly nothing to have her running for the nearest policeman. Nothing more in fact than a table and a pair of chairs, something that looked as though it may serve as a narrow makeshift bed against one wall, and a large blackened pot hanging down from the chimney over the remains of a fire whose ashes she discovered to be quite cold. The only other thing in the room, indeed in the whole cottage, was a wooden trunk half hidden in a cobweb-festooned corner, and it was to this object that Lydia directed her attentions. The trunk itself wasn't covered in thick dust or cobwebs and neither, she discovered, was it locked. The lid complained quietly as she heaved it around stout brass hinges and settled it against the wall.

She took a deep breath and let it out slowly, listening for a few moments in case she wasn't alone. But all remained silent in the cottage, except for her own rapid breathing and pounding heart. In the trunk were several items of clothing, including a couple of black kerchiefs and eye-masks, which Lydia had little doubt were used for concealing someone's identity. Two black capes, edged with satin and closely resembling the one Luke had worn the night she met him, lay folded in half, partially concealing a pair of feather trimmed three-cornered hats. The rest of the cavity held an assortment of pistols and a couple of swords; one in particular caught her attention. It was longer than the sword she remembered seeing at Luke's left hip, and she picked it up tentatively using two hands. It wasn't light, and she found herself having to balance it carefully, as it was also very sharp. It sported a curved ornamented hilt of filigreed silver curling almost into a full circle forming a protective cup for the user's hand. It was a marvellous piece of craftsmanship, and after a few moments of admiring said weapon, she laid it on the dirt floor of the cottage and began to examine the rest of the articles in the trunk.

Pistols, powder flasks, lead balls, and the bag that, she was certain, had been carried in by the man a while ago. Tugging open the leather binding of the oilskin, she found it to be filled with dark grey powder—gunpowder and lots of it. She whistled silently. Maybe this guy wasn't just a simple highwayman. Perhaps she'd uncovered another gunpowder plot, and he was all set to try and blow up the Houses of Parliament, a second time. Her mouth was suddenly dry and she noted a direct correlation between her heart rate and her breathing. She had to find someone who could help her, someone she could trust. But who? Could she perhaps trust Luke? Wasn't there a chance he was innocent in all of this? Fat chance, but it was possible. Maybe she was here to save Luke? Should she tell him everything and leave him to deal with it? He would uncover a plot to overthrow the government, and she would find herself back in her own time—just that simple.

She piled everything back into the trunk as neatly as she had found it and closed the lid. Taking a deep reviving breath and feeling better for having made a decision, albeit one that she may live or die to regret, she left the cottage.

The mare continued to eat its way through the sparse crunchy grass with apparent contentment and offered only cursory resistance to the ride home. Lydia rode out by the road and immediately began planning what she would say to Luke. She formulated several sentences she would be able to rattle off without conscious thought in case His Lordship wasn't inclined to give her his attention. Yes, she'd tell him first of all about seeing the man at the cottage and what she'd found there, let him mull that over for a moment or two, assess his reaction, and then she'd ask him why he was keeping company with the man. Then if all went well and she could satisfy herself Luke wasn't involved in some dastardly plot to blow up the government, she would give him the letter and be done with it. Then she might be able to go home. She sighed. "That's what I really want to do, you know," she said to the horse. "I really do." Deep down she knew there were other things she would wish for given the opportunity.

The twenty-first century with the dreadful Darwin hovering in the wings didn't seem too favourable a prospect when there was an eighteenth-century lord who could turn her to mush with one blaze from his infernal blue eyes, and set her on fire with the merest touch of his hand. Oh, yes, there was a lord, but what chance did she have of gaining his favour sufficiently to make it a legal and binding relationship, which was the only way she would have him. God forbid she should have an affair with him and find herself pregnant and alone in this century, or indeed, what if she returned to the twenty-first century in that condition, it would take quite an amount of explaining. She shuddered at the idea.

Judd appeared on cue and opened the gate, nodding his head once or twice before inviting her indoors for a belly-warmer as he put it.

Seated by the warmth of a blazing fire, Lydia relaxed and waited for the cup of hot spiced alcohol to appear; her problems seemingly less urgent for the time being. "Judd," she said, as he appeared with a jug and began pouring into two mugs, "was there a robbery last night? A coach I mean. A highway robbery."

He leaned to take the kettle from its place in the hearth, a thick cloth in his hand. "No, I ain't heard o' no robbery last night." He lifted the kettle and filled the mugs, replacing it on the hearth and passing a mug to Lydia. "But then news ain't quick around 'ere."

"I see." She felt strangely deflated, having been certain that the man she'd seen was a highway robber. Perhaps she should give more attention to her other theory that he was setting out to blow up Parliament. "Well, cheers, thank you again for this." She laughed. "I'll be depleting your rum supplies if I carry on."

"Don't ye be worryin' none about that, miss. There be plenty more where that come from." He winked. "An' good brandy if ye likes it."

"Smuggled?"

"Best not ask 'bout that, if ye understands me, miss."

"Sorry, I keep forgetting there are things best left unsaid." She grinned at him. "This drink is even better than the one yesterday. Another of your concoctions?"

"Aye, that it be, but part o' me wife's recipe." His eyes twinkled, and he continued speaking. "Mebbe she'll be back in a couple o' weeks or so an' ye can meet 'er. She'd like to meet ye."

"I should like that, and I hope she gets back soon. I can see you miss having her around. How long have you been married?"

"Nigh on five and thirty years." He gave a wry smile. "Not bad eh?"

"No," Lydia sighed. "I doubt I'll ever be able to say that."

"Ye never knows. Ye ain't so old, an' all it takes is for a gentleman to come along an' who can say?"

"If you knew my luck with finding Mr. Right, you'd not have so much faith," Lydia grunted. "Look, this is what I have left from my last disastrous relationship." She held out her left hand.

Judd gave a low whistle. "That be worth a pretty penny, I don' doubt."

She nodded. "I tried to throw it away, into the reservoir, but it wouldn't come off. Then I tried to sell it outside the Blue Bell so I'd have money for lunch, but again it wouldn't budge, and I nearly ended up having my finger ripped off." She stopped, her thoughts flashing to the coming conversation she intended to have with Luke Waverly.

"'E left ye, did 'e? Scoundrel."

"Not exactly. He did some things I wasn't prepared to tolerate, and so I finished it."

"What sort o' things, if ye don' mind me askin'?"

"Things like other women," she said flatly. "That's not what marriage, at least to my mind, is all about."

"The missus once told me that if I went a rovin', she'd well, she'd take a carvin' knife to bits o' me, if ye understands me meaning."

Lydia started to laugh. "Oh, Judd, I think I'm going to like your wife." She got to her feet. "I have to be going now. I need to talk to His Lordship."

"Doubt 'e be awake; only come in early this morn 'e did. Them up at the 'ouse said 'e 'ad head like gamgee." He shook his head. "Shame 'bout the way 'e behaves."

"It's nothing to do with me, but I intend to talk to him whether he has a head like whatever it is you said or not," Lydia tossed over her shoulder as she opened the door. Outside the air had turned decidedly chillier, and she tugged the cloak tightly around her before walking around to collect the mare. Judd followed and saw her safely mounted before turning back inside.

"Judd, is my bicycle back in the cubby-hole?" she called.

"Aye, miss, it be back where it were. Funny thing that, 'is Lordship takin' it out."

"Do you ever see"—she hesitated with the question—"I mean, does His Lordship ever entertain visitors? Have you seen him with a man, lately? Rides a big bay horse."

Judd scratched his head then shook it decisively. "Can't say I 'as, miss. Ain't come through these gates. Should I keep a watch out?"

"Oh, no, I was just wondering if the man I met in the village, at the pub had come by. He said he might drop in for a visit."

"Nobody been 'ere, not to my knowin', but if they does I'll tell ye."

"Thanks, Judd, see you later." She rode steadily up to the house. So Judd didn't know who the man was, yet it appeared he was a close acquaintance of Luke's from the way they were carrying on with her bike. There was only one way to find out, and that was to ask.

* * *

Luke nodded in agreement to Jack Palmer's suggestion, somewhat relieved if he were to admit it.

"Aye, Luke, 'tis the best we can do. Either she shall not be involved at all, or she will panic and make a slip up. Whichever way it goes, you and I will have a better idea of where we stand and of whom we need to be cautious. I'm sure 'twill all turn out for the best. Don't look so worried." Palmer slapped him on the back.

"Easy for you to say. She is a guest under my roof, and it could be very difficult if she's adversely involved in all this." Luke turned and poured himself a drink.

"Just keep it thus," the other said grimly. "Aye, I'll take a nip with you as you appear to have forgotten your manners."

Luke scowled and poured him a drink. "What mean you, by that, Jack?"

"I mean keep her at arm's length. She's an attractive wench, and I know you too well, my friend." He raised his eyebrows.

"Do you know how long it is since I availed myself of female charms?"

"Likely last eve," Palmer laughed. "I hear you were at the Bell."

Shaking his head slowly, Luke looked steadily at the other man. He was about to set the record straight when a disturbance in the hallway caught his ear. "She's back. I'll call her in." He glanced behind him briefly as a panel in the wall opened and closed again with barely a low click.

Setting down his glass, Luke walked to the door and opened it; there was no one in sight. He would wait a short while, fastidious as Lydia was about cleanliness she was likely washing after a day in the saddle. He would give her a short while before having her summoned.

*   *   *

Lydia looked at herself in the mirror. She had washed her face and hands and it would have to do. She wasn't about to fuss around until she lost her courage. Indeed, a long relaxing soak after her talk with His Lordship would be the best thing. She took a great lungful of air and marched purposefully out of her room and along the hallway, having already ascertained Luke's whereabouts from one of the servants.

The door was ajar, and she knocked upon entering, fully intent on maintaining an air of confidence.

Luke stood by the fireplace, tall and imposing, a frown upon his face. He looked up as she entered, somewhat surprised at her sudden appearance. "Lydia, I was hoping to speak with you. Would you care for a drink?" He was already pouring a brandy as he delivered the question.

"I need to speak to you first," she said hurriedly. "It's really important. About those horses and that cottage in the woods and . . . ," she stopped. He was smiling at her in that infuriating fashion he had.

"Calm down a little. Here," he indicated a large comfortable chair, "sit by the fire." He seated himself opposite. "Before you say anything, I wish to apologise for my outburst last eve. However, I stand by what I said."

Lydia felt her fingers tighten around the glass. "You mean about my minding my own business? Don't worry, I'm not about to ask you where you were until dawn this morning."

"We'll not go into that," he said tightly, running a hand through his hair, which hung thick about his shoulders, unrestrained by its usual ribbon.

How she wished he wouldn't do that; it was very distracting. In fact, having his hair hanging loose was doing strange things to her breathing. "I like your hair down," she said, changing the subject from his nightly adventures to one that she quickly realised could ultimately land her in far hotter water. His blue eyes blazed, and she could almost feel his hands on her body and his mouth seeking her own.

"Lydia?" He wanted to ask more about why she found his hair agreeable but checked his words.

"Mmm, yes, what?"

"Lydia, there's someone I want you to meet." He maintained his composure. "We shall speak of more intimate things later if you so desire it, but for now, there is a gentleman, a business acquaintance of mine, would you mind?"

"No, not at all," she said looking around, a puzzled frown on her face. "Where is he?" Luke nodded and allowed his eyes to indicate a part of the room behind her chair.

She stood and turned just in time to see a man apparently step through to what to all intents and purposes was the panelling of the wall. She gasped and almost dropped her glass as the man came towards her, his step light and his gaze steady. He took her free hand and placed a light kiss on the back of it.

"Jack Palmer at your service." He made a short bow.

Luke watched intently, determining that her first reactions would give away anything she might then try to hide. Lydia stood in silence, looking first at one man then the other.

"You, you're Jack Palmer?" She shook her head in disbelief. "But why didn't you tell me that when I met you?" She turned to Luke accusingly. "What's going on?"

"That is precisely what we would like to know," Palmer said quietly. "Please be seated and be assured there is naught for you to fear; we just need answers to a few questions that's all."

"Don't we all," Lydia muttered under her breath and gave Luke one final glare before sitting down.

"Now, you came to the tavern looking for Jack Palmer," said the man himself. "What is it you want with me?"

Lydia shifted uncomfortably in her seat. This wasn't quite the situation she had envisaged. How could she warn Luke that his supposed business acquaintance was likely in the business of blowing things up when the man was sitting right here? And just how involved was His Lordship?

"Lydia," it was Luke who spoke, "just tell us why you wanted to see Jack. "You don't need to tell us anything else," he added pointedly.

"All right." She'd been given a hint there. Mr. Palmer, it seemed, knew nothing of her being from another century—one less person to accuse her of heresy. "I was witness to a murder," she said quickly and waited for a reaction.

"We know that already," Luke said gently. Getting to his feet, he came and stood by the side of her chair, laying his arm across its back. "What about Jack?"

How could she tell them that the man had asked her to find Palmer without giving the reason why? She struggled for something to say.

"No need to be afraid. Tell her, Luke, we are not about to do her harm. Unless of course, you have something to hide from us?"

"Nay, Jack." Luke shook his head.

"Merely an observation," Palmer clarified.

"Lydia," Luke continued, "'tis only that we need answers, and perhaps at some later date we shall be able to tell you more of this."

"More of what?"

"There are things happening in England of which you likely know naught, and 'twill be safer if you remain in such ignorance," Jack Palmer said.

"Well then," she collected her thoughts and spun a small lie, "it was as that poor man was being murdered he sort of yelled out your name."

Palmer leaned forwards in his seat. "What did he say?"

"I'm not too sure." She looked around the room; she'd never been a good liar. "Something about not giving any information to anyone but—well, yourself." Was Palmer truly Luke's business associate, or was he in collaboration with a gang, intent on undermining the English government? And did Luke know? She certainly couldn't tell him she had discovered gunpowder and things at the cottage. Lydia sighed and realised both men were looking at her.

"Is that it?" Luke asked.

"Yes, I think that's all he said, but you know, truthfully I can't remember it too clearly. I'm sorry." She looked from one man to the other and was rewarded by a slight pat on her shoulder from Luke.

"So that's the reason you wanted to find Jack Palmer," Jack said, rubbing his chin. "The only reason?"

"Yes."

"You don't want to buy a horse then?"

"I have a very nice horse, thank you," she replied and breathed a sigh of relief. What about the letter? That damn letter should have been in Palmer's hands by now. But then what? She had to find out more before she committed the information into the wrong hands. Luke's hand had come to rest on her shoulder. Did it belong to a traitor or indeed a murderer? She hoped neither. It was a strong, firm hand, the fingers long enough to suggest sensitivity yet the nails trimmed short, business like, and functional. It was also the hand that had wound into her hair and thumbed her cheek softly as his mouth took her own in a flurry of hasty passion.

"Ah, so you have no more complaints about the mare leading you astray," Luke laughed.

"Aye, His Lordship tells me the mare ran off with you into the woods, and you happened upon a cottage and what was it, now?" Palmer rubbed his chin thoughtfully. "Two black horses, wasn't that what you said, Luke?" He looked innocently at Lydia.

"Yes, there were two of the most beautiful horses I have ever seen." Now she definitely didn't trust Palmer. The man was shrewd, and there was more to his words than idle enquiry. *Concentrate on the pretty horses,* she told herself. "Really gorgeous they were." She turned and looked at Luke for support. He was staring at Jack Palmer; a look of acute displeasure on his face.

"Like I told you, Jack, the bloody mare ran off with her, and I've a need now to find out who keeps such animals on my land." He smiled quickly then said. "In fact, if you've a mind you can set yourself to the task."

"Aye, I can do that. Perhaps you'd better stay out of the woods, pretty miss."

It was a scarcely veiled warning. "Well, then I'm stuck." She forced a grin. "Can't go out on the highway and can't go into the woods."

"There is an abundance of parkland, sufficient for your needs," Luke said stiffly. "And if you insist on riding the public highway, I see no alternative than to accompany you."

Lydia looked up and widened her eyes. "Thank you, Your Lordship."

Luke muttered something incomprehensible and took a sip of brandy. "So, we conclude our business. 'Tis time you readied for dinner, Lydia. Jack and I have further business to discuss." He stood and took her hand, placing the lightest whisper of a kiss on the back of it.

Lydia took her leave and left the room. All things considered, she'd come out of her introduction to Jack Palmer quite well, although she felt more confused than ever. She had also been advised to stay away from the cottage, which she had no intention of doing, not until she found out what they were up to, particularly Palmer. It stung that Luke had known the identity of the man she had met in the Blue Bell and was obviously aware of her conversation with him. The two of them were involved in something serious, and she intended to find out what it was.

If it were the last thing she did before going home.

NINE

Luke didn't say much at dinner, and Jack Palmer wasn't present, so Lydia found herself with no more information by the end of the evening than she'd had at the beginning. She returned to her own room, prodded the fire a few times with the poker, and sat down in a large comfortable chair very disgruntled and wishing this were all a bad dream and she would soon wake up. A hot bath was what she needed, and perhaps some chocolate. She got to her feet and stretched, cursed her stays, walked to the bellpull, and yanked on it twice.

Sometime later she crawled from a rapidly cooling tub of water and towelled herself dry in front of a blazing fire, having dismissed the maid. Several new gowns and robes had been supplied, and she chose a wrapping style of heavy ivory silk and pulled it on over her bed gown, securing it at her waist with a large silver brooch, one of several pieces of jewellery that had been delivered to her room along with two more pairs of shoes. She slipped her bare feet into her slippers and gave a swift glance in the mirror at her hair, still damp but forming a corn-coloured halo around her ears.

Taking a candle from the mantelpiece, Lydia left her room. She padded along the carpeted hallway and down the long curved staircase, gripping the smoothly polished rail firmly to avoid a tumble down the dimly lit stairs. It wasn't a long way to the kitchens, but she managed to lose her way a couple of times, eventually clattering through the doorway and tripping over a pile of wooden boxes.

"Ouch! Bloody hell." The candle fell from her hand and extinguished. She shoved a stray box out of her path—grateful her candle hadn't set fire to anything—and continued through the darkened kitchen, the only light being that of a feebly glowing moon gaining entrance through a small high window. Lydia felt her way carefully through various sacks, tables, and a small cat, which grumbled its way out of one corner and slunk off into another. She knew there had to be a stash of eighteenth-century chocolate somewhere close by; she'd drunk enough of it recently. There would be a particular place for dry goods, or so she imagined. Feeling her way along one wall, she found the place she sought and paused awhile hoping her eyes might become accustomed to the dark a little more. They didn't, so she proceeded to fumble around on the shelf and felt around until her hand curled around a box of what she imagined might be chocolate. She peered at the faint writing and uttered a soft but triumphant, "Yes,"

"I see you were unable to sleep."

Lydia jumped a foot in the air, and swore. She juggled with the box of chocolate for a brief moment then gave up the struggle and let it fall to the floor, her heart pounding at the sudden interruption. She cursed again and turned to face the intruder. Luke's tall frame was barely visible in the semidarkness, but his face, a glorious sculpture of shadows and angles, was clearly defined in the glow of the candles he held. She stared. He wore a long robe, tied with a sash around his middle. "I . . . I suddenly felt the need for chocolate," she stated and squatted down to begin the recovery of the box, which miraculously had retained its contents.

"Allow me to assist you." He placed the pair of candles behind him on a shelf.

"Thanks," she managed to mutter, sensing rather than seeing him come to kneel down beside her. "Oh, good it's still in tact." She raised her face to smile her relief and found herself looking into a pair of questioning eyes. Caught in the glow of the candlelight they glimmered with an increased vividness. She wobbled and almost lost her balance, but a steadying hand behind one arm restrained her, and in an instant she was on her feet staring once more into those devastating blue eyes, both her arms held gently yet firmly.

"You almost fell," Luke observed sliding his hands along her arms to her hands and raising them to his lips. "Do you still desire chocolate?" he breathed, aware that his voice was barely audible and that he was trembling.

Lydia had little idea just what she desired at that moment, her heart was doing flip-flops and she was having severe difficulty drawing breath. "I'm not sure," she whispered, allowing her body to relax as his hands moved around her back pulling her forwards to his chest.

"Oh God, Lydia." He groaned. "Why do you wander around in such a state of undress? You'll drive me insane." He hugged her against him; it was the only way he could avoid looking into her face. The only trouble was he could feel every inch of her soft body, devoid of the usual trappings of underwear, pressed close against his own rapidly hardening one. "Lydia?"

"Yes?" Raising her head, she looked through the darkness and into a face that was becoming very familiar and far too desirable. Her arms had somehow found their way around his neck and her fingers slipped easily into the thick waves of his loose hair.

"In truth you already have driven me to madness." He slid one hand down lower onto her backside pulling her more firmly against him then lifted the other to stroke her cheek. "You're beautiful."

Lydia opened her lips very slightly in response to a finger brushed lightly across them, and was rewarded by a throaty groan from Luke who removed his finger, then slipping his hand behind her head bent to cover her mouth with his own.

She was aware of a slight taste of brandy and a great heat raging through her as she met the sweet and passionate onslaught of his mouth without resistance. The thought flashed in her mind that she was being too eager, but as suddenly as it came, it was gone, and nothing else existed but the feel of warm hard flesh pressing close, and a mouth so intense yet gentle over her own and slipping down, over her throat, now kissing her ears.

"Lydia, Lydia," Luke whispered huskily against her neck, "what say you we take ourselves somewhere else. The kitchen is not befitting, this er . . ."

Lydia attempted to nod her head. He wanted her, and there was no denying she had the hots for him. She just couldn't return to her own time without experiencing his love making; inadvisable though she knew the action to be.

With a swift sudden movement, Luke swept her up into his arms as though she were weightless, kissed her firmly on the mouth then leaned to blow out the candles before negotiating the darkened kitchen and its obstacles. He walked swiftly out into the hall and up the staircase to his own room. At the door, he halted.

"Hold me tightly," he said and moved to open his door.

Lydia held on around his neck, her breath grazing his throat and the temptation to trace tiny patterns on the sensitive flesh of his neck with her tongue too strong to resist.

"Wait, I pray of you. Inflame me no more." He strode into his room, kicked the door shut, then walked to his bed and placed her on it. He sighed and shook his head slowly. For the moment, all he could do was look at the dark eyes and the ridiculous tangle of short boyish hair around the head of the beautiful woman lying on his bed. "Now," he said softly, and sat down on the edge of the bed, "now you may continue in your work, my love."

"I don't need to beg you then?" She laughed softly.

"Nay, never worry on that."

Heat seared her veins like a molten rock flow, as her gown slipped away, removed by obviously skilled fingers, which then moulded themselves to her shoulders, throat and down lower to trace the contours of her breasts. Then his mouth was on her flesh again teasing, whisper-light and driving her to tug at his hair in her need for something more substantial. It was almost too much pleasure to bear, and she wanted to scream at him just to get on with it, but then what else would she miss out on? If this were merely foreplay, it was better than anything she'd ever experienced—better than chocolate, almost better than the real thing, and that was yet to come.

Her hips lifted, unbidden. "Luke . . . I, oh, that feels so good," she said softly and gave herself over completely to his attentions. What did it matter what he'd done before? They were here now, together in this time. But for how long?

"Let's have this robe off you, my pretty," he groaned, and pulled the garment wide so only the thin fabric of her shift lay between his hands and her breasts.

Lydia felt as though a bolt shot through her head. My pretty—he'd called her that name again. Damn him! She was just anyone to him. A serving wench at the tavern would have done just as well. "Damn you!" She shoved him hard away from her. "My pretty indeed. I'm just another in a long line aren't I?"

"No, but nay . . . Lydia my love. Please," he protested as she shoved him again and swung her feet off the bed.

"You unspeakable pig!"

"Believe me, 'twas a slip of the tongue."

"Don't you dare touch me!" Stay angry she told herself, unwilling to submit to the tears she felt welling in her eyes. She turned to face him, her eyes blazing. "You're no different to bloody Darwin. I'm just a piece of flesh to you. You were probably at the Bell with some wench last night. Well, I'm telling you now . . ." She continued to berate him with a few choice words then with a final glare tugged her robe into place and grasping the fabric close ran from the room. She thought he called out once, but didn't delay entering the sanctuary of her own chamber and slammed the door shut behind her.

Luke sat on the edge of the bed and cursed himself. Of all the damnable things he could have said to her, he'd chosen that. It really had been a slip of the tongue, but a very unfortunate one, and one she wasn't likely to forgive in a hurry. Now she considered him lower than a serpent for having tried to take her to his bed as he would a common serving wench. He groaned, stood up and secured his breeches, thankful that at least his anatomy had returned to somewhere near its less-enthusiastic self—that last look she had thrown him had been sharper than the knackerman's knife. A brandy was the first thing that came to mind. He poured himself a small one and sat down by the fire. It was going to be a long lonely night, and he wasn't inclined to visit to the Blue Bell, though hearty company may just be the thing he needed. He damned himself again for his stupidity and lack of sensibility. "Damn it, man, you were raised a gentleman," he said out loud.

"Aye, that you were. What's up?"

Luke started from his seat and turned to find Jack Palmer grinning at him. "Damn it all, Jack, stop creeping up on me like that. I may just shoot you one day."

"You wouldn't be the first that's tried."

"And besides that, there's my privacy to consider," Luke continued, indignantly.

"Oh aye, you've never bothered about that afore." Jack Palmer raised his eyebrows. "Mind if I pour myself a drink, as you don't seem about to offer?"

Luke waved a hand. "Help yourself; you know where everything is." He resumed staring into the flames.

"So," Palmer said, seating himself, "as I said, what's up?"

Luke raised his eyes unwillingly to meet the other man's. "Nothing you'd be happy to hear." He paused then said, "Unless, of course, you've been eavesdropping."

"Nay, Luke, save your ill humour for someone else." He took a sip of his drink. "Overhearing a conversation or two from the dining room or drawing room I don't deny, but even I wouldn't stoop to listening at a gentleman's bedroom door—especially yours."

"My apologies, Jack," Luke said almost wearily, "my words were uncalled for. I'm a little unsettled as you see."

"Aye, that you are. Now for the third time of asking, will you tell me what ails you?"

"I almost did what you advised me not to."

"How mean you?"

"Lydia, I found myself alone with her and . . . ," he trailed off.

"Hah!" Jack Palmer slapped his thigh. "I knew it! You couldn't bear to have such a tasty morsel under your roof without partaking of its delights. But I warned you only because as yet we have no certain idea as to her identity and reason for being here." He looked at him shrewdly. "Unless are you withholding information, my friend."

"Nothing but would further ascertain her innocence in all of this."

"Then pray tell me, for I'm not as convinced of her innocence as you appear to be. Though I do deem her to be an honest wench and a pretty one."

"*Pretty*, that's a word indeed." Luke scowled miserably.

"Luke, man, talk to me. I've not seen you in this state afore." Palmer hesitated then said, "'Tis late but what say you we take ourselves to the Bell for a bevy or two?"

"Nay, Jack, I'm in poor humour for company, but I'll tell you the gist of my story." He related the events of the evening briefly, receiving no verbal response until he'd finished his tale.

With a nod of his head Palmer said, "'Tis likely a good thing you were thwarted in your efforts. Could you but imagine the implications had you gotten her with child?"

"I should have wed her," Luke said with a shrug of his shoulders.

Palmer's eyes narrowed. "You are indeed a man smitten, and I believe you to be sincere. I've known you long enough to see how you are when it comes to the fairer sex, and the like of this I've never seen."

"'Tis of little matter now. I doubt she'll look at me again. I insulted her beyond belief; you've no idea."

Jack Palmer began to chuckle. "Tell me again, the words she told you."

"I will not," Luke growled. They'd not been ladylike, and they carried truth, which he was fully aware applied as much to him as any man—at least before this night.

"How did it go? Ah, yes, she said all you needed was somewhere warm to put it," Palmer chortled. "She got you aright there."

"Jack, when you've quite finished." Luke drew himself upright in the chair and with much consternation said, "I will agree there was a time it may have been the case." He stopped speaking seeing the smirk spread across his friend's face.

"Was a time? When wasn't there a time? Oh, my friend, in truth you are something to behold, indeed you are."

"If you won't hear me out."

"Indeed I'm all ears. Go on with your tale and I'll contain my mirth." Palmer pushed his hand against his mouth.

"I tried to tell myself that's all I wanted from her; time and again I told myself that story, hammered it into my skull, but I know now that I want more. To tell the truth, Jack, I don't know how to explain what I feel, or what I want. 'Tis all new to me."

Jack Palmer nodded his head knowingly. "You're in love, man. Simple as that. It happens from time to time. 'Tis a strange affliction."

"Love I know little of, but 'tis a mighty strange feeling, to that I'll acquiesce." Luke thought a moment, wondering at the other man's words. "'Tis like a hunger, but more than just desire, raging as it does in a man." He looked up from the fire, "Nay, 'tis an emptiness when she's not near me, when I don't hear her voice and now . . ."

Palmer chuckled again. "Carry on and you'll be writing poetry my friend."

"That I doubt," Luke laughed. "But, Jack, what to do? I offended her badly."

"It seems to me that even though she is offended now, give her a little time to come around, and she'll understand what you're about. I credit her with a good head on her shoulders, and considering her own words I don't think she's quite as sensitive as you may be inclined to believe."

"Think you?"

"Indeed. But I still beg caution of you." He chose his words carefully, "We have a task before us which must be accomplished."

"I give you my word, Jack, I'll not lay claim to any part of her 'ere this thing's done and over with. All supposing she'll have me," Luke added miserably.

"Have you ever had trouble convincing a woman before this day?" There was a twinkle in his friend's eye. "Confidence, my friend, and all shall be well. Confidence and caution."

"By the way, why are you here at this time of night, or should I say morn?"

"Ah, I'm glad you asked," said the other, stroking his chin. "I was party to a little information earlier this eve. It appears we may have our quarry by next week. A dawn coach direct from London, a change of horses two miles out of the city—in itself an unusual thing, then headed north, straight for the border. What think you?"

"Aye, could be," agreed Luke. "I hope so. This thievery is getting quite beyond my passion. And how am I to return the things I've taken so far? There's a veritable pirate's hoard in my cellars."

"Don't look so dismayed. If you are indeed intent on returning the goods, it shall be done anonymously. Although there are some whom I desire to bemoan their losses."

"There's one at least who'll not see his precious gold again." Luke had never hidden his dislike of Lord Fulford. "Aye, there are many charities up at London only too willing to accept the indulgence of a philanthropist such as myself, without too many questions asked."

"There now, you're back in your normal spirits, and I'll drink to that." Palmer glugged the last of his brandy and reached for more.

"You drink too much, Jack. You'll be falling off that horse of yours one day."

"She'd stand and wait for me, don't you fret. She's a good mare. Less trouble than a woman," he added with a smirk.

"Damn you, Jack."

"As I've said before, I may well be. Now, will you not tell me more of your dear-heart? Something perhaps, that will truly convince me of her innocence. Whence she came for instance?"

"That, I cannot do. In fact, even I cannot fully comprehend some of the things she told me."

Jack Palmer looked puzzled for a moment. "How be that? You're as intelligent a fellow as ever there was; you've travelled, you're well read. What is it you don't comprehend?"

Luke shook his head. "In truth, Jack, if I felt certain it would cement her innocence I should tell you all, but I fear it would only serve to confound you."

"Don't you trust me then?"

"Jack, 'tis not like that, naught at all to do with trust." He looked up from the fire. "Trust, nay. *Incredible* is the word. If I tell you that she herself is involved in some strange goings on, shall you leave it at that, at least for the time being?"

Palmer appeared to consider for a moment before speaking. "Luke, if her story is good enough for you, then I accept it. I just hope your judgment isn't being influenced by your prick."

Tempted to swipe the poker from the hearth and wrap it around his friend's neck, Luke took instead a very long deep breath and said quietly, "No, you may rest assured, 'tis not."

"Now I do believe you to be in love with the wench." Jack Palmer laughed loudly. "In more sane moments you would have made some ferocious attack upon my person, which would have resulted in two pairs of black eyes followed by a bout of hearty drinking down at the Bell."

"Aye, well, now you know."

TEN

Lydia couldn't sleep, and sat at her window, staring first at the moon when it deigned to make an appearance from behind the ominous dark clouds of the night sky, and then at the wisps of white mist that heralded the arrival of a pale, chilly dawn.

Periodically she rose and went to sit by the fire that still blazed in the hearth. Eighteenth-century houses weren't the warmest of places unless one happened to be in direct proximity of the fireplace. She was miserable, and the worst of it was she knew it to be totally her own fault. There had been other bad experiences in relationships, not least the long-term one with the dreadful Darwin, so why hadn't she learned from it?

She had known from the beginning that His Lordship had no scruples and even fewer morals. Still she had allowed herself to be influenced by his charm and those devastating blue eyes. How many more times would she fall for false promises and lies? However, to be fair, Luke had never promised her anything beyond that which he offered at the time. What would it have been like with him? It could have been the most wonderful, glorious thing in the world if his reputation had not gone before him. She sighed, half wishing her pride and scruples hadn't got in the way, but on the other hand, if he slept around so much the chances of catching some awful disease were likely very high. She'd done the right thing, she convinced herself, and in not mentioning she'd seen Jack Palmer out at the cottage and of all the stuff she'd come across there, she had also done the right thing. What she needed was an ally someone who could help her sort out this mess. To whom could she turn to in her hour of need? She stared out of the window, over the trees, and through the slowly creeping daylight to the land beyond.

*   *   *

Two days later, she sat in exactly the same position, having spent the last forty-eight hours wandering the house and deliberating her future. Luke had been absent, and as no one else appeared concerned, she hadn't bothered to ask where he might be. I seemed there was only one avenue open to her. Lord Fulford couldn't live too far away, and although it was his coach that had almost caused her to meet her maker, and the impression Judd had given was less than favourable, he seemed like the only alternative she had.

Around eight o'clock she made her way to the dining room uncertain whether breakfast would be available. His Lordship kept greatly varying hours, and it was a fact that Lydia had overheard the staff grousing about on more than one occasion.

No one was around, and she was about to leave when a servant appeared and enquired as to madam's preference for breakfast. She ordered the quickest thing she could think of and shortly sat down to a large plate of scrambled eggs and a pot of steaming coffee. At least someone had remembered what she drank.

The plan in her head was somewhat vague as she left the house and made her way to the stables. She didn't have the horse brought around to the front of the house, deciding the less fuss she made, the less chance there was of Luke's apprehending her before she could leave. She was certain he wouldn't approve her intention to visit his neighbour, and as he had pointed out it wasn't safe for her to ride the highway alone, but what alternative did she have? What if she were mugged? Or murdered? Or even worse raped and murdered? *Don't think about it,* she told herself sternly. *Fear could only be an enemy.*

"Mornin', milady." The stable lad touched his hat.

"Morning, Peter. Would you saddle my horse?"

"Be off again? You rides more than I ever seen a lady ride you does."

"I'd still like to use an ordinary saddle," she muttered under her breath, noting several very nice looking ones sitting nearby. She determined to try one some day soon, when it wasn't too cold or windy, when her skirts wouldn't fly up over her head and she'd end up showing her bare bum to all and sundry.

"Mare's ready, milady."

Lydia roused herself from thoughts of how uncomfortable it might indeed prove to be riding astride in long skirts and without knickers, but she supposed there might be a way of sitting on her petticoat, if it would stay in place. "My shorts," she mumbled. She noticed the lad staring at her. "Ah, yes, thank you, I was thinking about something."

"My dad says it be unhealthy to think too hard."

"He might be right," she agreed and followed the pair to the mounting block.

"Should I tell 'is Lordship when you be coming back, milady?"

Lydia knew this to be a demand and not a request. Luke had her covered—so to speak. "I'll be back in time for dinner." She settled herself in the saddle and urged the horse forwards knowing the lad was about to insist she be more specific. Well, damn Luke and his blue eyes. He wasn't her keeper.

She rode to the gatehouse, and after accepting Judd's offer of a quick drink and a chat she had gleaned enough information, she hoped, to find Fulford Manor.

The general direction was easy enough, and she rode on regardless, taking a couple of turns as Judd had instructed, and keeping her eyes and ears open for any unwanted companion who might happen to be skulking around.

"I should have brought a pistol," she observed absentmindedly as the horse trotted along the unfamiliar dirt road. "Should learn how to use one anyhow, don't you think so horse?" The animal said nothing. "Mind you," Lydia continued, happy in her own company and with the sound of her own voice, "from what I've heard of these eighteenth-century firearms, they're about as likely to blow up in your face as to fire properly. Maybe I should get myself a bow and arrow."

The mare pricked its ears and snorted.

"Now what's wrong? Lydia scolded and prepared herself for an equine performance. A low rumbling caught her ears, the same rumbling she had heard the day she was knocked off her bike. She listened, as did the horse, not wanting to continue in its forwards motion and fully intent on awaiting the rapidly approaching noise behind them. Which side would he be driving on? Lydia had no idea, and was still deliberating the question when the mare began to sidestep into the middle of the road.

The crashing of a coach and horses drew closer, and Lydia cursed for not having both legs down the sides of her horse. "How can I use my legs like this?" she wailed and wished she had learned to ride side-saddle properly. She turned and looked over her shoulder just in time to see a pair of horses rounding the bend a couple of hundred feet behind them. "Horse, don't do this, you're going to get us flattened." She pulled and kicked helplessly, but her efforts were ignored. The horse continued to snort and patter around, and Lydia had already decided that the coach driver was blind, stupid, or a homicidal maniac.

He wasn't slowing his horses down.

As if sensing real danger from her equine associates, the mare spun on her quarters and made a sudden dash across the road with Lydia clinging gamely onto the saddle.

"Whoa, whoa! Get out of the way, you fool," the coach driver shouted. He stood and hauled on the reins apparently just coming to his senses in the realisation he might actually kill someone.

"I'm bloody trying . . . and fool yourself," Lydia yelled back and struggled to regain control of her mount.

"What the devil's going on? Stop the coach, and get control of the horses, man."

Lydia heard the second voice and thought she recognised it. The mare was merely bouncing up and down now, and she took the opportunity to glare at her would-be assassin who peered at her from the window of his coach. She was in no mood for pleasantries; these clowns had almost had her in a ditch a second time. She gathered her wits about her. "Do you always have your coachman drive so fast? You could have unhorsed me, and then what would you have done if I'd been hurt?"

The man in the coach simply gazed at her, a slightly startled expression on his face.

"Well? Can't you speak?" She was angry and scared.

"Madam," the man said at last, "would it be fair to say that you appear to be in very poor control of your horse?"

"That's not the issue," she spluttered.

"Aye, but it is. My coach has right of way on the road, and should I come to grief simply because some person cannot control his mount"—he paused—"you would find yourself in very deep water."

He smiled and it was nothing short of hideous to Lydia's mind.

"Damn you!"

"Coachman! Tarry no more," he spat at his driver. "Leave this wench to her own devices."

Lydia was about to fling the juiciest morsel of twentieth-century verbal abuse that she could summon, but the mare made a violent manoeuvre in objection to the departure of its four-footed friends. "No! Stop it, no." She wrestled for a few short seconds as her feet became dislodged and she dropped her whip, then with skirts not quite over her head found that she was airborne. She hit the earth and lay there unable to move whether out of fear, shock, or actual damage, she wasn't sure. Footsteps approached and a hand reached down and grabbed her roughly by the arm in an attempt to haul her to her feet.

"Get off me! Let me go," she spluttered and realised she couldn't be badly injured just by the volume of her own voice. She struggled more violently as the man held on and cursed her thoroughly. She cursed him back. "You wait 'til His Lordship hears about this." Why she said it she wasn't sure, but she needed some sort of back up just in case.

"Let her be," the man from the coach called, suddenly appearing by her side. "Are you hurt?"

Lydia stopped struggling the second her arm was released, and after a fortifying sniff or two, she looked up to face the man who spoke to her. "I don't know yet, do I?" She'd been about to mention the need for X-rays and a CAT scan, but held her tongue.

"Perhaps I could offer you the hospitality of my home until we are certain you have taken no bodily hurt. 'Tis but a few miles." He indicated the general direction with a wave of his hand.

Lydia studied him a moment or two. "Are you by any chance Lord Fulford?"

"I am, and might I enquire as to your name?"

Lydia scrambled to her feet and brushed her skirts down around her. "I'm Lydia McKenzie. Pleased to meet Your Lordship." She stuck out her hand then remembering where she was, dropped a quick curtsey and offered the back of her hand instead.

"I'm afraid you have me at a disadvantage, my dear." He took her hand lightly and bowed his head.

"Mmm, yes, I suppose you don't know me, but I was on my way to see you actually." It had never even crossed her mind to plan what she would say to this man, and now she found she had nothing suitable in her vocabulary.

"Well, you were on your way to see me and you mentioned something about His Lordship not being pleased. Who might His Lordship be?"

Lydia began to sway, and little blacks spots danced wildly in front of her eyes. "Luke Waverly, the . . ." Vaguely she felt herself carried then placed on what felt like a seat, and a blanket pulled around her.

"Fetch her horse, man and bring it along. Make haste now; 'tis damnably cold to be sitting around."

The coach squeaked and rocked as Lord Fulford climbed in and seated himself. Lydia tried to open her eyes, but each time she experienced such an acute wave of nausea, that she determined not to try for a while. She felt the coach lurch, and they were on their way. In the dark confines of the blanket, she was able to manage coherent thoughts and had about formulated some plausible excuse for wanting to visit Lord Fulford when the coach, which had been rattling along a good old rate, suddenly swerved and shuddered to a halt. The driver and the horses cursed seemingly as one at some outrage.

"Stand and deliver!"

Lydia heard the words plainly enough from inside her dark refuge and had the foresight to slide a little flatter onto the seat where she hoped she may not be so conspicuous.

"Hold those horses, man." It was the same voice as had uttered the previous order. "Now get down. Now!"

Lydia found herself trembling. It was all very well to play highwayman and to dream of being abducted—in a nice way, of course, by a handsome gentleman of the road, but to meet one in the flesh, and after all the gruesome tales Judd had told her, she wasn't quite sure she was up to this. Maybe he wouldn't see her if she remained still and under the blanket.

The highwayman requested Lord Fulford step down so he might relieve him of his valuables.

Fulford haughtily replied that he had little on his person as he was in fact returning from a business journey involving no frivolity or need for much coin or jewel. Apparently, his words fell on deaf ears, and he was informed that his fine clothing would have to do in that case. A second later Lydia found her hand exposed and her engagement ring somehow forced from her finger. She blinked, surprised at its removal. She'd been trying for days, and thanked God that today her hands were really cold and she had apparently lost a little weight. Otherwise she was certain she would have forfeited a digit in the process.

"Who's that?" the highwayman demanded.

"Well, you know how it is," Lord Fulford replied silkily, dropping the now ringless hand. "Even business has its upsides. She had a little too much to drink, that's all."

Why would he say that? Why didn't he just admit to the truth? Lydia moved slowly, working the blanket free just enough that she was able to peek out through its folds. The highwayman had his head bowed slightly, and she cold see nothing below the feather trimmed edges of his three-cornered hat. He began speaking again, and without the muffling effects of the heavy wool around her ears, it was a voice Lydia had heard before. And then he looked up, almost straight at her. He wore an eye mask and a kerchief, but she'd know that steady gaze anywhere. She gasped and ducked her head, seeing clearly behind her own closed eyes the face of the highwayman, masked but not disguised, to those who knew him. Something, perhaps fate, had held her back from delivering that letter into his hands. Palmer was set to blow up Parliament, and he was a thief as well. She shuddered. Now she was certain Luke had nothing to do with this nefarious business and was unaware of this man's real business pursuits. At least she had her answer about the horses and the clothing in the cottage. But how to tell Luke, and should she tell Lord Fulford she knew the identity of the man who had robbed him? The immediate answer which sprung to mind was, no. She would think of a way to tell Luke and let him decide Palmer's fate. She relaxed a little inside the confines of the blanket as Lord Fulford regained his seat, her indignation growing by the second at the way the man had just taken her ring and handed it over to a thief. She pulled the blanket from her face just in time to hear the parting words of the highwayman, and watched dumbstruck as he set the mighty black beast he rode to a full standing rear and raised his hat in salute. She was further surprised to note that he appeared to have a full head of hair.

"Dick Turpin thanks you, my lord," he shouted and spurred the horse away.

Lydia nearly threw up. She had just been victim to a hold up by Dick Turpin, the most infamous highwayman in history, and who just happened to be one of Luke Waverly's business associates. Not only that—he wore a toupee.

"Scoundrel. I'll have him hanged, just see if I don't," the man sitting next to her snarled.

"You gave him my ring," she said, turning to look at him. "Why?"

Lord Fulford appraised her thoroughly before he spoke. "Surely, you do not expect me to undergo the humiliation of disrobing in public? He was satisfied with your jewel it seems."

She sighed. "I suppose." Anyway, she had tried to throw the ring away, so what if a highwayman had it now? She smiled suddenly and said, "Just wait 'til Darwin finds out."

Lord Fulford looked at her for a brief second as though about to ask a question, but then he turned away, uninterested, and stared out of the window, remarking briefly that they would be at his home within the half hour.

Lydia didn't feel at her best, and so the lack of conversation was to her liking. She huddled under the blanket, horribly

aware that she hadn't the foggiest notion of how she was
going to get back home again, and by home she wasn't certain
whether she meant her own abode in the twenty-first century
or the house she'd come to think of as home this past couple
of weeks. There had to be a way of returning to her own time,
but she wasn't convinced it would be easy. Climbing on her
bike and returning to the place she fell off might work, but it
was getting colder day by day, and as had been pointed out to
her many times, the roads weren't safe for a traveller alone,
particularly a woman. Hadn't she just witnessed the fact?

"Are you all right, my dear?" Lord Fulford enquired
suddenly.

"Oh, I'm fine, but I may have sustained a concussion; I've
a bloody awful headache coming on." She may as well rub it
in. She did feel a headache starting, and she just might have
a concussion. Bugger it, Lord Fulford deserved to feel at least
a bit guilty, though she doubted he would. She was having
second thoughts about asking him for help. He didn't seem
the helpful type, but perhaps she shouldn't judge—he may
be a perfectly nice man under that perfectly vile exterior. She
drifted off into an uneasy sleep, her head flopping around with
each jolt of the coach until at last they came to a crunching
halt.

Lydia felt herself shaken by the shoulder and raised her
head slowly on a stiff neck to look around her. "Oh, yes.
Nice house." It was. Not so large as Beckham, but beautifully
detailed and well appointed amidst tall poplars and large
stone archways.

"Thank you, my dear, I think so. Now if you please." He
indicated the open door where a footman stood ready to assist
Lydia out of the carriage.

She stepped down, a little wobbly on her feet and glad
of the footman's steadying hand. Another liveried servant
appeared to assist her and, with a short bow and an indication
of his hand that she should accompany him, led her into the
house. They entered a large hall, and she was immediately

ushered into a large drawing room where a blazing fire roared in a tremendous hearth and warmed the room to a very comfortable level. Lydia sank down in a deep chair and was relieved of the blanket she continued to clutch defensively around her person.

"Would milady care for something warming to drink perhaps?" The man didn't wait for a reply but strode from the room carrying the blanket.

Well, this was quite a predicament. Here she was with some unknown lord, a man who apparently disliked Luke's family intensely but who might be the only one she could turn to for help, even though she herself didn't find the man pleasing company—and that was putting it mildly. The fact he'd not been inclined to offer hospitality until she had mentioned Luke's name was worth consideration. What was he after? More importantly, how was she going to leave? Lydia knew she wouldn't be able to ride home in her present condition, not on that bloody animal anyway. Damn the beast; she'd order its oats cut to half ration when she got back.

"Milady." The servant returned and placed a goblet of heavy cut glass on a small table by Lydia's right elbow. It steamed deliciously, and she felt her spirits rise. Having sampled Judd's famous brews she was certain this would help her regain her strength.

"'Tis hot, milady; be careful you don't burn yourself," the man continued. "I took the liberty of fetching you this if you still feel a chill." He lifted a quilt from where he'd placed it on a chair back and handed it to her.

"Thank you, you're very kind," she said with a smile and a gratitude she actually felt. The quilt was thick and stuffed with feathers, and the silk casing made it extremely comfortable after the initial one second of icy cold contact. Lydia hugged it around her.

"Any thing else, milady?"

"No, thank you, you've been very helpful. I'll be sure and tell His Lordship."

"As you will, milady." He gave a wry smile. "If you'll beg my pardon for saying so, he won't care a fig."

"Oh, I'm sure he will," she faltered, unsure whether to add to her statement.

"Be you staying long, milady?"

"I don't think so. Why do you ask?" She laughed suddenly. "Trying to get rid of me already?"

"No, milady, for certain, no." The man looked at her steadily.

"I was joking, I'm sorry."

"Of course, milady. I was merely wondering about having a fire lit in one of the guest rooms for you."

"To tell the truth I'll likely be off as soon as I've finished my drink and got warmed through."

"You certainly will not!" a voice boomed from the doorway. "Be gone with you, man, and fetch me a good hot toddy. I see my guest already has hers. Don't stand there tittle-tattling with your irritations."

The man retreated from the room.

Lydia took pains to prevent an unpleasant frown settling on her face and forced something of a smile to her lips. "This is very kind of you, Your Lordship." *Stay as formal as possible,* she told herself, *the safest way.*

"Think nothing of it, my dear. May I call you, Lydia?"

She desperately wanted to refuse his request, but he was the one person she may have to turn to for help. She needed to stay on his good side. "Of course, er, Your Lordship."

"Good, good, ah, here is my drink. Not hot enough to raze my palate, I trust."

"No, milord. As always, moderate, to your liking." The servant gave a swift glance in Lydia's direction and hurried from the room.

"Devil's, they've been known to set the bloody stuff on fire afore bringing it to me in the hopes I'll lift the skin off my gums. They tried it twice; I made them pay."

"I see." Lydia felt herself squirm. What sort of hatred drove servants to do such a thing, and what had Lord Fulford done to exact his payment?

"Very likely you don't, but 'tis of no matter." He held up his glass. "Cheers, my dear."

"Cheers." What else could she say?

They sat in silence for a while. The hot toddy had the desired warming effect, though not nearly so potent as Judd's home concoction, and Lydia began to feel more like her old self.

Ready, and able to flee if the need arose.

Lord Fulford turned out to be a most genial host after insisting she inspect the rooms that were to be hers for the night, or for as long as she wished, and being very attentive to her opinion of them.

"They're very nice, but I don't wish to impose any further on your hospitality." She found herself responding favourably to his politeness.

"Nonsense, my dear. 'Tis growing colder outdoors by the minute. In fact, I should not be surprised to find we have snow on the morrow. Besides, that fall you had most certainly knocked the stuffing out of you. No, you must remain the night under my roof."

There was no use in protesting; it was already late in the afternoon. What would Luke think when she didn't come home? Likely he wouldn't even notice. He'd be out on the town tonight, down at the Blue Bell with some floozy, getting what he hadn't managed to get last night.

Lousy philandering pig.

"Well, in that case, thank you."

"Enchanted, my dear. Now, you mentioned that you were in fact coming to see me, and I am still wondering for what reason I should be accorded such an honour."

"Well," she cast around for words as she tried to push her groggy mind into gear, "it's a funny story really. You see I got lost a while ago. Another knock on the head when I took a fall from my . . . er, horse." Dear God, she hoped the man didn't remember coming across her in the dark, on her bike. Still, she could swear she was on horseback, and they'd be none the wiser about the bike. A sudden vision of Jack Palmer riding her bike sprang into her mind. She started to giggle; it rose in her throat, uncalled for and uncontrolled. She let out a shriek before clapping her fist to her mouth and choking behind her hand, feigning a coughing fit.

Lord Fulford stared for a moment then ran from the room shouting for assistance, clearly having forgotten the bellpull in his haste.

Lydia finally exploded, unable to control her laughter any longer and was about to roll on the floor when the servant entered, ran to her side and hoisted her to a standing position.

"Milady, what is it? His Lordship said you were taken with a fit. Sit you down." He forced her into a chair and held her by the shoulders until her gurgles subsided, and she wiped her eyes and hiccoughed.

"Don't worry," Lydia assured him between the diminishing gurgles and sobs, "I'm fine. I'm not choking, and I'm not possessed or anything, if that's what you're thinking."

The man looked at her steadily and said nothing.

"You wouldn't understand if I told you," she continued, trying desperately to forbid a vision of the thigh-booted, velvet-clad figure pedalling her bike furiously through the trees from reappearing in her head.

"You never know, milady."

"But I do." She began to snigger again and finally exploded in a fit of laughter. "Dick Turpin on a mountain bike!" She grasped her stomach and rolled off the chair onto the floor, tears streaming down her face. "I told, you," she gasped at length to the man staring at her. "You couldn't possibly understand."

Nor did he. Apart from catching something about Dick Turpin, the notorious highwayman, he had no idea why she'd taken on so. But his task was to calm the lady, and he intended to do his best. Kneeling beside her, he patted her hand and nodded comfortingly.

At length, Lydia regained her sanity and climbed to her feet with the help of Andrew as she discovered his name to be.

"Thank you, Andrew. I'm sorry to put you to all this trouble, and you may tell His Lordship that I'm quite recovered from my . . . er, fit. Brought on by my fall you understand." She began to giggle again as thoughts of Dick Turpin trundling around on her precious mountain bike flitted through her mind's eye.

"Milady," Andrew cautioned, "begging your pardon."

"Thank you, I'll try and stay under control, but honestly you've no idea how funny this is." She sniffed and coughed in a businesslike manner. "I'm glad His Lordship took so long in getting back," she said.

Andrew lowered his voice and said, "He's waiting down the hallway. He's afeard to come back in case you take on a real fit, like you were possessed. Squeamish he is, don't like blood or vomit." He paused. "Neither the other."

The other? Lydia was about to ask, when the disgusting realisation of his meaning struck her. Had Lord Fulford really expected she might . . . ?

She was saved from further indulgences in the workings of the human bowel by the entrance of said lord, looking a little pale around the gills.

"I'm fine now, Your Lordship," she assured him. He didn't seem about to disagree, and that cheered her immensely. "Just a little upset from my fall."

Unconvinced, he merely grunted his assent before seating himself close to the fire and continuing with his toddy.

Lydia continued to chirp at him. "I wasn't sick, I mean I didn't vomit, and I didn't do any damage to the furniture." She paused as he turned a dreadfully pale gaze upon her. "Or to myself, and there's no blood anywhere." She smiled in a reassuring fashion and reached for her own drink before sitting back down in the chair. "And none of the other," she added with a sly grin.

"Madam! Do you mind, I am of a delicate disposition when it comes to things of that nature, and besides," he stated petulantly, "'tis almost time for dinner. Come." He stood.

Lydia smirked into her glass. Was this really the man who wanted to steal Luke's land? What a spineless toad he was turning out to be. "Thank you once again, Your Lordship, for your hospitality." She took the offered arm, wishing it were Luke's arm she held even though he was a philandering pig, and walked through to the dining room where a table was set splendidly for two. Perhaps she and Lord Beckham could just be friends. So far, she had withstood his advances, but how long could she go on if he persisted? With a sinking heart she remembered her parting words to him; she'd be lucky if there were even a place for her to sleep at Beckham House when she returned.

"If you have concern regarding your absence from Beckham, fret not my dear I have sent word that you are safe and well, and that I have offered my hospitality for a few days," Lord Fulford said suddenly.

"A few days?"

"I thought it best in the circumstances," he continued, quite apparently well recovered from his temporary bout of frailty. "You are, of course, free to leave at any time, but we must not take chances with your delicate health."

Lydia felt her eyes widen. "Actually, I'm in pretty good health," she contested.

"Ah, but, my dear, there is no need to be brave."

He was a loony, a squeamish loony, and she wanted to tell him to go to hell right there and then, but eighteenth-century protocol dictated otherwise, and Lydia felt just a little inclined to abide by some of the rules of the century in which she found herself. At least the squeamish loony hadn't made a move on her. She gave the man a good old-fashioned cheesy grin across the dining room table as her chair was scooted under her backside by yet another liveried member of staff.

"I can see you are a woman of spirit," he observed.

"I try," she commented. "Seriously, though, I'm of quite a hardy disposition. I have a stomach like a horse and an asbestos mouth when it comes to curries."

"Frankly, my dear, some of your words befuddle me."

Oh, dear she was babbling future stuff again. "Sorry, we have some different words where I come from." She leaned back slightly as soup was delivered to her. "You have a very nice home." She hoped he wouldn't ask the obvious, but she knew he would, and after several mouthfuls of soup, he did.

"Where exactly are you from? I believe you were about to tell me a strange story as you put it when you were taken with your, er, when you were indisposed."

"When I started choking, you mean." When you left me to choke, she thought silently.

He was waiting for an answer.

"I'm not from these parts as you may have already guessed."

"Indeed I had gleaned that much."

"This soup is delicious."

He was still waiting.

"I'm from just outside Leeds," she said, at last deciding the truth would do as well as any.

"Do business there myself."

"Oh, you do?" She tried not to sound too concerned. There was little chance he would expect her to know anyone in particular.

"Perhaps you know Lord Sedgemere, or Sir Douglas Arnold.? They move in the most fashionable of circles."

"I only go there shopping, at the new centre; the parking's easy." She swallowed and stopped speaking. Talk about putting her foot in it. She was glad she wasn't a centipede. Looking up, she saw His Lordship was staring at her in a most peculiar way.

"I should be pleased and less confounded if you would explain your observations to me, after dinner. Then we shall have an abundance of time, and you will have my undivided attention," he added and continued eating.

Lydia ate slowly and steadily everything that was put in front of her, anything to delay the moment of truth. The moment when she'd have to explain why she had come to see him in the first place, and all the rest he would want to know.

Some two hours later, she leaned back in her chair and held in the biggest burp imaginable. She had eaten far more than she could comfortably manage and was now paying for that indulgence. "I'm full," she sighed, "and I've got indigestion." She was certain it existed in this century under a different name. "Pain, here," she clarified and held her stomach.

"I'm hardly surprised," Lord Sainsbury said with ill-disguised gravity. "Never, have I seen a woman eat as you do."

"Oh, I do it all the time when the food's as good as it was here tonight, and then I suffer for it." She groaned. "I usually take to my bed immediately afterwards." She noted he was still frowning. "Otherwise I get really ill . . . my insides start churning, if you know what I mean." Good, he was turning pale, and the grimness on his face was giving way to acute distaste. She offered a wan, slightly nauseated-looking smile and was adequately rewarded.

"I bid you goodnight then, madam. We may perhaps continue our conversation on the morrow?"

"Yes. Oh, and thank you again for a really delicious dinner. I'm so looking forwards to breakfast. Lots of it I hope." She beamed at his ever-increasing pallor, bobbed a curtsy, and made her way, assisted by a maid, who it appeared had been hanging around for just that purpose, to her room.

"Anything else you needs, milady, just pull there." The woman indicated the thick braid dangling from the ceiling. Lydia dismissed her, convincing the woman she really and truly was capable of undressing herself as she wasn't wearing a corset. She ignored the fleeting disagreeable frown she received and shooed the woman out of the door, locking it securely in her wake. Then with a groan, she threw up into the thing that served as a toilet and wished she were dead.

ELEVEN

Lydia stretched, and yawned, feeling much better for having a good night's sleep and a resilient digestive tract. She looked around at her surroundings. It was a very nice room and warm too. How had it stayed so warm throughout the night? She flung back the covers and stared.

"Mornin', milady," a maid kneeling by the hearth greeted her. "Got the fire goin' early for you I did. It can be a bit nippy like, these morns." She grinned and turned back to her work sweeping ashes.

But how? Hadn't she locked the door herself? "Good morning," Lydia responded finally.

The maid stood with her bucket of ashes held carefully in one hand doing her best to prevent the hot metal swinging against her petticoats. "Do you want your door lockin' again, milady?"

Lydia wanted to say there wasn't much point, but merely shook her head, noticing the bunch of keys the girls wore at her waist. Lord Fulford or anyone for that matter could have snuck in her room during the night; so much for security. She considered the fact briefly, but as she'd not been accosted there seemed little point dwelling on it. Slippers and a robe sat on the end of the bed. She donned them, walked across to the windows and drew back the drapes. The day was dull and pale looking, and a soft mist hung in wisps like Christmas garlands over and around the many Poplar trees surrounding the house. Lydia stared appreciatively and had to admit the place was beautiful, set among low hills, equally as well appointed as Beckham, and the grounds were definitely more ornate, and perhaps a little better kept. But the lord of *that* house had other things on his mind, most of the time. She turned as two maids entered the room, each carrying what appeared to be a fully laden tray covered with a white cloth.

"His Lordship said he thought you might like to take breakfast quietly in your room," offered the first girl. She placed her own tray down on a table then turned to instruct the other girl how to set everything.

"Thank you," Lydia said and waited until both had left the room before she allowed herself a fit of the giggles. Obviously, last night's performance had given Lord Fulford no stomach for her company at breakfast. Good, that gave her more breathing space to fabricate some plausible story for visiting him. It would also give her time to consider her options should she find having him for an ally not to her liking. She looked at the mounds of food before her and groaned. No way in hell could she even start to demolish this lot, but what to do with it? His Lordship mustn't suspect she'd purposely made herself ill last night to avoid his questions. She lifted the lid to a tall silver pot, sniffed, and curled her nose in distaste.

She picked at the food for about half an hour, even managing to down several mouthfuls of tea to aid her digestion, but eventually giving up the battle and conceding she would have to risk his finding out the truth. A thought struck her, and she staggered to her feet taking a few deep breaths before walking to her door and peering out along the hallway. His Lordship was nowhere in sight, and neither was anyone else for that matter. She dashed back into the room and grabbed the silver teapot. Somewhere at the end of this hallway, near the top of the stairs, stood a very large plant in a very large pot, and she remembered it looked as though it needed watering. Water, tea, what was the difference? She found the plant and disposed of the tea in a worthwhile manner, noting, as she turned, a line of marble busts sitting atop short pillars and placed at intervals along the wall. Someone once told her that the pillars were often hollow, and she hardly dared hope as she gently shifted one of the marble heads to one side, taking care not to move it overly far lest it proved too heavy for her to support. Her heart took a leap, and she quietly returned the object to its resting place and ran back to her room.

In record time, the breakfast trays were depleted. She took care to leave a little of something on each plate, realising it wasn't humanly possible for her to have eaten it all without being extremely ill. Lydia nodded with satisfaction. The busts were heavy enough to seal in the smell of the food inside their pillars for a few hours at least, and she would be long gone by the time it began to decompose. For a moment, she experienced a sudden pang of guilt, but it quickly passed. If indeed Lord Fulford turned out to be an ally and someone she could trust, she might come clean about the food and apologise profusely; then again . . . she may just avoid him like the plague.

As it turned out, His Lordship had been called away on urgent business, leaving instruction that she be accorded every courtesy and that he would arrive back in time for dinner at six. Lydia hadn't planned on staying another night, and she certainly didn't intend to be around when the breakfast in the busts started to stink. Several hours were all she had mind to remain, just long enough to ascertain her chances of help from His Lordship, and since he wasn't here, there was nothing for it but to ride back to Beckham on the mare. She cursed under her breath having fully expected she would ride in the comfort of Lord Fulford's coach and determined to make the mare canter the whole way back to Beckham. Keep her moving forwards, tire her out and she shouldn't give too much trouble. Lydia grunted and touched a tender spot on her hip where she'd made first contact when she landed in the dirt.

"Oh, but His Lordship was quite specific," a man stated some time later, as he barred her way into the stables. "He gave instructions you were to remain for dinner. Concerned for your health, milady, that's all. You had a terrible fall yesterday, you did, and it be too nippy for riding."

"Do I look injured?" she growled and wondered if she could dodge the man, but then what? She couldn't outrun him wearing a dress.

"Never can tell, milady." He pulled a face and shook his head. "Never can tell."

"Bugger!" She ignored the servant's surprised frown and marched back to the house and into the drawing room where she'd sat the previous evening.

"You be feeling all right, milady?" It was Andrew.

She let go a long sigh. "Not really. I wanted to go home. Back to Beckham," she clarified.

"His Lordship seems fixed on your staying a while longer. Sent your horse back he did."

"What? You mean I don't have a horse to ride?"

Andrew shrugged. "I suppose he thought it pointless to keep your horse here when he intends sending you back in his coach."

"Yes, but when? I have things to do," she wailed. Things like warning Luke Waverly that his business associate was really a notorious highwayman who was possibly planning another gunpowder plot.

"I wish I could help, but the lads out in the stable have been told you're to stay here."

"Stay today, tonight you mean?" Lydia was experiencing discomfort, and it was nothing to do with her digestive system. The servant wasn't looking at her directly, and she noticed he shuffled his feet. "Andrew, please tell me the truth. How long am I to stay here?"

He spread his hands in a helpless gesture. "I truly don't know, but I did hear"—he turned to glance at the door—"that there's some business Lord Fulford wants to see finished afore he lets you return to Beckham. For your own safety, he said. Least that's what I heard from the staff."

"For my own safety?" She shook her head. Maybe Fulford was a good guy, and she'd been too blinded by her own lust and Lord Beckham's charm to see the truth of the matter.

"Aye, that's about it, so not to worry, eh?" Andrew concluded. "I'll fetch you some tea."

"Coffee perhaps."

"As you wish."

He duly returned with coffee and an assortment of extremely fattening pastries. Lydia looked them over with disgust but realised she could be tempted if she tried hard enough. Anyway, she needed to think, and she always did her best thinking when she was eating. The fire was warm, she was comfortable, and with a steaming pot of coffee to hand and a plateful of sickeningly sweet pastries, she put on her thinking cap. Things were not falling into place, at least not as she would have them, but that was just too much to hope for. Life just wasn't like that. Firstly, there was the murdered man. Who was he, and who was he working for? Obviously not the people who murdered him, so who were they working for? She took a bite of an apple-filled pastry. Then there was the letter that was to be delivered into the hands of Jack Palmer, who, although he pretended to be a legitimate businessman, was actually Dick Turpin the highwayman and might also be planning to blow up Parliament. Therefore, she warmed to her subject and wished she had a pen and some paper to write all this down, casting Jack Palmer as a bad guy, who then were the good guys so to speak?

Hadn't Lord Fulford been robbed at the point of a pistol? It wouldn't seem likely that Turpin was in his good books. Was she really getting any further with this? Her previous allusions as to Luke being involved in the nefarious goings on at the cottage seemed less remote due to the discovery of Jack Palmer's real identity. Still, Luke might just be playing highwayman for the hell of it—the aristocracy often became bored. She sighed for the tenth time that morning. What sort of information could a letter destined for the hands of a highwayman contain? Of course, wasn't it obvious? Information about a coach load of goodies, gold perhaps, or people wearing lots of it. It was a bit drastic, to murder someone for that sort of information, but then again no, it wasn't. The eighteenth century was a tough place if one wasn't highly placed in the hierarchy, or had pots of money. And what was one murder compared to a lifetime of comfortable living. Supposing those men had succeeded in getting that letter?

Lydia felt her blood run cold. What if someone had seen her and until now they'd kept quiet, waiting for the right time, the right place? What if Turpin knew she had the letter and was just biding his time until he got her alone? She sat bolt upright in the chair. The ring. He had her ring. What were the chances he didn't realise it was hers? After all, he had seen it quite clearly outside the Blue Bell and on one occasion after that. Now he knew where she was, alone, and no Luke Waverly to protect her. She found herself almost looking forwards to the return of Lord Fulford and decided it best to hang around for him after all. He could alert his staff to her danger, and surely he would offer protection—at least until he found out what she'd done with her breakfast. She winced at the thought and decided there and then to come clean the first chance she got. She would also tell His Lordship about the letter; then he could take her back to Beckham to retrieve it. Luke would hardly be involved at all, which was just as well seeing how he was so closely associated with Palmer, Turpin, damn the man, whoever he was. She had liked him, and though not trusting him completely, Jack Palmer hadn't struck her as being a hardened criminal, certainly not an evil man. But she'd seen him in action with her own eyes, robbing people and waving a pistol about in a most threatening manner.

Andrew re entered the room and enquired if there were anything else he could get for her. Lydia said a chat would be nice and convinced the man to take a seat by the fire. Just for a short while, she assured him.

"How long have you worked for Lord Fulford?"

"Less than a year. I was recommended when my previous employer died," he answered.

"You must have come with glowing references then," Lydia observed.

"I like to think so."

"Where was your previous place of employment, if you don't mind my asking?"

"Lincolnshire. Are you familiar with it, milady?"

"Somewhat, but I can't say I've actually spent much time there. It's a bit flat isn't it?"

"Aye, the lands are low towards the costal side, but 'tis a pretty enough place," Andrew said, with a nod of his head.

"Andrew, do you . . . I mean. Well, you've heard about Lord Beckham. Do you know him very well?" She thought she imagined some hesitation in Andrew's manner.

"I do know of him. That is to say his reputation goes before him." He smiled wryly. "I'm sure you yourself have heard stories."

"I have," Lydia said quietly. "Although it appears he's changed for the better these past couple of years, or at least that's what I gather."

"Aye, he's turned the estates around since he came north. If you beg my pardon, milady, what that man needs is a good wife with a firm mind to keep him in check."

"I've heard that said before," she laughed. "It seems he has no such intentions though."

"Stranger things have been known to happen, milady." Andrew shrugged his shoulders and rose to his feet. "Now, if you'll excuse me I have things to attend to. Are you certain there is naught else I can get for you?"

"No, nothing at all thank you."

Andrew nodded, then turned and silently left the room.

Lydia watched him go and wondered why everyone kept hinting that Luke needed a wife. Did he have such intentions? She sighed. It was going to be a long, dreary day unless she could find something extremely time consuming to do. Eventually, she decided that fresh air or a good long soak in a tub was what she needed, and since no one had offered the latter, she chose to stroll around the gardens. The air was brisk, typical of an English autumn day and pleasant enough if one wrapped up well and enjoyed the feel of a chill wind. Lydia strolled along a wide gravel pathway, her cloak hugged tightly and just taking her time. After all, she had the whole day to herself, a whole day to reflect on the incredible turn her life had taken, and a whole day to decide what in the hell to do about it.

It all came right back down to that blasted letter. The letter she never should have accepted in the first place. The letter she ought to have opened and read. She almost slapped her forehead in disgust. How stupid could she be? The contents of the letter would almost certainly indicate who was involved in felonious activities, and from that she could glean who wasn't. Never mind that the letter was confidential and sealed with a great glob of wax, and bugger waiting about for Lord Fulford's return. She needed to leave now. The sooner she opened the letter, and the sooner she warned Luke of Palmer's double identity, the better—unless he already knew. She wanted to discount the possibility. But could she?

The low walls of the ornamental gardens gave rise to a small archway leading around towards the back of the house. Lydia continued walking, mulling over the possibility of stealing a horse. What she wouldn't give to have her mountain bike to hand. The path wound on and around, making a loop that appeared to return to the front of the house and the main driveway. A few small buildings not too far away looked as though they might warrant further inspection; it struck her that her horse might not have been sent back to Beckham after

all and might be hidden away. Cautiously, she approached the
first building, which on closer inspection looked as though
it might have been a brew house at one time, but now it lay
silent, seemingly redundant. The second building didn't look
much more promising, but as she approached she heard the
sound of men's voices, and they seemed to be arguing about
something. Thanking the good Lord for making her light on
her feet, Lydia crept nearer, having no desire to be discovered
eavesdropping. Hearing her name, she froze. They were
discussing her and in a not-too-friendly manner it appeared.

"I can't sees why we 'as to keep 'er 'ere at all," snorted one
man. "Just send 'er back to Beckham, let 'im 'ave the trouble.
Or even better let 'em find 'er on the road and lay the blame
at Turpin's feet."

"Seems like 'is Lordship wants to keep 'er as surety just in
case," said another voice.

"Surety against what? No one saw us do 'im in, an' there
weren't nothin' when we searched 'im. An' what's so important
in a letter? Now the wench, I could 'ave a bit o' fun with." He
guffawed loudly.

"I think it be more'n a murder 'is Lordship be harkin'
'bout. There be more goin' on than we knows, mark me,
you'll see," a third man drawled. "An' if I was you I wouldn'
be makin' remarks like that for 'im to hear. Got designs on
'er 'imself likely."

Lydia's blood turned to ice in her veins. These were the
men she had seen commit murder; she recognised the voice
of their leader.

It was a voice she would never forget.

Shrinking back against the wall, she turned and retraced
her steps along the path until she was at the far end of the
house, almost at the garden where she'd begun her stroll. She
breathed normally at last and walked as casually as she could
back through the front doors.

Into the house of a murderer.

Straightening her spine and fingering her hair behind her ears, she walked into the drawing room and hauled on the bellpull. Andrew appeared a few moments later.

"I was wondering if I could possibly take a bath."

"Lord Beckham's habits have rubbed off." He smiled suddenly. Then just as suddenly, he was serious again. "I'm afraid we have no real facility for bathing, but a tub of sorts may be found. I'll have it brought to your room. Would you like a hot drink while you wait?"

"Yes, thank you." Lydia realised she had begun to tremble. Her voice wobbled, and her teeth weren't faring much better. "P . . . perhaps a toddy."

"Of course." He made to leave the room then stopped and turned. "Milady, are you unwell?"

"I . . . I'm fine, just a little chilled," she assured him.

He bowed and walked out of the door.

Lydia collapsed into a chair, grateful it was large and seemed to afford a degree of protection, which was exactly what she felt in dire need of. "Luke," she whispered, "please help me. Please." She was crying before she had any chance to check the tears. Whatever else Luke Waverly might be, she was certain he wouldn't let these men hurt her. She sobbed louder. Now it wasn't just Jack Palmer, a.k.a. Dick Turpin who was after her; there was a band of murderers who were not exactly extending the hand of friendship, and should they discover she'd been a witness to their vile deed—heaven forbid.

She was dead meat.

So much for seeking the alliance of Lord Fulford. She shuddered at how close she had come to divulging the secret of the letter to the very man who'd sent his thugs to murder a man for it.

Andrew entered the room and she turned her head to wipe her eyes on the cloak she still wore.

"You are cold perhaps," he observed. "This should warm you a little, and there will be hot water and a tub in your room shortly. Nothing so grand I fear as you are used to at Beckham."

She sniffed and blinked a couple of times then said, "That cold wind made my eyes sore; a hot steamy bath is just what I need. I don't care what the tub's like." She took the glass Andrew had placed on the table. Its contents steamed. "Do the glasses ever break when you pour the hot drink into them?" she asked, desperate for something to say.

"Aye, they can, and I find it best to use pewter, but for you, milady, glass is what I choose." He continued, "If the glass is warmed gently first with warm water and placed on a wooden surface whilst it is filled, there is generally little problem with breakage."

"I see." She managed a smile. Well, she had asked.

"Are you sure you're all right, milady? Your eyes appear very sore indeed."

She nodded vigorously. "I'm sure. I'll be fine. You're certain His Lordship has sent word to Lord Beckham to let him know I'm here?"

"I'm certain it will have been attended to at the same time your horse was taken back there. Now, I think I hear them beginning to take the tub up to your room. Take your time with your drink, and I shall call you when the water is ready."

"Thank you, Andrew. You're very kind."

"Think nothing of it."

But she did. He was being uncommonly attentive. The remark he'd made about Lord Beckham's habit having rubbed off on her bore no hint of sarcasm nor had it contained any innuendo. It was an honest to goodness observation made by someone who knew more about Luke than just the local gossip. Did he know Luke personally, and if so, how? This was not looking good. What if Andrew had worked for Luke or his family at some time and had been employed by Lord Fulford as a sort of spy? "Lydia Mckenzie," she muttered, "you have an overactive imagination."

An hour or so later she sat, tightly curled in a wooden tub that looked like it was one half of a beer barrel. She'd not complain about her tub at Beckham House ever again given that she got the chance.

"Milady," enquired the young girl who'd brought a second hot toddy, courtesy of Andrew, "they be wantin' to know if you wants to eat in your room seein' as how 'is Lordship's not coming back tonight."

"Not coming back? What do you mean?"

"Sent word 'e won't be back for a couple o' days. Oh, but you be free to ask for whatever you wants. You bein' a guest an' all."

Lydia gulped. A prisoner more like. "Thank you, yes, I'll eat here. You can go now I'll manage."

The girl bobbed and left the room. Lydia was certain she heard the lock click home but was too weary to crawl out of the warmth of the tub to check. She found herself glad of Fulford's absence for the night. There was no telling what he had in store for her on his return. Now she didn't feel at all bad about hiding breakfast inside the marble busts.

The water, cooled rapidly. Lydia disentangled her legs and scrambled from the tub remembering her own words to Luke, words that had left her burning with embarrassment and him with a very strange look on his face. If not worried half out of her mind, she could have giggled at the memory, but even a vision of Mr. Turpin on her mountain bike couldn't raise a smile at the moment. She dried herself and donned a heavy robe before taking a seat by the fire.

What to do now? There really was nothing for it but to wait for rescue, or be murdered. No one was likely to come for her if she were honest. In all likelihood, Luke had been told she was spending a few days here and would be brought back in due course.

Saved from further dark thoughts by the soft sound of a key turning in the lock, she looked up as the door edged open.

"May I enter?"

"Andrew," she didn't hide her surprise, "what brings you here?" Noting he came empty handed she added, "Not my dinner obviously."

He put a finger to his lips and quietly closed the door behind him. "Listen to me. I needs must speak quickly."

She looked at him wide eyed. Gone was the hesitant politeness he had demonstrated earlier, and gone was any hint of servitude. He was speaking to her as an equal. She listened intently to his words.

"I heard some of the staff speaking, and they led me to believe that Lord Beckham was not advised of your being here." He paused. "I had further suspicion, and it appears your mare remains in the stables, out of sight. You have, to all intents and purposes disappeared."

"Or am about to," she said miserably.

"Eat your dinner tonight," he continued, "as though naught were amiss. Dismiss the servants and retire to your bed. Stay awake and be dressed. I shall come for you when the house is asleep."

"How will I get my horse?"

"Fear not the stable lad is easily bought."

"I'm not sure I know my way back to Beckham in the dark."

He appeared to consider for a moment then said, "I'll have the lad ride part way with you. You'll have naught to fear."

"I, I don't know. What about highwaymen?"

Andrew was at the door. "Think not on that. Now, remember, act as though naught were amiss. All depends on it."

Lydia nodded dumbly, hardly daring to believe she was about to make her escape like some heroine in a Gothic novel, riding out on a wind-swept night, along a ribbon of moonlight and across the purple heath. She almost wept with relief, but not yet. Not until she was safely back inside the walls of Beckham House.

TWELVE

The clock on the mantelpiece struck twelve. Lydia sat by the fire and listened; not a sound in the house anywhere. Would Andrew be true to his word and help her return to Beckham, or was it just some horrible ploy to get her out on the road tonight? She remembered the words she had heard spoken earlier that day about laying the blame for her demise at Turpin's feet. How easy it would be to bump her off somewhere tonight, and tomorrow an unsuspecting soul would find her dead in a ditch and she would have gone there a willing victim, like a lamb to the slaughter. She was of half a mind to refuse to go with Andrew.

A soft sound caught her ear, and she turned warily as her door inched open. Andrew stood there, his face lighted by the flame of the single candle he carried.

"Are you ready?"

"I'm not sure." She hesitated. "I . . . that is."

"How can you trust me?" He stood a moment his eyes unwavering, "You cannot, but you have to. Come." He held out his free hand.

Lydia rose from the chair and took the offered hand as they stole into the darkness of the hallway, Andrew holding the candle low so it cast barely a light to aid them.

"Trust me," he whispered.

"Like you said, I have no real alternative," she whispered back

They crept along a short distance until Andrew pulled her to a halt and put a finger to his lips and then passed her the candle to hold.

She watched as he moved tentatively forwards then beckoned her to follow. They stopped again, and Lydia groaned as Andrew reached for one of the marble busts. She hid her face in the darkness and watched him attempt to shift the whole item. He grunted a couple of times before quitting the struggle.

"Step back if you would," he said softly, then proceeded to lift the bust from its pedestal.

Lydia cringed. Did this one contain the ham, the eggs, or the various sweets and sundries? She couldn't recall but knew the bust certainly to be one of her chosen pair.

Andrew sniffed the air, ignored his nose for a moment, and then placed the bust silently on the floor. Without so much as a hint that he found anything amiss, he shifted the pedestal to one side.

The whiff of fermenting eggs—and she had forgotten about the smoked fish—permeated Lydia's olfactory senses. The strange aroma wafted around them like a thick cloud, and she almost felt the need for some sort of explanation. Andrew's next action rendered such explanation unnecessary as the wall emitted a slight groaning sound, and as she watched one of the panels slipped out of place just far enough that he was able to reach in with a hand. After a second or two of fumbling, he appeared to find what he was feeling for and gave a sharp tug, pushing his shoulder against the wall at the same time. Half the panel rotated, and he stepped aside affording Lydia a full view of what was a narrow but accessible opening, to where she had no idea, and she hesitated as he motioned her forwards.

"Why me first?" She resisted the hand on her arm.

"I needs must replace the marbles," he said quietly. "Please, go through, take the candle with you and hold it high so I may see."

She went and stood, barely in the entrance, as he shuffled first the pillar into its place and then replaced the bust on top before backing himself into the opening. Lydia found herself being forced farther into the tunnel and prepared to grab Andrew by the hair if he so much made a move back outside. She had read too many stories of unwanted people being shoved into secret passages and left there.

He paused to wipe his hands down the front of his breeches his hands having come a little too close to the contents of the pillar. Then he took the candle and holding it high he pulled the panel back into place and gave Lydia a wry smile. She caught his face briefly and noted a hint of humour in his eyes as he said, "I shall not even ask . . . ."

"Where does this lead?" she hissed, grateful for his diplomacy.

"We should exit, if my memory serves me, by the south gate. Outside the walls, of course."

"But that's miles, it has to be."

"Not miles but far enough for our needs. If the stable lad does his work well, there is little chance of our being discovered."

"You're not coming with us?" She tripped and stumbled forwards, falling hard against Andrew's back with a curse.

"Nay, but steady yourself, I should like to have you out of here in one piece."

"I'll go for that," she agreed. "So you'll come back here?"

"'Twould not do to arouse suspicions by my absence."

"But what about the stable lad? Ouch!"

"Watch your head."

"Thanks. What will Lord Fulford do to him?"

"Nothing that isn't worth his while for what I paid him. He'll also receive a fairly innocent but convincing bump on the head after he returns. He'll be found in the stables with a story that he was set upon from behind and knows naught else about the matter."

"Will they believe him?" Lydia asked doubtfully.

"Like I said, he's being paid handsomely for his troubles. Of course, he won't be paid in full until I am assured of his loyalty."

Lydia could swear Andrew had a self-satisfied smirk on his face even though she couldn't see it. "Clever."

"Thank you. Now take a little more care. We're almost at the outer foundations of the house and the passage begins to descend more quickly here."

"You're not kidding." Lydia slithered and slid down the rapidly increasing slope and on more than one occasion ended up on her backside and was hauled to her feet by an ever-vigilant Andrew. "I'm glad it's dirt and not concrete," she reflected as he hauled her back into position for what seemed like the zillionth time.

"Aye," Andrew agreed, having not the slightest idea what she was talking about.

At last the passage levelled off, and Lydia could only assume they'd travelled below the walls of the house and were now tramping under the grounds. A distinctly musty smell turned rapidly into a very nasty one, and upon enquery, Andrew advised that they were close to the cesspits, a fact he appeared inordinately happy about.

Lydia tried not to breath and remained silent for the rest of the way. Finally, they began to climb towards the surface, starting with a slope in the passageway and then a steep roughly hewn staircase supported by thick planks of wood. She waited, her need for fresh air suddenly urgent, while Andrew shoved hard on a heavy trapdoor above them. It wasn't budging.

"The stable lad must be able to hear you banging. Why doesn't he help?" she asked, a note of concern creeping into her voice.

"I thought it unwise to allow him knowledge of this place." Andrew responded, taking a brief respite from his labours. "The less known, the better."

"I suppose so. We could get out back where we came in though, I suppose?"

"I couldn't be certain of that. I've not tried."

Oh Lord, they were lost down here forever. She would die in a hole in the ground with a stranger. Lydia felt a scream start to form but extinguished it in a flash as the trapdoor gave way with a mighty creak, and a gush of cold night air rushed into the tunnel.

"Come, give me your hand," Andrew instructed as he heaved the trapdoor clear of the opening and climbed out.

Lydia did as she was told, noting the top few stairs to be in poorer condition and less solid than the rest, probably due to rainwater seeping in over the years. At last, she stood under the sky and on solid earth. She breathed a great sigh of relief and watched as Andrew replaced the trapdoor and hastily threw loose dirt and sod over it.

"'Twas covered with live earth, which tore out when I forced it," he explained. "That's why it was so difficult to open. I'll return later and conceal it better."

"You're not thinking to need it again any time soon, are you?" Lydia shuddered.

"One never knows, but come, we must make haste."

The candle extinguished, they walked carefully by the light of a scant moon until they rounded a small thicket, where a figure stood holding two horses.

"Everything all right? Anyone see you?" Andrew asked as the boy approached.

The stable lad's eyes were wide, and his face bore a starkness, whether from fear or cold Lydia wasn't certain, but he didn't look happy.

"Nay, sir, I came out jus' as you said when they be all passed out wi' drink. That stuff you put in the pitcher worked well."

"A little something I had access to," Andrew said in response to Lydia's questioning glance. "Now, let's have you on your horse and back to Beckham before anyone here is the wiser you've gone. Lad"—he turned to the boy who had already mounted the other horse—"ride only as fast as the lady is able. 'Tis a poor moon this night and we want no falls. Take her as far as the crossroads at the Burley turn-off then return here and clean the sweat from your mount immediately. There must be no suspicion it has been ridden this night, or you yourself will be under that suspicion," he added ominously.

"Aye, sir," the lad replied with an unmistakable warble in his voice. "I'll do just as you say, sir."

Lydia was impressed at Andrew's show of authority. He had demonstrated quite a propensity for it since this little adventure began. She gathered her skirts, her cloak, and her reins. "Andrew, I don't know what to say, but a thanks a million. I'll be sure and tell Lord Beckham what you've done, so if you need another job anytime soon—"

"Don't worry, milady. Just ride fast and safe. Boy, remember what I say."

They rode off into the darkness. Lydia turned to see the vague outline of a man slip into the grounds through the south gate. She hoped Andrew would make it safely into the house undetected.

Night riding was not to Lydia's liking. She preferred to have full view of the land prior to her horse's hooves cantering over it, but the lad seemed sure of himself and she followed unquestioningly in his wake. The mare was behaving well enough, and Lydia hoped things would continue in that vein once the other horse left, and when that would be she had yet to discover. The crossroads at the Burley turn-off meant nothing even though she must have passed by there yesterday either on horseback or in the coach.

"How far is the turnoff where you leave me?" she hissed at the lad riding in front. He seemed not to hear, so she urged the mare forwards bringing them alongside the other horse.

She raised her voice a little and said, "I said, how far is the turn-off?"

Without turning to look at her he replied, "Not too far now." His voice was strained and nervous.

She couldn't help but feel sorry for him. Even though it seemed he was to be paid very generously for his work, there was still the matter of the knock on the head. It was a bit drastic to Lydia's mind, but necessary according to Andrew.

Just who *was* Andrew? Not a regular run-of-the-mill, tug-your-forelock sort of servant for sure; he had too much authority for that. Lydia's musings were cut short, and she pulled the mare to a trot as the lad leaned over and took hold of her horse's reins, whispered a few directions, and pointed the way she should go. Then he turned his horse around and headed off at a gallop in the direction they'd just come.

Lydia sat for a moment then made the mare walk the way she supposed the lad had pointed, but it was confusing. There were two roads, and she didn't know whether he'd said right or left. It was fifty-fifty; not bad odds all things considered. She decided the lad's arm had pointed mostly to the right and set the mare out in that direction. Keeping her eyes and ears peeled for anything that may be familiar, she held the horse at a steady trot for a couple of miles. It was the fastest pace she felt safe with in the scant moonlight. She listened as she had never listened in her life before, trying to go beyond the very obvious thud of her horse's hooves, beyond the fragmented sounds of sleepy birds nestled high in the surrounding of trees, beyond the moan of the chilly breeze and the rustling of fallen leaves. She wished there weren't so many trees. They made easy hiding places for those who didn't wish to be seen. Barely had this thought manifested when a dark shadow presented from the shelter of said trees.

"Hold there."

"Oh Lord," she breathed. The mare stopped dead in its tracks as though sensing that the man sitting astride his horse in front of them meant exactly what he said. Lydia urged the horse to go around the shadowy figure, which remained motionless. The mare refused to budge.

"Hold there, I say." The instruction was repeated.

Lydia's heart all but left her chest. It was him, Palmer, Turpin, whoever he was. Now what to do? She certainly couldn't outrun the man, and she didn't have a gun to shoot him—even if she had the guts, which she doubted. She sat still and said nothing.

"That's better." He wore his mask and kerchief, and spoke quietly, but so precise was he in his speech that every word rang clear through the cold night air. "Tell me how a pretty miss comes to be along this way in the darkness, and by herself?" The animal he rode moved forwards at some unseen aid from its master, and before Lydia could recover her senses, Turpin had grasped her horse's bridle.

There was no escape.

No sound came when Lydia tried to speak. Adrenaline coursed through her blood, leaving her hands and feet floppy and useless, while her heart continued to bang away like a demented drummer, and she found herself hyperventilating. If this was the flight-or-fight response, she wanted nothing to do with it. Again, she opened her mouth.

"Well, it appears I have struck you dumb," the highwayman said. "But I'd make a guess that you're lost."

Lydia thought she saw a twinkle in the man's eye, and forced a reply of sorts through chattering teeth. "No, I'm not lost, and I'll thank you to let me be on my way . . . please."

He let go of the bridle and leaned back in his saddle. "If you're on your way to Beckham House then I know you're lost," he continued.

"What makes you think I'm headed there?

"Put up your claws pretty one and I'll accompany you safely to your destination. Follow me." He turned without further communication.

Lydia realised he was giving her the opportunity not to follow, but what else could she do? Nothing appeared even vaguely familiar, and if she really were lost . . . She sighed resignedly and gave herself over into the hands of fate, which it appeared had a never-ending bag of goodies in store for her.

She rode several yards behind the highwayman not taking her eyes from the back of the be-cloaked figure in the feather-trimmed, three-cornered hat, who rode so easily over the darkened earth he may just as well have been riding in broad daylight. It struck Lydia that it was probably all the same to him, he no doubt had lots of practice at night riding.

He turned once or twice and gave her a brief glance but said nothing until they came to the edge of a small clearing. Lydia recognised it at once as the area where the cottage stood, but they had approached from a different direction, and the cottage, at least now in the darkness, was nowhere in sight. They continued to the small gate that opened on to Beckham lands, and Turpin jumped from his horse. He opened the gate with a flourish and waved Lydia through.

"'Tis best if you continue alone, as I'm sure you'll understand," he said and began to fumble inside his cloak.

"Er, yes, of course." Now what was he rummaging around for? Lydia was half of a mind to race for home, but intrigued at his struggles and colourful curses, she hesitated.

"One more thing." He swore again and continued to root around in his clothing.

Lydia waited. She sat silently, not quite able to comprehend the complexities of the situation, and the fact that Dick Turpin had just helped bring her home. She didn't know why he'd helped her but felt certain there had to be an ulterior motive. She just didn't know what it was yet.

"Aha, here it is." He came close by her side, leading his black horse. "Yours, I believe."

Lydia could scarcely believe her eyes as he handed back her ring. He *had* known it was her in Fulford's coach. Had he known she was at Fulford Manor? What he didn't know was that she recognised him for Jack Palmer. Her mind spun.

"Thank you," she said quietly. "And thank you for helping me back here. You were right I was lost." She found herself giving a slight smile at the covered face.

"I would ask that you say nothing of this little encounter. To no one, do you understand?" the highwayman said keeping his eyes fixed on her.

"Yes, I think so."

"Your word. I would see you bound by it."

"I give you my word."

"Very well. I helped you this night when you were in need, and we shall leave it thus." So saying he led his horse back through the gate, and was on its back and had disappeared into the darkness of the trees before Lydia had a chance for further reply.

Without more ado, she urged the mare forwards and rode off across the park. Lydia thought hard. The highwayman had saved her from heaven knew what, and he quite understandably didn't want anyone knowing of his movements or his whereabouts, or the fact he was the one keeping horses and a chest full of gunpowder at the old cottage. She had to decide if Luke knew that Palmer wasn't the business associate he claimed to be, and even then what should she tell him. If Palmer's true identity were discovered, he would know she hadn't kept her word. She gulped and decided that *caution* was the word of the day—and she owed Palmer something.

She would just play it by ear. Maybe she could warn Luke enough so he would be a little leery of his business dealings with Palmer in future. Lydia scowled, remembering the letter—a letter for a highwayman, and a letter for which a man had lost his life. As soon as she was back in her own room and had slept a little, she would open it and then perhaps she'd have a better understanding of what was going on.

Lydia entered the yard as quietly as possible, not an easy endeavour given the strike of iron shoes on cobbles, and slipped from the mare's back. She jumped a foot in the air at the sound of a voice, begging her pardon and requesting she not be alarmed.

"His Lordship tol' me to wait up jus' in case you decided to come back tonight, milady." The lad touched his hat. "I'll take the mare now an' bed 'er down real well."

"Well, goodnight then, Peter, or should it be good morning?"

"Likely it should, milady."

At least Luke hadn't written her off. She wondered at his having had the lad wait up, as he'd put it, just in case. Had he actually worried about where she might have been these last couple of nights? The creep had probably been down at the Blue Bell and come home too drunk to even notice she wasn't there. For all Luke Waverly knew she could have been dead in a ditch and likely would have been if not for Andrew and, of course, Turpin. She wished he weren't Jack Palmer; it would make things a whole lot easier, and she dearly wished she'd not given her word to say nothing of their meeting. If only she'd had the chance to cross her fingers. She walked to the house.

The door swung open, and a woman holding a candle in one hand beckoned her inside. "C'mon in, milady, afore you catch your death. There be a hot meal waitin' in your room." She turned and led Lydia up the staircase, lighting a couple more candles along the way.

It was a relief to be once more in her room. It felt as near to home as it possibly could given the circumstances, and it was warm. A fire blazed heartily in the hearth, and several silver dishes sat upon a table. Lydia groaned—more food. Could she force herself? She found that a quick wash with good hot water, a clean shift, and a small glass of brandy somehow enticed her appetite to return, and she prepared to tuck into her meal.

The door of her room flew open. Lydia froze. Her eyes wide. It was Luke, and he looked furious. Furious and, she suspected, drunk.

"What the devil do you think you're playing at? Disappearing for nigh on two days, and then coming back at all hours without so much as a word." He grabbed a glass and poured a drink then threw himself into a chair. "Well, I'm waiting."

Lydia slammed her utensils on the table. "How dare you. You've no idea what I've been through." She jumped to her feet. "Why don't you get the full story before you start going off like a madman? Damn you! If you didn't spend all your time f . . . fornicating with your floosies"—she waved a hand in the air—"you might have a better idea what's going on around you." If she expected an angry response to her outburst, she was disappointed.

Luke merely raised an eyebrow. "So then, tell me, pretty one." He smiled lazily and without humour.

"Don't call me that!" Tears threatened. Lydia took a very deep breath and continued in a quiet voice. "I fell off my horse when that fool Fulford came by too fast in his coach—again." She noted a twitch at the corner of Luke's mouth. "I wasn't feeling well, and he took me to his place, and he wasn't going to let me go. Then a servant called Andrew helped me escape, and now here I am. And it wasn't very nice," she snuffled. "So don't go shouting the odds at me. I've had about all I can take, thank you." She glared at him, damning his blue eyes—they still held an inescapable fascination for her.

"I see," he drawled. "Well then, since you're back safe and sound I'll say no more. It seems you were not entirely to blame for your absence." He stood and stared deeply at her, seemingly a little unsteady on his feet. "You are certain there is no more to your tale?"

Her heart skipped a beat. "No," she said quickly. "Nothing I can think of at the moment. I'll let you know if something comes to mind."

She watched him leave the room and breathed a sigh of relief deciding to get some sleep then get her act together and work out what to do. The glass of brandy stood, untouched, on the floor, where Luke had placed it. How much of a creep he was, remained to be seen. If only he could refrain from calling her by that stupid name, but then what? She knew what he was, and a man like him wasn't worth bothering about. It could only lead to heartache, or worse, and after all, she had dumped the dreadful Darwin because he was unfaithful.

It seemed her knight in shining armour just didn't exist.

She crawled into bed and dreamed of him just the same.

THIRTEEN

"Well?"

"As you told me, she's in good health."

"I mean, well, did she tell you?" Jack Palmer watched Luke's face intently.

"She said Fulford had all but made her a prisoner at his house and that a servant by the name of Andrew helped her escape."

"That's all?"

"Aye, indeed," Luke said with a grin.

Palmer nodded his head. "Good, it seems she can be trusted. Now we need to seriously consider the fact that Fulford is further involved than we had thought."

"It seems so. Bloody hell, Jack, do you think he was keeping her as a hostage to bargain with?"

"Either that or he thinks she knows something about all this." Palmer scratched his chin thoughtfully. "As, did I."

"You've changed your mind then?"

"Aye, I believe I have. I think we can trust the pretty miss well enough, tho' I still feel 'twould be safer for her to be kept right out of it."

"Aye," Luke agreed, "but she has this infernal curiosity, and it seems my word doesn't dissuade her—she does exactly as she pleases." He gave a wry smile.

"As do you. Did she believe your supposed drunkenness, this eve?"

"Well enough to berate me for spending all my time fornicating with a floozy at the Bell." He grimaced and said, "She has a poor opinion of me, Jack, you do realise that."

"'Tis best to keep it that way until we're clear through this lot. Then," Palmer added with a slight smile, "we shall see."

"Jack."

"Aye, what is it?" Palmer poured himself a drink and sat down.

Luke remained standing and bent to retrieve the poker then began prodding mindlessly at the fire; a habit he had acquired when nervous.

"Whenever you're ready."

"I've fallen in love with her, Jack. Now, I'm certain of it."

The brandy swirled around in Palmer's glass, and he considered it for a moment before speaking. "If advice is what you're after, I'm not the one to give it, excepting to say what I already have. But *love* is a strong word, my friend, and I wonder at your comprehension of it."

Luke turned and scowled. "You do me a disservice. Am I so cold and unyielding to your eyes then?"

"I merely state that perhaps you misinterpret lust for its finer counterpart. Remember, I've heard you swear undying love before."

"Aye, usually with a partially clad wench on my lap and a tankard of strong ale in my hand."

"That be as it may, I beg you think carefully on your words." Palmer took a deep breath. "Luke, I'd be the last to deter you from finding someone who'd keep you in line, but heaven only knows you've one hell of a reputation. Do you really believe you can be true to one woman? Look at me and tell me that you would keep the marriage vows in their entirety." He waited and watched as Luke shifted position by the fireplace.

"I would, Jack. I truly believe I would."

Jack Palmer gave a long and somewhat exasperated sigh. "Then, let us agree to keep the pretty one out of this affair, and safe until such time you are able to offer her your hand. But, Luke, I've quite taken a liking to her myself, and should you find your intentions wavering, I beg you desist from any action that would hurt her."

Luke looked up in surprise. "You soft sod, Jack. I never took you for a romantic. Nay, damn it, man, we're not much different you and I, excepting you've worked for your crust whereas I had mine handed to me, aye, and wasted much of it. But fear not. Should she come to me, I'll have her and give her no reason ever to doubt me." He laughed then said, "In fact, Jack Palmer, you'll be godparent to our firstborn."

"Are you sure you weren't at the Bell this eve?" Palmer commented over his glass.

"Never further from my mind."

"I wish it could be so, but you have your reputation to uphold, remember. We have need of your dalliances a little while longer. 'Twould not do for you to seem respectable."

"Worry not. I pay that wench down there enough for her silence. She doesn't care about much more than the money I pay her."

"Keep it thus."

"I intend to. Now, let us to business. We seem to be going around almost in circles. At least none of my forays has unearthed much," Luke said and frowned. He replaced the poker in its usual position on the hearth and moved from the fireside.

"Aye, it seems we are apprehending every conveyance we are able yet none bearing what we seek," Palmer agreed.

"There's more intelligence afoot than we imagined, I'll warrant, and I wonder at our own identities being secure. What the devil happened to that letter?"

"I'll guarantee our man was killed for it," Palmer said. "Whether his assailants found what they were looking for, I have no idea, but I am positive now that Fulford was responsible for the attack."

"Aye," Luke snapped. "Damn the man. If I discover he so much as laid a finger on . . ."

"On your love," his friend offered.

"On Lydia," Luke continued. "Aye, my love, as you will. Damn you, Jack."

Jack Palmer laughed softly at his friend's discomfort. "Now, Luke, if you will but turn your attentions to more serious matters. It seems we are not to have the information we expected, which would have assisted us in our endeavours. That being as it is, we really have little alternative but to continue intercepting each and every conveyance between London and the borders, before anything else comes to pass."

"Aye, Jack, that's true, but we have time constraints."

"'Tis right enough," his friend agreed. "Should those instructions and the gold that is already finding its way north, reach the intended recipients . . . I hesitate to dwell on the outcome. Damn the French, and the Scots."

"Be calm, my friend, England has seen worse than this upon her shores."

"Seems forever she is beset by enemies," Palmer groused.

Luke inclined his head. "We've been the aggressor too and many times."

"Not without reason," Palmer responded. "The French are ever at our door."

"'Tis true we have not seen eye to eye with the French for many a year, but the Scots now, that may be a different matter. They should, by rights, be our allies."

"But they are not." Palmer rose to his feet.

"'Tis not my doing or your own, Jack. Sit down."

"We could do with help, that's for sure," Palmer grumbled. "What about the Earl of Westmorland? He's a damn good man and not too far away."

"Aye, he's a good man, but I fear he has troubles of his own at the moment."

"What mean you?" Palmer looked up.

"His wife recently gave birth to a son then took it upon herself to die. The man is left with a new born babe and a son barely a man."

"Oh aye, I'd forgotten Westmorland's wife. Who's the boy's father? Not Westmorland himself, I'll warrant. Pour me another drink, will you."

"No one is certain. Neither is anyone bound to speak of it. The babe apparently has the dark hair of his sire, but not his eyes," Luke concluded.

"Aye, now I remember hearing something of it." Palmer scratched his chin and thought a moment, then grinned and took the glass he was handed. "I remember hearing about the bairn having light blue eyes. You wouldn't be having anything to do with it, would you?"

"Damn you, Jack." Luke couldn't avoid a laugh as he spoke."'Twould be more likely the babe is your own given the lack of hair on his pate."

Jack Palmer was swift and accurate.

Luke froze and held his position a second or two before reaching for the dagger that protruded from his coat sleeve and pinned him very decisively to the wall. He pulled it out. "Damn it, Jack, I was only jesting."

"I know," the other said, "and I was only practicing."

"You wouldn't need to carry a bloody dagger if you didn't insist on keeping that damnable hefty rapier at your side," Luke said finally, coming to sit by the fire and handing back the knife. "Why you don't carry something a little lighter, I don't know."

"'Twas good enough for my father and it has done service well by me," Palmer said blithely.

Luke shook his head slowly, a smile upon his face. "I say no more. Have it your own way, but desist I beg of you from unleashing your weapons upon my person." He looked down at his waistcoat sleeve. "This silk is bloody expensive."

"Now that's something," Palmer mused.

"What?"

"I remember a time when Luke Waverly wouldn't have cared a fig about the expense of his clothing. Perhaps there's hope for you yet, my friend."

"Damn you, Jack."

"Likely I shall be."

"We were about to discuss business as I recall." Luke took a sip of his drink.

"Aye, it concerns the coach heading straight for the border that that we spoke of, travelling on the Great North Road, and now it seems there shall be another a couple of hours later, some twenty five miles away at the Tadcaster crossing; the choice is yours to make. I chose the Tadcaster, and you took the Bryerly last time, so this one's at your will." He slapped his thigh. "That was something, eh? Made for merry conversation at the Bell. Two coaches in one night."

"Aye." Luke smiled. "Turpin certainly made a name for himself that night. I'll take the Taddy this time round. Shouldn't want you to get bored."

"Not bored, my friend, but old. I fear the years are running away with me at times."

"You're a couple of years younger than I am." Luke laughed. "And I certainly don't feel life is running away with me."

"That's because for most of your days you've been running away with life," Palmer remarked dryly. "And look at your bloody head, covered with those dark locks, and look at mine. No, on second thoughts, do not. There is no justice in the world."

Luke began to laugh at his friend's indignation. "Ah, Jack, hair or not you've done fair with your life. Which brings me to a point I've been hesitant to raise. He recovered himself and said soberly. "Did you consider my offer?"

"Your offer?" Palmer looked mystified for a second then said, "Oh, you mean about working for you?"

"Working *with* me, Jack, *with* me. I need someone with a good head on his shoulders, and above all, I need someone I can trust. This is a large estate, and as time goes on it seems business often takes me up to London and the counties. I really do need a good man here at all times. What of it?"

The other fidgeted with his glass. "I'm still thinking on it. It has its merits certainly, but whether 'tis for me," he said, shaking his head, "I know not."

"But why not, Jack? Come, man, think about the benefits of a place to call your own and a good steady income. What say you?"

"I say let it be for now. We've other things to see to. I shall think it over."

Luke knew he'd get no better reply. The man would do exactly as he wanted.

Jack Palmer was a law unto himself.

FOURTEEN

Lydia slept past noon, occasionally raising her head to sniff the air and deciding it was far more to her liking to remain in bed a while longer than to brave the chill of her room. The fire had slipped to a mere glow, and she guessed the maid had stayed out of the room so as not to disturb her. She was about to emerge from the goose feathers when a young girl ran in, bobbed a curtsey, and apologised profusely for having let the fire get so low, but what with all the commotion.

"What commotion?"

"Ooo, milady, it be that poor mister Judd. Last night. Beaten 'e were, an' left for dead. A couple o' men found 'im by the gates. Terrible state 'e be in. Terrible."

Lydia was out of bed in a flash. "Where is he now?"

"They brung 'im indoors at the instruction o' the master. 'E be downstairs."

The maid was still talking as Lydia dashed from the room pulling her robe around her. She raced down the stairway almost colliding with a servant carrying what looked like clean sheets. "Where's Judd?" Barely waiting for response, she followed the direction of the woman's eyes and raced ahead into a room where a group of men stood talking in low voices. They turned as she entered and she saw Luke among them.

"Lydia, this is no place for you." He strode purposefully towards her and grabbed her arm.

She pulled away. "Is he alive? I heard . . ." She stared wide eyed at Luke. "Tell me, oh, please?"

Luke took both her arms and held her until she became still. "Listen to me, Lydia"—his face held an unusual grimness, and he appeared to struggle for words—"Judd is badly hurt. The physician is attending him, and 'tis best we let him do his work. We shall know more then."

"You mean he could die?"

"As I said, he is badly hurt." Luke ground the words between his teeth. His trusted servant had been the object of a vile and murderous attack, and Lydia could certainly be at risk of the same; this had been a warning. He felt her body tremble and watched for a moment, as the colour drained from her cheeks then he pulled her tightly against his chest, his hands around her back and cradling her head. He did what he could to subdue the great racking sobs she seemed powerless to control, but he was unused to this sort of thing and merely made what he considered were soothing noises and stroked her hair as she wept. Given any other occasion, holding her thus would have driven him insane, yet not a lecherous thought crossed his mind. Neither did the heat rise in his loins. This was a new experience, something he'd not known before, an emotion that left him trembling almost as much as Lydia, and he had no idea how to control it. Damn his heart. It pounded so hard in his chest she must surely feel it against her own. He slipped a hand under her chin and raised her tear-stained face. "I want you to go to your room and remain there." She gulped and looked as though she hadn't heard him. "Lydia, listen to me." He held her chin firmly. "There's naught to be done at this time. Please." He turned and called to a young woman who held a bowl of water for the physician. "You, girl."

"Yes, milord," she said and bobbed a curtsey.

"Watch what you're doing, girl," the doctor said sharply as water splashed from the bowl onto his feet.

"I want you to leave what you're doing," Luke continued, "which appears to be bathing the good doctor's feet, and take your mistress upstairs. See she has a good fire, and have some brandy brought to her." He watched as the maid manoeuvred Lydia out of the room; then he turned and beckoned to the doctor.

The man finished drying his hands as he walked to where Luke stood by the fireplace.

"Well, doctor. What are his chances? Quietly, if you please."

"I'd say reasonably good by token of the fact he was thoroughly inebriated when he was attacked. He likely passed out in a matter of seconds, thereby giving his attackers a false impression of his injuries. Safe to say they imagined him to be far closer to death than he was, by a long chalk. Lucky for him."

Luke barely hid a smile. "Aye, he's a lucky old devil at that. So you think he'll recover?"

The doctor nodded. "'Tis most likely."

"Doctor Green, isn't it?"

"Aye."

"Doctor, I have need of a favour from you," Luke said quietly.

"If I am able, Your Lordship."

"That man was attacked for a reason. It was a warning, and though I may tell you little about the nature of the situation, 'tis suffice to say that England's very security may rest, at least in part, upon your actions this day."

The doctor turned his back to the two men remaining in the room. "What mean you?"

"It must be made known that master Sparks did not in fact recover from his injuries but died without regaining consciousness. Believe me when I say 'tis imperative you do this. The men who attacked him have an employer, and I wish that he remain secure in the false knowledge that he will not be implicated through the identification of his men. I do not wish to alarm him, if you understand me."

The doctor nodded. "I will do as you ask, but what about those two?" He glanced at the men in the room standing near where Judd Sparks lay on a couch.

"'Tis surprising what coin will procure . . . and failing that," Luke raised his eyebrows, "there are other ways. Now, should we need you again, I'll send a man for you, but no one must know of his," he nodded at Judd, "continuance to live."

The doctor picked up his leather satchel and made his farewells. He left the house shaking his head sadly and muttering about what an evil world it was that death should come so brutally. He left behind a half dozen wailing women and several stern faced men.

Luke nodded with satisfaction then turned back into the room and closed the door behind him. "You two pay attention. I have something to say and you'd best mind my words."

The two men came closer and looked at each other a couple of times before turning their attention to His Lordship, who seemed a might more authoritative than usual.

"I am quite certain you're wondering why the good doctor did that. 'Twas because I told him to, and now I'm telling you that Judd Sparks died this day, and until I say otherwise that's the way it stays. Do you understand me?"

"Aye, milord, if you says so," one man said, nodding rapidly to the other.

"I do, and for your troubles . . ." Luke pulled a pouch from his waistband and handed each man two coins. "Do we have an understanding then?"

This time the men chimed their assent in unison.

He pierced each man with an icy stare. "Should you decide otherwise, remember I can have you hanged on a moment's notice; the magistrate wouldn't even bother to ask the charge. Work with me, and you'll have no gripe." He paused, pleased with the anxious looks on the men's faces, then added, "Work against me, and you'll wish you'd never slipped from your mothers' bellies."

"You can rely on us, Your Lordship, be certain of it," the first man assured him frantically.

"Good. Now, I need sacks filled with something heavy, about the weight of a man's body, and make certain no one sees you. I'll have a coffin brought as soon as possible. Put the sacks in it and secure the lid. Firstly, though we need to move Judd somewhere out of ears and eyes, and I think I know the place. Know you the staircase in the far-north wing of the house?"

The two men thought a moment, and then one said, "That be the door what's locked. It ain't never been open in all my years 'ere."

"Aye, that's the place. I want you to bring him up there. You man, go tell the staff to assemble in the kitchen and to wait there for me then get yourself back here in haste."

Having ensured the staff was safely secured in the kitchen, Luke directed the two men, carrying Judd Sparks in a sheet between them, to the north end of the house. He halted by a narrow door and unlocked it with no slight difficulty, damming the bloody thing and continuing to grumble as he climbed the narrow winding stairway holding a candelabrum high in front of the two men, who grunted with every step. He hoped there wasn't anything untoward in the room above, something long forgotten, some awful family relic. It was years since anyone had been up here he was sure. As it turned out, the worst the room had to offer was an abundance of spiders and dust-laden webs.

"Put him down over there." Luke watched as the men laid their burden carefully down on a small trundle bed, which, after having the top cover shaken off, seemed reasonably acceptable. "And bring some wood for a fire; it's damnably cold in here. I want to keep Judd's whereabouts a secret, not freeze him to death. I'll go down and keep everyone in the kitchen for a half hour while you fetch enough fuel for several days. Clean this place, and then go about your business. I'll see you suitably rewarded." He turned and left the room wondering what he would say that was so interesting it would take a half hour. He wanted badly to go to Lydia's room, to comfort her, to reassure her. And he badly wanted to run a sword through Fulford's heart. A cold sweat broke out on his forehead at thoughts of Lydia's narrow escape. He'd never really considered losing her, but then he'd never, until last eve really known for certain how much he wanted to keep her.

As it turned out the men did their work quickly, and assured everything was in order, Luke hurried from the kitchen to the north wing, locked the door of the stairway, then headed straight to Lydia's room and knocked lightly, waiting for a response before entering.

The maid rose from her seat by the fire and bobbed him a curtsey. "Milady, 'ad some brandy, Your Lordship."

"Thank you. You may leave us now."

Lydia looked up briefly as Luke walked across the room to the window and stared out. He closed the drapes, walked back to the door, opened it, and turned his head left and right. Then he re-entered the room, closed the door and locked it behind him.

Still Lydia said nothing. He came to stand by her side then moved to pour himself a drink and sat down opposite her. She raised her eyes, and Luke felt he might almost have wept at the sadness there. "Lydia," he said quietly, "Judd's not dead." She sprang suddenly to life and would have shouted her relief had Luke not silenced her with a shake of his head and a finger to his lips. In a low voice he said, "Judd is alive, and the doctor says he'll very likely return to his former state of health, given time and care." He watched spellbound as the sadness washed from her eyes in a flow of soft tears, tears of relief. "Allow me continue." Then he found himself kneeling by her side and unable to say another word. He took one of her hands in his own and simply held it as she sobbed softly.

"Why, but why," she sniffed eventually, "did you let me believe he was dead? The maid said . . ."

Her voice was barely a whisper and for that, Luke was glad. "Believe me I have good reason, and I shall endeavour to tell you what I may, though I fear 'twill be little enough to satisfy your curiosity." He let go of her hand and got to his feet, glancing at the clock as he sat down. He pulled a piece of crumpled paper from his pocket and handed it to Lydia. "This was fastened to Judd's jacket when they found him."

Lydia looked at him questioningly before unfolding the paper. She read the words twice then asked, "What does it mean?"

Luke retrieved the paper. "Remember there are others dear to you," he read. "'Tis a warning. A warning that should I continue to interfere in a certain business I have been party to undermining, there will be repercussions. I fear not for myself, and they know it, but Lydia, I give you my word naught shall befall you. I would die first and kill any man who attempted harm upon your person." He stared at her momentarily. "As an aside, did anything befall you at Fulford Manor?"

Lydia sat wide eyed, not because it was apparent someone just might be of the mind to do her in, but she had just heard Luke Waverly say he'd lay down his life for her. She was stunned, and that was putting it mildly. "I . . . no, no, thankfully."

Luke heaved a sigh of relief. At least he was saved a journey to kill the man this night; there was other business that required his attention.

"I'm not really sure why we have to pretend Judd is dead?"

"I do not wish to give our adversary further cause to effect his defences. I should like him to feel secure and mayhap he shall become a little slipshod. If he were aware that Judd still lives and is able to identify his attackers . . ."

"But wouldn't that solve everything? I mean if you can prove who is behind all this"—she spread her hands—"conspiracy or whatever it is."

"Nay, would that it were so simple. We have a far-greater prize to hand. All I can tell you is that I am on God's side for England."

She grunted. That was a bit heavy. "Can I see Judd?"

Luke thought for a moment. "I don't see why not, but understand that no one must know he still lives, or his whereabouts. You may see to his needs, though I suspect him to be sleeping for sometime yet. Come, I'll show you where he is." He stood and held out a hand. "We must be silent. Follow me." He led the way by the light of a single candle, Lydia hanging on to his free hand until they reached the door to the stairway. "Hold the candle would you?" He unlocked the door with scant less trouble than before and cursed it mildly.

"This is creepy," Lydia whispered as he ushered her up the spiralled stairway and into the small room.

"Your words are not familiar," he said entering the room behind her.

Judd lay softly snoring under a pile of blankets on the small bed. A fire flickered comfortingly in the grate. Lydia ran forwards and stooped by the side of the bed, unsure what to do next.

"I'd not thought but who is to tend the bloody fire," Luke grumbled.

"I don't mind coming up here to see to it," Lydia offered. "Judd will want a drink or some broth or something, won't he?" Gently she eased a blanket away from the old man's face and stepped back, horrified.

"I'm of a mind that he'll sleep through the night and likely wake with a fearful head," Luke said wryly. "Apparently he was as drunk as a parson when he was set upon, and it likely saved his life."

"I'm not quite sure what you mean," Lydia said staring down at what was visible of Judd's face. Both his eyes were blackened and his nose, which had long since quit gushing blood, bore a thick congealed mass of the stuff that plugged his nostrils and made his snoring so much more forceful.

"The doctor surmised that he passed out with the first few blows, and his would-be murderers assumed they'd done sufficient damage and he was near death. It appears they curtailed their attack much sooner than they would have, had Judd remained conscious. To all intents and purposes he was dead in their eyes."

"Bloody hell," Lydia mumbled, "and they say drinking's bad for your health."

Luke felt a smile tug at the corner of his mouth. "We must be off." At the bottom of the stairs, he closed and locked the door. "Watch where I put the key." He ran his fingers over the top of the door frame. "See here, bring the candle," he instructed. "This piece of wood is broken; the key will just slide behind it far enough to be out of sight. Try it and make certain you can find it."

Lydia nodded her assent and reached up. After running her fingers along the wood and coming away with a splinter stuck under one of her nails, she assured him she would be able to find and replace the key. "This hurts," she moaned, sucking her finger. "I don't suppose you have any tweezers handy?"

"Let me see." He held the candle closer. "'Tis fair buried in your flesh. Back to your room and I'll see to it."

"How will you do it?" she asked, finger in mouth, as they entered her room and he bade her take a seat.

He proceeded to light a dozen or so candles then came to kneel in front of her. "Will you trust me? 'Tis the best way I can think of."

She nodded and found her finger suddenly between his lips. She trembled.

"I hurt you?" he said raising his light eyes to her briefly.

"No, no, you didn't hurt me." She sucked in a breath and held it while he teased the tiny splinter, which to Lydia felt as big as a tree trunk, between his teeth, occasionally allowing his tongue to linger on her fingertips. Her eyelids slipped quietly shut, and she silently determined to have several more mishaps with splinters if this sort of attention would be the consequence—*just think of the interesting places one could get a splinter.*

"Are you asleep?" Luke touched her cheek with the back of his hand.

She jumped, a little embarrassed to have been caught napping so to speak. "Oh, it's out. That was quick."

"And painless, I hope." From the look in her eyes, he was certain she would have him that very moment, and dear heaven he wanted her, but Jack was right; there must be no liaison until after this affair was cleared. Damn, Jack Palmer, did he always have to be right?

"It was painless, yes." And very, very nice. Could they do it again sometime?

Luke got to his feet quickly before he was further tempted. He looked at the clock. "Almost seven. I'll have dinner sent up here for you, and I would ask that you lock your door."

"Are you going out?" His look said it all, and her stomach took a dive. He was off out again, and no doubt to his usual haunts. She wanted to say something about it being a shame he wouldn't forgo his entertainment, considering what had happened to Judd, for just one night, but knew it to be a worthless exercise. He would go anyway.

He slipped a hand under her chin and bent down, brushing her lips very gently with his own. "Trust me, Lydia." Then he turned and strode from the room.

Lydia stood, walked to the door and turned the key in the lock. She dismissed the idea of running after him and sucked her finger, as she walked to the window and pulled the drapes open a little. The night sky was remarkably clear, and it seemed a thousand stars twinkled on their backdrop of dark velvet alongside the faint silver glow of a crescent moon. It was an evening made for romance. *You're a fool, Lydia Mckenzie,* she told herself. Here she was, just out of one lousy relationship and ready to fall headlong into another. Falling hook, line, and sinker for a totally unsuitable man—a man from another century no less. *Yes,* she answered her own unspoken words, fully aware that if talking to oneself were a true sign of madness, then answering was even more certain to have her committed to Bedlam or whatever the place was called these days. Luke Waverly was a womanizer of the highest magnitude, and she was a fool for a pair of blue eyes and a charming manner, not to mention an incredible physique, as she guessed from the way his body felt against her own. His kisses, limited as they had been, left her only too willing, if not a mite over-eager, to sample more.

A whole host of other attributes came to mind as she tried to reason with her own common sense, and she realised that the list of why she should fall into Luke's arms with complete abandonment was becoming astonishingly lengthy.

And the list of why she shouldn't was looking very sick indeed.

FIFTEEN

Lydia picked at her food. Dinner was a miserable affair, taken alone in her room, the door securely locked as Luke had asked. What was His Lordship doing? The question raised its unwelcome head yet again. She didn't want to think about it, and anyway, it wasn't her business, that much he'd told her.

But not tonight.

Tonight he had asked that she trust him, and she could only take that to be a good sign, but of what she wasn't sure. Could leopards really change their spots?

The clock chimed softly. Nine o'clock. Outside, there was a faint clatter of hooves, and despite her resolve to remain uninvolved, Lydia threw down her knife and fork and ran to the window, barely in time to see a horseman leave the premises at a smart canter.

Luke. No doubt on his way to the Blue Bell.

She ran her tongue over her lips as though expecting to taste him there, but all she tasted was highly seasoned pheasant. Turning from the window, she scowled at the idea of sitting alone in her room. Judd. She would visit Judd and make sure the fire was okay. The house was quiet, and she was certain she could get to the staircase without anyone seeing her. She recalled the secret panel that Andrew had used in their escape from Fulford Manor, and remembered Jack Palmer's sudden appearance in the library. Anyone who knew this house could appear or disappear at will it seemed, and Lydia wished she knew a few secret passages. She gathered some untouched portions of her meal and wrapped them securely in a dinner cloth, then took a taper and lit a pair of candles. With a swift glance into the darkened hallway, lit only by a scant candle here and there, she stepped out of her room. Candles held high in one hand, and the bag of food securely in the other, she set off down the hallway.

It wasn't as easy as when she'd gone there with Luke, and she made several wrong guesses before finally arriving at the small door at the end of the long hall. She placed her bundle and the candles on the floor then ran her hand carefully along the top of the door, found the key and struggled with the lock for a moment. She uttered a couple of curses and recalled having heard Luke do a similar thing. The door wide, she retrieved the bundle, then placing the candles on a step entered the stairway and pulled the door closed behind her. Not wishing to alarm Judd should he be awake, she stole very quietly up the stairs.

"Judd, Judd, are you sleeping?" Judd gave a couple of grunts and pulled the covers more firmly over his head. "You've got a hangover haven't you, Judd Sparks?"

He remained silent.

"I'm sorry. I know you've been beaten up as well. I didn't mean anything by that. How are you feeling?" She came to sit by the bed on a small stool. "I have some food here if you can stomach it," she encouraged.

Slowly the covers slid away, and Judd poked his bruised and battered face out to greet her, squinting as best as he was able through swollen eyelids. "Thank ye miss," he mumbled and attempted to sit up.

"Oh, Judd, I didn't realise how bad it really was." She stared, horror-struck at his battered face, the severity of his injuries becoming clear. "I'm sorry I made that remark when I came in, truly I am. You look awful. Let me get some water and clean you up a bit."

There had been more bleeding since her visit with Luke, and dried blood plugged not only the man's nostrils but covered his throat and neck. Several pieces of linen and some clean towels lay piled on a table by a jug of water. The water was tepid, but it was clean and served its purpose. Gently she dabbed away at the congealed blood and cleared Judd's nose.

"I'm sure His Lordship had intended someone look after you better than they have," Lydia said and remembered Luke's remark about Judd sleeping through the night, and as long as he had a good fire there was little else to do. She supposed he was right, but it seemed a bit unkind to leave the old man by himself. She did note that he had been undressed and now wore a clean if slightly bloodied nightshirt. "I'll stay with you awhile, Judd, if you like."

He nodded his head. "I might be able to manage some o' that food ye were talkin' about."

Lydia helped him to sit more securely and watched as he nibbled tentatively on each morsel until it was small enough to swallow.

"I aches everywhere. Feels like a coach run over me, I do."

"I almost experienced that," Lydia growled. "Judd, do you remember anything about the men who attacked you?" she asked and rose to throw more coal on the fire.

"Oh, I knows 'em I do, no doubts. Fulford's men all right."

The poker in Lydia's hand clattered to the hearth. She turned and reached out a hand to steady herself on the mantelpiece. "Lord Fulford? You mean he was the one who . . . ?"

"Aye, miss, 'twere 'is men. Bad lot they be. Aye, an' there be somethin' . . . somethin' I 'eard 'em say." He scratched his head tentatively. "What were it?"

"Maybe it's not as important as you getting a good night's rest." Lydia was still reeling over the revelation that Fulford's men had beaten old Judd. God alone knew what they'd have done to her had she not escaped from that house. "You really should sleep."

"Ah," Judd said suddenly, a piece of partly chewed game falling from his mouth, "I remembers. An' I need to tell 'is Lordship. Important it be." He moved as though trying to crawl out of the bed. "I 'as to . . ."

"No, Judd. You have to stay where you are." Lydia ran to his side and pushed him back. He was quite animated, and considering he might have a fever, she was ready to call for assistance and more tepid water. "Just try to relax, Judd. It's all right."

"Nay, ye don't understands, miss. There be an ambush planned at Taddy. I 'as to tell the master." He stopped. "Jus' in case."

"Just in case what?"

"Where be . . . ?" He started to cough.

"If you mean His Lordship," Lydia responded stiffly. "He's out. Left about a half hour ago."

Judd recovered himself. "Stop 'im . . . miss." He recommenced coughing and grabbed her arm. "Got to . . ."

"It's too late, Judd. I told you, he's already left."

"Don' mean that," Judd mumbled, his coughing fit resolving.

"Then tell me what you do mean, and just maybe I can help," Lydia said, becoming exasperated with his ramblings.

"I don' know as I should." He winced. "But I be so hurtin', miss, I ain't up to seein' to it meself."

"Tell me, Judd," she encouraged, "I can keep a secret."

"Well," he said, whispering as though the whole world were trying to eavesdrop, "'tis like the master knows I knows, but I don' let on I knows."

Lydia tried to digest that then said, "What is it you know that he knows you know but—oh hell, Judd, please, just tell me what you want me to do."

"The master, 'e been ridin' out at night."

"Well, I know that. The whole bloody county knows that," she said scathingly. "The Blue Bell's his second home."

"No, no, miss, not that. "'E be a gentleman o' the road, 'e be. Sometimes like, when the fancy takes 'im. Dunno why 'e does it, with 'is money an' all."

Lydia stared as Judd continued to babble. "Judd, are you telling me that His Lordship is a highwayman?" Her feet and hands had turned numb, and she recalled her own similar thoughts, which she had dismissed as fanciful.

"Now I ain't sayin' 'e be the one what's been doin' these robbins lately." He shook his head. "Turpin takes the credit for most. But, I don' wants take no chance it might be 'is Lordship out this night, 'avin' 'is fun."

Lydia felt it far more likely that Luke was all set to have his fun somewhere much more cosy but refrained from saying as much.

"Ye 'as to warn 'im, miss. Ye 'as to." As though he thought she might refuse, he added, "Remember the night ye came 'ere, remember 'e be shot that night. 'Twill be far worse for 'im at Taddy if they be waitin' for 'im."

"What's Taddy?" Lydia asked, stalling for time until she could make up her mind what to do.

"Uh?" Judd grunted.

"I said, what's Taddy?"

"It be a crossing on the Tadcaster road. A coach be 'eld up there a week o' more ago." He grinned. "Two coaches in one night, an' twenty miles apart. They all says Turpin did 'em both. But I knows better."

Lydia hesitated. What to do? She could do nothing and hope Luke wasn't out doing highway robbery tonight, but what if he was, and if he were killed . . . "All right, Judd." Her heart pounded. The last thing she wanted to see was Luke with a half-naked wench in his lap, but neither did she want to see him lying dead. Another thought crossed her mind. What if

the highwayman at Taddy was in fact Turpin? She owed him
something too, didn't she?

"Go, quick as you can, miss. Go to the Bell. Like as not 'e
still be there."

"I'll need to bribe the stable lad to keep quiet, or everyone
will know about this before morning for sure. And you're
supposed to be dead."

"Aye, that be a point." He scratched his head.

"I don't have any money," she admitted. "His Lordship said
he'd give me some, but somehow he never got around to it."

"Look in me trews; they be over there."

Lydia looked with distaste at the filthy trousers and vowed
to teach Judd the merits of washing his clothing, and possibly
himself, now and again. She picked them up.

"See inside the top. I keeps a sixpence in there. It be
security like."

She took the coin, promising to replace it as soon as His
Lordship coughed up. "Now is there anything else you need
before I go?"

"Nay, all I wants is that ye warns the master."

"I'll be off then." Lydia flew down the staircase, locked the
door and replaced the key above it, then ran as fast as her gown
would allow back to her room. Hastily she struggled into her
petticoats and stays. Even if Luke was taken up with his floozy,
she intended to look halfway decent. Leaving the stays a little
looser than usual, she pulled a heavy velvet gown around her,
secured it with a brooch, and tucked a handkerchief across the
neck. She was glad of the boots and a pair of warm woollen
socks, and grabbed a pair of gloves just for good measure. It
would get very cold as the night wore on.

There was little need for caution as she stole down the
main staircase, her cloak tightly held around her. It appeared
the rest of the household had retired or were, Lydia suspected,
sitting in the kitchen exchanging horror stories about the
day's grisly happenings.

*   *   *

"I need my horse saddled," she said quietly.

The stable lad jumped off his bench with a shriek. "Milady, you startled me!"

"Sorry, but I need my horse." She paused a second. "You're not Peter."

"No, milady. But, milady, no one ain't supposed to leave the premises."

Luke had given orders. "There's coin in it for you, and as soon as I see His Lordship, I'll make sure there's some more. Here." She held out the sixpence. "It's all I have right now. Please, this is important. Don't ask questions. His Lordship's life may depend on it."

Still the lad hesitated.

Lydia found herself hopping up and down in agitation. This conversation was getting her nowhere. Finally, she glared at him and with as much of a menacing tone as she could muster said, "Listen, you little twerp, you know what happened to Judd Sparks." Ah, she had his attention now. "His Lordship will not go lightly with anyone who was involved, and as you seem reluctant to help me I can only conclude that perhaps you may know more about—"

"Nay, milady, not I," the lad gasped, already pulling the saddle from its rack.

It seemed like three minutes flat, and Lydia was sitting atop the mare. "Here, you've been most helpful." She handed the boy his sixpence. And tomorrow there'll be another for your silence. Do you understand?"

"Aye, milady." He touched his cap.

It suddenly struck her that there was no Judd to open the gates. How did Luke leave?

"Tell me is there another gate, not the main gate, out of the grounds?"

"Aye, down that side o' the park." He pointed in a general direction. "Follow the walls down to where a beck runs across the path, cross it an' after half a mile or so you'll come to a gate. 'Tis unlocked. His Lordship uses it sometimes."

She sensed the lad's discomfort and didn't bother to ask when or why Luke used it. All she needed to do was to find it, find her way to the road, and head for the Blue Bell.

The beck proved to be little more than a gently meandering puddle, though Lydia suspected that in the right season it would swell to a minor torrent. She pushed the mare onwards, keeping her eyes peeled for the gate. There wasn't much light, but she was becoming accustomed to peering into the darkness and making out the shape of things. As the lad had said, there was a gate, and it proved to be unlocked. It was a struggle to reach the latch from horseback, but one well worth the effort as it meant she wouldn't have to remount.

A short while later they came out on the main road, and Lydia could hardly believe her luck, they were nearly half way to the village, and soon a cluster of buildings swam into view. The lights of the tavern glowed dimly through thick glass windows, where clouded shapes could be seen moving around inside, and since the landlord considered the premises a coaching inn, there were a couple of lanterns hanging outside. Lydia pulled her horse to a stop beneath the yellow glow and prepared to dismount.

Her heart firmly in her mouth and pounding away so much it was making her teeth chatter, she looked around for Luke's chestnut gelding, but it was nowhere in sight, and neither was anyone else's horse. She remembered the boy who took horses and groaned inwardly; she had no money tonight either. Sure enough, the boy appeared the minute she disengaged herself from the saddle.

She stopped him before he had chance to open his mouth. "I've no money tonight either, so you may as well not bother to ask me. I'll just fasten my horse here." She looked around for somewhere to tie the mare.

"I knows who you are now," the boy said with a sly grin. "An' seein' 'is Lordship be inside, I daresay 'e won't mind paying for your 'orse." So saying he took the reins from Lydia's hand and walked off with the mare.

She steeled herself and made it to the door of the tavern, took the biggest breath she had ever taken in her entire life, and pushed her way inside. If the noise was incredible, the smoke was worse. Lydia blinked rapidly in an effort to see through the swirling haze. The place was packed. She was reluctant to shove through the crowd and was saved the task as a deathly hush descended on the assembly and several people stepped backwards to get a good look at her. She wished she could dissolve and disappear through a crack in the floorboards.

"Well, lookee, 'ere," came a man's voice.

Several others, none sounding too friendly, joined in, and Lydia was about to grab her skirts and run when she felt an arm encircle her waist. She turned, half frozen with fear, then sighed with relief. It was Luke, but he didn't look happy.

"What the devil are you doing here?" he hissed. "I told you . . ." He grabbed her arm and led her through the hoard of men gathered about them, who moved aside without so much as a murmur as he strode through.

"Just listen will you, and don't pull me about so much." Lydia tried unsuccessfully to free her arm. "I don't appreciate it."

"Would you rather I let you be? You wouldn't care for the company you'd receive, I assure you," he said darkly.

"Just don't pull me around so much, that's all."

The look on her face intrigued Luke. To be truthful it had him slightly worried. Forcing a smile, he said, "So, my pretty, you fancied a bevy with your lord, did you?"

His remark brought forth several chortles and crude remarks as the crowd returned to its normal raucous self. Lydia glared at him. God forbid, but she would kill him if she got the chance. For now though she needed his undivided attention, and it looked as if it might be difficult to get.

Luke relieved her of her cloak and placed her none too gently into a hard wooden chair, then took up the one next to it and shouted for someone to bring him more ale, and something for his pretty miss. "Now"—he leaned close as though they were in intimate conversation, allowing his hand to slip onto her thigh—"what the hell are you doing here?"

"Don't—"

"I have my reputation to think of," he said and patted her leg. "Don't you even think about, you know what," he added, mentally crossing his legs.

Lydia nodded mutely and was about to explain the reason for her journey when a young woman drifted alongside Luke and plonked a mug down in front of him. Then she plonked herself in his lap and proceeded to toy with the bunch of lace at his chin.

Lydia gaped.

"Sal, my pretty, you'll have to wait your turn." He laughed. "I'm discussing business at the moment."

"Well, then just a kiss, milord." She cast a sly glance at Lydia.

Luke obliged, and it seemed to Lydia that it was no hard task for him. She felt her heart slip from her mouth and sink rapidly into her boots, leaving a very empty feeling in her chest.

"Off with you now." He tipped the girl off his knee. "And fetch my lady here a drink." He paused and fixed Lydia with his eyes. "She has need of warming."

A few more choice guffaws issued forth from several men standing close by, suggesting how he might accomplish the task without the aid of drink.

"I told you not to come here," he said quietly. "'Tis not a place for such as you, leastways not at night."

"And it's yours?" She saw thunder rolling into the light blue sky of his eyes. "Luke, listen to me. Please, Your Lordship." Now she had his attention. "It's important."

"Very well." He leaned an elbow on the table.

"I can't shout," she mouthed, above the din of the room.

He leaned closer. His lips caressed the lobe of her ear, and he said very softly, "Is this close enough?" He shifted in his seat, his breeches suddenly not affording him their usual degree of comfort.

Lydia shivered, wishing there wasn't so much company, although by the looks of several couples rolling around in a corner, nothing was sacred or private. She turned slightly so he could see her face and read her lips if the need arose. She concentrated on his chin, willing herself not to look into his eyes or at his thick dark hair, restrained in a queue by a wide black bow. "Judd says there's an ambush set at the . . . the . . . oh, I can't remember where. It was that funny name."

Luke raised an eyebrow. "Well, you've had a ride in the dark for nothing it seems, and a damnably foolish one if I may say so. Didn't I tell you to stay at the house."

"Taddy," she said.

"What?"

"There's to be an ambush at the Taddy, and Judd thought . . ."

"What's it to do with me?"

"You know very well," she hissed.

"I do? Sorry to disappoint you, but I have no idea what you're talking about." He leaned back in his chair. "I'm in the middle of an evening's entertainment, or I was until your untimely appearance. But nay, we'll have a drink together then I'll set you safely on your way—with an escort." He scowled at her then began to speak in a loud voice. "So, my pretty, you rode all this way because you were lonely. Couldn't bear to be without me." He laughed harshly at his own joke. Lydia shrank a bit more with each word he spoke. Why was he being so obnoxious? A mug of mulled wine appeared in front of her, and she nodded a brief thank-you, but the girl was already gone.

"Cheers," Luke said, lifting his mug.

Lydia slipped a still-gloved hand around her own pewter mug and lifted it to her lips. "Bloody hell!" She almost threw the mug back onto the table then clasped a hand to her mouth. "It's red hot," she gasped, and stared at Luke with wide watery eyes.

Luke was already on his feet and striding across the room, scattering anyone who happened to get in his way. "Sal!" he roared, and grabbed the girl's skirts as she attempted to disappear into the crowd. "Get you here, girl, and answer to me!" He pulled back and took hold of both her arms.

The saucy look disappeared from the girl's features as she found herself hauled around to face a very angry Lord Beckham. "I . . . I, milord, I . . ."

He leaned close to her face. "I know what you did, and 'twas no accident. But hear me, Sal. 'Twill not go well for you if you lose my favour. Do you understand?"

The girl's eyes widened with each word he spoke, and she nodded vigorously. "Aye, milord, I do. I be sorry, milord."

Releasing her arms, Luke turned and spoke to another woman before returning to where Lydia sat tentatively touching her lips. "Let me see." He moved her hand. "Your lips are not burned badly, tho' I dare say it might prevent me from kissing you for a while."

Lydia was speechless for a second. "Damn, but you're arrogant." She marvelled at the slightly lopsided grin he gave her, and sighed inwardly. Arrogant he may be, but he was also hot.

"Aye, that too," he agreed. "Now, here's another drink for you. He looked pointedly at the woman who brought it.

"'Tis a bad thing she did, deary," the woman said to Lydia and touched the mug with her bare fingers. "This one'll be just to your likin'." She made a slight curtsey and left them to their drinks.

"Once again, my pretty. Cheers."

Lydia eyed her drink suspiciously. "What is it?" she asked, poking a finger into the froth at the top of the glass.

"Lambswool."

"What's that?" She sucked her finger. "Not bad; tastes of apples."

"Aye, roasted and spiced, atop hot ale." He held his mug aloft.

"What are we toasting to?"

"Aught you would wish," he said with a twinkle in his eyes.

"Well, then," she said quietly, "how about you being shot dead on the road tonight?"

Luke glared. "Damn it, Lydia, still your tongue. That sort of talk could get you hurt."

"Well, if that's all the thanks I get, go out do what you bloody well want. Just don't blame me for the consequences." She made as though to stand, but a hand placed heavily on her shoulder prevented it.

"Sit down, immediately."

There was an edge to his voice she'd not heard before, and she considered telling him to go to hell, but the alternatives to his company were not encouraging.

"I am," he said, removing his hand when he was certain she wasn't about to make a run for the door, "quite able to take care of my own life and to bear the responsibility of it, aye, and the consequences too."

"You wouldn't think so hanging about down here with, with . . ." Lydia felt tears sting the corners of her eyes and hastily blinked them away. "Smoke," she informed him.

Luke appeared not to notice. "It appears you have distaste for my lifestyle and my means of entertainment. Are you then offering an alternative?" His lips twitched slightly. He hated himself for speaking thusly but saw little other way.

"What do you mean?"

"Judging by the sour look on your face when that girl sat upon my lap. Like you were eating gooseberries without sugar," he clarified. "I'd say you were jealous. Would it be that you desire to replace her?" He was well aware of Lydia's darkening glare but ignored it. The angrier and more disgusted she was, the more likely she was to leave him alone.

Lydia set her mouth in a straight line and said nothing. Inside she felt turmoil and hurt like never before. Why was he being like this after asking her to trust him? One minute he was talking of kissing her, and the next he was . . .

Luke interrupted her thoughts and said, "No, I take it."

"You'll end up getting syphilis," she snapped. "And serve you bloody well right."

"Would you care?"

"No," she lied.

"Then pray allow me to conduct my life as I see befitting a gentleman of my nature and standing. Ah, Lydia"—his eyes and mouth were laughing—"what shall I do with you?"

"Nothing," she replied haughtily. "I'm not one of your floosies to be bought and used for a price. I wouldn't sleep with someone just for his money."

Luke raised his eyebrows. What was she saying? He remembered she had mentioned her maidenly virtue not being in tact. "Aye, I remember you once said you were not innocent in these matters."

"That's true, but neither do I go sharing it around on a whim."

"I see." Would he be considered a whim? "Finish your drink Lydia and have another. I have needs must convince you I should prefer to spend a little longer in your own company than that of another."

The man was impossible. "You don't have to do that for me," she grumbled.

"For myself then." He raised a hand and called for more drinks. "My lady is not yet warm enough," he concluded.

A gang of rough-looking women lounging by the fire with a group of equally rough-looking men cackled with gusto. One of them rose to her feet and jiggled her bosom, which was all but clear to view, her stays being partially unfastened.

"There be some 'ere what needs a warmin', milord," she cackled and was immediately pulled on to a man's lap.

Lydia watched in amazement as the man shoved his hand down into the woman's clothing and apparently squeezed her breast a little too hard. He received a brief verbal chastisement for his troubles and then continued his foraging in a less-robust fashion, which appeared to please his female companion.

"You look shocked," Luke observed.

"It's a bit public for my liking. Not that there isn't anything similar in my time." She proceeded to explain all about male reviews, with hunks leaping around in next to nothing to the delight of a roomful of shrieking women, and watched with satisfaction as Luke's eyes narrowed in disbelief.

"This is true?" he asked, taking a sip of his drink. She nodded, and he continued, "And what pray do men of your," he lowered his voice, "time, think to this?"

She shrugged. "I guess most of them don't mind; there have been strip clubs around for years," she said blithely. "It's where men go to watch naked women do, mmm, things."

"You mean an equivalent for men?"

"Yes, and I'm not going into details, so don't ask."

Luke pondered her words for a moment. "Have you, do you frequent these places for women? To look at men?"

Damn, he actually looked concerned. She wished she could tell him that of course she did, all the time, and keep a straight face, but the truth would have to suffice. "No, I never have."

He looked relieved and slightly smug.

"What's the point in looking if you can't sample the goods," Lydia quipped and watched the smugness slip from his face.

"You would want . . . ?" He was lost for words. It was one thing for a man to want these things but for a decent woman—for Lydia . . .

"No, but you know what they say."

"What, do they say?" He regained his composure.

"What's good for the goose is good for the gander." She grinned and held up her glass. "Cheers."

Luke started to laugh. "Ah, my pretty you—"

"Don't bloody call me that. I've asked you not to, and now I'm telling you."

"And you would prefer perhaps . . . ah, let me see." He paused, never taking his eyes from hers. Dearest God but they were eyes to seduce the very devil himself, dark and haunting, yet now they glared hotly at him, their owner in an extreme state of irritation. "I have it. You shall be called mistress. How's that?"

Lydia felt a giggle rising and said, "It makes me sound ancient."

"But think of the implications," Luke said, his eyes twinkling. "You could be my mistress."

"Oh, don't start that again."

"Well, 'tis time to think of getting you home safely. Simon," he called to a man standing a short distance away.

If Lydia harboured any hopes of his accompanying her back to Beckham, they were dashed at his words.

"Half a crown to see this lady safely back to Beckham. You'll be paid upon your return."

Lydia's heart sank. What had she expected? He'd come down here to enjoy himself and that meant—she found the words stuck in her throat—spending the night with someone.

"Come," he stood and held out a hand, "I'll see you to your horse."

"That's to pay for as well," Lydia mumbled. "Seeing as I don't have any money."

"My apologies." He reached inside his frock and pulled a pouch from his belt. "I did say I would furnish you with sufficient funds for your stay here."

"Don't you dare hand me money in here," she hissed.

Luke laughed softly and drew back the hand he'd dipped into his purse. "So, it seems the pretty one is sensitive after all. Take her home Simon and return only when you see her safely into my house. Take the path by the side gate; the main gate remains locked at this time." He turned to face the rest of the room. "You have no doubt heard of the unfortunate demise of my gateman at the hands of as-yet-unknown assailants." He paused to allow his words to take effect. "Rest assured, I intend to find out the identity of the murderers and see them hanged, and I offer a handsome reward for information leading to that happy day."

Lydia averted her gaze, not certain her expression could be relied upon to give nothing away. Luke it seemed was determined to ensure that Judd's death was common knowledge. The men in the room mumbled their agreement that the murderers should indeed hang.

The girl called Sal watched and smiled slowly at Lydia before flicking a lock of hair from her face and turning to converse with another woman. Lydia turned her eyes back to Luke, but not before the girl swung around and flashed a malicious glare in her direction.

"You'll be safe with Simon," Luke said, propelling her out of the door. "He wants his payment."

"I'll be perfectly all right riding back by myself. You needn't waste your money," Lydia snorted. "I did get here by myself, you know."

"Where's that boy?" He whistled into the darkness. "Aye, and now that you're here I look upon it as my responsibility to ensure you return to Beckham in one piece."

The boy appeared around the corner of the building.

"Bring Lady Lydia's horse around." He turned to Lydia. "See how I gave you a respectable title, and a bloody mouthful 'tis too."

"You could take me home," she ventured.

He shook his head. "Nay, I cannot."

"Well," she said with finality, "at least if you're here with someone you won't be out somewhere getting shot."

Her words caught him unawares, and Luke felt a strange warm glow pass through him. Did she care? He wanted to pull her to him to hold her tightly and whisper words of comfort. His hand strayed to a renegade curl and lifted it from her face. "Your hair grows rapidly," he remarked. "Perhaps . . ." Thoughts of that hair framing her face as she lay gazing at him from the pillows of his bed flooded his mind.

"Horse, milord."

Luke shook himself back to reality. "Lydia, come, let's have you on the mare." He handed the boy a coin. Lydia stood by her horse awaiting the customary boost. "I'll go carefully," he assured her before he hoisted her into the saddle. "I should not wish to give you cause to make further upon assault my manhood."

Lydia bit her tongue knowing her words had told what her heart had known all along. She would rather see him in the arms of another woman than see him dead.

"Off you go then." He slapped Lydia's mare on the rump. "See her back safely Simon, or you'll answer to me."

Lydia gripped the reins tightly. How could she possible be in love with a man like this? A man who had, according to his reputation and partly by his own admission, slept with half the population of England and who was now undoubtedly off to pursue some of the same. She felt the dampness of a tear sneak from the corner of her eye and was glad of the darkness, lit only faintly by the lamps of the tavern.

"Lydia."

The sound of her name on his lips made her turn in some sort of expectation, but of what she didn't know. Luke had paused in the doorway and now stood there as nothing but a tall dark silhouette. "Yes?"

"Don't wait up."

SIXTEEN

Lydia thanked Simon, who firmly refused to let her out of his sight until she disappeared inside the doors of Beckham House.

Opening the door to Simon's hefty blows, the maid eyed Lydia suspiciously but said nothing and returned to her own quarters the instant she was dismissed.

A welcoming fire crackled in the hearth, and Lydia flopped into a chair with a great sigh. She kicked off her boots then unfastened her cloak and gown. What an evening. It had in fact been one hell of a couple of days, and it likely wasn't over by a long chalk. She stood up, sat down, stood up again, and proceeded with the tedious business of removing her stays. She heaved a great sigh as her ribs expanded, and throwing the offending restriction onto the bed, she walked over to the window and moved the drapes slightly to one side. The sky remained clear, and a crescent moon cast a soft light across the darkness of the night, and she remembered Luke's words about the moon being a good light for a gentleman of the road. Damn him. Would he be out there tonight? Something in her gut told her he would. But what could she do? She'd tried her best to warn him. If indeed, as Judd had told her an ambush had been set, Luke would ride straight into it.

She couldn't let him do that. She just couldn't.

*   *   *

Luke watched as Lydia rode off with Simon then turned back into the tavern. Pulling his watch from his waistcoat, he glanced at it briefly. It marked a quarter to eleven. He grimaced at the thought of the next few hours, three of which he would spend in one of the upstairs rooms of the tavern, waiting until most if not all the patrons had departed before he himself left. If nothing else it was good for his reputation. He feigned a yawn and looked appraisingly at the three women clustered around him. As always, he needed an alibi. There wasn't much difference between the females so far as general appearance went, but he trusted the one who called herself Anna. She took his coin, asked no questions, and she kept her silence as needed. The girl Sal had endeavoured to gain his attentions for some weeks; yet he had been surprised and not a little disturbed by her obvious animosity towards Lydia. The girl was watching him now through lowered eyelashes.

"Thought ye might be fancyin' somethin' a bit more on the fresh side tonight, milord," she said in a silky voice and sidled against him until he was forced to pay her heed. "What think ye, milord, somethin' younger?" She sucked suggestively on her finger and then placed it against Luke's lips. "Mmmm?"

"And risk the wrath of pretty Anna?" He laughed. "I think not." He nodded, indicating the men sitting by them. "See, men aplenty and only too willing to partake of your charms."

She glowered at him and mumbling something he took to be a curse, she turned amidst bawdy offers from several men and flounced away from the table.

Luke engaged himself in conversation with another of the women and some of the men who were telling tall tales of their exploits that week. He checked his watch again. "Well, Anna, what say you? Shall we retire?" He finished his drink then stood and offered the woman his hand.

"'Bout time, milord. I were thinking ye might not be of a mind this night."

"Always of a mind with you." He patted her playfully on the backside and allowed her to pass in front of him.

At the top of the stairs he paused. Would Lydia really wish him in the arms of another woman than see him dead? Did she merely want him to remain alive for her own security, or was it possible she really cared for him?

He closed the bedroom door behind him. The room was dark except for the light of two candles, and he watched as Anna made herself comfortable in a chair by the fire. "The room is warm tonight," he observed mildly and put his hand to his head.

"Something amiss, milord?" Anna stood and came over to where Luke had flopped down on the bed and now sat with his head in his hands.

"Anna, who brought that last drink I had?"

"Don't rightly recall, milord. Why'd ye ask?"

"You've been seeing to it that I received watered ale all eve, have you not?" he asked, looking up wearily.

"Of course, I always see it done. What of it?"

"But the last one," he responded noting a slur in his voice, "you were sitting by my side as I recall."

"Truth be, Your Lordship, I ain't sure. You be laughing wi' the rest, an' I were about business for a bit. I don't recall who filled your mug. 'Twern't me."

"Ah, by the grace of God, I should have been more alert this night. There is much at stake." He'd noticed a bitter taste in that last ale and now cursed himself for his foolishness. Lydia had filled his mind, and there had been room for naught else.

"Mayhap you need to sleep," Anna suggested, assisting him to his feet as he attempted to rise from the bed.

"Water, I need cold water." He staggered to the basin and sloshed his face with the warm water there. It helped a little, but his mind was becoming increasingly fuzzy.

"What the hell, Anna. What have I taken?"

She helped him to a chair and stood shaking her head. "I dunno, milord, but it were none o' my doin' honest."

"I believe you," he croaked, "but I may not sleep. I must not sleep. Open the window. I need fresh air." Oh Lord, he was seeing double and could barely raise his head. He had to ride this night.

Had to.

"I knows a woman what might help. She fixes 'erbs."

"Go then," Luke groaned, "and quickly."

She ran from the room, and Luke barely heard the door close behind her. His senses were fading rapidly.

The feel of ice-cold water over his face and head roused him. Someone was trying to force him to drink. He pushed away but was restrained and a cup shoved to his mouth.

"Drink this, milord," someone was saying. "'Twill help lessen the need for sleep."

"Aye, milord, take what you can."

He recognised Anna's voice and relaxed a little, allowing the liquid to trickle down his throat. He coughed and forced his eyes to open. He lay on the bed, an old woman beside him. She was nodding her head slowly.

"Take more if you will, milord," the old woman encouraged.

Luke did his best to swallow more of the foul-tasting brew then threw out his hand. "Enough! I can take no more." He gazed around the room, no longer seeing two of everything, although his vision was still far from clear. He put a hand to his head.

"'Twill keep you awake for a few hours; then you will fall into a deep sleep that even I cannot prevent," the old woman said.

"How long?" he gasped, struggling to his feet. "Tell me, old woman, how long do I have?"

"Two maybe three hours. 'Tis difficult to predict, not knowing how much of the draught ye took. But you're a strong man; you may do better than that."

"What was I given? Do you know?" He held his head in both hands; it throbbed like the devil.

"I can't be sure what it might 'ave been. Now, milord, take your rest for a while longer. Let my herbs do their work an' you'll be lively enough soon. You'll get your money's worth." She flashed a toothy grin at Anna. "He'll manage what he needs to."

Luke groaned and leaned back against the head of the bed. That was the story Anna had given the woman. He almost managed a laugh. The old woman had brought her herbs and her skills in order to assist him perform for the night. It was the last thing on his mind.

"Bring me some water, Anna. Aye, to drink." His senses were returning. A clock somewhere struck the hour of two—it was time to leave. The tavern would be empty of revellers. He would go unseen, collect the black gelding, and get to his position at the Taddy in readiness for the early coach. He reflected upon Lydia's warning. It was an unscheduled coach, and even Jack had remarked on it. There was no way in hell he could let it pass without intervention, no matter if Lydia's warning had been true.

He would simply be careful.

SEVENTEEN

Lydia paced the room, worried and uncertain. What could she do? She cursed herself for returning to Beckham and leaving Luke at the tavern. Perhaps she should ride out again and somehow prevent him going to the crossroads. And how would she do that? If he'd not listened the first time, what would be the difference in a second attempt? She laughed at the thought that she could force him to do anything he didn't want to. Perhaps she could catch him before he got to the crossroads if she knew where it was. Her thoughts turned to Jack Palmer, Dick Turpin—where was *he*? She flopped into a chair, feeling completely helpless, the energy drained from her, but determined to try somehow to prevent Luke coming to harm. If it meant going out again in the dark, so be it. A thought struck her. She would be able to ride much faster if she rode astride. Her mind whirled. Where to get clothing at this time of night? There was nothing for it, she leapt to her feet and dragged the wooden chest from behind a table. Throwing it wide, she pulled out her shorts and shirt and hastily dressed herself. Her boots weren't exactly made for wearing with thigh length spandex shorts but they'd have to do. Impulsively, she donned her petticoat for a bit of extra warmth and threw her cloak around her shoulders.

Something crackled and dug into her hip. The letter!

Pulling the letter from the pocket of her shorts, she took a seat by the fire, broke the seal, and unfolded the paper. The script was unfamiliar and difficult to read, but she persisted. The message was succinct and to the point, and Lydia's heart sank in her chest as she read the few lines written there.

"Oh no, please no," she said quietly with a shake of her head. Retrieving her gloves from the bed, she ran from the room and made the bottom of the narrow staircase in record time. She unlocked the door and raced up into the room calling to Judd as she went.

"Judd, oh, Judd, are you awake?"

"Aye, miss." He struggled to make out her form in the scant light of the candle she carried.

She knelt by the side of the bed. "Judd, you've got to tell me how to get to the Taddy crossroads."

"What ye be sayin', miss?"

"Oh, Judd, I've done something really stupid, and I've got to stop His Lordship. Oh, I told him what you said, but he didn't believe a word, and now I know that he'll certainly be riding into an ambush if he goes there. I have to stop him, Judd. I have to." She wiped her hand across the tears that ran freely down her cheeks

"Nay, miss don' take on so."

"Judd," she pleaded, getting to her feet, "tell me the way, please."

One minute later, she pounded down the small stairway and locked the door, replacing the key above it. Under her cloak she wore Judd's filthy but warm frock. She'd donned it at his insistence, and was grateful for its extra insulation as she stepped out into the cold night air.

The stable lad blinked at her sudden arrival and at her second request for the horse that night, but he offered no resistance and only mild surprise at her request that he tack the mare with a man's saddle. She quickly adjusted the stirrup leathers and checked the girth before trotting the mare into the yard and mounting. Her petticoat firmly wrapped around her legs, she set the mare at a canter and thanking the heavens for the faint but available moonlight headed past the front of the house. The main gate remained locked, and the quickest way to reach her destination was out by the old cottage. Lydia turned the mare through the trees and pushed faster across the moonlit park, crouched low in the saddle. They made the gate without mishap. Lydia jumped from the mare's back, and they were through and on their way within seconds.

The clearing swam into sight; Lydia slowed the mare to a trot and steered directly in front of the cottage noting the sound of horses chomping feed somewhere in the dark. Straining her eyes, it seemed that she glimpsed a movement by the barn. She gathered her wits and rode around, passing by the animals, which were plainly enjoying their late meal. Wide eyed she stared at the black, only just discernable in the dark, and at its companion, a stocky bay, an animal she knew quite well. "Oh, no." She felt sick in the knowledge that Dick Turpin was out this night—Jack Palmer, the man to whom she ought to have given that bloody letter in the first place and saved everyone all this trouble. Hauling the mare around, she dug her heels in. Damn! Who would be at the Taddy? "Sorry, beastie, but we have to go and now." She had to warn the highwayman—whichever one it happened to be. Within seconds she had the animal racing across the clearing in what she hoped was the right direction. She paid little attention to her petticoats billowing high and wild around her, held barely in check by the borrowed frock and her cloak. It shouldn't take much more than half an hour to the crossroads at the rate they were going, but as Lydia reminded herself, she had no idea what time the coach was due or when Luke had left the tavern, whether he would ride to the cottage or go straight to the crossroads. Did he ride even ride one of the black horses?

She didn't know. Did he know who Palmer really was? She didn't know that either.

She was scared witless, and that was an understatement. What if she got to the crossroads and herself became a victim of the supposed ambushers? She shivered; her hands and feet were turning numb with cold—or was it fear?

They rode on, and Lydia wished she had taken the trouble to tuck her petticoats around her bare knees, which were rubbing unmercifully on the saddle. Still what were her sore knees compared with Luke's life? Or Turpin's for that matter? She berated herself for a fool as they flew across the countryside. If she had she given the letter to Palmer in the first place . . .

Fate certainly had a way of spicing up one's life, and Lydia decided then and there never to complain about her lot in life, ever again.

The mare's hooves clattered on hard dirt, and Lydia guessed they had come to the main road. It should be plain sailing the rest of the way, unless she was beset by footpads, or a highwayman. The thought crossed her mind that she might be shot by Palmer if she took him unawares, and she determined to call out a greeting immediately if she caught sight of his shadowy form. She laughed. The chances of her spotting the man before he saw her were slim; he was probably out there watching her right now. Surprisingly, she hoped he was.

Lydia turned her attention back to the darkness and the shadows lurking there. They reached the crossroads, a small affair with a four directional wooden signpost, and it was now that she realised she had no plan of action, and all she could hope for was to spot Luke or Palmer before anyone else did. She rode into the security of a thick cluster of trees and hoped she wouldn't fall asleep or freeze before the night was out.

*   *   *

Luke's head throbbed, and his eyes were heavy. Even the chill of the night air didn't serve well enough to wake him to the level of alertness he would have wished. His exit from the tavern had gone unnoticed, and he had ridden like a madman, through the grounds of Beckham, across the back of the house, and exited the park at the gate leading to the clearing. He had spent more time than he should at the ministering of Anna and the old woman, and now he had need make haste in order to be well in position and out of sight before the arrival of the coach, aye, and to be certain no would-be assassins were lurking in the trees. He was not of a mind to die this night and still desired to find out who had slipped the sleeping potion into his drink. God forbid it should turn out to be Lydia. The thought swirled around in his brain, and he could only construe two possible motives she would have for doing such a thing. The least palatable was that she had involvement in this business and contrived to prevent the apprehension of information on its way to support the Jacobite cause. She had failed in her attempts to dissuade him from riding against the coach this evening with her tales of an ambush. Had he been a fool? Had her story been naught but lies? Another possibility tapped at his mind, and it was a far more welcome solution. Could it be that Lydia had drugged him in an attempt to prevent his being killed, because she cared? He remembered trying to convince himself earlier that evening that she not only had his well-being at heart but was also romantically inclined towards him.

Jumping from the chestnut's back, he hurried it into the enclosure telling himself to keep his mind on the business to hand. The black had finished its fodder he noted gratefully as he threw a saddle on its back. He couldn't afford the animal to colic. He took a few minutes to adjust the lay of the bit before fitting the bridle and securing the animal to the fence. Shedding his surtout, he ran to cottage, returning within seconds hastily fastening a black cloak around his person. He tucked a pistol in his belt, shoved another deep inside his waistcoat, and pulled his three-cornered hat down on his head with a hard twist so that it almost met with the mask he wore across his eyes. A kerchief hung loose at his throat, almost obscuring the bunch of white lace he knew would stare like a beacon into the night once he pulled the black silk into place over his nose and mouth. His left foot barely grazed the stirrup, and he swung effortlessly into the saddle, crouching low under the trees as the horse left the clearing at a gallop knowing its rider to be secure and competent.

Luke thanked the good Lord for the moon this night and noted the glint where it struck the hilt of his sword, and danced and flickered. Reflected on inlays of gold and silver, it reminded him of Lydia's eyes, dark yet set in a face so fair and bordered by short curls a little darker than the colour of ripe barley. He sighed. She was a beauty, and a prize he was willing to fight for.

He approached the crossroads from the west, circling around several times to ensure there were no assailants awaiting him. Satisfied he was alone he sat back to wait. He hoped he'd not missed the blasted thing; coaches were not particularly known for their punctuality. Jack should be headed back to the cottage by now, from way across the Great North Road. Luke grinned. Yet again, Turpin would be seen to execute an incredible feat of horsemanship. Strange how Jack actually appeared to enjoy all this while he really didn't see the appeal of it. The first couple of times there had been the coursing of blood in his veins, and the tingling excitement that ran through his bones had aroused him almost sexually. Yes, danger certainly provoked the maleness in him, but he was inclined to prefer arousal in a different manner, and in more comfortable surroundings—it was damnably cold out tonight. Luke shivered, shook his head, and blinked.

The black pricked up its ears. Luke steadied the animal, which appeared also to feel the rise of heat through its belly on such occasions even though it had recently lost its claim to manhood. "Steady, my boy," he whispered and shook his head in an attempt to stave off the drowsiness he felt creeping over him. He watched, staying as keenly alert as he was able but saw nothing. Still the horse kept its interest and stamped impatiently. Luke's stomach tightened; he was always nervous when his horse sensed something he himself couldn't see. Eventually, he settled the animal and sat back to wait. Some minutes later a barely audible rumble caught his ear, and he slipped the pistol easily from his belt and pulled the black kerchief over the lower half of his face. The dark shape of a coach and six, weakly lit by ineffective coach lamps, loomed out of the darkness. Luke touched his heels against the horse's flanks and launched the animal into the road, effectively blocking passage of the vehicle. The team plunged with alarm as the coachman stood and hauled hard on the reins in an effort to control them. Luke sat easily atop the black and allowed it to rear once before demanding compliance and immobility. The horse stood and merely snorted. Levelling his pistol at the coachman, Luke made his demand.

"Stand I say! Stand and deliver."

His voice rang loud and sharp in the crisp air, and in a tone that brooked no defiance.

* * *

Lydia jumped and sat up in the saddle with a start, awake if not fully aware. Bloody hell, she had fallen asleep and was dreaming while the mare had ambled farther into the trees and almost out of view of the crossroads. She froze. A familiar voice barked orders from somewhere close by. She pulled the mare around and stared out into the moonlit road, first at the coach and four, and a driver who was being advised in no uncertain terms to throw down his weapon, and then at the figure giving the order.

Luke!

Movement in the trees to Lydia's left caught her attention. She saw moonlight glint on metal as several figures guided their mounts quietly towards the road. Opening her mouth she screamed Luke's name at the top of her lungs and watched him swing the big black around full circle as all hell broke loose around her. "It's a trap, Luke! It's a trap!" she yelled. "Get out of here!" How she wished she had a pistol, but she was powerless to help and watched as at least half a dozen men tumbled from the coach and began shooting.

Luke fired his pistol, and took a man down. Then dashing the spent firearm to the ground, he drove his horse across the road into the trees closely pursued by four riders, who took up the chase at full gallop.

*   *   *

Luke's mind whirled. Had he really heard Lydia's voice shouting a warning? Where was she? He rode low and fast, twisting and turning the gelding through the trees in an attempt to throw off his attackers, his thoughts barely with his own survival. If she were out there, was she captured? Unwittingly he jerked the reins. The black faltered and then plunged forwards again into a swath of close trees. Luke cursed himself for his inattention and slowed the horse a little to negotiate low branches that threatened to knock a man senseless if he were unaware. He would go back for Lydia as soon as he had confounded his pursuers.

A shout off to his right, left him in no doubt that such an action at this time would indeed be foolish, and he swung the horse further into the woods. Too late, he realised his mistake and snatched the second pistol from inside his waistcoat. He fired the instant his aim was sure, and not a second too soon; his assailant was barely a sword's distance away and fell screaming from his horse directly into the path of a second horseman. Luke pushed the black harder, not minding the sweat, mud, and saliva that flew into his face. Hell, but he'd not experienced this before. Even the time he took lead in his arm, escape had been assured. This time his fate was uncertain, but he had a good horse that could outrun almost anything in the county, provided it didn't stumble in the dark at this breakneck speed. He blinked and remembered the old woman's warning that sleep, after the short respite she had promised, would come quickly and with little warning. The remaining horsemen were still in pursuit, and Luke knew if he could make it to open ground, sheer speed alone might be what would save him this night even though he'd be an easy target.

They were almost out of the trees. He shook his head. His eyes were heavy and his senses dull, his mind slowed, and he thanked God his horse did not. Though the way was unfamiliar, the gelding raced boldly ahead, and Luke glimpsed the soft glow of the moon spreading out over open land not too far distant. He forced the horse to more speed and prayed he wouldn't lapse into unconsciousness.

The dull report of a pistol being discharged alerted him almost before the pain awakened him. He gasped in shock at the sudden heat that tore through his side and forced him to struggle to remain in the saddle. "Go, just go," he rasped and dug his heels in hard for good measure, laying himself low along the gelding's neck as sense and awareness began to slip from him. For the next few miles, he rode as a mere passenger hoping his horse would find its way to the cottage, and not become confused given the hullabaloo around them. He could do little to direct the animal but relaxed slightly in the knowledge that they appeared to be leaving their pursuers far behind. The pain in his side became an intense throbbing, and he was aware of a growing wetness seeping through his garments.

He was losing blood—fast.

Luke sensed the black slowing its pace but had neither the strength nor the thought to take any note of why. He felt himself begin to slip from the saddle and clung desperately to the thick mane under his hands for as long as he was able. As the horse stopped moving, he felt his limbs weaken, and he gave in to darkness.

*   *   *

Lydia sobbed with frustration. Luke lay at her feet bleeding to death right before her eyes, and she was unable to do anything about it. She was helpless, powerless to do anything but watch him die right there.

She had ridden off when the men galloped from the trees but had lost everyone, including Luke, after a couple of miles. Pistol shots had given some clue to the general direction, and she had followed the sounds as best she could, uncertain where he would go but eventually coming to the conclusion that Luke would try for the cottage if he could lose his pursuers first.

Bringing her mare to a trot as they entered the clearing, Lydia saw the dark form of a horse standing quite still. She jumped down, relief written all over her face. Then she had taken a deep breath, and her heart had almost stopped. Luke lay by the black's feet, unmoving. He was large and heavy, and at the very least senseless—and he was bleeding profusely. The night air was damp and cold, but there was no way she could shift him into the cottage, and in any case it was no warmer in there. She threw off her cloak and quickly slipped out of Judd's frock. Folding the cloak, she laid it over the upper half of Luke's body and draped the frock over his thighs. Blood saturated his clothing; he would certainly bleed to death if she didn't do something fast. Throwing aside the cloak, she opened his waistcoat and tugged his shirt free, then with great determination ripped away the bottom half of her petticoat and scrunched it up. Taking a deep breath she knelt by his side and pressed the ball of fabric into Luke's torn and gaping flesh. He groaned. Lydia jumped, releasing the pressure slightly and was rewarded by a gush of fresh blood.

"Damn it, keep pressing you idiot," she mumbled to herself. Somehow, she had to get help, but how could she leave? Luke couldn't be left alone. How long would it be before anyone realised they were gone? Would anyone in fact miss them? Luke often stayed out all night, and she came and went as she pleased. Palmer could be anywhere, and Judd was the only one who knew where she had gone.

The moonlight was almost non-existent, obscured by thick banks of cloud slowly shifting around, and a few spots of rain pattered around Lydia. "What can I do?" she wailed. "Oh, someone, please help me." She turned at a faint sound in the darkness. Seeing nothing, she turned back to gaze at the face of a man very close to death and whom she knew without doubt, she loved.

She listened again. Hoof beats, steady hoof beats muffled by the thick carpet of autumn leaves—someone was coming. She strained her eyes but saw nothing in the darkness. A soft crunch heralded the sound of a dismount. Lydia trembled. Had those men followed them? There was a pause followed by the sound of boots treading earth somewhere by the barn. She gasped and clasped one hand to her mouth afraid she might just cry out. The boots stopped moving, someone coughed and then slapped a hand against a horse several times.

"Who . . . who is it?" she called through chattering teeth knowing there was little point trying to hide; they were sitting ducks.

A shadowy figure loomed through the darkness. "'Tis I," boomed the voice of Jack Palmer. "What the hell's going on?"

"It's Luke," Lydia sobbed. "He's been shot. Please, please help him."

"What mean you?" Jack Palmer sprinted the last few yards between them. Dropping to his knees he stared briefly then said, "Luke, man, can you hear me?" He slapped Luke's cheek.

"It's all my fault. Oh, please help him." Lydia looked into Palmer's face—it was ashen.

Palmer stared down at where she held the bundle of blood-soaked petticoat. "God's sake, he's bleeding to death. We have to get him to Beckham. Nay," he said more quietly, "he's bleeding too badly for that." He shoved Lydia unceremoniously out of the way, and with some difficulty hoisted Luke to his feet and begged him stand until he was able to get a good grip of his person then staggered into the cottage and placed him in front of the fireplace. "Do as you were." He indicated that Lydia should continue to stem the bleeding then he dashed outside for firewood and had a fire crackling in the hearth in a matter of minutes. "Stay here," he ordered, ripping his dark cloak from him and stashing his pistols and rapier in the trunk. "I'll go for help. Aye, and remember your promise. Not a word of who I might be to anyone."

Lydia nodded glumly and watched as he raced out into the dark night. She did just as she was told, and apart from throwing an occasional lump of wood on the fire didn't move from her position and kept her petticoats pressed firmly against Luke's side. Her hands dripped warm blood. He was still bleeding. "Oh, please, please," she whispered, "don't die. I'll do anything, anything at all."

Luke twitched occasionally but otherwise made no movement or sound. His face had drained to a sickly grey colour, and Lydia pressed two fingers to his throat feeling frantically for a pulse. It was weak but it was there. She sighed with relief and prayed help would arrive in time.

Jack Palmer returned in what Lydia was sure had to be less than an hour, but it had been the longest hour of her life. He dashed into the room followed by Dr. Green, who hastily began to remove Luke's clothing.

"'Tis a nasty wound," the doctor observed, "and he has lost an amount of blood I'll wager. Still, he yet lives and he is young. We shall see what can be done."

Lydia sat back on her heels and watched with growing fear as the doctor examined the wound, shaking his head and tutting periodically.

"Can I help?" she whispered.

"Aye, you can stop snivelling and find something to boil water in." He glanced at her briefly and continued his work.

"Out in the barn," Palmer said grimly. "Hurry, now."

"'Tis likely he'll not make it," the doctor said matter-of-factly when Lydia was out of the room.

Palmer nodded. "Luke, man, stay with us," he encouraged, uncertain whether his words were being heard by the intended recipient or not.

"The ball passed into his left side," the doctor continued. "It broke a couple of ribs, but thank the Lord it was deflected and found exit through his chest wall." He further commented on the lucky fact it had not travelled a few more inches to the right, or it would certainly have pierced Luke's heart or lungs.

Lydia returned with a bucket and sat stunned as the doctor worked; his arms covered in blood up to the elbows. She had never seen so much blood in her life and almost gagged at the sight of Luke's flesh being pulled open and held there by Jack Palmer while the wound was irrigated. The doctor commented on the fact that Luke had escaped the complication of a perforated bowel, and she watched awestruck as he threw what scant surgical instruments he possessed into the pot of now-boiling water and performed surgery without anaesthetic. Finally, after the last shards of broken bone were removed, Dr. Green closed the wound with deft stitches of catgut.

Lydia was still contemplating his sterilization of the instruments when he spoke.

"The rest of your petticoat; give it to me."

"I . . . of course." Swiftly she doffed the remainder of said garment and watched as he tore it into strips.

"Help me roll him. I need to bind the wound; to support his ribs." The doctor directed his words at Palmer, who carefully moved Luke's senseless form by rolling him first to one side, then the other.

"'Tis the best I can do," the doctor said at last, getting to his feet. "The rest is up to him." He turned to face Lydia. "He cannot be taken to Beckham yet. A few hours more and mayhap we may venture to transport him. Shall you remain and tend him?"

She nodded mutely then said, "Dr. Green, about what you did . . ." She glanced at Palmer who was staring at the fire and paying them no heed.

"Aye?"

She kept her voice low. "You sterilized your instruments. I didn't think . . ." She hesitated.

"Germs?" he prompted.

Lydia gasped and nodded.

"I thought there was something about you," he continued quietly.

"You, you're from the future?" Her eyes widened.

"Nay, not I, but there are those I learned from." He reached out and touched her hand. "You must say nothing."

Lydia nodded again. "Thank you for helping Luke. I'm glad it was you. He has a good chance of recovering, doesn't he?"

"Keep him warm." The doctor's face showed little emotion. "Get him to drink warmed water." He appeared to think a moment then said, "There is little else you can do, except pray."

She did.

EIGHTEEN

Jack Palmer gazed at the figure of his friend, lying as though in death upon the dirt floor of the cottage, and covered for warmth by an assortment of outer garments. He looked at the young woman, in whose lap his friend's head lay, and wondered. Lydia wore her own cloak again, and Palmer remembered how at first she had resisted his attempts to wrap it around her, arguing that Luke needed it more. Never in his born days had he seen clothing such as she wore this night and was surprised the doctor had not commented on it.

He watched how she allowed her fingers to stray through Luke's thick hair, now heavy with sweat, and he considered that keeping Luke warm enough might be the least of their problems over the next few days. He had seen men live three or four days in an agony of fever, only to die, consumed in the end by its ravages. Lydia looked up as he crouched by her side. "You've not eaten all day," he said. "Are you not hungry?"

She shook her head. "No, thank you. I don't feel like eating."

It was late afternoon, and the weather had taken a turn for the worse. Rain lashed down in torrents, at times blown almost vertical across the small clearing by freezing cold winds. Palmer had said they would wait awhile yet before attempting to move Luke, though the quicker they got him back to Beckham, the better his chances would be.

"You need to keep up your strength if you've a mind to help him," Palmer continued.

She nodded. He had gone out earlier and brought back the essentials of a meal and arranged that a carriage be driven to the cottage. It would take some time, he told her, as they would have to come around by the road. The carriage couldn't make it by way of the park entrance.

"Jack? Do you mind if I call you that?"

"Nay, 'tis my name."

"Jack," Lydia found her voice barely a whisper, "will he live?" She searched his eyes for an affirmative answer but found none.

Palmer pressed his lips tight together. "I don't know, lass. I just don't know." He saw the tears well in her eyes and wished he knew better how to give comfort. He gave an uncomfortable cough and rose to his feet. "I'll get you some food."

Between salty tears and the stream of thin snot that ran unheeded from her nose, Lydia managed to swallow some bread and a small piece of game washed down with a swig of robust red wine. She had to admit to feeling somewhat revived, and at Jack Palmer's insistence left Luke in his care and walked to the doorway to stretch her cramped limbs. She opened the door and looked out. The weather was lousy and showed little sign of letting up. Lydia sighed and turned back into the room, closing the door behind her. "Jack, we need to get him back to Beckham."

"I tend to agree except that we have to wait for the carriage and 'tis filthy weather. Shouldn't be too long," he added, trying to sound encouraging.

There was a sudden, hasty thumping on the door.

Lydia turned to open it, regardless of whom it might be.

"Stay yourself," Palmer said quietly and leapt to his feet, pistol in hand. "Behind me." He motioned her out of the way and stepped to the door.

Lydia ran to Luke's side and sat wide eyed, her hand resting lightly on his cheek.

Jack Palmer stood a second then wrenched the door wide and levelled his pistol at chest height. He cursed mildly and stepped back into the room followed by another man wearing an oilskin cape pulled over his head.

Lydia looked up expectedly and tried to make out what the two men were saying.

"Bloody hell, man, how long?"

"Don' rightly know, sir," the man in the oilskin replied. "What wi' this weather an' all."

"What's wrong?" Lydia asked, noting Palmer's extreme agitation.

With a sigh he said, "The carriage is stuck in the mud nary a mile from here, but the mud is so deep the horses are sliding onto their bellies. It could take hours." He cursed foully and began to shoo the man out of the door.

"Wait." Lydia thought for a moment. "Use the door. Carry him I mean."

"The door?" Palmer rubbed his chin. "Aye, we could indeed carry him between the two of us." He looked at the man who nodded in acquiescence.

"And there's me," Lydia said eagerly. "I can help."

Jack Palmer grunted. "Fetch an axe man, and you'll find a jemmy somewhere in the barn."

The door was duly hacked and wrenched from its hinges without too much difficulty, and Lydia helped the two men wrap Luke in the oilskin then watched as they lifted his helpless form onto the makeshift stretcher. She wrapped her cloak tightly around her, considering it wise to cover the scant spandex shorts and top, the like of which she was certain would attract more than just a few stares from the men with the carriage.

Outside, the rain continued its onslaught and the oilskin cape blew from Luke's body on more than one occasion. Lydia fought valiantly to keep it over him, as the two men carrying him slipped and slithered, and struggled to keep their footing in the heavy mud. It was slow going, and although Jack Palmer showed no sign of fatigue, the other man was clearly becoming weary. Fearing he may drop his half of the door, Lydia edged the man to one side and took up part of the door herself, not caring if he were offended.

It seemed they took forever to get to the carriage, and Luke was becoming agitated. Lydia noticed a slight twitch of his hands and face muscles and he moaned frequently, but he never opened his eyes. Finally, they loaded him as comfortably as possible into the vehicle and got the horses turned around. A window had smashed during the fast and very rough drive from Beckham and already the inside of the carriage was soaked.

"Take care with your load," Palmer instructed then turned to Lydia. "I shall meet you back at Beckham. I'll bring your mare." With that, he strode off the way they had come, his head bowed to the elements.

*   *   *

Lydia sat with Luke hugged against her own body trying to cushion the jarring of the carriage as it banged over the rough ground. Once they reached the road it was an easier ride, though by no means smooth, and Lydia kept her head bowed partially to protect her eyes from the stinging rain, and partly to ensure that the man lying by her was still breathing.

She recognised the grey walls of Beckham and wondered vaguely who was in charge of the front gates; they were open. It crossed her mind that Judd was still in his attic, and she hoped someone had remembered to feed him.

Jack Palmer met them at the front of the house and strode across to the carriage, giving instruction that Luke be moved slowly. "I want him disturbed as little as possible," he barked.

"Will the doctor come here?" Lydia asked as three men laid Luke carefully on his bed.

"Nay, there is naught else he can do," Palmer replied. "Careful there, careful with him. Just leave him." He watched as the men left the room then looked doubtfully at Lydia. "He needs to be undressed."

"I'll help. It doesn't bother me."

"Well, maybe I should fetch . . ."

"Let's just do it, Jack." She began to pull away the garments, taking great care to move Luke's body as little as possible. "Could you have some clean warm water brought up? He needs to be washed."

Palmer nodded and walked to the bellpull and tugged it twice.

Sometime later, Lydia leaned back in a chair by the fire, a glass of brandy in her hand.

"He's sleeping soundly," Palmer remarked. "You did excellent work."

"At least he'll be more comfortable." She looked at the pallor of Luke's face, drawn and grey against the white linen of the pillows. She had insisted he be propped up a little and had explained the problems of fluid settling on his lungs to a very interested Jack Palmer. Luke was washed and out of his filthy clothing, and at Palmer's suggestion they'd not struggled to force his damaged body into a nightshirt. Lydia hadn't argued, not wishing to spend further time in such close contact with his naked body. If things had been different, she was certain she would have said he was quite magnificent. But as things were she barely remembered noting any particular part of his anatomy apart from the bloody wound at his side, which she washed carefully and rebound with clean linen.

She looked at the man sitting opposite. What sort of a man was he? He'd certainly done everything he could for Luke and had offered his concern for Judd. "By the way, did you find out if someone tended to Judd?"

"Aye, 'tis seen to. Remember, apart from our three selves and a couple of fellows well paid and sworn to secrecy, everyone else must continue to believe Judd is dead."

She nodded. "At least he'll be sober for a while."

"I've been meaning to ask," Palmer said, twirling his brandy in its glass. "Where come you by your garments?"

Lydia hugged the borrowed robe around her. It was Luke's, and it covered her well down to her ankles in thick folds of soft blue silk. She hesitated, wishing dearly that she could run off and take a bath to avoid this question.

"Well?"

"It's a little difficult to explain," she mumbled.

"I imagine." He sipped his drink. "I won't press you pretty miss, not this night. You have my friend's well-being at heart, and that is good enough for me. We shall see him through this, and then perhaps you'll satisfy my curiosity."

"Thank you." She was certain he was about to ask her about the bike, and she shuffled uncomfortably in her seat. A slight crackle emanated from the pocket of her shorts, and she pressed her hand against it. "Jack," she whispered. "Oh, Jack, I forgot." She got to her feet, placed her glass on a table and turned her back to him while she fished inside the robe. Slowly she faced Jack Palmer and held out her hand.

"What's this?"

"I . . . I didn't know what to do with it," she whispered, feeling suddenly uncertain of her legs. She sank back into the chair, trembling.

Palmer took the letter and unfolded it. He began to read and glanced up twice at Lydia before folding the paper again and stuffing it inside his waistcoat.

"I didn't know who was, that is . . . Oh, Jack, I'm so sorry I didn't trust you. But there were so many secrets." With that she broke down completely, racked by wave after wave of great racking sobs, her head bowed and supported by her hands. "And now if Luke dies, it's all m . . . my f . . . fault." She started to hiccough.

Jack Palmer stared at her tear-stained face as she raised her eyes to look at him. What could he say? Everything she said was true, yet her actions were blameless. He rubbed his chin and said, "All is not lost. Dry your tears, and tell me exactly how you came by this paper. The truth mind, now."

Lydia sniffed and wiped her arm across her face. He had demanded the truth, but he hadn't said the whole truth. She began her story.

He sat back after a while and said, "I'll not ask why you were out on the road in the first place, but the rest of your story appears reasonable."

"I just didn't trust anyone," Lydia sniffed.

"What do you intend to do? Do you intend to stay here for the time being?" Palmer leaned back in his chair, crossed and uncrossed his legs, never taking his eyes from her.

"I'm not sure," she fumbled her words. "You see I can't really explain enough to tell you what my problem is."

"Did you explain your dilemma to Luke?"

Lydia shifted uncomfortably before replying, "Yes, yes I did."

"Yet you cannot tell me?" He raised his eyebrows questioningly. "Could it be you still do not trust me?"

Lydia felt embarrassed by his frankness. "It's just that, well it's very convoluted."

"And you think I would not be able to comprehend?"

"Oh, no, I didn't mean that."

"Worry yourself not. If you desire to tell me than so it shall be, if not . . ."

"I'd like to talk to Luke before I tell anyone else, that's all," she concluded.

"So be it." Palmer looked suddenly serious. "There is the matter of this letter and the quarry we seek. 'Tis but three nights hence."

"And if I'd given you the letter in the first place, Luke wouldn't have been out there last night." She picked up her glass and brought it to her lips with barely steady hands. "Jack, I've messed things up, I know. Is there anything I can do that will help in all of this? I mean, I still don't know what's going on."

He looked at her steadily for a few moments. "We are not after riches, nor even the consignment of gold this conveyance may or may not bear, that is easily retrieved. 'Tis one man we seek, a man carrying information to the enemies of this great England." He gave a wry smile. "Should the information reach its destination . . . 'tis instruction for an uprising, and the gold is French gold." He looked steadily at Lydia. "The enemies of the king are planning to turn against him with a union of Scottish and French forces."

Lydia squirmed under his gaze. "You thought I was involved, didn't you?"

"It crossed my mind," he admitted.

"Be honest it was more than that, and it's why you didn't tell me you were Jack Palmer."

"We have to be careful in these times, and that's why I believe you acted as you did and showed wisdom in withholding the letter. I could have been anyone."

Lydia felt grateful for his assurances. "I suppose so but . . ."

A groan from Luke set them both on their feet. Lydia was first at the bedside, her hand on Luke's forehead.

"He's burning up, Jack. We'll need cool water and plenty of cloths."

"I was afraid of this," Palmer muttered. He strode over to the bellpull and gave a couple of vicious tugs. He rattled off orders to the servant who appeared.

Luke began to twitch fearfully as a maid ran into the room with water and cloths.

Lydia grabbed the cloths and threw them into the water. "Get more, of everything," she instructed the girl, sharply.

"Quickly. Help me, Jack. Wet cloths everywhere you can put them. He's starting to convulse."

Between them, they covered Luke's body with cool wet linen.

"The minute they start to get warm, replace them. We've got to get his temperature down and fast," Lydia gasped, hastily wringing out and re-applying the cloths to Luke's flesh. How she wished for a modern emergency room or some medication to bring his fever down, just over-the-counter normal, everyday stuff. Trouble was there was no friendly pharmacy around the corner; no convenient branch of Boots the Chemists.

Luke's fever raged the whole night and through into the next day. Periodically he would thrash about and cry out in some sort of unseen torment as sweat poured from him, and repeatedly severe chills followed, leaving him trembling but silent. Lydia held him as tightly as she dared each time his body convulsed and watched helplessly as he dropped back against the sodden sheets, exhausted. She stayed by him, refusing to leave his side except for necessary matters of hygiene.

Jack Palmer watched in quiet admiration, occasionally insisting that she drank a cup of water or a glass of wine. He noticed she wept silent tears and spoke to Luke as though he could truly hear her words.

"Please hold on, Luke. Don't die. I'll try to go home, yes I will. I've cost you too much already." She found Palmer at her side shaking his head slowly. "Oh, Jack, I forgot you were here."

"I've not left you, lass, nor shall I. Excepting for the work I must do."

"You mean tomorrow night?"

"Aye, these past two days have been hell, but I fear I have to leave this very eve. I have needs recruit a trustworthy soul to aid me."

"Luke would have been that one, wouldn't he?"

"'Tis not to be." He thought for a moment. "There is Captain Norton. Andrew to you."

Lydia turned and looked at him. "You mean Andrew who helped me get away from Fulford's place?"

"Aye, the very same. A good intelligence officer he is, but I fear to approach the Fulford residence, so close is our quarry. 'Twould not do to alert them, and the captain is needed where he is for a while longer." He walked to the fire and threw on more coal. "Now, my plan . . ."

"What plan?" Lydia said flatly. "It's all gone to hell since I got muddled up in it. You may as well be honest, Jack. I've buggered things up right good and proper."

If the situation hadn't been so dire, Jack Palmer knew he would have laughed. "I needs must have a riding mate tomorrow eve. Someone to stand with a pistol at my back should the need arise. This will be no run-of-the-mill hold up."

"Take me."

"What?" He didn't turn to look at her.

"I said, take me. It's the least I can do. I mean it," she finished as he slowly turned and regarded her.

"Far too dangerous for a woman."

"If you show me how to use a pistol, that's all you need to do. You know I can ride."

"Aye, that you can," he agreed. "And damnably well if you travelled as fast as you must have from the Taddy to the cottage."

"Tell you what. At least think about it. We have until tomorrow evening. If you can't get anyone else, promise me I can help." She stared at him.

He nodded. "Very well, and I go now with the full intent of recruiting someone who will negate that necessity."

Lydia grimaced. What had she done?

Wasn't offering to ride with Dick Turpin a bit like sticking your neck in a noose?

NINETEEN

Lydia yawned and wished she'd not drunk so much coffee; she needed to sleep. Luke's temperature seemed to be staying within reasonable limits, and he was resting. The coffee had certainly helped her through the last couple of exhausting nights, but now her body cried out for rest, and her mind refused to grant it. It was nigh on impossible to sleep comfortably in a chair, she concluded, and turned first one way and then the other, looking forwards to sleeping in a bed sometime in the near future.

It was early morning, and so far, there had been no word from Jack Palmer as to whether or not his recruiting had come to anything. On the one hand, she wanted to help, but on the other she was loathe to leave Luke in the care of anyone else in the house—he wasn't out of the woods yet.

"Lydia?"

She shuffled in the chair. Good, she was asleep. She was dreaming.

"Lydia." It was more of a gasp than a word.

She sat bolt upright and swivelled her head to look at the bed where Luke lay, his eyes barely open, nevertheless, open. She grabbed her robe around her and sprinted to his side.

"Luke," she said, trying to hide the silly grin that threatened, "you're awake." Hitherto restrained tears rolled down her cheeks. "Thank you, God," she whispered.

"Sit by me." He moved his hand, and she took it instantly with her own. The sparkle had gone from his blue eyes, his face was gaunt and his voice so weary it was barely audible. In short, he looked awful, but to Lydia, he was the most beautiful sight in the world.

"You've been very ill," she said after a few moments of mutual appraisal.

"So it seems. A drink, would you?" He tried to move himself up on his elbows against the pillow but twisted his face in pain and quickly gave up the attempt. He cursed under his breath at his apparent state of helplessness.

"Don't move, please," she begged. "You might start bleeding again. You've already done it twice with your thrashing around, and you've lost a lot of blood. Wait a minute while I get you a drink of water then I'll help you sit up a little."

"I don't want bloody water," he groaned. "Get me a brandy."

"You're having water and like it," she said and walked back to the bed with a cup. "Alcohol won't do you any good as you are."

"Damn it, I'll have what I . . . *aagh*." He grasped his side and scowled. "Damnation that hurts."

"Listen," she said bending close, "I've looked after you for three days now. You can't move by yourself, so don't try, and water it is. Don't argue. When you assure me you're not going to choke, I'll have some broth brought in."

Luke took a deep breath. He wasn't used to being told what to do, but it seemed he had little choice in the matter. "Water it is." He smiled weakly.

"Good, now let me lift your head, and sip it slowly," she ordered.

He indicated he had drunk enough after a couple of mouthfuls. "Have I passed the test? May I have some brandy now?"

"No, not yet, but I'll have the broth brought up." Lydia rose and walked over to the bellpull. "Cook has some ready and waiting for you. Are you warm enough? I opened the window a bit for some fresh air."

"Aye, but come back here. I fear my voice is too weak to reach you over there." He waited until she sat on the bed by him before he spoke again. "Tell me what's happened and how I came here. The last thing I remember is your voice screaming at me." He paused to gather breath. "Then I spun my horse around and not a moment too soon."

"What do you mean?"

"Had I not made such a manoeuvre, I should likely have gotten a ball in my chest. A man at the carriage window, aye. I saw him clearly as I turned. I saw the flash of the powder, but your shout had alerted me." He attempted a weak smile. "Thank you, for my life."

Lydia grunted. If he knew the truth, he might not be so grateful. She said nothing.

"So, come, enlighten me. How did I get here?"

"You don't remember being shot then?"

"Nay, as I said the shot missed by inches." He thought for a moment. "I was riding fast. I recall hearing the report of a pistol and then . . . Aye, I remember, but only just. That potion the old woman gave me was wearing off, which brings me to another point, but first I must rest."

"What potion?"

"Truly I need rest, I beg you." He closed his eyes and shuddered slightly. "I'm cold, Lydia."

"I'll close the window," she said and made to rise.

"Leave it be. I like the air."

"I'll get more blankets then."

"Nay, no more they weigh me down." He emitted a low groan as if to make a point.

"Well what then?" Was he being purposefully exasperating? Still with his eyes closed, he said softly, "Come, lie down beside me."

"What?" She gasped. "You've not changed much. You're at it again." She tried to hide a wry laugh.

"You must stop this pretence and feigning distress. I know you better." He opened one eye. "Besides, I am only a man, albeit an incapacitated one at present time. You have nothing to fear." He closed his eye.

She really would like to lie down. Oh, to stretch out and perhaps even manage to sleep. It sounded like heaven. Why shouldn't she? After all, she would be on top of the covers and he was underneath them. "All right, I'll lie down but don't start anything," she said warningly.

"I am in little position to, as you say, start anything." He opened his eyes and watched as she sat down at the edge and swung her legs onto the bed before lying down. He closed his eyes again and smiled.

"That really feels good," she sighed. "I've not been to bed in three nights."

"Closer."

"Uhh?"

"Move closer, remember I'm cold."

She did as he bid, and found herself touching the full length of his form and not knowing quite where to put her hands. Eventually she clasped them together on her chest and lay there staring at the ceiling.

"Thank you, Lydia, for tending me these past nights."

"Not a problem. I'm just glad you're on the mend."

"So it wasn't you who slipped a sleeping draught into my drink at the tavern?"

She sat up with a jolt. "Sleeping draught, what are you talking about?"

"'Tis of little matter at the moment. Tell me, has Jack been here?"

Lydia lay back against the soft pillows, very aware that Luke's hand had strayed onto her belly and rested there. "Jack's been here most of the time, but he had to go out on business. He should be back sometime this morning." There was no point trying to tell Luke everything that had happened. He would only worry and could do nothing in his present state.

"Did he say anything?" Luke continued.

"I thought you needed to rest."

"I appear to have regained a little strength. Now would you be so kind as to reach over me." He indicated an area by his right shoulder. "'Tis fiercely uncomfortable, just here. The linens mayhap."

"I'll come around and look." Reluctantly she raised herself onto her elbows.

"There's no need. You'll see my discomfort if you but lean over me." He half opened his eyes and kept them trained on her face as she leaned across him.

"What is it?" She prodded a hand under the back of his shoulder finding nothing amiss with the bed sheets.

"A little farther down . . . aye, more . . ."

"There's nothing bunched up. Can't . . . feel . . . anything." She grunted and began to slide back to her side of the bed.

"Wait."

She was suddenly very close to his face, and his hand, not strong but insistent, slipped into her hair and brought her head downwards as he barely raised his own.

His kiss was gentle, closed mouthed, and almost hesitant. Lydia heard herself give a little gasp and then a sigh as he released her.

Luke sank back on the pillows, exhausted by his efforts. "I must stink," he muttered.

Gathering her thoughts, Lydia lay down and once again stared at the ceiling not knowing quite what to say. "I'll wash your hair for you when you're up to it, and you probably want to bathe as soon as the wound is healed well enough."

The words had popped right out before she gave them thought.

"So long as you'll be there to tend me," he said softly, and knew she smiled at him.

"Never give up, do you? Now leave me alone; I need to sleep. Good morning."

"Good morning, sweetheart," he whispered and dropped his hand back softly onto her belly.

A light rapping sounded on the door. "The broth, milady."

Lydia groaned through slightly bared teeth. "Come in. I'd forgotten about that. Luke, are you still awake? They brought the broth, and I think you should try and eat some."

The young man bearing the broth set it on a table then, at Lydia's request, assisted her in bringing Luke into a semi-sitting position and propped him firmly on pillows.

"Now," she said, holding a spoonful of broth to his mouth, "you'll eat some of this and then tell me what it is you're babbling on about, this potion or whatever it is."

"You're very authoritative." He looked at her with a sly smile. "I doubt I would dare call you, my pretty . . ."

She sucked in a deep breath and exhaled slowly. "Please, don't start that again."

"I needs must have something to call you," he complained.

"How about my name?"

Luke said nothing more and concentrated on drinking the broth without choking. He was determined she would bring him a brandy and be damned.

"Would you like some more?"

He shook his head slightly. "Nay, 'twas hard enough work getting that lot down lying thus. Would that I could sit by the fire."

"No, not yet. You need to rest more. Maybe tomorrow when everything's sorted out." Lydia bit her lip. Damn her big mouth.

"What mean you?" Luke raised his tired eyes and scoured her face questioningly.

"Just when it's all over, you know . . . ," she trailed off.

"Where's Jack?" Luke said suddenly. "I mean, where is he, now?"

"That's something else I wanted to talk to you about," she said quietly. "I know you and Jack are together on this conspiracy thing, but I'm still not completely certain you know who he really is." She paused. "Now, before I tell you anything, I want you to know he saved your life. I couldn't have got you back to Beckham alone." She winced at Luke's piercing stare. "And he saved my life. Luke he knew I was being held at Fulford's place. I like him and I trust him, but he's not . . . who you think. He's not Jack Palmer. And I promised not to tell, but . . ."

Luke gave a long sigh. "Aye, 'tis true, his name is John Palmer, but he prefers Jack."

"I don't mean that," Lydia continued a little irritably. "Please listen to me . . . I'm just concerned you . . . well . . . and him . . . you could get yourselves hanged."

Luke's eyes widened. "We could?"

Lydia gritted her teeth. "He needs to be careful."

"He does?"

"Listen to me, damn it all. He's *that* highwayman. I can't tell you any more."

Luke inclined his head then nodded slowly. "*That* highwayman?"

Lydia scowled and opened her mouth. She remained open mouthed, as the door opened and the man in question stood there, framed in the opening, wide and solid.

"Lydia was just telling me . . . ," Luke began and waited.

Lydia wanted to curl up and slide under the bed as the eyes of both men turned on her.

The figure standing in the doorway pulled off his hat with a flourish and made a low bow. "Richard Turpin, at your service."

"I . . . I . . . ," she spluttered and turned to Luke. He was grinning from ear to ear. "You knew all the time."

"Aye, and I'll thank you not to cause me mirth. It damn well hurts like hell." He tried desperately to stop the slight shaking that threatened to cause him untold agonies if he succumbed to the intense desire to laugh. "Come, Jack, sit down, and tell me all I can bear to hear.

"I feel stupid," Lydia mumbled and rose from the bed taking the empty broth bowl with her. She walked across the room and set it on a table.

"Nay, lass, 'tis naught to feel stupid for," Jack Palmer said. "I feel honoured you saw fit to keep my secret so long." He grinned. "You've known since I held up Fulford's coach, have you not?"

She nodded then looked at him. "You knew it was me in the coach under all those blankets?"

"Aye, by your mare tethered to Fulford's coach, and your ring the minute Fulford handed it to me. I saw you hazard a glance out of your wrappings, and I knew at once that you recognised me; you had me worried for a while."

"So . . . you . . . were both in on my escape from Fulford Manor?"

"I rode back here post-haste and informed His Lordship of your plight. We decided to assure ourselves that you were in no way adversely involved and informed Captain Norton that he should keep an eye on you." He let out a long breath. "And then things changed, and it was decided to get you out of there as quickly as we could." He spread his hands. "You know the rest."

Lydia sat down, not quite taking it all in. She looked first at Jack Palmer and then at Luke, who lay bare-chested with a bemused look upon his face. "Thank you, Jack."

"Well, to business. We've a problem, Luke."

"Aye?"

"The man we seek travels north this very day. The coach carries no extra guard, but all will be armed, of that I am certain. There shall have been three changes of horses afore Stamford Bridge, and I intend to take our man five miles south of there when the horses are weary after the incline, at Poacher's Hill. 'Twill be around four of the morning."

"Poacher's Hill? That's too open, Jack. Even without a moon, they'll see you coming a mile off, and there's a fair moon tonight, if I'm not mistaken."

"That's exactly the reason I choose it," Palmer commented. "'Tis all in my plan."

"'Tis a death wish you have."

"Did you find someone?" Lydia asked hopefully.

Palmer looked at her and rubbed his chin. "Nay, I did not."

"What are you two about?" Luke asked suspiciously.

"You can't ride," Lydia said, finding the words tumbling from her mouth, "and Jack has to have someone with a pistol to protect his back."

"You are not serious." Luke tried to pull himself farther up in the bed, but was overwhelmed with pain and resigned himself to staying put. "No, Jack," he groaned. "No, Lydia, please." He grimaced as another wave of sharp pain from his broken ribs stabbed through his body.

Jack Palmer indicated Lydia should stay where she was. "Pour me a brandy, would you, there's a good lass. I needs must speak with your lord and master," he added with a half grin.

She almost told him to go to hell, but for the sake of peace and Luke's wound, she said nothing and did as he bid her.

Palmer sat down by Luke's side.

"Jack, don't do it. For pity's sake," Luke whispered. "'Twill be like taking her to the gallows. And nearly as certain."

"Luke, man, I don't know what else to do. Did she tell you aught of what's happened?"

Luke frowned. "Only that I was shot, and you brought me back here."

Palmer sighed. "Luke, she had the letter all along." He motioned that Luke should keep his voice low.

"She did? Bloody hell, why on earth didn't she give it to one of us?" He stared at Lydia's turned back.

"She had her reasons, and she was scared, but the issue now is the coach. Luke I need a man at my back, and I dare not remove Norton from his post, tho' I have sent word he should be in readiness for action. We may need him at Fulford a while longer yet. No, Luke"—he held up a hand—"'tis too late to send for the earl's help, and the Foxworth men remain on the continent. There is no alternative. Believe me, my friend, were there any other way, I should take it and willingly."

"She can't shoot," Luke protested.

"She shall, by this eve."

"I still don't understand how you intend to stop the coach in such an open area. They'll see you before you get within pistol range."

Jack Palmer stroked his chin and looked uncomfortable. "That's another reason to engage your lady."

"No, Jack. No, I shan't allow it. Lydia!" He lurched up in bed and immediately cried out with pain.

"What?" She was by his side in a flash. "What did you say to him, Jack? Luke, please lie back down." She smoothed the pillows under his head and pushed him into them.

"Jack, you've not told her, have you?" He turned his light eyes on her and looked into a face he was certain he wanted to look upon the rest of his born days. It would not do for Jack Palmer to take her out and get her killed.

Lydia turned. "What haven't you told me, Jack?"

"I need you to stop the coach so I can get close enough, quickly enough. I need you to distract their attentions." He looked uncomfortably at the floor.

"How . . . do you mean?"

"You will be a decoy. You will run your horse to them crying out you have been attacked and er . . . harmed. You will feign bodily injury, and they shall assist you as you will appear to be a lady of means."

Lydia was feeling queasy. This was becoming far more dangerous than she had ever considered. She found Luke clutching her hand and turned her head. There was a look in his eyes, and it was fear. She had never seen it there before. "I have to, Luke," she whispered. "I owe you both that much. Don't you realise that if it weren't for my stupidity you wouldn't have been shot in the first place—you wouldn't have been out there?"

"Lydia, you did nothing wrong, and I beg of you not to ride tonight."

"From what Jack's told me, England may be under threat of invasion if this information gets where it's supposed to. Luke"—she squeezed his hand—"I want to do this. In fact," she said slowly, "I think this is why I may have come here. Don't you see? I was meant to be instrumental in preventing this uprising, a bit like a quest."

"Aye," Luke growled, "and such quests often end in death."

"I don't have too bad a feeling about this though. I was sent here to do a job, and when it's done I . . ." she stopped, suddenly aware of what she was about to say.

"'Tis time I gave you instruction with a pistol." Palmer broke the awful silence in the room.

"Yes, I suppose it is," she replied and smiled at Luke in what she hoped was a reassuring manner. "We won't be too long; then I'll come back and see you've everything you need before we leave this evening." She followed Jack Palmer out of the door and closed it without a backwards glance.

TWENTY

"We should go well out of sight," he said, leading the way across the back of the house and into the trees.

"Jack, about this evening. You said I was to look like a lady of means."

"Aye, that I did," he agreed.

"Well, it's just that if I'm expected to ride as fast, I'll have to ride astride. I can't do it side-saddle."

He looked at her for a moment. "I was going to ask you about that. I noticed your mare's saddle and wondered at it."

They continued walking a short distance more until Palmer called a halt. "Here will do."

"Do I need to learn how to load it?" She looked suspiciously at the weapon he held, remembering all she had ever read about their suspect reliability.

"Nay, you'll have two pistols, both loaded. 'Tis all you'll need."

"I've been thinking," she said as he handed her the firearm, "about riding astride. It was difficult with my petticoat; it kept blowing all over the place."

"Concentrate on this for the minute. Now, keep your arm in line, look at your target, that tree stump. See it?"

Lydia nodded, squinted along the barrel, and pulled the trigger. The noise wasn't nearly so bad as she'd expected it would be at close quarters, and she watched in quiet fascination the cloud of greyish white smoke that spread around her.

"Not bad. You were close. Here," he said handing her a second pistol. "Try again."

By the end of two hours, Lydia had gathered the rudiments of firing a pistol. She just hoped she wouldn't have to fire it at anyone.

"You'll do," Palmer said with a grimace. "Come, let us see what His Lordship is up to."

"Jack, you didn't hear me out, about the riding I mean."

"Tell me, then."

"If I wear my gown without my petticoat but with my cloak over the top I can still look like a lady, at least from the back and sides, and I'll be able to ride fast."

"And what about the open front of your gown?" Palmer said knowingly.

"That's where you can help."

"I shall try."

"Get me a pair jackboots and some breeches; it's too cold just to wear my shorts—the things I was wearing the other night," she clarified.

He stood a moment and rubbed his chin thoughtfully. Then he continued walking. "It might work, they would be aware only of your gown and cloak and you would indeed appear as a lady at least until we had them stopped then it would be of no matter. Aye," he said and clapped her on the shoulder, "it might just work."

Lydia couldn't quite hide her smile at Jack's enthusiasm as they returned to Luke's room. The man actually appeared to be enjoying this.

Luke was sleeping.

"Let him sleep," Palmer suggested. "We needs must plan our evening's entertainment."

The man was mad. Now she was convinced of it. "I'm glad you can think of it like that. I'll be glad when it's all over."

"Brandy?"

She nodded. "But only a small one—I need all my faculties in tact."

"Aye, there'll be time for celebration when we see the next dawn."

Lydia grew increasingly nervous as the day wore on and the sky began to darken. Jack had found her a pair of breeches and a reasonably well-fitting pair of light jackboots, for the cost of a half crown to the stable lad, he told her. She briefly remembered saying that the boy would be rich if things carried on, but at the moment, she could barely remember her own name. She pulled her gown over a borrowed shirt, having shunned the stays in favour of her bra, and stretched each limb in turn to ascertain the freedom of movement she would have. She picked up her cloak and a feather-trimmed three-cornered hat with a veil attached, partly to cover her features and partly because Jack told her many ladies wore such hats. Wishing she had a sweater to wear, Lydia left the security of her room and hoped she would actually see it again. Her own words had plagued her since she had uttered them. What if, when her task was completed, she just disappeared? Her unhappy mind conjured up visions of the dreadful Darwin and days sitting in a computer cubicle. She didn't want to go back—but did she have a choice?

She knocked and slowly poked her head around Luke's door. He lay propped on the pillows nodding at something Jack Palmer was saying.

"May I come in?"

Palmer nodded approval. Luke's jaw dropped.

"I think I'm going to be cold," she said quickly.

"A waistcoat, leave it to me," Palmer said immediately.

She watched Jack leave the room then turned slowly to face a very troubled-looking Luke. "Please, please don't say anything. I just want to get this over with." She remained standing by the door at a complete loss what to say or do. "I would ask only that you reconsider," he said. "I have to do it, Luke. It's partly my fault, and like I said before, and I really think it's why I'm here."

"And I also remember you were starting to mention what may happen once you have completed your task. Come here, Lydia. I would have you close."

She was on the point of tears as she walked to his bed and sat down. "Please don't say anymore. I don't want to think about it."

With her assistance, Luke slung an arm around her shoulder. "And I don't want you to leave," he said softly.

"I don't think it's anything we can control."

"Mayhap you're right, but do you have to make it so easy?"

"What do you mean easy?"

He noted the slight indignation in her voice and said, "For fate, I mean."

Lydia looked up at him and wondered what she saw in his eyes. If she had been fully compos mentis, she would have sworn it was love. "I have to go, but I intend to come back, for a bath at the very least—in your tub. It's bigger than mine."

"I'll look forwards to it." He bent as best he could and brushed her lips lightly with his own.

Lydia was about to advise him that she fully intended to bathe alone, when Palmer returned.

"'Tis time we were off. Unless you intend to fly that is."

Lydia couldn't make out whether his words held some innuendo and didn't ask. She got to her feet and looked at Luke. "Before you say anything—that's why I'm wearing this lot."

"I had meant to enquire, but was somehow distracted. From the back you look quite normal excepting for the lack of bulky underpinnings, and from the side you look passable."

Lydia was glad he was making light of this; she needed some humour. "Thank you."

"But, nay from the front, Lydia, I know not what to say." He appraised her long legs, clad as they were in slightly too tight breeches and thigh length boots, visible where her gown spilled widely away from her waist to her ankles. She wore a man's shirt with a belt holding the whole thing in place about her waist.

"Waistcoat," Jack Palmer offered the garment. "Not the stable lad's this time."

The garment was large and fitted easily over her gown. No one would see it under her cloak, and Lydia was certain she would be grateful for its light padding and long sleeves later that night.

She looked down at her self then walked to a mirror. "I look like the bloody Pied Piper," she grumbled.

The two men looked at each other.

"I mean the colours. She was glad her sister couldn't see her. She'd have a fit. The gown was of midnight blue silk with gold robings; she wore black breeches, white shirt and . . . she looked one more time at the scarlet waistcoat and shook her head. "All I need is a green hat."

"Black will have to suffice," Jack said. "Now, we must be off."

"Just a minute, Jack." Luke's voice was harsh as though strained from effort.

"Aye, my friend."

"The chestnut mare, she can't keep pace with you, and God forbid something should go amiss, she has neither the speed nor the stamina."

"Already thought of it, Luke. Worry not. We're not taking the mare."

"Just a minute. You didn't tell me I wasn't riding my horse. What am I riding?" Lydia stood right where she was awaiting his answer.

"Jack, no! She must not ride my gelding. He's far too strong. The beast still thinks he's a stallion."

Jack Palmer gave a long suffering sigh and looked at one then the other before he spoke. He addressed Lydia. "You shall ride my bonnie, Black Bess." With that, he turned and walked out of the room.

"Me? Ride Black Bess?" Lydia turned and stared at Luke incredulously. "Oh, my."

"You're familiar with the animal?"

"She, she's famous through history and . . ." Luke had his finger at his lips.

A servant entered the room. "Come to mend the fire, milady." She curtsied and got on with the task. Luke frowned slightly, not sure he liked being so thoroughly ignored in his own home. Lydia, it appeared, had secured her place as mistress there. Well, he could live with that.

"I have to go now, Luke." Lydia attempted to keep her back to the girl by the fireplace. It wouldn't do to have too many inquisitive eyes on her strange garments.

"I should be obliged if you could finish your task quickly, girl," Luke gasped and lay back heavily against the pillows with the effort of speaking loudly.

Lydia waited. She hoped there weren't too may more people hanging around downstairs. Finally, the girl straightened up, curtseyed again, and left.

"Right, now I have to go." Lydia walked purposefully across the room. "That coal's awfully smelly, and the smoke fumes aren't good for your lungs either." She needed to get out of the room before her courage deserted her and she broke down and wept.

"Lydia?"

Please, she thought silently, *don't say any more to dissuade me. It just might work.* She had the thought that perhaps he was about to say something ridiculous or just plain awful as he had a couple of times before. She turned slowly the door handle grasped in her hand. "What is it?"

Luke didn't know what Lydia was seeing. He probably looked like hell, but he was looking at the most beautiful face the world. He took a breath and winced when a sharp pain caught him, as he knew it would.

"If you've something to say." She couldn't fathom the look in his eyes. It was there again as it had been earlier.

"I love you." There. He'd said it. Not for the first time he had to admit, but it was the first time he had ever meant it. He watched her face noting little emotion there. "Go now, and may God bring you safely back."

Lydia gulped, suddenly wishing she didn't have to go with Jack Palmer. "I have to go."

With one last look at the expression on His Lordship's face she fled from the room.

TWENTY ONE

Lydia ran through the house, out of the front door, and down the steps. She desperately wanted to sit down and think about what Luke had said. Should she believe him? Did she want to believe him? There wasn't time to think or to do anything, she realised, as her feet hit the gravel. Jack Palmer stood holding his own bay horse and the chestnut mare tacked up with a man's saddle.

"Let's away," he said sharply and vaulted astride his mount.

Lydia jumped on board as quickly as her gown would allow. "Just give me a minute, Jack. I need to get this robe under my backside." She tucked herself around and nodded that she was ready.

The bay took off at a fast canter, Jack Palmer nothing but a low dark shape on its back.

"I hope I'm up to this," Lydia muttered. She put her heels to the mare's sides, quickly aware that it wasn't necessary; they were already past the first row of trees that bordered the beginnings of the park proper and keeping a good pace in the wake of the bay. They passed through the gate at the park boundary without mishap and trotted into the clearing by the cottage just as a pale half moon appeared over the trees.

"Good, we have light to ride by," Jack commented grimly. "Tho' it means we shall be more easily visible to others. "Bring your mare in here." He led the way to where a pair of crude stalls held buckets of grain and water. "Tie her there, but leave her tack on. You may need to change horses quickly." Lydia nodded; her voice was not forthcoming. "Are you all right?"

This time her voice obeyed her. "I'm fine."

He nodded and strode off in the direction of the cottage, returning a few minutes later wearing his heavy, satin-bound cloak and carrying four pistols. He wore the rapier at his side.

"I'll keep hold of the pistols for now. I feel safer that way."

"Yes," Lydia managed. Ten minutes later, she stood by the side of the big black animal that was hers for the next few hours, and watched in wonderment as one of the most notorious highwaymen in England whispered soft words in its ear and stroked its velvet coat.

"Aye, my bonnie Bess, you'll do fine this night with your precious load. Come along now." He turned to Lydia. "Up you get."

"Good girl, Bess," she whispered and patted the horse's neck, feeling her hand tremble, but whether it was from fear, cold, or the fact she was sitting astride this mountain of a horse that she had only read about in history books, Lydia didn't know. She gave Jack Palmer a brave smile.

"She'll take care of you, never worry," he said reassuringly. "Not like this bloody great thing." He struggled to still Luke's gelding then leapt into the saddle. Cursing, he wrestled a second or two until the animal merely snorted and pattered a dance with its front feet as he tightened the girth.

Lydia hoped so. She was grateful not to be riding the gelding.

"Follow me closely. We needs must ride fast. I want to be certain we are not followed."

Lydia didn't remember too much of the ride except, as Jack had forewarned, it was fast. Black Bess, calm and surefooted, stayed a respectable distance behind the gelding as though planted there, and Lydia found she was able to relax little and encouraged herself to take fortifying deep breaths. She would need all the oxygen her lungs could endure.

Finally, they pulled up in a small copse, Bess coming alongside the gelding of her own accord. Lydia stared across a wide expanse of rolling countryside bathed in stark shadows and pale moon glow. "I can see for miles," she whispered.

"Aye," Palmer agreed, "so can our quarry, and that's why they'll not think we'd risk an attack here. Now, are you clear on what you shall do?"

"Yes, I think so." So saying she stood in the stirrups and untucked her robe then pulled it around her, allowing her cloak to drape over the top.

"Good," Palmer said approvingly. "Unless they are extremely observant, they shall never be the wiser of your attire, or of your riding style. At least," he added with a grin, "until 'tis too late. Now"—he reached inside his cape, pulled out two pistols and handed one to Lydia—"shove this one in your belt." He waited until she had the weapon safely secured. "Can you ride and carry another pistol? So you'll have one at the ready. Just in case."

"I think so," she said, accepting the second pistol.

"Be certain to keep your hand concealed until I give the order. If 'tis seen that you carry a weapon, 'twill all be over." He reached once more into his clothing and pulled something out.

Lydia strained to see what it was and hid a smile when he pulled off his three-cornered hat and stuck the toupee on his thinning scalp, securing it around his ears with something she couldn't make out. He replaced his hat and said nothing.

"Now," her companion continued, "'tis likely there will be more than our passenger on board. Do not, and I repeat, do not be intimidated by anyone or anything. I shall be with you. And do not be swayed by any grievances offered, and if heaven forbid we have a swooning woman, leave her be. Do not, and heed my words, on any account dismount. Stay on Bess's back, and you shall be safe."

Lydia felt visibly paler, the gravity of her situation hammered home by the intensity in the highwayman's voice and the grim mask his face presented. "I understand."

"One last thing. Take this." He handed her a kerchief. "Don it only after the coach is in my control. Until then keep your head down and your hat pulled low. We cannot take the chance of your being recognised. And do not under any circumstances call me by name." He tapped her shoulder and said, "Make good pretence of a distressed female."

"If I'm not careful," she responded, tying the black silk firmly around her throat, "I'll soon be a distressed female. No pretence required."

"Wait! Look, there. The brow of that hill." He pointed.

Lydia screwed up her eyes but through the haze of her veil could see nothing. "I don't see anything."

"Watch. You'll see soon enough, and then you must be off. I need them stopped directly below that hollow as I showed you earlier." He tied his eye mask swiftly around his head.

"I think I see it now. Yes, yes, I do. Oh, Jack, they're galloping all out."

"Aye, and a six horse team. They have a mighty pulling force, but all to our advantage. Once they are stopped 'tis not easy to coordinate six frightened horses and get underway in haste."

Lydia's fingers were cold but not frozen, and she thought she could feel sweat trickling down her back. She would be happy if that were the worst spontaneous bodily function to occur before the night was over.

"Ready?" Palmer took up his reins.

Black Bess trembled slightly, and Lydia knew she was conveying her own fear to the horse and endeavoured to relax. She glanced at her companion. His eyes glittered keenly through the holes of his mask showing not fear but pure excitement.

"Remember," he said, "straight across and cut them off. Scream with all your might. You must alert to driver to your presence and then be convincing enough that the passengers will agree to his stopping to aid you."

Lydia gave him a dark look and wished she had taken drama classes at school.

"Go!" he hissed before pulling his kerchief across his mouth.

She dug her heels hard into Bess's flanks and found herself launched upon a black rocket and flying, barely in the saddle, down the hill and across the open meadow. Lydia screamed until she thought her lungs would burst. It was difficult to scream and breathe at the same time, and it wasn't easy to control the rocket with one hand and keep the pistol well out of view, as they galloped towards the path of the coach, which was drawing closer and showing no signs of slowing down. It crossed Lydia's mind that her luck with coaches had so far not been good, and she screamed louder, lacing her screams with a few entreaties for assistance.

"Please, oh, please help me!" Quite dramatically all the pent up emotion of the last few days flowed from her in a torrent of tears and uncontrollable blubbering.

"Hold there!"

Lydia was unsure whether the driver was yelling at her or his horses, but she saw with relief that he was attempting to arrest the travel of the coach.

"Please, please," she sobbed, bending low on Bess's neck and slowing the horse to a canter as the coach, still moving at a fair old rate, rumbled and crashed alongside. She had to stop the coach before it went much farther, or Jack wouldn't have time to cover the distance without making the coachman suspicious of the situation.

She took a risk, let go of the reins, and flung herself dangerously to one side.

"Stop the coach!" a man's voice shouted. "She's falling off."

"I be trying, damn it!" The driver cursed and with a last-ditch attempt hauled the team to a plunging, snorting halt.

"Come on, Jack, come on," Lydia whispered. She kept her head low and gave the appearance she may well be slipping into unconscious as Bess cavorted around, unsettled by her rider's sloppy attentions.

The driver set the brake and leapt from his seat followed by the guard. Lydia peeked out from the folds of her cloak and noted with satisfaction that he left his blunderbuss behind him.

Where was Jack?

Two men tumbled from the coach, and Lydia's heart sank as one man made a move in her direction holding out a hand as though to quiet her mount. If he came any closer, she knew her cover would be blown. "Come on, Jack, pleeeese," she whispered.

"Hold, there! Stand I say," a voice snapped.

Lydia let out a huge sigh of relief. The voice was loud and insistent and it came as music to her ears. She adjusted her hat and pulled the black silk over her mouth and nose; then sat upright and removed the net from her eyes.

"You there, step away from the coach, and you, sir," the highwayman spoke to the male passenger already halfway to Lydia's assistance, "be so good as to come over here."

Lydia took up the reins in one hand and with a flourish, which even she had to admit was quite impressive, produced the pistol from under her cloak. Black Bess, sensing the familiarity of the situation, responded with admirable calm to her rider's heels.

Jack rode the gelding around the coach and ordered the remaining passenger, a woman, to descend; then he trotted up and down his line of victims, perusing them one by one. Lydia watched, her hand steady on an extended arm holding the pistol in the general direction of the passengers while sweat continued to bathe her in chilly dampness. It was miserable, though she had to admit there was an excitement to all this, albeit it a rather perverse excitement and not one she wished to repeat. *Please don't move*, she silently willed the passengers. It was one thing to fire at a tree stump, but a living person was a very different matter. She watched wide eyed, as the passengers were relieved of their jewellery and purses in a most courteous fashion. Jack certainly was a professional.

Neither the passengers nor the coachmen showed any sign of opposition, and at his instruction that they each remove their outer garment did so wordlessly and without dissent. Only the husband of the woman dared to voice a mild objection at his wife being treated in such an inappropriate manner.

Palmer looked at the woman. "Madam, you may retain your cloak, but if you would be so kind as to collect these articles and convey them to my associate." He inclined his head in Lydia's direction. "One at a time if you please."

Lydia's felt herself blanch as the woman approached carrying the driver's surtout. She was small, and her pale features gave the impression of a childlike frailty. Lydia felt sorry for her and wished she could assure her everything would be all right. But she remembered Jack's words and immediately straightened her spine, sat tall, and tried to look fierce. What was she supposed to do?

"My associate will examine your garments to ensure you hide nothing from me. No hidden caches of jewels," he added. "Madam, move back to your husband while the task is completed.

Lydia took the surtout with a trembling hand, grateful to Bess for remaining stationary. She worked her way through the layers of heavy fabric then shook her head at Jack who sat calm and relaxed watching the proceedings. This was repeated until all the outer garments had been examined, and each time Lydia gave her answer with a shake of her head.

"Damn it, man!" It was the single male passenger. "You have our valuables. Can you not see we have no other? We are freezing to death."

Jack rode very close to the man and poked his pistol towards him.

Lydia tightened the grip on her own pistol and watched. She hoped he wasn't about to do something to get them both hanged.

"I have a feeling," the highwayman said, "just a feeling that there is something one of you is concealing. An extraordinary jewel perhaps?" His eyes smiled humourlessly through the holes of his mask.

"Nothing, sir," the woman cried out and ran forwards. "We are but on our way north on my husband's business. You have all we possess. Now, shall you let us pass?"

Lydia had to admit the woman had guts.

"Aye, madam, but first gentlemen, be so good as to remove your coats and waistcoats." He waved his pistol in the air. "'Tis cold this night, and I fear that if you don't make haste, you may well freeze."

The four men complied and stood shivering in breeches and shirts while Lydia duly went through their clothing. The husband's coat was difficult to search, but she struggled gamely with the heavy brocade and stiffened skirts under the watchful eye of everyone. The other three men wore frocks, and she delved through the large pockets with little difficulty, finding nothing. The waistcoats proved equally fruitless. She saw Jack Palmer frowning at her as she emptied the contents of yet another pocket and found nothing excepting mundane items of little value.

They should have found something by now, surely.

"Shirts! Boots!"

"Surely not, man," the single gentleman gasped.

"Now!" Palmer barked. "Do as I say or you'll suffer for it."

Stripped of their shirts and footwear, the four stood shivering, saying not a word. Lydia went through their clothing as quickly as she could, aware of all eyes on her, particularly those of Jack Palmer. She saw him shuffle in the saddle. He was becoming anxious.

He waved the men farther from the coach and instructed them to lie face down on the ground then he rode to Lydia's side. "'Tis not as I had hoped," he hissed. "Cover me well." With that, he jumped from the gelding's back and approached the coach driver, the first in line. He ran his hands over the man convinced this wasn't the party they were looking for. Next, the guard. Nothing. He moved on.

"Stay yourself," Palmer growled as the single gentleman shuddered at his touch. He intended to be most thorough with this one.

Lydia wished her eyes were on stalks so she could swivel them behind her. It occurred to her that the longer they stood here, bathed in moonlight and clearly visible to anyone passing relatively close by, the more chance there was of being set upon. She watched the woman who stood unmoving near the coach then her attentions drifted back to where Jack was running his hand over the last man's clothing, and it seemed he wasn't having any luck. A movement caught the corner of her eye. She resisted the temptation to turn her head in an obvious way and shifted her gaze only slightly wishing again for swivel eyeballs on stalks. The woman was edging slightly closer to the open door of the coach. It wouldn't do her any good to leap inside: it wasn't going anywhere. And it struck Lydia that perhaps she wanted to get in out of the cold. Whatever the reason, she intended to keep half an unnoticed eye on her.

Jack Palmer straightened himself and stood over his last victim. He wore a grim frown. "I still have this feeling," he said, "that one of you carries something that would be exceedingly valuable to me." He turned, still pointing his pistol at the head of the husband who lay panting in terror on the ground. "In the coach mayhap?" He waved his pistol with a flourish.

What a showman! Lydia reminded herself this was real whilst marvelling at the way Jack took everything in his stride and, in fact, seemed to thrive on it.

"Seems you needs must shiver a while longer yet," he said and briefly glanced down at the men on the ground.

Whether it was movement or intuition that alerted Lydia, she never discovered. Her pistol swung almost of its own volition in the direction of the woman who had carefully placed herself by the edge of the door and now slipped a hand down low inside the coach by one of the seats. "Hold there!" Where her voice came from, she never discovered either, but her voice it was that roared out the command.

Palmer spun into action and was at the woman's side even as she jumped back in surprise at Lydia's shout—surprise that caused her to lose her grip on a pistol, which tumbled from the coach.

Lydia felt the hateful glare of the woman's eyes upon her and stared right back a little shocked by her own fortitude and amazed at how she was slipping right into her new role.

The highwayman stood silent for a moment, conscious he had his back to the four men but confident Lydia was watching them. He kicked the pistol right under the coach. "It seems, madam, you seek to do me harm. What should I make of that, I wonder?"

Come on, Jack, let's get out of here ran through Lydia's mind. The men on the ground hadn't moved an inch. Maybe they had frozen there. That would be murder, wouldn't it? She glanced at the coach and blinked upon seeing the transformation that had come over the woman. No longer did her face hold the vindictive glare she'd directed at Lydia. Now her features were soft, as she spoke in dulcet tones to Palmer who was listening, it appeared, with great interest.

The woman pleaded with him to let her husband go and to allow them continue on their way post-haste. He had a weak constitution, she continued, and might succumb to a fever were he to remain out in the cold.

Lydia watched fascinated by the woman's acting, for it certainly was just that, and it seemed Jack was listening most intently to her story, nodding his head in an understanding manner. He seemed on the point of acquiescing to the woman's pleas and offered her his arm.

"I fully understand your dilemma, madam." He stopped and turned her around so that her back was to him. "But you see I have needs must ensure you carry no other valuable. Take off your cloak."

"Sir, I must protest!" The woman's husband made as though to rise from the cold ground.

"Stay right where you are, or I might have to use this thing." Lydia waved her second pistol in the air. It suddenly occurred to her that if Black Bess took off she had no means of control. She'd be up the creek without the proverbial paddle.

The cloak lay on the ground where Palmer had thrown it in disgust. He stood and thought for a moment, relying solely on Lydia to protect his back while he made his search. The fact that the woman had begun crying unnerved him only slightly; he was used to a show of tears when ladies thought themselves about to be relieved of their finery. "Ah, I see you dress sensibly for travel," he remarked, noting the well-cut jacket and waistcoat of red damask snugly fitted over a petticoat of contrasting velvet. Remove your jacket."

The woman appeared to hesitate for a brief moment then did as he asked before turning to face him. "Please, sir, have mercy. Surely you do not mean to bare me before others. Nay, sir, even my husband does me the courtesy of extinguishing the candles," she simpered.

The word *yeuk* came to Lydia's mind. Was Jack being taken in by all this play acting? There was something about the woman tugging her jacket from her shoulders that wasn't quite right. She glanced at the woman's husband and felt sorry for him. He obviously cared a great deal for his wife, and no doubt, the thought was in his mind that she may not be divested only of her garments but possibly ravished. Lydia looked back at Jack and the woman; her tears were running freely enough, and she was obviously distressed.

"Please, sir," she gasped. "No more." She huddled her arms around herself, shivering and sobbing. "No more, I beg of you."

"Nay, madam, I have to be sure you carry naught on your person." Palmer's voice held a hint of agitation.

"If, if I remove my waistcoat"—the woman put her hand to her forehead and moaned softly—"and prove I have nothing, then will you see it in your heart to release us? My husband is very ill indeed."

The husband had suddenly gone from a weak disposition to needing open-heart surgery, and Lydia found herself shaking her head in wonderment at the woman's tale. Her eyes didn't carry the same emotion as her words. Something was amiss.

Jack scowled at the female passenger, crying and whining in front of him. "Remove your waistcoat then if you will," he snapped.

The woman began to unbutton her garment, looking all the while into the highwayman's eyes. She slipped it from her shoulders and stood silently, her breasts heaving at the top of her richly embroidered stays. She dropped her eyes then returned them to the man who still trained his pistol on her and in a tremulous voice said, "Oh, sir, I beg of you. Oh, no, you do not mean to, to . . ." Her eyes rolled up in her head and she crumpled to the ground in a dead faint.

Lydia briefly saw Jack look heavenwards, but had her own attentions suddenly diverted as the woman's husband scrambled to his knees. "Stop right there!" She had to stop the man, or Jack would in all probability shoot him. "Back over there. Lie down, face in the dirt. Now!"

The man seemed to hesitate and then made a move forwards. "Cannot we resolve this like gentlemen? I am Earl Granby, and this is the countess—"

"Stay!" Damn the man, he would do anything to save his wife's honour it seemed—even get himself killed. "If you come any closer," Lydia snapped, "I'll let her have it." He stopped moving and was looking at her with an incredulous expression on his face.

"You wouldn't. Nay, lad, I think you would not." He raised a foot to take a step.

"I'm a bloody woman," she snarled feeling suddenly very conscious of her hair. "And I think my partner might just be paying too much attention to your lady there. You had better hope he restrains his carnal desires, or I may just have to remove the object of those desires. Now, back on the ground!"

He went.

Lydia trembled and realised her hands were shaking badly. She couldn't take much more of this. Palmer grasped the woman under her arms and pulled her to her feet where she stood unsteadily for a moment or two hanging on to his sleeve. Her breath came in huge gulps as she struggled for breath.

"Please, sir, please."

He scowled. "Countess, eh? Move aside while I look in the coach." He unlatched her fingers from his coat. "Cover me well," he shouted over his shoulder and shoved his pistol into his pocket before stepping into the coach. He pulled the furnishings from the seats opening the tops to rummage around further; then he pulled a dagger from his boot and began to rip at the upholstery.

All the while, Lydia kept a close watch on everyone. She felt like a movie camera panning the set as she looked first at the four men shivering and slightly tinged with blue, lying on the ground, and then at the woman, who appeared to have regained her composure with surprising speed. Too quickly to Lydia's mind. She waited until Jack reappeared at the door of the coach with a foul look on his face then called, "Check her petticoat." It had occurred to her many times the past few weeks how much one could conceal under a petticoat. And there was something definitely suspicious about the woman's behaviour.

He said nothing as he stuck the dagger back inside his boot and looked at Lydia, for a moment of half a mind to reject the suggestion, but Lydia had proven herself not given to frivolous notions. He looked at the woman standing before him. She had looked sharply at his partner on the horse at hearing the words, and now as she looked back at him he saw her tears had dried. He also caught a glimpse of something else he couldn't quite put a name to, but it looked like hatred.

"Your petticoat. Remove it."

The woman looked aghast and stared to cry again. Begging and beseeching she pleaded that she be spared the humiliation.

"Do not force me to lay hand upon you," Jack roared his patience finally at its limits. He pulled the pistol from his coat and, pointing it at her chest, said quietly, "Do it, now."

The woman gulped and reached behind to unfasten the ties of her petticoat. "Perhaps you could turn your back?" She blinked at him with great wide eyes.

He turned and rolled his eyes at Lydia who stifled a laugh. Amazing, even in these dire circumstances, Jack Palmer could still summon humour.

"Are you finished, madam?"

"Yes, and as you can see my petticoat holds nothing." She held the garment out in front of her and shook it lightly in Lydia's direction.

Lydia watched and scowled. Never had she seen such a tiny waist, and the woman's chest positively poured out from the top of her stays, she was the stuff Hollywood heroines were made of—demure, petite, and slightly helpless.

Or was she?

"What say you?" Jack called out. "Does her petticoat contain that which we seek?"

"I can't tell from here. You'll have to check it."

He turned back immediately and, disregarding the objections he received, reached to take the petticoat, which the woman held defensively against her body.

Lydia groaned as the woman casually put a hand to her head and looked as though she would faint again. But she didn't faint. She removed the small hat she wore and pulled at the pins of her hair allowing it to tumble loosely about her shoulders. Lydia's mouth dropped a notch. The woman was all set to seduce Jack, and all for the sake of his searching her petticoat. It didn't make sense; she was already out of the damn thing. If she'd had little patience with the doll-like woman before the removal of the hat, Lydia had far less now. No one could have hair so gorgeous. It just wasn't fair. She looked again at the golden, silky tresses.

No, it wasn't fair.

Impulsively she called out, "Check it and be bloody quick about it. These guys down here are freezing their bollocks off." She hoped her use of the vernacular would shock Jack into action. He was standing there looking dazed.

He snapped to life. "Aye, indeed, madam, refrain from your flirting. I think your husband would not approve. He reached out and tugged the petticoat from the woman's hand.

She screamed and lunged forwards, clawing at his face. Taken aback at the sudden assault, he didn't move fast enough and received several deep scratches down his cheek.

"Bloody hell!" He recovered swiftly and caught one of her hands. He slipped his pistol into his belt and used both hands to grasp her firmly.

"Let me go, damn you! You don't know what you are about, you ignorant lout." She bent her head and bit him hard on his hand.

If she were expecting him to release her, she was disappointed. The highwayman pulled her close against him, snarled a few choice words into her face and then flung her to the ground.

Lydia continued to watch, not sure where all this was leading, but it was beginning to look as though the letter had contained false information. Damn that bloody letter. She thought of Luke lying in bed close to death. Then she thought of Luke, lying in bed, naked. The second thought was by far the most pleasant, and she decided to stick with it.

Jack retrieved his pistol and stood over the woman. "Over here, come here." He motioned to Lydia.

Bess responded to a slight tug on the rein and pressure from Lydia's boot heel and came close to Jack without trouble.

Keeping his eye on the woman, he walked backwards a step or two and caught up the petticoat. "It appears the lady has a problem with my looking at her undergarment." He thrust it at Lydia. "Check it, thoroughly."

Lydia stuffed both pistols into her belt and took the voluminous petticoat in two hands and turning it inside out ran her fingers along the thick folds of velvet inch by tedious inch. The petticoat had a wide, flat pleat at the centre front and smaller pleats running backwards from it; she slid her fingers into every one. She was about halfway around when she reached a pleat sewn a little differently than the rest.

And it crackled.

"Your knife."

Without a word, Jack slipped a couple of fingers inside his right boot and pulled out the dagger. "Be careful, 'tis sharp," he advised needlessly.

Lydia took the knife and dug the blade under a row of stitches.

The woman screamed for her to stop and was shoved back onto the ground by a now very irate Jack Palmer, as she attempted to rise.

"Got it," Lydia said, pulling a long narrow roll of paper from the seam. "It's sealed." She held it aloft for Jack to see then leaned down to give it to him.

"No! Damn you, you witch! Give it here." The woman flew to her feet and made a lunge for the paper.

Jack grabbed her and pinned her hands behind her back while she continued to struggle and curse at Lydia in a most unladylike fashion.

Lydia sighed. "Oh, do shut up," she said witheringly.

"Hold still." Jack tried hard to hide the laughter in his face. "In . . . the bag, my . . . saddle." He regained control. "Rope, get it for me."

Lydia wasn't sure he meant Bess's saddle or the gelding's, but she took a chance and dug into the saddlebag where she sat. She found a coil of thin rope and handed it to him.

Within minutes he had the woman's hands firmly tied behind her. He dragged her towards the coach and threw her in then threw her clothing after her. "You lot," he roared, striding across to the four men on the ground. "Up!" He waved his pistol menacingly. "Gather your clothing and be gone."

"But, don't we need to keep her?" Lydia asked as Jack mounted the gelding.

The woman's husband hissed a threat at the pair as he climbed into the coach carrying his clothing and began trying to console his wife, who it seemed, was having none of it and spewed forth every curse she could lay tongue to.

Lydia looked at Jack awaiting her reply.

"Would you wish to keep her?" he said grimly.

"Let's go. Can we?" Lydia felt suddenly very tired.

He nodded. "You have something for me?" Jack held out a hand and took the roll of paper. Tempting as it was, he knew the seal must remain in place and undisturbed. "Ready?" He turned and fired his pistol in the air.

The six horses snorted and reared, and were underway even before the coachman had scrambled into his seat and picked up the reins. The single gentleman amidst the tangles of the woman's clothing and her husband's embroidered coat, held grimly on to the coach, valiantly tying to clamber in and close the door. And the countess could be heard clearly cursing her husband in a most colourful fashion.

The gelding reared at a touch from Jack's heels, and Lydia watched fascinated as the highwayman raised his three-cornered hat. "Dick Turpin thanks you." Then laughing loudly he called out, "Ho, my bonny Bess. Ho."

Black Bess rose on her hind legs, and Lydia shrieked. She flung her arms around the mare's neck and stood in the stirrups. It couldn't have been more than a few seconds, but it seemed like forever until Bess's front feet hit the ground and the horse leapt away in the wake of the gelding, Lydia clinging on for dear life.

A couple of miles on, Jack pulled his horse to a halt and waited for Lydia to come alongside.

"Well?" He said, pulling the kerchief from his face.

She looked at him. "Well?"

"Ha-ha-ha," he roared and slapped his thigh then removed his mask and wiped tears from his eyes. "I think you make a most worthy partner. What say you?"

Lydia pulled a face and divested herself of the black silk. "I shouldn't want to do this for a living; it's too stressful." She put a hand to her mouth and yawned. "Can we go home now, please?"

"Indeed. I am in good spirits this day, and I look forwards to a good brandy in front of a blazing fire with my friend Luke, and of course my partner. Now, let's be off to the cottage and see to these horses."

TWENTY-TWO

Lydia dropped from Bess's back, her knees buckled and she sat down unceremoniously in a pile of wet leaves. Jack assisted her to her feet, grumbling, as he held a hand to his face for a second then withdrew it and looked at the residue.

"Some claws that one."

"I'll clean it for you when we get back," Lydia said, and yawned feeling her eyelids flicker closed for a moment.

"You're exhausted. Let's get your horse."

She nodded and followed him to where the chestnut stood idly crunching on a few residual wisps of hay.

"Are you all right?" Jack said, booting her into the saddle. "Able to ride to Beckham alone?"

"I think so. I'm just so tired."

Tired or not she rode back to the hall faster than she had ever done her mind a jumble of incoherent thoughts. Thoughts that she'd just taken part in an armed robbery, thoughts that the man she was in love with had told her he loved her, and she couldn't quite bring herself to trust him, and thoughts that she might somehow suddenly find herself back in the twenty-first century. She pushed the mare as fast as she dare, glad of the slowly creeping grey light that edged its way through the trees. It would be daylight in a short while, and here she was just getting ready to go to bed. She and Jack had been away only a few hours, but already fears for Luke's wellbeing nagged at her. What if the fever had started again? Would anyone cool him down properly?

The mare's shoes clattered on the yard, and Peter ran forwards to assist Lydia from the saddle. She groaned a thank-you and staggered off towards the house, where she was met by two maids and escorted to her room. "How is His Lordship?" she asked and, upon hearing he was well, collapsed on the bed. She refused the girls' entreaties that they undress her; she just wanted to lie down. "He's sleeping?" she said hopefully, deciding that as long as Luke was well she would go and see him later.

"Nay, milady, 'e been up this past hour or more, sitting by the fire."

Lydia groaned. The damn man. She just hoped he hadn't opened his wound.

Another girl appeared at the doorway and spoke quietly. "Beggin' pardon, milady, His Lordship requests you come to his room."

"Oh, no," Lydia groaned. She didn't have the strength to roll over in bed, let alone crawl to Luke's room. Every inch of her flesh cried out for rest. "Tell him I'm really very tired. I'll see him in the morning, or make that afternoon."

"But, milady, 'e be most insistent you go," the girl said nervously. "We'll help you," she encouraged. "You looks all in, you do."

Against her better judgment, Lydia allowed herself to be escorted out along the hall to Luke's room quite certain she would be asleep by the time they got there.

*   *   *

Luke shifted in his chair. It was large and usually very comfortable, but this hour he cursed it for the damnable discomfort it caused him. His side hurt like hell and damnation, but it was nothing compared with the pain in his heart that had plagued him all night until he received news of Lydia's return. The door opened.

"Lydia!" He pressed a hand to his side and took a couple of shallow breaths. He wanted to run across the room and take her in his arms, but here he was, helpless as a baby.

Lydia raised her drooping head and aimed her best attempt at a smile right into Luke's beautiful light blue eyes, wondering yet again at what she saw there.

"Take her in there," Luke said, his voice far weaker than he would have liked.

"W . . . where are you taking me?"

"You shall be bathed, and then you may sleep."

"Don't you want to know what happened? I mean . . . I thought." She cast him a weary glance. "I thought you'd want to ask me a million questions."

"Nay, we'll speak later of the night's events." He hesitated. "'Tis enough that you are safe."

Lydia smiled and felt tears prick the corners of her eyes. She allowed the maids to guide her into Luke's bathing room, where she was duly divested of her clothing, amidst several strange stares, and immersed in a huge tub of steaming water. Three times, she slid down into the water as sleep overtook her, and three times the girls recovered her swiftly. The hot water was comforting, and it smelled of lavender. Lydia felt as though she were floating in a dream. A dream about a man with long dark hair and incredible blue eyes, a man who not too long ago had said he loved her.

"Milady, you be lookin' like a prune if you stays in there much longer," one of the maids advised.

"Mmmmm," she said, "prunes sound just fine." Nevertheless, she allowed them to assist her out of the water and stood, unabashed at her nakedness, as they towelled her dry and wrapped her in a robe of pale green silk.

"How are you?" Luke asked, as Lydia lay down on a couch loaded with feather pillows, opposite where he sat.

She stretched her arms and legs and looked at the man sitting in the chair by the fire. "I should be asking you that. What are you doing out of bed anyhow?"

"Waiting for you, of course."

"Thank you. Oh," she sniffed, "and what's that smell?"

"Apple wood. I thought you'd like it since you complained about the coal. I remembered we had trees cut last year, so 'twas easily arranged to have the logs brought in. And I thought you might enjoy a bath after your adventures." He raised an eyebrow. "Did you have fun out there?"

"Thank you," she said softly, "for the fire and the bath. I feel much better now. As for having fun, I think Jack might have been enjoying himself, at least until he was clawed."

"Clawed? What were you tackling? Dragons?" Luke allowed himself a slight grin then curtailed it with a grimace.

"Almost, and I'll tell you all about it if you promise to stop squirming about so much."

"Indeed, I should relax more if I had a little less discomfort. A brandy perhaps if my esteemed nursemaid will allow it?" He looked at her hopefully and tried not to laugh at her open mouth. She was the most beautiful creature he had ever seen, even as now, staring at him as though she were only half in control of her senses.

"Nursemaid am I? Well, I think I'll have a brandy. You, mister, can get your own." She rolled to her feet and staggered to the small table where the decanter stood.

"Lydia, love."

"What?"

"I obeyed your command not to partake."

"You did?" She poured one drink. "Didn't have any at all since I left?"

"Nay, not a drop. You see, I listened."

Lydia was, if she were to admit it, quite impressed. But he was laughing at her. Not perhaps with his mouth, but his eyes glinted with a wicked humour.

"In fact, I find it perfectly pleasant to allow you control," he continued.

"If you really want a drink, you'd best stop talking. You're just digging yourself in deeper."

"Aye, love, as you say."

She laughed, and poured another drink. "Here you are."

"Now, I'm quite content." He sipped his drink. "Make yourself comfortable, and tell me the whole tale. But first, did Jack get what we were after?"

She nodded. "Yes. He said he'd come straight back here when he's finished doing whatever it is he has to do."

"Thank the Lord, 'twill soon be over. Now tell me of your ride on Black Bess."

Lydia felt herself drop off to sleep periodically during her storytelling, and each time she awoke with a guilty little jump. She struggled to stay awake but eventually succumbed to slumber.

From Lydia's story, it appeared the night had not been easy, and Luke expected she would sleep for many hours. Three sharp raps on the door roused him from his thoughts, and he called out as loudly as he was able.

Jack Palmer strode into the room. "Good morning."

Luke nodded his acquiescence and couldn't help but smile at the wide grin that spread across the other man's face. "Damn you, Jack, quit that smirking. It hurts like hell when I laugh."

"I see your lady is resting." Palmer glanced at Lydia, gently snuffling in the pile of pillows. He poured himself a drink and then pulled up a chair. "Did she tell you what befell us?"

"Much of it, and most importantly that you got the information."

"Aye, there'll be no rebellion this time, but plenty of trade for the topsman I'll warrant. We have names, dates"—he paused and took a swig of his brandy—"and the location of most of the gold they were to use for financing."

"You're smirking again, Jack."

"'Tis an interesting thing that a great hoard of gold and weapons was discovered in the cellars of Fulford Manor."

"You look like a cat that's got the cream, my friend." Luke grinned.

"What . . . where's a cat? Show me . . . oh, I." Lydia pushed herself up onto an elbow and smiled sleepily in her embarrassment. She blinked and then caught sight of Jack palmer. "Hello, Jack," she said and stuck a fist into her mouth as she yawned.

"Ah, you're awake," he observed.

"Only just and probably not for long." She yawned again.

"Now as to the cat that's got the cream, aye," Jack continued. "I've never had any fondness for Fulford, but he's taken care of or will be within the next twenty-four hours—he's hidden himself, but not for long. Norton's after him. And now I have better things to speak of."

Luke looked at Lydia who seemed just as baffled by Jack's words as he. "What mean you?"

"The conduct of this lady." He turned to Lydia and waited, just to ensure his words had the desired effect. "She was bloody marvellous, Luke. Just bloody marvellous." He held his glass high. "To you, my ferocious and formidable partner."

Lydia accepted the toast with a giggle then lay back and listened as Jack retold his own, exceedingly animated version of their exploits. Luke shook his head slowly, and glanced several times at Lydia in amusement.

"I sincerely recommend," Palmer said and rose to his feet, "that you do nothing, my friend, to irk the pretty miss." He feigned dodging a blow.

"I'll let you off this time," Lydia laughed. "I'm too tired to strangle you right now."

"Worry not, Jack, I have little intention of it," Luke responded. "In fact I have every intention of ensuring she is at my side and not opposing me."

"You have?" Jack Palmer walked to the door. "Well then, I'll leave you to it. I needs must clean myself."

"Oh, Jack, I'm sorry." Lydia started to crawl from her pillows. "I promised to see to those scratches for you."

He held up a hand. "They are but scratches, and I believe there are other, more important matters you should attend to."

Lydia watched him leave the room and stared at the closed door for a few seconds wondering what he meant.

"Lydia," Luke said. "Lydia, help me up would you."

"What do you want?"

"I wish to sit by you," he said simply.

She tottered half asleep to his chair and, taking him carefully by one arm, helped him to a standing position then slipped an arm around his waist. Luke wore a silk robe, heavy enough for warmth, yet not too heavy to disguise the hard contours of his muscles where her hand rested. Even in his weakened state and without his normal arrogance he was one hell of a man, and a strange tingle ran through Lydia's body. She shuddered.

"You shivered," he said.

"Mmm, come on let's have you sitting down before you fall down and take me with you."

"'Twould be interesting. Ouch! Steady."

"Sorry, but you went one way, and I went the other."

"The way of things," he agreed. With a groan, he allowed her to assist him onto the couch.

"You should go to bed you know," she suggested.

He looked at her suddenly, waited until she sat down then said, "Is that an invitation?"

She sighed. Some things never changed. "I'm saying nothing, but you just don't give up do you?"

"I do not. I intend to pursue you and make you mine," he said casually.

"I beg your pardon. You talk as though you're hunting me. Is that what I am to you, a trophy?" She turned her back and snuggled into a pillow.

Luke sighed. He wasn't doing too well. He was tired and likely his mind was not as sharp as it should be; mayhap he should leave this until he was more alert. He considered for a moment. Lydia had come into his life unexpectedly, and it was possible she might leave with equal lack of warning. Still, he had lived his life happily enough before she came—hadn't he? He wasn't sure he had an answer. There seemed to be a great void behind him that he had once called his life. He looked at her, curled up beside him, and reached out a hand to touch her shoulder. She needed to go to bed and to stretch out those wonderful long limbs, but he didn't care to let her out of his sight. He recalled her words about what may happen when her task was completed.

"Lydia, I didn't mean it to sound that way. Please, look at me." She grunted but otherwise didn't respond. He sighed again. "I want you to get into my bed. The linen is fresh. I had it changed an hour or two ago."

"What?" She sat up slowly and turned. "You want me to get into your bed? You just get worse," she snorted with disgust.

"I'm hardly in any condition to lay a finger on you, and I demand, nay, request that you desist from besmirching my character further."

Lydia looked at him sheepishly. "I'm sorry, but you say some of the damndest things. All right, I'll go and sleep in your bed. It's warmer in here than my room will be."

"Shall you swear at me when we're wed?" he asked suddenly.

She was halfway to his bed. What had he just said? He was at it again with his tasteless jokes. She ignored him and pulled back the covers. There was definitely more than enough room for two, and a nice cuddle would be quite cosy. She

SOMEONE LIKE YOU   283

remembered who he was, laughed silently, and crawled into bed.

"You didn't answer my question, Lydia," he called softly to the mound in the bed.

"Can't hear you."

"Nor do you want to it seems." He waited a moment hearing nothing but a few little snuffles. She was sleeping. He could wait a few more hours, and for now, he would just keep a watchful eye on her. "You may not be a trophy, but you're a prize worth fighting for," he said quietly, knowing she didn't hear. How could he prevent her from disappearing, if that was indeed what fate had in mind? He determined to ask her more about her own time. Perhaps then he could ensure she didn't return to it.

TWENTY - THREE

Lydia blinked a couple of times before recollecting where she was. The drapes were drawn, and the room was in darkness except for the light of a few candles. She rolled over, loath to get out of the warm comforting folds of goose down, and came face to face with a pair of light blue eyes.

"Good afternoon, love. I wondered when you would wake." Luke lay on his side, watching her.

"You scared me half to bloody death. What are you doing?" she asked suspiciously.

"Watching you. I wanted to make certain you didn't disappear."

"Why should I do that?"

"You've completed your task, have you not?"

She frowned. "I'm not sure."

Slowly he eased himself closer and, with a groan and a curse, bent his head. His kiss was light, and he restrained a passion that craved for more. "Lydia, you didn't answer my question." He spoke between kissing her mouth, her cheeks, her throat knowing she could barely make out his words, but he didn't care. He'd just keep on asking.

"Stop it." She struggled to turn her head away.

Luke grinned. "Are you hungry?" he asked and rolled onto his back. He lay there looking at the ceiling.

Feeling slightly miffed by his sudden change of mood, Lydia grunted and pulled herself into a sitting position. "Have you been there all the time?" she said accusingly.

"A few hours. I needed my rest you said so." He grinned at her.

She considered the facts. He was on top of the covers, and she was under them, quite the reverse of last time. He wasn't in any position to take advantage of her, and very likely if he decided to kiss her again, she wouldn't object.

"Are you struck dumb this afternoon?"

"This afternoon? Is it really?" She looked around the darkened room.

"'Tis almost four o'clock. Now, are you hungry?"

"I could eat a mouthful."

"Give me a moment," he said quietly. "Allow me another moment to gaze upon your beauty."

"I wish you wouldn't make fun of me," she said stiffly and began to climb out of bed.

"Lydia. Look at me."

She stood, turned, and looked him full in the face. "I'm looking, Your Lordship."

"You want me, don't you? I think you do."

"I . . . I . . . damn you!"

"If you don't want to answer that, help me to my feet. 'Tis difficult without help."

She walked around to his side of the bed. "I should shove you on the floor and leave you there," she grumbled as she assisted him towards a chair near the fire.

"You love me too dearly for that."

Lydia blew out her cheeks and pulled the bell. "What do you want to eat?"

"I am content for the moment to feast my eyes upon you, my love."

"Just stop it, will you. I don't . . . ," she started to berate him but stopped as she heard a sharp knock at the door. "Come in," she called, grateful for the distraction.

Jack entered. "You're up and about I see. Did you sleep well?" He nodded to the pair.

"I slept very well thank you," Lydia said tartly. "It was when I woke up things started to go wrong."

He looked from her to Luke then said, "What's he done now?"

"He's gone mad. Really, Jack, I think he's delirious."

"Luke, my friend what have you done to upset my partner?"

"I merely asked her a question, and she seems intent on ignoring me and defaming my character." Luke put a hand to his side and leaned back in his chair.

"Have you ordered food yet?" Jack asked glancing at Lydia.

"I rang the bell."

"Good, I already informed the staff to bring dinner as soon as you rang. In fact, I think I hear something." He strode to the door and opened it just as three young men arrived bearing several large silver dishes. "Come, let's forget our differences and eat. I would have more of your own tale if you would permit it."

"Jack!" Luke frowned.

"She can speak for herself, and should she wish not to speak, then so be it," the other returned with a knowing smile.

"How much do you know?" she said.

"Nothing at all. His Lordship refused all entreaties to enlighten me."

"Nothing? That's not true." Lydia gave a quick grin. "You know all about my bike, and it seemed to me you were having a good old time. I'll tell you only because I trust you and"—she paused—"because I like you."

Jack laughed quietly. "She has us pegged, Luke. Ah, this pie is excellent."

Luke couldn't hide his own smile. "So you saw us?"

She nodded. "You were like a couple of schoolboys. I must admit though, Jack. You were doing very well."

"You're not angry?" Luke inched himself into a more upright position.

"No. In fact I haven't laughed so hard for a long time," she said. "Now where should I begin? Cars, trains or planes?"

An hour or so later, Jack Palmer sat back in his chair and gave a low whistle. "What I wouldn't give to see all this."

"Don't even consider meddling in it, Jack," Luke advised. "Naught good could come of it."

"Tell me, did I ever become famous?" Jack laughed.

"I . . ." Lydia looked helplessly at Luke who simply shook his head. "Well, I suppose I've read some things about you, in history books," she said warily. "You achieved fame by riding the distance between London and York in about fifteen hours. Black Bess went down in history for that," she concluded.

He looked aghast at her revelation. "Nay, I fear you have it wrong there, lass. That ride was done by Nevison. Aye, Swift Nick was known for his reckless riding. I should never do that to my bonnie Bess. In truth I would not."

"Well, perhaps I got it wrong. I never was very good at history." Lydia breathed a sigh of relief when he seemed satisfied with her answer.

"It sounds an intriguing world, this twenty-first century. What say you, Luke?"

"Indeed it does." Luke shifted slightly. "Damn this wound. It still hurts like the devil when I move."

"Mayhap we should look into visiting for ourselves."

"Are you mad? 'Tis all I can think of to keep this one from suddenly disappearing back there." He nodded towards Lydia.

"Ah, so you're thinking of keeping her, are you?" Jack Palmer's eyes twinkled.

Lydia watched them, like little boys with a secret they were perhaps about to share. She gasped at Luke's next words. To play around with his silly banter when they were alone was one thing, but for him to involve Jack was embarrassing.

"Aye, I fully intend to keep her." He cast a glance and held her dark eyes with his own light ones. "If she'll have me."

"See," Lydia snapped, "he's at it again." Neither man was listening. She watched as Jack left his food, rose to his feet, and assisted Luke to stand.

"Careful there, I hurt like hell," Luke groused. He came to where Lydia sat and proceeded to lower himself to one knee, aided by the other man.

"What are you doing now?" Lydia could barely keep a straight face. So intent was he on his mission.

"Jack, don't go too far. I shall likely require assistance to my feet," Luke advised.

"Take your time. I'll be outside."

"Where's he going?" Lydia asked suspiciously.

"Lydia, listen to me. I mean really listen." Luke took her hands and kissed them. "'Tis bloody painful in this position, and I intend to ask you this in some haste."

"You do?" She had to agree he looked very uncomfortable.

"Lydia, will you marry me?"

"You're at it again." She tried to pull her hands away.

"I am as sincere as I ever was. Please answer me gladly and quickly for I'm in bloody agony. Lydia, I want you for the rest of my life, at my side. I promise to protect you and care for you . . . What else can I say? Shall you accept me?" He looked at her expectantly.

"And will you be faithful?"

Her question caught him unawares. He hesitated, and he knew she took it as a sign of his own doubt. "You will believe what I tell you?"

"Try me."

"Aye, I give you my total assurance I will never take another." He knew his words to be sincere, but did she? He considered her narrowed eyes and sceptical expression.

"You have one hell of a reputation, and you've been with who knows how many since I got here. You might have some awful disease."

He scowled. "I assure you I do not have some foul disease. As for my nightly visits to the Blue Bell . . ." He grinned then said, "I never touched anyone there. All were paid for their silence that is all. 'Twas was my alibi for being abroad at nights, and a way of perpetuating the idea that I was little but a mindless philanderer."

"So you weren't out . . ." Lydia found she was beginning to smile.

He leaned close to her ear and whispered, "I've not bedded a woman in nigh on a year but keep it a secret. 'Twould not do to sully my reputation."

Lydia's smile turned slowly into a soft laugh. "I don't know what to say."

"Just tell me you'll have me, and then I may get up from the floor. If I don't do it soon I fear I never shall." He gave a long groan. "What say you?"

She shook her head and knew herself for a fool, but a fool in love. "I will," she whispered. "I will."

"Tomorrow. 'Tis all settled then."

"Tomorrow!"

"Aye, have you objection?"

"Well no, but you aren't well yet."

"Ah, you fear for my performance. True. I needs must wait before . . . a few days."

Lydia felt herself turning pink. "That can wait; I'm not desperate."

"You appeared enthusiastic though, as I recall," Luke said with a sly grin. "I look forwards to such pleasures, but I am content to have you as my wife in name only for as long as 'tis necessary." The truth was he felt she was less likely to disappear if he gave her his name and she became part of his world. He hugged her against him as tightly as he was able.

The tears rolled freely down Lydia's cheeks. "Do you mean it?" she whispered.

"Which part: marriage, being faithful, or waiting to make you mine?" He held her fast as she pulled back and said quickly, "Love, I mean all those things. I love you very much, Lydia." He lifted her chin and looked deep into her eyes. "I do."

"And I look a bloody awful mess," she sniffed, and then she laughed as he wiped the tears from her eyes with the sleeve of his robe.

Luke kissed her softly, tasting the salt of residual tears, and he felt a low groan rise in his chest. Damnation but it would be murder to wed her, to have in his bed, and not be able to consummate the marriage, and it would be few days more at least, until his bloody side was secure. "You look beautiful."

"You really can be nice sometimes, can't you?"

"Aye, when the mood strikes me. Come, pretty one, help me to my feet or call Jack."

Lydia tried to summon a glare at his words but was unable. His eyes were the brightest blue she'd ever seen them, and his dark hair, wild and loose over his shoulders likened him to the glorious knight of her dreams. Who needed the shining armour? She remembered the first time they'd met, and the first time he'd kissed her, she remembered the night they'd met in the kitchen . . . when she'd said . . . and determined not to go there. He was right, she had wanted him, but not under any old circumstances. Now it seemed things had fallen into place quite well.

"I'm waiting to get back into my chair," Luke reminded her with a slight groan.

"I take it you need help?"

"Is there not something else you wish to say?" Lydia looked puzzled and said nothing. Luke gave a quick smile and called to Jack, who immediately entered and helped him very slowly to gain his feet.

"Well, are congratulations in order?"

"Indeed they are. Jack, be a good fellow and call for a bottle of my finest champagne."

"Smuggled?" Lydia asked.

"What other is there?" Luke grinned and slid an arm around her waist, pulling her closer to him. He watched Jack walk to the bellpull then breathed, "Would that I could show you this night how much I love you. Lydia, refrain from looking at me thus, or I may indeed forget I am wounded."

"Perhaps you should," she murmured. She hadn't really meant to say that. The words just slipped out of their own volition. The merest touch of his knuckles gently stroking her cheek kindled flames she knew would be difficult to control. "Perhaps we should sleep in separate beds until . . . until you're all right." She trembled again and heard a soft sigh from somewhere.

"I once said you wanted me as much as I wanted you. Now I know 'tis true." He brushed her lips with his own. "But I forbid absolutely that we should sleep in separate beds. There are many ways to find pleasure," he whispered.

"Luke, man can't you wait?" Jack shook his head and laughed loudly. "Give the lass some space."

"Jack, you have ears like a ship's rat. Nay, never heed that my friend. I desire that you ride to the town, find that fool of a vicar, and bring him back here post-haste. I intend to wed this eve. Shall you do it?"

"What says your lady?" Jack Palmer rejoined with a bemused smile.

Lydia found she was unable to say anything. Her gaze fixed on the man at her side who awaited a response, and she saw nothing beyond his face.

"She appears to suffer some malady this day," Luke stated.

"No, no, I'm all right but . . . can you . . . I mean can we just have a wedding, I mean spontaneously, like that?"

"You forget who I am. I can do mostly anything I wish. Now, Jack, shall you do this for me?"

Jack was already half way to the door laughing as he went. "You'll need a ring for the lady," he called over his shoulder.

"I shall see to it that you have the perfect ring of your own choosing. There are many precious stones in the family coffers," Luke said. "But for now, what to do?"

"Do you have any pigs?"

"Pigs?"

"They wear rings in their noses, don't they? You know just like the owl and the . . . No, forget that; you've not heard it."

"No, indeed but I'm relieved you haven't suggested using your previous ring," he said.

"No way, I wouldn't insult you. It stays where it is, locked in that trunk. I don't mind what I have; pull one out of the curtains for all I care." She giggled as he kissed her and kept on kissing her until she could barely breathe.

"Nay, I can do better than that. Walk over to that cabinet." He indicated a piece of furniture on the far wall. "You'll find a box in the left lower drawer."

Lydia rose and walked across the room. The cabinet was delicate and intricately carved, and she knew that in the twenty-first century this bit of craftsmanship would fetch a pretty penny. She slid the drawer open and reached inside. Carefully she pulled out a small box and shut the drawer. "This box is beautiful. What's it made of?"

"Olive wood with pearl inlay," Luke replied. "My grandfather brought it back with him from Spain, and it's been in that drawer for as long as I can remember. It contains a few items that belonged to my grandmother; there might be something useful, only temporarily of course. Open it."

Lydia sat down and spun the small catch with her thumb. She opened the lid of the box and gasped. "Are these real?"

"Real enough," Luke said, laughing at her honest astonishment, "though not particularly extravagant by my grandfather's standards. Do you see anything that would suit?"

"There must be twenty rings in here," Lydia said, poking around in the box. "Oh, and look, this necklace matches this one, and this. Now this is nice and . . ."

"Lydia, love you shall have whatever your heart desires, but for now just choose a bloody ring that fits."

"Sorry, my lord," she grinned. "Oh, wait. Look at this one." She passed the ring to Luke. "Is it gold?"

"Aye, forged from the purest gold. 'Twas commissioned by my grandfather." He held the ring between his thumb and forefinger turning it in the light so that the different colours of gold gleamed red, yellow, and white against the flicker of the candle glow.

"And these pearls, Luke, they're beautiful. They're pink."

"Gathered on his many travels. Try the ring," he suggested.

It fitted as though made for her. "It's perfect." Lydia took it off and handed it back. "This is the one I want."

"For now 'twill suffice."

"I'll be very happy to have this as my permanent wedding ring."

"'Tis not what I had in mind, but we may discuss it later." She nodded. "It's a deal."

"Off you go then."

"Where?"

"To don your best gown."

"What are you wearing then?" She cocked her head to one side. "Your Lordship."

"I fear 'twould be an impossibility to dress."

"In that case," she slipped her arms around his neck and snuggled against him, "I'm getting married just as I am."

"Oh, you are, are you? Have you not noticed by whom you sit? I may be infirm, but I'm still a red-blooded male." His eyes twinkled, and he pushed her gently away, holding her at arms length. "You wouldn't want me to break open my wound."

She shook her head vigorously. "How long before it's healed . . . I mean so you can bathe properly and do things . . . ride," she added lamely.

"I'm not sure if you're in heat for me or 'tis that I stink."

"Neither," she laughed. "I'm concerned for your well-being, that's all."

"In that case stay by me like you were." He pulled her arms back around his neck. "And don't look at me in that way you do, at the very least until I am able to do something about it."

"Tell me, there's not another reason you're in such a hurry to get married? There's not a family fortune at stake, is there?"

He made an attempt at laughing but stopped as a sharp pain caught him. "No. My fortune is secure. But that leads me to consider introducing you to my family." He frowned. "Invariably, my father and I find each other's company disagreeable for more than a short period of time."

"Will our marriage be a problem?"

"Indeed not. They will be pleased enough that I take a bride, and after meeting you they shall be entranced, just as I."

What could she say? The most wonderful man in the whole of her world was hers by his own choice, and she'd only had to leave her own century to find him. It was a good trade-off.

"Do you regret anything?" he asked suddenly.

"Such as?" She couldn't imagine regretting anything except that she'd not met him earlier and most certainly before the age of the dreadful Darwin.

"Is there anything you will miss from your own time?"

"Modern sanitation and my sister. I wish I could let her know I'm okay. I still can't fully comprehend that I'm here to stay. Oh, not that there's any reason to go back." She hugged him too tightly and felt him wince. "Everything I have, everything I want, is right here."

"I hope by that you mean me." He kissed her cheek and slowly migrated to her mouth. Strangely, when he kissed her, held her, felt that roaring furnace in his belly and his body harden, there was very little pain in his side, perhaps if he were to move with extremely slowness and care . . .

Lydia pulled her mouth free. "No, Black Bess," she said, laughing. "Of course I mean you, silly. My Lord Beckham."

"Very well. Now, we should discuss where I should take you after we are wed and settled. Would you perhaps like a journey to Paris or Tuscany?" He tapped his finger to his lips. "Or perhaps the estates in Ireland; they are beautiful beyond belief. Almost," he whispered, "as beautiful as you."

Lydia realised she could easily cope with this sort of flattery and the blushes it brought to her cheeks. She was certain Luke wouldn't understand if she told him that men in her century generally didn't speak this way. "Ireland sounds lovely."

"I was thinking that perhaps we would wed again in church. Somewhere more befitting my bride."

"We'll discuss it later." Lydia disengaged herself from his body. "I'm off to put a shift on under this robe. I suppose I ought to appear slightly respectable before a man of the cloth."

"Very likely he's potted by now anyhow," Luke remarked.

"It can't be more than six o'clock."

"Seems to be the holy order of things. I've seen him in the Bell by three," Luke grinned.

Lydia frowned. "This marriage will be real? I mean if the vicar's drunk . . ."

"Indeed in the eyes of God, and 'twill be recorded according to law. Have no fear"—the wickedness crept into his eyes again—"you shall be a very properly wed woman on your wedding night. Now go, don your shift. Jack should return shortly with the old sot."

*　　*　　*

"Are we married then?" Lydia murmured later that evening. "I'm wearing a ring, so I suppose we must be."

"Aye, at least I recall saying a few words." Luke lay on his back, his arms folded across his chest. "And you, my love, I believe, also spoke your part."

"It all seems like a dream, and I'm so tired now." She rolled on her side to face him. "Fancy, I'm going to go to sleep on my wedding night."

"'Tis as well. A few days only, perhaps. And then . . ." He flashed a wicked grin. "I also recall that you promised to obey me. I wonder how long that will last."

"You might be surprised." She laughed and kissed him quickly on the cheek. "Just keep me happy, and you'll be all right."

"Old Judd has a saying," Luke said softly. "Happy wife, happy life."

"Sensible man," Lydia agreed.

"I'll keep you happy, never fear."

As he turned to kiss her, she knew he would.

TWENTY-FOUR

The days passed blissfully, and Lydia occupied her time with things she had never dreamed of, not least planning a ball for their real wedding as Luke put it. He was determined, it seemed, to introduce her to the echelons of society in the correct and proper manner even though Lydia had assured him she was happy just to be his wife; the thoughts of meeting a crowd eighteenth century aristocracy were somewhat daunting.

She sighed. What was she worried about? Luke would be there by her side when she met the multitude of strangers that would descend upon them in a few short weeks, and his family couldn't be all that bad. The Beckham staff knew what it was about when it came to organizing an occasion of this magnitude, and Lydia was grateful that everyone seemed to have taken a liking to her, in particular the cook who had offered the most extensive menu Lydia had ever seen in her life. It seemed that at least the culinary arrangements were under control. The invitations were more of a problem; she didn't know anybody. Luke would have to be in charge of names and titles. She blew out her cheeks in exasperation and looked up as Luke walked into the drawing room.

"Keeping busy?"

She nodded. "I am, but I'd much rather be spending time with my husband."

"That's just what I was coming to speak to you about." He waited a moment then continued, "Would you like to take dinner in our room this evening?"

"That's fine by me." She grabbed the hand he offered and found herself spun around and crushed against a broad chest.

He laughed. "There are a few more things I should attend to first, but I do have time for a kiss, my love."

"I can manage that, particularly since you didn't call me that other thing."

"Nor shall I, since it appears to offend you." He bent his head to meet the upturned face that watched him closely and wondered how he had lived so long without this contentment and love in his life. He felt need of nothing else, and the way his wife responded to his kisses left him in fear for his sanity. "I'll see you there at seven does that suit?"

"Fine, but what's the occasion? Or should I even ask?"

"Just join me for dinner." He winked and walked out of the room.

Lydia was as happy as she could hope to be, but a worrying little voice kept popping into her head unannounced. Would she ever be certain she was here to stay? Was there anything she could do to ensure she remained? It was a subject she had deliberated upon, finally arriving at the conclusion that she could stay but the bike and the ring had to go back. First thing in the morning she would see to it.

*   *   *

Luke sat by the fire wearing a robe of dark blue silk, his legs stretched luxuriously in front of him, a glass of brandy in his hand. Lydia sniffed the air appreciatively having become quite fond of the smell of burning apple wood.

"Hello there. This is nice." She walked behind him and bent over his shoulder, allowing her lips to linger on his cheek. He'd shaved, and his skin felt smooth and smelled faintly of sandalwood. His hair, loose and still slightly damp, hung about his shoulders just begging Lydia's fingers to tangle into it. "You smell good." She lifted a strand of hair then let it fall as he spoke.

"Thank you. I thought 'twas time to bathe. I've not felt clean in a week."

"You bathed? Was it safe? Your side, I mean."

"Come here." he reached around for her hand. "I mean right here."

Lydia found herself pulled down onto his lap. She sat there tentatively not daring to move lest she cause him pain. He was smiling in a most infuriating way.

"'Tis healed well enough, and I fear this night may prove a sleepless one. What say you, wife?"

She found she couldn't say a word. The arms around her were unrelenting, as was the mouth that teased and played on her own, kissing her with a restrained passion she was barely able to match, so fierce was the pounding of her heart and the swirling heat that seemed intent on consuming her inch by delicious inch.

"Lydia, Lydia, I'm going insane for you," Luke gasped between kisses. "These past few days have been torture." He ran a finger around the neckline of her gown and allowed himself a low growl of pleasure.

"Me too," she whispered.

"Aye, my love," he breathed, "and tonight, you shall have your wedding night." He grinned suddenly and held her at arms length as best he could while she still sat upon his lap. "First we'll eat, and then you shall be bathed."

"What do you mean, shall be bathed?" she asked in wide-eyed innocence.

"Surely you would not deny your husband the pleasure of washing your skin with the finest perfumed soap and then gently caressing you with scented oils before he takes you to his bed."

"I guess not. I just never took you for the type to . . . do . . . that . . . sort . . . of . . . thing," she managed between more kisses. She turned her head. "In fact, I think I might quite enjoy it."

"Quite enjoy it?" he grunted. "I find that a little disheartening."

"You'll live, my lord. Now shall we eat? I see it's all ready." She pulled away giggling and ran to the table.

"I've almost lost my appetite," Luke said and rose to his feet, advancing until he had backed her fully into a corner. "I remember the last time I did this. For a second it seemed as though I might receive another kick in the bollocks, but as it turned out you were rather more than enthusiastic"—he grinned wickedly—"my love."

"I was not," she said haughtily.

"But you were." He pressed the length of his body against her, noting with pleasure the little sound that escaped her throat. "Just as now." Before she had chance for further response, he laughed and grasping her hand led her back to the table.

"I was thinking, maybe I should have my bath first and then dinner."

"I fear you would not eat this night if I were to bathe you first."

"In that case," she acquiesced, "dinner first."

*   *   *

Lydia had never had anyone bathe her since she was a child, and although she had seen her husband's naked body and had enjoyed mutual caresses the past few days, this was quite different. It was wonderful as it turned out, and the

embarrassment she felt soon evaporated in the warm water
and she surrendered herself completely to the heady scents
of the soaps and oils he smoothed gently over her body. She
giggled when he patted her dry and then slipped a gown of soft
chambray around her, swung her into his arms, and carried
her to the bed.

"Your wound?"

"Never worry." He laid her gently down.

"Well, thank you that was . . ."

"Shhh, wench, do as you're told for once."

Indignation was the least of her responses as his hands
traced around her ears, her face, her throat. It struck her
briefly that he was very skilled, and he must have learned
those skills somewhere else, but that was in the past; he was
her husband now, and she was determined to enjoy every
minute of him.

"God, Lydia," he murmured, "I can scarce control myself,
though I promise to do so." His hands slipped over her
shoulders and stroked their way almost casually to her breasts,
taking with them the fine fabric of her gown and pulling it
awry. Luke groaned again and said something unintelligible
before allowing his mouth to follow his fingers, his tongue
beginning a slow gentle trail across her flesh, teasing and
tantalizing. He knew he trembled with the efforts he made to
control his passion, and his wife trembled even more when
he slid a hand down over her belly. It was almost more than
he could bear and began to loose control of his own senses
at the feel of her hips lifting willingly to him and her nails
lightly raking his back.

Lydia kissed his face and his fingers every chance she had,
and wound her hands in his luscious dark hair, holding him
tightly, her body screaming for his invasion as she felt him
press against her, big and hard where he lay close to her thighs,
almost there, almost touching her own soft flesh.

She wanted him.

"Luke, Luke, oh, it's too much . . ."

"I remember," he said, flicking his hair from his face, "you once said you wouldn't have me if I were the last man on earth." He moved and kissed her belly.

"Mmmm, perhaps . . . oh, Luke."

"I also said that I'd not have you unless you begged of me," he said, his eyes twinkling. He stroked a finger, light as a feather, between her thighs until she squirmed and gasped. "Now, shall you beg me?"

"You, you . . ." She groaned. "You . . . pig . . . oh, please."

"Indeed, my love." He laughed softly and closed his eyes briefly before he moved over her, wondering at how she trembled for him.

He was hot, hard, and just a vague pressure. Then he moved, long, slow and deliberate. Lydia wanted to cry out, but her voice deserted her and all she heard was a soft moan deep in her throat. Her mind wanted to shout to the heavens at the impossible sensations tearing her apart with pleasure, as her body took on a life of its own and moved in perfect symmetry with her husband's. She was aware of very little for a long while, except an all-consuming, ever-raging tide of incredible delight that ebbed and flowed spiralling her onwards and upwards on a seemingly endless flight, soaring through the boundaries of all credible pleasure. Lydia heard her own voice. She heard Luke's voice as the whole world crashed and sang around her. Was she screaming when she finally let go? She didn't know, and she didn't care as she tumbled down, down on a glorious helter-skelter of ecstasy that left her sobbing and spent and holding on tightly to the man she never intended to let go.

"You're crying, my love," he said and leaned to wipe a stray tear.

"Just happy," she whispered. "Just very, very happy."

TWENTY - FIVE

"You should be here to say good-bye to Jack later today," Luke said, slipping a hand inside his wife's gown and around her naked waist.

"He's leaving?" She turned from the window and swung around to face him.

"Aye." Luke kissed her.

"But I thought you'd asked him to stay on here?"

He held her tightly in a comfortable embrace. "I tried to convince him."

"Where will he go? I mean what will he do? Will he . . . ?" She watched her husband roll his light blue eyes heavenwards.

"He could have gotten a pardon, I'm sure of it. There are some who think favourably of him."

"You mean he'll go on being a highwayman." She looked at the carpet.

"That and a few other things." He lifted her chin with a finger. "He's a fine judge of horseflesh, remember," he said and smiled.

"Oh, Luke, he shouldn't go back out there." She lowered her eyes and refused to meet his gaze.

"You know things. But I entreat you not to repeat those things." He put a finger to her lips. "You cannot, nay must not, interfere with fate, my love. Do you believe me?"

She hesitated and chewed her lip a moment. "You're right."

"One never knows what fate may have in store. Mayhap, by token of your being here, things may change. We shall no doubt see."

"I hope so." She grimaced. Perhaps she had already changed the highwayman's future. "When will he be here? I want to be certain I don't miss him." Lydia grinned suddenly. "I like Jack. I like him a lot and I trust him. He'd do anything for you, you know." She stopped, realising her eyes were misting.

"Aye, I've known him some years, and I too trust him—with my life. Now come, what say we try a ride this fine morn? I believe I'm quite well healed."

"You're sure? It's one thing to make mad, passionate love the whole night, but galloping about on a horse, well, I don't know." Lydia widened her eyes and blinked.

Luke raised his eyebrows. "Perhaps then I should make mad, glorious love with you again instead?"

"Mad, passionate love," she corrected.

"This gown comes off with little effort," he whispered into her ear. "Though it need not even come off," he mused, shuffling his hands further into the folds of the material.

"For you to have your wicked way, you mean, Your Lordship?" She leaned up and kissed his mouth while her hands pulled loose the sash at his waist and opened his robe.

Luke growled low in his chest, loving the way she leaned on him and pressed against his hot, eager flesh, snuggling herself around him. She wanted him again.

"Lift me up," she whispered and fixed her arms firmly around his neck.

"As you wish, my love." He did as she asked and felt soft, naked flesh yield to him.

"You won't drop me, will you?" she gasped.

"Nay, love, I can hold you well enough. Wrap your legs around me and hold tight with your arms; I'll soon have you firm." He grasped her backside and shifted his feet to improve his balance, letting out a low groan about the same time as Lydia gave a little shriek and a long-drawn-out sigh. "There now"—he bent his knees slightly and began moving her hips against his own in a slow rhythmic swaying motion—"I have you firm, very firm indeed."

He moved steadily, and then all restraint gone he staggered backwards, his breath short and drawn. He barely made it to the bed before he lost his balance.

"I couldn't stand straight," he gasped and managed to lay her down on the bed without disengaging himself. "Love, I think you shall surely kill me." He shuddered at her nails raking his back in frenzied desperate need as she curled her legs high about his waist and held him there.

Lydia had scant coherent thought and saw, through half-closed eyes, the pleasure and agony that tightened her husband's face as uncontrollable ripples rocked her against a raging tide, suffusing her body with fire, intensifying with every thrust his hard flesh made inside her. She cried out her need, begging that he take her higher, "Luke . . . don't stop."

"Lydia," he gasped, "I . . . oh, my love . . ." He drew out the last word in a strangled cry—he had no intention of stopping.

* * *

Lydia lay in a sweaty embrace and murmured something incomprehensible to the wonderful blue-eyed man at her side, who was idly stroking her face. "Oh, my," she murmured, "it's eleven o'clock already."

"Aye, I needs must dress myself," Luke said lazily and gently stroked an errant lock of hair from her face. "Your hair, it grows at a rare old rate. 'Tis wild like you," he laughed and licked her cheek.

"Ick!" She giggled and rolled away. "Do you really think it's growing?"

"Aye, an inch or more since you came here."

"Good, and it seems in better condition that it used to be."

"'Tis the eighteenth century air," Luke laughed. "Damnation, eleven o' clock you say. I should make ready to meet with Jack and go over any details we may have forgotten. I'm afraid our gallop will have to wait until another time." He kissed Lydia and jumped up from the bed.

She watched him walk across the room, naked. He was a finely built specimen, heavily muscled, yet he moved with the grace of an athlete. She gave her best Hollywood-heroine sigh a little more loudly that she had intended.

He turned around. "You are sighing for more? Wife, you may almost be too much for me. Or have you needs must feast you eyes upon my naked body just to be certain all 'tis not a dream," he said with a wicked grin and continued walking into his dressing room.

"I must admit you're not bad when it comes to the bed and the body thing," she shouted after him and shrugged her shoulders. Although she couldn't see him, she knew he'd be listening intently, no doubt waiting for some other compliment, be it as it may a back-handed one. "I'd say you're a bit above average," she called out happily.

"And I'd say you're one devil of a liar," he called back. "At least that's the impression I get when your legs are wrapped around me, begging me to . . ."

"Luke! Shhh . . . there's someone at the door." She could still hear him grumbling away to himself about his prowess between the sheets as she answered the knock. "Come in."

A servant entered and enquired whether they would take lunch in His Lordship's chamber or the dining room.

"We'll eat in the library in an hour," Luke called out then waited for the man to leave and walked back into the bedroom, his breeches partly fastened. He held the waistband together with a hand while he wiped his face on a towel. "I'll see you in the library in a while, my love. Allow us half an hour." He finished fastening his breeches and pulled Lydia against his bare chest. "'Tis the worst job donning breeches such a short while after partaking of your sweet delights, and damnably uncomfortable, if you must know. And now, my love, I must go."

"The poet quite becomes you." She smiled sweetly. "Now get your bloody shirt on, and go meet Jack in the library. I'll be there when I've washed and dressed."

"Now I have the answer to that question of mine," he called as he left the room.

Lydia frowned and took her time wriggling into her shift and stays, drawing them only moderately tight. She had moved most of her clothing into Luke's room at his suggestion even though it would have been quite normal for her to retain her own room. He had plans to have a wall or two demolished and extend their bedchamber to include private dressing rooms, but had fiercely objected to her having a separate bedroom. He seemed convinced it was the reason many marriages floundered and said he had no intention of his marriage floundering because of a lack of intimacy. The aching Lydia felt in targeted areas of her body each time she moved was testimony to that fact.

She was happy. She had everything in the world to be happy for, except not being able to let her sister know she was alive and well; perhaps somehow she could insert something in a history book or leave something in the keeping of a solicitor. But then, wouldn't she be changing history? Never having considered the possibilities deeply before, she couldn't work out what changed if something happened before a future event or after it, but she knew the ramifications were far reaching and inevitably held an element of danger.

After twenty minutes, Lydia realised she should have called her maid. Even dressing in a simple wraparound gown would have been easier with assistance. Nevertheless, she dressed to her satisfaction and took a last twirl in front of a huge mirror, her gown secured with a diamond-encrusted brooch Luke had given to her along with the rest of the stuff from his grandmother's box of trinkets—as he called them. Lydia snorted. Trinkets indeed. She supposed he would call the crown jewels mere baubles. She looked down at the ring on the third finger of her left hand. It was simple yet surprisingly intricate when viewed closely and care taken to note the fine weave of gold, brushed like hair and turned into a golden braid of shimmering colour inlaid with five small and perfect pink pearls.

She knew Luke wasn't too happy for her to exhibit it as her permanent wedding ring, but for now he appeared content, and Lydia was just certain she would talk him around. She remembered Darwin's ring. It and the bike had to go back. She shoved her feet into a pair of slippers and opened the bedroom door just as a maid was about to knock. "Yes?"

"Oh, milady, I jus' come to mend the fire, that's all."

"I thought perhaps you'd come to hurry me along to see Mr. Palmer before he leaves," she said with a grin.

"Mr. Palmer ain't been by today, leastways not in the past hour 'e ain't."

Lydia thought a moment then said, "Well, not to worry eh?" She picked up her skirts and made her way along to the library. Jack was up to his tricks again, sneaking in through the panels in the wall whenever he wanted his presence unknown. He could appear and disappear without a sound, and she still found that a little unnerving.

Luke sat in the library trying to straighten the folds of his shirt inside his breeches without removing his waistcoat.

"You should dress yourself properly before you receive visitors," Jack observed.

"Told me to get my bloody shirt on and about threw me out of the room," Luke grumbled good-naturedly.

"I see she's a match for you. Now I may leave you in safe hands."

"Aye, that you may. Rest assured, Jack, I'll care for her well." He answered the question he was certain his friend would ask.

"She's a fine woman, and she'll make a fine mother. Mark my words, Luke, you'll have a brood at your feet in no time." He held his glass in the air. "To you and yours."

"To his and which?" Lydia entered the room and laughed, holding out her hands as Jack strode forwards. She offered the side of her face and giggled when he planted a kiss, first on one side then the other and again on the first one.

"I am part French you know, somewhere," Jack announced and laughed.

"Enough with my wife, you lecherous scoundrel," Luke interjected. "Lydia, Jack has something for you."

"For me?"

"'Tis a gift I thought of the night we rode out."

"You're giving me Black Bess," she said, open mouthed and beaming from ear to ear.

Luke burst out laughing at Jack's abject look of horror.

"Nay, I fear . . . I . . . could never . . ."

"It's all right, Jack," Lydia assured him. "I was only joking. Believe me, I'd never wish to take Bess from you. Though of course, if you ever want to bring her by for me to ride, I wouldn't object."

Jack Palmer let out a long breath. "She had my heart racing there, Luke. Nay, lass, here's what I have for you." He lifted a package from the floor and handed it to her.

"What is it?" Lydia said, foolishly holding the string and doing nothing else. "It's quite heavy."

"You might try opening it," Luke suggested dryly.

She stuck her tongue out at him then proceeded to pull the package to bits. She gasped as yard upon yard of midnight blue velvet tumbled down around her feet. "I don't know what to say, Jack. It's beautiful."

"I hoped you'd like it. I remembered the woman in the coach was wearing a riding habit, and I thought something of that ilk would suit you, so with the permission of your husband . . ."

"Thank you, Jack. I'll have it made up as soon as I can. I love the colour." She plopped the material in a pile and rushed to hug a surprised Jack Palmer and planted a kiss on his cheek. "Thank you again. It's lovely."

"That's twice now," Luke commented drolly from his seat.

"What?" two voices said in unison.

"That you've kissed him, that ruffian, Palmer. I demand you come here and offer me the same favour."

"Oh, he demands so much, Jack. What do you think?"

"I've seen him throw a tantrum a time or two," Palmer said. "I'd say you should placate him forthwith."

Without further ado, Lydia sauntered across the room, sat on her husband's lap and kissed him softly on the lips. "There, satisfied?"

"As much as I am able, while we have company." He grinned. "Well, Jack, shall you not reconsider?"

"Nay, I must take my leave of you. I have a desire to travel south again."

"To London?" Lydia said, glancing at Jack.

"Aye, indeed. Now, Luke will you have a man bring the sorrel from the cottage? I have no further need of it for the time being."

"I'll fetch it myself in the morn," Luke assured him. "The less prying eyes out there, the better. Though I trust we'll not need to use the place for such purposes again."

"It would make a nice retreat," Lydia put in. "You know somewhere to go to be quiet and alone. Peaceful."

"Fanciful ideas these future women," Luke said and gave her a squeeze.

"I wish you and your lady good health and happiness," Jack said rubbing his chin thoughtfully. "Mayhap you might invite me to a christening sometime soon." He winked at Lydia.

She got to her feet, aided by a little shove from Luke who came to stand behind her. "Take care, Jack," she said softly. She wanted to throw her arms around his neck and hug him again, but if she did the tears would come and she would likely blab everything she'd ever read in the history books about Dick Turpin.

Jack studied her face for a moment. There was something in her eyes, something she wouldn't say and he wasn't about to ask. "I'm off then." He took Luke's offered hand in his own and pulled him forwards, slapping him soundly on the back. Then he stepped to the panelling and slipped his fingers behind a carving. The panel pushed back easily at a seemingly light pressure from his hand. He stepped through the opening and turned briefly. "Fear not, pretty miss; they'll not pull the cart out from under Dick Turpin's feet." With that, he disappeared into the darkness, sliding the panel closed behind him.

"How does he manage without a candle?" Lydia said mindlessly, still mulling over the highwayman's last words.

"'Tis almost a straight run, and he knows it better than the back of his own hand. Come, love, sit with me by the fire." Luke took her hand and pulled her into his lap. "You must forget these future things that plague you. Fate will do what it will." He kissed her nose. "It brought you to me." He kissed her nose again. "And I pray God it shall allow you to remain," he added quietly.

This time Lydia beat him to it and kissed him quickly on the mouth. "I'll have the dressmaker start on my riding habit tomorrow. I can hardly believe Jack thought of it for me."

"Something I should have thought of myself," Luke groused.

"You were nearly dead as I recall. The trouble is with a wonderful new riding habit I'll have no excuse for wanting to ride astride," she grumbled.

"You, my love, may ride however you bloody well want. I'll have breeches made for you, and propriety be damned." A wicked glint stole into his eye corner. "You're the wife of Lord Beckham. He's well known for his wild ways and doing just what the devil he pleases."

"We'll tell everyone it's what they wear in Outer Mongolia or some such place," Lydia laughed and wrapped her arms around him. "And you know, I think I like Lord Beckham's wild ways, within reason, of course." She sighed happily. "Who'd have thought I'd ever end up with . . . ?"

Then she was silent as he wove his fingers into the back of her hair, and a pair of light blue eyes held her for a second before he leaned forwards and brushed her lips with his own.

"Someone like me," he offered before kissing her deeply.

"Mmmmm . . . ," she managed. A shudder ran all the way to her toes, and suddenly she was completely absorbed by her husband's mouth—unaware that anything else existed.

TWENTY-SIX

Lydia glanced at the clock on the mantelpiece. There was time before dinner to take the bike up the road, stick it in the ditch, and walk back. She would tell Luke what she had done after the fact—he'd only fuss. Pulling her cloak tightly about her, she tucked her arms inside its folds, Darwin's diamond engagement ring firmly gripped in her fist. She shivered and looked up at the desolate grey sky. Autumn would soon turn to winter and then to spring. Lydia pondered the idea of spring in the eighteenth century as she trudged towards the gatehouse. The door to the cubby-hole was locked, so she walked around and knocked on the gatehouse door. Judd was home, still nursing a bruised skull but otherwise back to his old self. He opened the door and grinned widely at her.

"Glad to see you back on your feet, Judd."

"Part in thanks to ye, milady."

"We have you to thank for His Lordship's life," she said quietly. "If you hadn't insisted I warn him . . . I can't even think about what might have happened."

"Seems it near on did. Aye, an' I 'ear 'twere that wench at the Bell give 'is Lordship that sleepin' potion. She be jealous

o' ye or some such thing. A bad do, that." He shook his head
and tutted.

"I should beat the living daylights out of her by rights,"
Lydia growled.

"Aye, but ye be a lady, an' ladies ain't supposed to do that
sort o' thing."

"Don't you believe it, Judd. If she tries anything else, I'll
throttle her, I swear I will."

"Ye would an' all."

"Judd, I need my bike, and the door's locked. Can you
open it for me?"

"His Lordship's orders, but I got the key 'ere on my belt."
He led the way around the back and began to fumble with the
lock. "Said it best be locked out o' the way o' pryin' eyes."

"That's probably true, but after today it won't be around
to be pried upon," Lydia said confidently. Tugging the bike
from the recess, she unzipped the little bag strapped to the
frame and dropped Darwin's ring unceremoniously inside.
Then she looked at the ring on her third finger. Even the
biggest best-cut diamond in the world could never be as dear
to her as the Spanish gold and pearls she wore on her left
hand. "You never saw this bike, Judd. It's important you forget
all about it."

"I understands." He nodded his head.

"When I come back I'll have a toddy with you." She nudged
him and said, "Might be the last chance we get before your
wife comes back, and then you'll have to behave yourself."

"Just like 'is Lordship." He grinned. "Ye be fair suited
together."

Lydia waved him a cheery bye and set off, peddling down
the road as fast as she dare, which wasn't very fast given she
was wearing an enormous skirt and a cloak. Batman, Mary
Poppins, even the prince of darkness flitted through her mind,
but she didn't care what she looked like as long as she wasn't
seen—and didn't disappear—along with the bike and the ring
back to the twenty-first century.

She reached her destination without mishap and dismounted. Autumn leaves lay here and there, herded into little mounds by the chill wind, and Lydia found it difficult to see exactly where her point of arrival had been. Grasping the bike firmly by the handlebars, she pushed it through the leaves and over a small hillock, turning to survey the scene. This was it; this was where it had happened. Taking a few steps backwards, she stopped and looked again, certain now that she was standing in the exact spot where she had arrived in the eighteenth century.

"I'll miss you, bike," she said ruefully and let it fall, complete with its little bag, into the leaves. Her hand strayed to her right hip and burrowed in the folds of her gown until she found the folded piece of paper she written on earlier. Should she send it? If she tried to send it and it wasn't supposed to go, what was the worst that could happen? Likely, everything would stay where it was. She dropped to her knees and unzipped the bag, then with a last doubtful look, she stuffed the piece of paper inside and closed the zipper.

With a long sigh, she stood up and stepped back hurriedly, in case fate got a bit too eager. Now she was here to stay, she was sure. Smiling to herself and with a sudden spring in her step, she turned and almost skipped out of the clearing. A faint rustle caught her ear, but she ignored it, far too happy to worry about some small scurrying creature in the undergrowth. There it was again, nearer this time and somehow it sounded heavier. She turned, and at the same instant her eyes widened in fear.

She screamed.

*   *   *

"Have you seen my wife?" Luke said casually to the man lighting candles in his study.

"Indeed, I have not, milord."

Luke had spent most of the day preoccupied with business and the latter part making lists of his inglorious relatives, all of whom would be most insulted if they were not invited to a splendid ball in honour of his recent marriage. He still hadn't decided whether Lydia and he should wed again somewhere grand and imposing, like the great cathedral at York. Lydia had stated that she wasn't concerned about a big wedding. That they were legally wed was all she needed to know. Luke had mentally puffed out his chest at this and realised for the umpteenth time how much he loved her—even though she swore at him now and again. He looked up as the clock struck three. Surely she had finished with the dressmaker, and he felt certain that's where she was. She'd been eager to start on the blue velvet.

"Begging your pardon, milord." The man lighting candles coughed a little nervously.

"Yes, what is it?"

"Now I recall seeing her ladyship leaving the house sometime afore two o'clock."

"She went riding then, no doubt." Why hadn't she come to find him? He would have taken the time to go with her.

"She went down the main driveway. Walking, milord."

Luke was on his feet. "Walking? Where the hell would she be walking to?" The answer hit him in a flash; she had gone to see Judd. Almost without thought, he reached for his sword, a strange unease creeping over him.

He pounded down the stairway and grabbed a surtout from its peg. It didn't take long to saddle a horse and ride it to the gatehouse. Luke dropped lightly from his mount's back and winced slightly at the pain in his side. The wound was healing fast but from time to time gave him a swift reminder of that awful night.

"Judd, are you there?" He banged on the door only once before it was flung, wide open. "Where's my wife, Judd?" He tried peering into the recesses of the room.

"She ain't 'ere, sir. She were, 'bout an hour ago."

"She didn't come to see you then, see how you are, I mean."

"Oh aye, sir, then she took that contraption somewhere, said something about it bein' out o' the way o' pryin' eyes fer good. Then she were comin' back to 'ave a toddy." He beamed at this last comment.

"She should be on her way back by now if she's taken the thing back whence it came," Luke muttered. "Thank you, Judd, I'll ride out and meet her." Damnation, she would be bloody freezing by now. Why hadn't she asked him to go with her?

Luke rode steadily, certain he would come across his wife at each bend in the road, but he didn't. He came to the clearing, the clearing where Lydia had seen a man murdered; the place all this had begun. His heart pounded in his chest, and he thought he might choke, so constricted was his throat. Had she had tried to bring the bike here, to send it back? He dismounted and walked towards the back of the clearing. She must be here—she had to be. Fate couldn't be this cruel. He gasped with relief as he spotted the bike in the leaves. Lydia would be here, somewhere. Of course, she had gone back by way of the cottage. It wasn't far and he knew she had a fascination for the place. It was still daylight, but dusk fell quickly this time of year, and darkness soon followed. If he rode swiftly, he could overtake her, and when he found her he would give her a few of his thoughts on the matter of her running off alone. Impulsively, he bent down and unzipped the little bag attached to the bicycle. As he had suspected, nay, hoped, she was sending her engagement ring back to the future. He gave it a last glance and pulled out a piece of paper. He knew no surprise at the words he read; she had written to her sister after all. He shook his head, wondering at the advisability of such an action but then replaced the letter and closed the bag. Reaching down he threw a few handfuls of leaves to cover the bike a little better and staggered to his knees as a tremendous gust of wind swirled across the clearing.

"Damnation!" He made and failed in the attempt to grab his hat and watched as it blew into some trees—sparsely appointed, very slender trees. Luke got to his feet and looked down at the bike, which hadn't moved then he stood for a moment, staring at his three-cornered hat. Slowly he turned around.

"Afternoon," a voice called.

Luke blinked.

"Bit chilly," a second man added and raised a hand.

Luke watched open mouthed as the two scantily clad riders sped by on their miraculous machines. Then he stared out over the great expanse of grey water where a forest should have been.

Dear God—he was in the future.

*   *   *

Luke shook himself and hoped he was dreaming. He closed his eyes and opened them again only to see the self same body of water staring back at him. It was all here just as Lydia had told him. The old forest was gone; in its place was a great expanse of storage water. He retrieved his hat and tugged it down onto his head. If Lydia were here, he would find her, and if she were not—he didn't want to dwell on that possibility. A chill wind blew from the north, and he pulled his surtout around his shoulders, looking once more at the bike as though it might suddenly produce Lydia if he stared at it hard enough. Reluctantly, he dragged it upright. He needed transport, and this machine would have to suffice, though he would have preferred a good fast horse. And he would have preferred to know where he was going. There was only one thing to do, and that was head for Beckham. Someone there would be able to assist him.

He encountered two or three people walking along the road, which he now noted to have a layer of hard black stuff on it, and those people stared at him. He tried to concentrate as he lost his balance yet again and wobbled precariously. It was damnably difficult riding Lydia's infernal machine wearing his jackboots and with his surtout flapping around like a mad thing, and he'd lost count of the times his sword had stuck into the wheel. He breathed a sigh of relief as the dark stone walls of Beckham swam into view. At least something was familiar. The gatehouse looked little changed, but now it bore a large sign. "National Trust," Luke read out loud. "And what pray is that?" He continued reading a brief history of his own home and the days it was open to the public.

"Closed only last week, mate," a cheery man with a dog advised. "Busy it is, right up until the end of the season. You visiting then?" He cast a long unabashed gaze over Luke's attire and grinned. "You with one of those historical societies then? Re-enactment?"

"I, sir, am Lord Beckham, and I wish to enter my own home." Luke drew himself up to his full height and looked down at the man who appeared totally nonplussed.

"Well you won't be getting in here 'til next year sometime. Like I said, it's closed. Locked and barred."

"Who lives here?"

"Well, I suppose there are caretakers, but no one really lives here full time," the man said. "It's been turned into a museum more or less. I haven't been inside it, but I hear it's marvellous, full of art treasures and such."

"What of the family?"

The man shrugged and whistled for his dog, which was foraging in a clump of weeds. It trotted over and began sniffing Luke's feet in a friendly manner. "Couldn't tell you, mate, sorry. Anyhow, best be on my way now; the wife'll have the tea on." So saying, he called the dog to heel and walked off.

Luke glanced down at his sprinkled boots, and then gazed longingly through the gates of what had once been his home. His and Lydia's. The world was desolate without the wife he was privileged to have had for a few short days, and if he hadn't known the futility of such an action, he would have sat down just where he was and wept. Taking a deep breath and a last glance at the gatehouse at Beckham, he set off towards the town, or at least he hoped he did. Who could say what may have transpired in the last few hundred years? He pedalled steadily, almost coming to grief as a terrifyingly noisy object on wheels screamed past him. He knew it to be one of the cars Lydia had told him of, but her description hadn't prepared him for actually coming face to face with the damn things. That he would be dead should one collide with his person, he was without doubt.

Dusk crept in, and Luke could see lights in the distance. Good, he was coming into the town. Another car flew past; Luke winced at the closeness and apparent abandon with which these drivers flung their carriages along. The lights grew brighter, and a low rumbling became a loud roaring.

He rounded a bend and came suddenly upon a great conglomeration of bright lamps set on long stems reaching high into the evening sky and organized in what appeared to be a circle. Cars and other extraordinary mechanized carriages flew in and out of the circle at a truly alarming rate. Luke's head spun. He stopped the bike and felt a trickle of cold sweat find its way under his shirt and down his back. Bloody hell, he had no idea what to do in this new world. If Lydia had been afraid in his world, he was damnably fearful in hers. As he watched, all manner of vehicles whizzed around the complex of roads, and he began to see the links with inventions in his own time, humble beginnings to be sure, but look what had grown from them.

It was growing colder and darker, and Luke reckoned his chances of survival were slim if he wandered about on these roads in the dark, and he didn't relish spending the night in a ditch. He had money; he would find an inn somewhere. He looked for the best way to cross the first of the roads and, making a decision, climbed off the bike and began to walk with it.

Eeeeeeoww! An enormous carriage almost took the back of the bike with it as it flew by. Luke moved to a run, spurred on by thoughts of self preservation, and found himself suddenly sprawled in the damp grass. A sharp pain shot through his ankle, and he grabbed it with both hands then rolled into a sitting position, noting the already apparent swelling. He tried to stand and found he couldn't put weight on his foot. He could manage to hop on one leg if he held on to the bike but was certain there were more of those blasted holes lurking out there just waiting to trip him. The alternative to reaching an inn at some distant point versus sleeping in the grass was the only thing that spurred him on—slowly.

* * *

"Charlie, cop a look at that." The truck driver's mate pointed to where the glare of the headlights picked up a figure hopping along the grass verge, on one leg and pushing a bicycle.

"Looks like he's limping," Charlie responded.

"Think he needs a lift?"

"He's limping pretty badly. Hang on I'll pull over."

Luke heard the strange new noise as air brakes chugged and squealed but didn't look up at first. Only when he realised one of the giant carriages was coming backwards towards him did he take notice and prepare to move very quickly out of its way if the need arose. The vehicle backed up slowly and stopped a few yards away. A man opened the nearside door and dropped to the ground from the high cab.

"Want a lift, mate?"

"Thank you," Luke called and attempted to hop more quickly. He didn't find the man's words familiar but he assumed they were an offer of help. "I most certainly appreciate your assistance."

The man standing by the vehicle wore a strange expression as he looked at Luke standing near the open door under the glow of the interior light. "Thank you again for your kind offer," Luke said, wondering at the man's sudden lack of communication.

"Come on, Bert, help him put his bike in the back, and let's be off," the driver called.

"Aye . . . all right," Bert said and moved to take the bike from Luke's hands.

"Climb up in the cab. Can you manage?"

"Indeed, sir, I am able," Luke responded to the unseen driver, and taking advantage of the grab handles hauled himself into the cab with little effort. "Good evening."

Charlie let the cigarette he'd been about to light fall from his mouth. "Bloody hell!"

Luke said nothing. His clothing would no doubt be cause for much speculation, and he may indeed have to think on that matter if he were to be stuck in this century for any length of time. He hoped he would not be, at least not without Lydia.

Bert climbed back in the cab and shut the door without saying a word.

Charlie put the engine into gear, and the vehicle crawled out into the lane of traffic.

Luke sat mesmerized in the darkness of the cab, watching as they sped around other vehicles and other vehicles passed them. "It was very kind of you to help me," Luke said at length unable to bear the silence. "I was looking for the town of Low Beckham. I hope to find accommodation."

"Think nothing of it," the man sitting on his left, muttered. "It's about a hundred feet under water. They flooded it fifty years ago when they built the reservoir."

Luke's stomach churned. He remembered vaguely having heard Lydia say something similar the day she showed him the man's body. He glanced at the driver, illuminated for a moment by the lights of another vehicle. The man looked as though he had seen a ghost. Luke realised it was probably his clothing and said, "I believe you think my clothing strange."

"A bit," the driver said.

"Historical re-enactment," he said, remembering the words of the man with the dog.

Both men visibly relaxed at his words and started to laugh.

"Historical re-enactment, you hear that, Bert? Well now that's all right then." Charlie chuckled some more and said,

"There we were thinking we had another like that lass we picked up couple or so years ago. This very stretch of road it were."

"No, the A64," Bert corrected.

"Oh, aye. Close enough though. That were something." Charlie glanced briefly at Luke before fixing his eyes on the road again. "Aye, we picked up a lass wearing all this historical clothing, barely able to walk. Frozen she were. 'Bout this time o' year too. Had walked all the way to the road from that place—what were it, Bert?"

"Some hall somewhere," Bert said. "Anyhows, where can we drop you? Seeing as how you'll not find Low Beckham."

Luke thought for a moment. "Faversham Park?"

"Can't say I know it," Bert answered. "But we're not so far off Foxworth. That's right, it was Foxworth she said she walked from. Is that any good to you? We can drop you pretty close."

"Foxworth! Home of the Somersby-Griffiths. Do they still live there?"

Bert blew out a breath. "We could drop him at the next intersection, and he can walk to the pub in the village; they do bed and breakfast."

Charlie nodded. "Can you walk at all?"

"Indeed, I believe I shall be able to make a short distance. How far is Foxworth from the er, pub?"

"Ten miles or so, not too far. There's likely a bus runs by there."

Luke didn't bother to ask what a bus was. In the morning, after a good night's rest, he would travel to Foxworth. Lydia's words about a quest had been praying on his mind. What if he were here for the same thing? Yes, he would return the bike whence it came and the ring to its previous owner. Damn the idea of having to encounter Lydia's former lover, but he would do it and gladly. Anything so he could return to his wife.

A few miles farther on, the vehicle chugged and squealed to a halt.

"Can't take this thing through the village," Charlie said, "but it's only a short walk. Think you can make it?"

"I believe so, and I thank you, sirs." Luke began to climb out of the cab. Gingerly he tested his foot on the ground. It still hurt like hell, but he could use it for balance.

"Hang on there, and I'll get your bike; you'll need something to hold on to." Bert walked into the darkness.

Luke hobbled after him supporting himself on the vehicle with one hand. "The girl," he said, suddenly recalling Charlie's words, "the one you said you found dressed strangely. What befell her?"

Bert scratched his head. "We took her to the hospital. She came out of it all right, but she still stuck to her story. Crackers she was, nice enough though."

Luke watched as Bert pulled the bicycle from the back of the truck. "What story was that?"

"That she'd just come from another century. Travelled in time she said."

Luke took a deep breath, suddenly very interested. "Which century, did she say?"

"Not sure. Ask Charlie; he's better at all that stuff. He likes history. Hey, Charlie?"

"What's that?" Charlie shouted from the cab.

"That lass, the one we picked up. What century did she say she'd come from?"

"Do you remember?" Luke said eagerly, taking hold of the bike and hobbling to the open door.

"Eighteenth I think. Late seventeen hundreds." The driver lit a cigarette then took a long drag and looked at Luke carefully. "You know a lot about history, I suppose, being that you do re-enactment."

"Aye," Luke nodded. Suddenly there was hope. If someone else had travelled . . . perhaps he could get help. If only he knew where to start looking. "You don't know where I might find this girl?"

"Sorry, mate, all I know is her dad paid us nicely for picking her up off the roadside," Charlie concluded. "C'mon, Bert, best be off."

Bert climbed back in the cab. "Take care of that ankle now. Red Lion." He pointed straight down the road.

Luke watched the tail lights fade into the distance.

"Strange one that," Charlie said and puffed on his cigarette.

"If you ask me," Bert said slowly, "he was from no re-enactment society."

"Think we should have told him the rest then?"

Bert shook his head. "Albert Thompson paid us well for helping his daughter and for keeping quiet about what she went through."

"True." Charlie grinned. "That young fella will find out what he needs to know without our interference, I'm sure of it." He changed down and floored the accelerator. "Come on let's get this load to the yard. I'm ready for a pint."

TWENTY-SEVEN

"Luke hopped and cursed his way down the road towards a huddle of lights. The Red Lion was thankfully at the near end of the street, and he pushed the bike into a small entry and propped it against the wall.

With a sigh he realised he hadn't a hope in hell of blending in with the local population and taking a fortifying deep breath, he pulled his three-cornered hat firmly onto his head. He would continue his pretence to belong to a re-enactment society, although he still wasn't quite certain he knew what one did, should anyone ask. He pushed open the heavy wooden door and entered the Red Lion, grateful it wasn't busy. A handful of men clustered around the bar, and only one or two turned to see who had come in. Luke found he was the centre of attraction for a few seconds until good manners and the need for a drink overcame the men.

"Good evening, sirs." He lifted his hat and replaced it on his head. "Re-enactment, hence my clothing," he offered hastily. "'Tis cold out tonight. I would have a drink to warm me landlord."

"Bitter?" the man behind the bar asked.

Luke paused, his glance straying to the glasses of the other men. "Your ale looks admirable."

"Bitter it is then."

"Come and stand over here by the fire," called a man wearing a corduroy jacket.

"Kind of you, sir." Luke hobbled across the room and bent down by the fire, rubbing his hands together in front of the welcome heat.

"Hurt your foot?"

Luke turned to face the man. "Aye, I slipped. 'Tis not broken but it hurts like the devil" He shrugged out of his surtout and laid it across the back of a chair, dropping his hat down by it.

The man nodded. "I imagine."

"Here you are then." The landlord pushed a pint glass of creamy topped beer across the bar.

"Of course." Luke turned back to the bar, unbuttoned his frock, and pulled out his purse.

"Some waistcoat," remarked a man standing close by.

Luke glanced at the gold and blue brocade of his clothing. "'Tis fashionable," he commented and pulled a couple of coins out of the purse and put them on the bar.

Several men burst into laughter. One slapped Luke on the back and commended him on his nice try.

The landlord shook his head. "Can't take these, mate."

Luke found his response cut short.

"I'll get that," the man in the corduroy jacket said.

"Thank you." Luke extended a hand. "Waverly, Luke Waverly, at your service, sir." He decided it prudent to keep his title quiet.

"Dennis Hardcastle," the man responded and offered a firm handshake. "Pleased to make your acquaintance." He fingered the coins on the bar. "Interesting coins. Where did you get them?"

"They were not dishonestly come by, I assure you, sir," Luke said with a grin, picking the coins up.

"No, no I didn't think for one minute they were. I'm a collector you see. He indicated a couple of stools and a small table at the far side of the fire. "Why don't we sit down."

Luke took his drink, followed the man to the table, and seated himself.

"Do you have any more coins, like those I mean?"

"You say you're a collector. Then you know about coins and history. For instance why Beckham Park is closed?"

"Probably the end of the season; I don't know it too well," Dennis Hardcastle said. "Let me see those again, would you?"

Luke watched as the man turned the coins over in his hand, then brought a little eyeglass out of his pocket and examined them closely.

"They're authentic all right," he said eventually. "If you need money, I'll buy these from you. And I'll give you a fair price."

Luke considered his situation a moment and agreed to the man's proposal. "Aye, I shall need money for a room tonight. In fact, I needs must ask the innkeeper what accommodations he has."

"You do well with your speech; you could almost be from the seventeen hundreds," the man commented. "Practiced a lot have you?"

"I have indeed."

"How did you get here?"

"I am riding a bicycle." Luke wondered at the man's interest.

"Dressed like that it can't be easy."

"Nay, 'tis damnably difficult. 'Twas as I pushed the bloody thing that I fell and wrenched my ankle." Luke thought for a moment. "Do you know how far it is to Foxworth Hall?"

"Aye, the Somersby-Griffith's pile. It's about twelve miles, a bit less maybe, but might I ask why you want to go there? I don't recall them doing any re-enactment, although they do a great Christmas bash since the new fella took it."

"You attend?"

"I know Sir Philip's father-in-law. It's a grand bit of a do with everybody wearing period clothing. You'd fit right in. Are you a friend of the family?"

Luke took a sip of his beer. "I know of them," he said carefully, wiping the froth off his top lip. "You say you are acquainted with Sir Philip's father-in-law?

"I am. Name's Albert. In fact, he might be in here later tonight. I'll introduce you if you like."

"Indeed, I should be most grateful."

Luke duly organized his accommodation, which proved to be a small room with a small bed, and an even smaller window overlooking the back of the pub, but it was clean and warm. He had future money in his purse with the promise of more whenever he wanted it in return for the coins he carried, and tomorrow he would think about new clothing; something less conspicuous. For the present, he would rest his ankle and satisfy his appetite. He looked at the plate of food before him.

"Albert just walked in." Dennis Hardcastle nodded in the direction of the bar.

Luke swivelled his head to look at a portly man of medium height wearing a flat cap and a large baggy woollen garment over brown trousers.

The man looked across and raised a hand. Then picking up his pint, he came to join them by the fireplace. "Don't think I know your friend here, Dennis." The man placed his beer on the table and pulled up a chair.

"Meet Luke Waverly. He's part of a re-enactment society. He fell off his bike and sprained his ankle. I just bought some coins, and quite remarkable they are. Oh, and he knows Foxworth."

"Coins, you say." The newcomer turned and looked first at Luke's boots and then at his breeches and waistcoat. His eyes lingered on the three-cornered hat. "The hat, I presume is yours? May I?"

Luke placed his knife and fork on the table and wiped his hands on his napkin before retrieving his hat from its place by the fireplace and handing it to the man.

The man in the baggy sweater studied the hat, turning it over several times, examining the lining. "Nice workmanship," he said and handed it back. "I'm Albert Thompson, by the way." He held out a hand.

"Luke Waverly, at your service."

"So, you're into this re-enactment thing, are you?"

"I am, sir."

"And you say you know Foxworth Hall?" Albert Thompson sipped on his beer and watched Luke closely.

Luke was aware of the man's scrutiny and a little disturbed by it. He picked up his own glass. "I know a branch of the Somersby-Griffiths." He stifled a yawn, painfully aware of his increasing fatigue.

"You know my son-in-law?"

Luke drank a couple of mouthfuls and placed his glass down on the table. "Not exactly."

Albert Thompson pulled a few notes out of his pocket. "Dennis, fetch us another drink would you, while I get to know this young man."

"Well, if you're paying." Dennis Hardcastle stood and ambled over to the bar.

Albert Thompson waited until the man was out of earshot leaned forwards and said, "Why are you here?"

"I . . ." Luke paused, suspicious of the man called Albert Thompson who appeared to see right through him. "I am, as I said, a member of a . . ."

He leaned closer. "You're no more part of a re-enactment group than I am. What are you doing here?"

Luke took a deep breath, uncertain of the man's motives, but what had he to lose by being honest? "I have no idea. 'Twas an accident, and I would like to get back. I just got married."

"Pretty was she?" The man gave a half smile.

"Beautiful," Luke breathed. "The most incredible woman I've ever known." Coming back to reality he added, "How did you know?"

"Let's just say I guessed. And your hat, there's something about the way that particular manufacturer put in his stitches. My son-in-law has one that's almost identical. An heirloom. It was his grandfather's."

Luke relaxed. The man was becoming quite genial. He picked up his drink then put it back on the table. "His grandfather's? Surely not?" He grinned over his glass. "I think perhaps a few more generations. I am assuming they"—he nodded at his hat—"are not normal attire in this century."

Albert Thompson looked at him without smiling. "Nor have they been for about two hundred years. Most certainly it belonged to his grandfather. Would you like me to introduce you to Philip?"

"You're saying then . . . ," Luke began incredulously, a feeling of trepidation rising in his chest, edging its way past the hope he held tight there.

"I'm saying that we'll say no more on the matter, and tomorrow if you like, I'll pick you up and drive you out to Foxworth."

Luke felt the hope surge within him. "I thank you, most sincerely."

"Here we are then." Dennis Hardcastle set three glasses of beer on the table and handed over the change.

"Your health, gentleman." Luke held up his glass and waited for the other two. For the first time in the last few hours, he dared himself to see light in the ever-increasing darkness that threatened to engulf him.

He dared to think he might see his wife again.

TWENTY-EIGHT

Luke looked down dubiously at the little red box Albert Thompson called *his Bessie*. Where his legs were going to fit he wasn't sure, but after an encouraging nod or two from the pilot he squeezed himself inside.

"Buckle up then, there's a good lad."

Luke knew he had a blank expression on his face. "I fear, sir, I do not understand."

"Like this."

He watched the short demonstration then followed suit, feeling quite pleased with his mastery of the restraint he was apparently to wear.

"Right then. Let's be off."

If Luke admitted to being a tad nervous, he was being less than honest. He was petrified and clung with his left hand to the door—out of sight of his driver he hoped. It had been one thing sitting in the high-fronted vehicle with Bert and Charlie, but this was a box. A very small, very low box and Albert Thompson threw it around in a most disconcerting manner.

"I called my daughter this morning just to let them know we were coming."

Luke wished the man wouldn't look at him when he was speaking. He would much prefer he keep his eyes on where they were going. "Aye, 'tis best I am not a surprise."

"Oh, you're a surprise well enough, no getting away from it. I just wanted to make sure Philip wasn't off playing rugby or some such thing; has to try everything that man does. Still," Albert Thompson rattled on, glancing at the road now and again, "couldn't wish for a better son-in-law. Got me tickets to the test match last year. You into cricket, are you?" He didn't wait for a reply. "Oh, and he's a really good father to those bairns."

"I take it he is also a good husband to your daughter," Luke put in.

"He is. Worried about her we did, for a while. Never seemed too interested in keeping a fella. Suppose she just hadn't found the right one. What about you then?"

"What mean you?"

"I mean your wife. What's she like?"

Luke felt his stomach lurch once then said, "Beautiful." He settled into a contented daydream and said no more until the car swerved and slowed suddenly, causing him to come up hard against the strap across his chest.

"Almost there."

They drove past two large wrought iron gates.

"The front gates are kept locked," Albert said. "Philip likes his privacy. There's another entrance through a private road half a mile or so down the way."

Luke gazed in wonderment at the well-manicured parkland. How was it that his home was a museum and this place, the home of mere baronets, was still a family home and in pristine condition? The walls demonstrated signs of repair but appeared intact, over eight miles of them as he recalled, smaller than Beckham, but Foxworth had survived.

"Is the house in good repair?" he asked suddenly, a pang of envy tearing at him.

"You'll see for yourself in a few minutes," his driver said and changed gears with a crunch, swinging the little car down a dirt road where a large sign bore the words No Through Road.

As they drew closer, the trees thickened, completely obscuring any view of the house. It seemed Sir Philip and his family indeed had their privacy. All appeared well tended, and a gardener or some such person raised a hand in salute to the little car, and paused to lean on his rake just long enough to watch the vehicle disappear around a curve, through a tunnel of huge beech trees.

The car's tyres scrunched to a halt and skidded slightly on coarse gravel in front of the house. Albert Thompson turned off the ignition and turned to look at his passenger who said not a word.

Luke was speechless. He had visited Foxworth twice that he could remember. Both times he had been fair game for a multitude of unattached young ladies, and both times he had declined all attempts at securing him for the purposes of a marriage contract, though he recalled having shared some mutual pleasures out by the rose gardens where there was a little rotunda. He wondered if it were still there. Nervously, he reached back and fingered the bow in his hair, shaking his head slowly.

"'Tis almost as I remember it," he said quietly.

"Philip had the plumbing done: bathrooms, central heating, all that stuff. My daughter insisted on it. Can't beat good plumbing I always say. Come on then, out you get. Don't forget your hat now."

Easier said than done, Luke thought as he struggled to unfold his legs and make sure they worked before he stood on them. He shivered slightly and pulled his frock around him, then reached into the back seat, glancing briefly at his sword and surtout, which he had been forced to remove in order to fit in the car, before retrieving his three-cornered hat.

"Good morning." A man stood at the top of a short flight of stone steps a girl of about ten at his side.

"Morning, Phil. Hope you've got the kettle on," Albert Thompson responded.

"Always," the man answered with a laugh.

Only then did Luke realise he was being watched. He straightened his breeches and strode purposefully around the back of the little car and joined Albert Thompson at the foot of the stairs. They walked up together. Luke had never felt so self-conscious in his life.

"Look, Dad, like you used to wear," the child said.

"Similar," the man remarked as he held out a hand to Luke. "Philip Somersby-Griffith, at your service."

"Luke Waverly, at yours, sir."

The man who took his hand in a firm grip was perhaps a few years older than Luke and matched him in height, being if anything a little broader. He wore a high-necked black garment over extremely tight breeches, a pair of striped socks reaching almost to his knees, and on his feet were some soft looking things bearing remarkable resemblance to fat furry rabbits. Luke quashed the desire to remark upon his host's footwear. More to his surprise was that the man wore his hair restrained at the nape in a manner similar to his own, slightly longer hair.

Philip hesitated then said, "Waverly, I know the name, but come inside, man. 'Tis bloody cold out here." He flashed his dark eyes once over Luke's person then led the way indoors.

Luke couldn't help but stare around as he was divested of his frock and three-cornered hat by the young girl.

"April, my daughter." Philip laughed. "She finds you quite fascinating."

The girl ran to hang the hat and coat, followed by a small boy who appeared as if out of nowhere, demanding he be allowed to do something. He satisfied himself by grabbing the skirts of Luke's waistcoat and holding on tightly.

"This gentleman is a guest. Remember that, Thomas," Philip admonished, detaching the boy's hands and ruffling his hair. "Why don't you two run upstairs and see if your brother is awake yet?"

The children ran off screaming and giggling, up the wide expanse of stairway to the first floor.

"This is magnificent," Luke said with genuine admiration. "'Tis as I remember it, yet much improved and certainly warmer." He realised no one had heard him and followed the others into a large kitchen, where a young woman was pouring boiling water into a teapot.

"Meet my wife, Robyn. Robyn, this is Luke Waverly, the gentleman your father told us about."

She turned, gasped, and about came to grief with the kettle. "Hell! Oh, I'm sorry, I just wasn't expecting the er, clothing. Dad didn't tell us everything, obviously." She cast a questioning eye at her father. "Well, pleased to meet you, Luke. Sit down and make yourself comfortable. Breakfast is nearly ready. We decided to wait until you two got here. Dad always makes us sit down again if we don't wait for him." She smiled fondly at her father.

Luke took the chair indicated by Philip and looked around the room and up at the ceiling. The lighting system of the future fascinated him. Just a flick of a little switch and a hundred candles came or went.

"Throw the butter in the microwave, would you, love. Fifteen seconds should do it," Robyn said to her husband.

Luke watched mystified as a rectangle of apparently hard butter disappeared into a black and silver box and re-appeared a very short time later ready for spreading.

He couldn't help it; he had to ask.

"Microwave," Philip told him and cast a look at his wife, who cast a similar one back. "I'm not sure myself how the bloody thing works. But 'tis marvellous for softening butter, as you see."

Luke nodded, for the moment satisfied but left wondering for the second time at Philip's manner of speech.

Nothing much was said over the first part of breakfast apart from the niceties of please pass this and that. Everyone, it seemed, had an appetite to satisfy.

Philip placed his knife and fork on his plate and took a sip of tea. "So, Albert tells me you may know my family."

"Luke finished chewing, swallowed his food, and said, "Aye, I do, though quite a way back." That was an understatement.

Philip looked thoughtful for a moment. "How far back? And if I may be so bold as to ask, do you always dress thusly?"

"The second question is most easily answered. I do, though it appears inappropriate at this present time, and I shall endeavour to procure something more suitable."

"And the first question," Philip prompted, not to be put off.

"Several generations."

"I see." He looked at his wife.

She in turn looked at her father who sat with a smug smile on his face. "You didn't tell us everything, did you, Dad?"

"Why spoil the fun," he said, shifting a wedge of grilled tomato around on his plate.

"I fear . . . if there has been some misrepresentation . . . ," Luke said slowly and made as though to get to his feet. "I am sorry to have taken your time."

"Sit down, lad." Albert Thompson waited until Luke re-seated himself before he continued speaking. "Phil, remember that tricorn of yours, the one that belonged to your grandfather?"

"Indeed, the best three-cornered hat I ever owned. They knew how to make hats in those . . . days," he finished uncertainly. "Why?"

He'd said it again. Grandfather. Luke tried to listen to the conversation while he attempted to recall the Foxworth household as he had known it.

"Wasn't it one of a limited commemorative number made a few years after the first Jacobite uprising? Isn't that what you said?"

"Where is this leading, may I ask?" Philip shot his father-in-law a warning look.

"This young fella has one just like it," Albert Thompson responded.

"I see." Philip seemed to consider his words carefully. "Your ancestor's?"

"No, sir," Luke said without hesitation. "'Twas purchased by my own hand, and as I recall I paid the outrageous sum of twelve pounds, ten shillings and sixpence for it, as likely did your grandfather, Frederick. We went hunting together that very week." He looked directly at Philip. "Your grandfather was a little reckless and put his horse at a hedgerow after imbibing several brandies. I'm sure you know the rest of the story."

Philip rose slowly to his feet. "You then must be . . . Damnation! My apologies, Your Lordship. 'Tis a great honour." He made a short bow. "This is incredible." He sat down again, shaking his head. "Robyn, love, meet Lord Beckham." He grinned. "A lord with quite a colourful history."

"Actually, I've read a few things about you," she said, her eyes twinkling. "Quite a life you lead, Your Lordship."

"Luke, please. And I have in fact given up the life for which, it appears, I was best known, and that is one of the reasons I'm here. I need your help."

"How can we help?" Philip said.

"Very simple. I need to return to my own time." He felt a silent lurch in his chest at the thought of his wife. Was she all right? Was she worrying for him? "I was recently married, and I should like to return to my wife."

"I imagine," Philip nodded knowingly. "Can you tell us more of the story? In fact why don't we all go into the drawing room. There's a grand fire blazing, and we can hear your story in comfort."

It was well into the afternoon when Luke finally got his tale out and the details had been satisfactorily digested by all.

"I'm not certain I can help," Philip said. "But I think the first thing is to find your wife's sister and this person called Darwin. It may indeed be as you suggest that returning the bike and the ring to their true places will effect your return home."

Luke nodded. Even though the sixth baronet of Foxwood and his wife hadn't come up with any magical solution, it was comforting to have their support. At their insistence, he agreed to spend the next few days as their guest, and a man was duly dispatched to bring the bike from the pub.

* * *

Philip had connections in the right places, and in less than a week both Lydia's sister and the dreadful Darwin had been unearthed.

Luke, dressed more appropriately in what he learned were jeans, and one of Philip's turtle-neck sweaters, climbed into a sleek silver Volvo wagon alongside Philip, with the bike secured to a rack at the back of the vehicle. Robyn waved good-bye to the children and her parents, who were watching them for the day, and clambered in behind the two men. She had insisted upon accompanying them, stating it would be too intimidating to approach Lydia's sister without her. Imagine you two great hulks arriving on her doorstep with news, as it were, from the grave, she had said.

The two men had nodded in agreement. Luke was somewhat disappointed not to be riding on the back of Philip's amazing two wheeled machine, which the baronet had assured him would do in excess of one hundred and thirty miles an hour and promised to demonstrate the fact as soon as an opportunity arose.

They drove for about an hour until they reached a recently built community of moderately sized houses, each with a perfectly landscaped garden, comprising of an ornamental fountain and slightly less-ornamental rocks.

"Lydia wouldn't have liked this," Luke grumbled, knowing he would have nothing good to say about the man who had been engaged to his wife.

"I wish we could have gone to see her sister first," Robyn said as she climbed from the car and stretched her legs.

"Aye, but if we don't see him today there might not be the chance again for a few weeks," Philip said.

"Going to the Bahamas with his girlfriend, indeed," Robyn snorted. "Didn't take him long did it. Oh, I'm sorry." She looked at Luke apologetically.

"'Twas my own thought," Luke assured her. "Come, we'll finish this as soon as we may." He strode to the front door and banged the brass knocker three times on the highly polished wood. He was nervous. Why he didn't know. He was a match for any man, especially someone like the one he was about to meet. All the same, it was comforting in this strange world to have Sir Philip standing right behind him.

A thin blond-haired girl wearing a smart black jacket and an exceedingly short red dress duly opened the door. Her ears sported large glittery stones, and every finger appeared adorned in similar manner.

Luke took a mental step backwards. *Good lord, was this the sort of woman Darwin lusted after?* His love was well out of it. "Begging your pardon. I am expected. Luke Waverly, at your service." He bowed stiffly and briefly.

The girl looked him up and down then smiled. "I'm very sorry," she said in silky tones, "Darwin called to say he can't get back. He said to take a message." She giggled. "I didn't realise I would be having two such good-looking guys visiting, or I might have put off my flight for a few hours." She tucked a stray piece of hair behind an ear and cast a long look at Philip, who rolled his eyes and felt himself shoved to one side.

Luke shuddered. When his wife did a similar thing with her hair, it about unhinged him, but when this person performed the action, it was nothing short of nauseating. He pulled himself together and to his full height, dwarfing the female even though her shoes bore long spiked heels.

"We need to see Darwin," Robyn snapped, elbowing her way to Luke's side. "You told my husband on the phone that he'd be here."

"And things change," the girl said with a soft laugh. "Look, lovey, he's not here, and I have a flight to catch. If you'll excuse me."

"Please, wait." Luke wished Philip would calm his wife who stood bristling as though she might make an assault at any time. "'Tis very important I speak with the gentleman in question; I have something I believe he would like returned."

"You do? What?"

Luke opened the hand he held down by his side. "This."

The girl's eyes almost popped out of her head. "What a rock!"

"Indeed, and I wish to return it." He allowed the girl to take the ring and saw her eyes light greedily as she held it to the air watching it sparkle even in the weak daylight. "If you please," he said, holding out his hand.

"I could give it to him."

"I think not," Luke said in a tone he remembered regretfully having used with Lydia from time to time, a tone that kept people at a distance and under some amount of control.

"We could drive to the airport," Philip said quietly to Robyn.

The girl sighed and handed the ring back. "I'll tell him, but I won't see him until tomorrow evening, when I get to the hotel."

"What," Philip interjected, "you mean you aren't meeting him at the airport?"

"No, in the Bahamas. And that's if he even gets there," she said dismally. "Last time I didn't see him for nearly a week and had to entertain myself."

"I'm sure you managed quite well," Robyn mumbled under her breath and felt a large arm slip around her waist and draw her against an equally large chest.

"'Tis a difficult situation," Luke grumbled.

"We could fly to the Bahamas," Philip suggested.

"It's that important, is it?" The girl appeared a little more interested. "Look, I'll tell him as soon as I see him. There's no point you lot flying out there. Like I said, he might turn up any time—or maybe not at all," she concluded.

Philip stepped forwards and handed her a business card. "Have him call me the second you see him. Have him reverse the charges if he needs to. 'Tis extremely important."

"I'll say. That rock must be worth thousands." Her eyes glazed slightly. "Thousands."

They left the girl standing on the doorstep, no doubt contemplating what all those thousands might be spent on.

"Well, what now?" Philip said as he put the Volvo into gear.

"I should like to visit Lydia's sister, as planned," Luke answered, but with little enthusiasm.

"Let me just say," Robyn interjected, "that if you found that last call unsettling, please be prepared for something far worse with Lydia's sister."

The two men exchanged glances.

"Think about it, you're coming in out of the blue to tell this woman that her sister is alive and well and living in the eighteenth century. How does that sound?"

"In truth I'd not thought about it thus." Luke turned to look at Robyn in the back seat. "You think then she will refuse to take the bike?" Her words unsettled him. Was Lydia in fact alive and well? He prayed it was so. "I have the letter Lydia put in the bag; mayhap that will assist us."

"Hopefully, but if she doesn't recognise her sister's writing, it won't prove a thing," Robyn said and tapped her husband on the shoulder. "I hope she doesn't go running to the police and accuse us of abduction or murder."

"It had crossed my mind," Philip agreed.

Luke felt himself shrink into the soft leather seat. If he had thought this would be easy, he realised he was very mistaken.

*   *   *

Two hours later, he sat in a comfortable chair in a future home, drinking something called a wine cooler. A young woman, a little older than Lydia, sat with both elbows resting on the dining room table while her husband stood by and made comforting noises.

Luke thanked the Lord that Robyn's prophecy of doom hadn't come to pass. Lydia's sister, Anne, had been tearful, angry, and somewhat disbelieving, but between the various stages of her distress had been willing to listen, willing to accept there might be something to his story. And so far she hadn't called the police.

"Lydia always had a vivid imagination," Anne sniffed. "Wanted to be a highwayman when she was little. We kept telling her that highwaymen were boys, but she didn't care. She did all right until she met that fool, Darwin. I'm glad she's away from him." She turned to Luke. "If what you say is true then, I think she's found a wonderful man."

He nodded, not sure how to respond. "You believe my words then, and the letter?"

"I'm trying, really I am," Anne sniffed.

"I had no idea she intended to send you a communication," Luke continued, "but 'tis a welcome thing."

"It's her writing, I'm certain of that," Anne said. "Only the night before she . . . disappeared, I had her write down everything she was thinking—to help her get Darwin out of her system." She shrugged. "It didn't work too well, and she ended up getting drunk. She said she had a hangover when she set off on her bike that afternoon."

Luke got to his feet and came to stand by Anne's elbow. "I wish there were some way I could prove to you I tell the truth, but I know none."

Could you leave something when you go back?" Anne asked tearfully. "Something we could find?"

Luke turned helplessly to Philip and Robyn. "What say you?"

Philip blew out his cheeks. "I cannot be certain. That which has gone before may be impossible to change. And if one were to go back and perform a deed not formerly performed, it might be construed as change. But," he added holding up a hand, "I really don't know."

"Do you know much about this time stuff then?" It was Anne's husband.

"Very little, I'm sorry to say," Philip replied. "The man who does, or perhaps I should say did, is no longer with us."

The bike, along with Lydia's letter, was given over to her sister's safekeeping, and Luke left giving firm assurances that as soon as he heard anything from Darwin, he would call Anne and let her know of his plans to return to the eighteenth century.

Damnation, he wasn't even sure he could get back there.

He cursed Darwin for his absurdity and for his very existence.

TWENTY-NINE

Three days later, the phone rang at Foxworth. Robyn answered it.

"Philip"—she glanced at her husband before continuing—"it's for Luke."

"Darwin, is it?" Philip strode outside to where Luke stood batsman in a game of cricket with April and Thomas. "Luke, man. Telephone." Luke turned, and Philip silenced his daughter's cry of disappointment with a look. "I'll stand in for him, one innings. How will that be?" he offered, and took up his position, grabbing the bat, which Luke thrust at him before racing into the house.

"Darwin?"

"It's Anne," Robyn said simply and handed him the phone, making sure he had the handset the right way up.

"Luke Waverly here." He nodded, grunted, nodded again, then raised his eyebrows in surprise and frowned in disbelief. He said his good-bye's and thank-you's, promising to do what he could. Wearily, he handed the phone back to Robyn just as Philip came into the room.

"Good news I trust." He spoke before seeing the expression on Luke's face.

Robyn shook her head. "I think not. Luke, sit down or you might fall down."

Luke sat and accepted the drink he was offered. "That was Lydia's sister. Apparently, Darwin telephoned her, said he saw no point in bothering me."

"Likely doesn't want to face you," Philip suggested.

"More like scared witless by the sounds of it," Robyn put in.

"He doesn't want the ring back," Luke continued.

Philip and Robyn looked at one another.

Luke made a poor attempt at a smile. "'Tis a bloody fake, and apparently a very good one. Something called a cubic zir . . . I can't recall."

"Cubic zirconia." Robyn let out a whistle. "The cheap bastard. Fancy telling Lydia all those lies about how much it was worth."

"A great pity she didn't think to have it valued," Philip remarked.

"My Lydia is too trusting for that," Luke said dully and slugged the remainder of his drink.

"Well, I don't think we can make him take it back if he doesn't want it."

Luke looked at Philip and shook his head. "Apparently he got money for it. I did not fully understand what Anne told me. Insurance? Could he do that?"

Philip groaned. "Aye, he could indeed, and very likely a pretty penny if he insured it at full value. Oh, 'tis not so difficult to insure one ring and then replace it with an identical one of inferior quality. People do it all the time so they do not have to wear their family heirlooms. They keep the real ones locked in a vault, or hidden somewhere. However, there are those who do it purposefully to defraud their insurance company, and of course, 'tis illegal. Nevertheless, he has in fact done it. And I fear there is little we can do about it."

"'Tis of no matter," Luke said quietly then was silent. He was lost, lost in time and without his beloved Lydia. "And I am still here," he said quietly.

"Philip, I want to get the kids ready for bed. You stay and talk to Luke. I'll call you when they've had their bath." Robyn leaned down and planted a kiss on Philip's cheek.

Luke watched her leave the room. "She's a fine woman, your wife."

"She is indeed. I consider myself a very lucky man. Would you like me to tell you how we met?"

Luke nodded. "I would, since I gather 'tis a story, similar to my own." He smiled ruefully. "Excepting that I no longer have my lady."

"But wait 'til you hear our tale," Philip said encouragingly. "It may give you hope yet." He settled himself comfortably on the couch, drink in hand, his feet stretched out before him—complete with bunny slippers.

Luke sat enthralled, hardly daring to sip on his very fine cognac, lest he miss some of Philip's story. He shook his head in wonderment. "All that and still you are together. 'Tis an amazing, nay, incredible story, yet it happened, and here you are with your family. That it could be this way for Lydia and me." He looked directly at Philip. "I don't even know where she is. I never found her that day, and I worry she may have fallen into unfavourable circumstances."

"Aye, I know. Luke, I didn't tell you much about how we moved from time to time, and I am acquainted only briefly with the details. As I said at Anne's home, I'm not the man."

"Then who?"

"His name is, or was, Sir John Ingleby. Years before I came to know him at Oxford he had discovered the secrets of time, aye, and indeed had travelled across the centuries. I only became involved when there was threat of worldwide destruction." Philip shrugged. "I had money and a taste for adventure."

"This man, he was the one who helped you come here, you say?"

"Aye, if not for him I should be dead. Philip leaned forwards in his chair. "Luke, next week is the anniversary of that terrible night when I almost lost my life, and the night Robyn left my century. Do you understand what I'm saying?"

"I cannot be certain I fully understand."

"I believe we may be able to access a time alignment." He paused. "'Tis a grave risk you would take, but one perhaps you may consider worthwhile."

"Think you I can travel back to my time in the same fashion you came here?"

Philip shook his head. "I cannot send you back to your own time; I cannot even guarantee sending you anywhere. We may only hope that you will meet with Sir John, and from there he is able to assist you. 'Tis a terrible long shot," he finished.

"Aye, but one I'm willing to take." Luke grinned suddenly. "Sir, you have given me the one thing I was without." The man wearing bunny slippers raised his eyebrows. "Hope, you have given me hope."

Robyn walked in. "Well, did you decide?"

"Robyn love, if you ever learn to be anything less than direct, I shall probably die of shock," Philip laughed. "Aye, we discussed it, and Luke here is willing to take the chance. Next week it is then." He raised his glass.

Robyn looked at her husband and inclined her chin. "And the other thing?"

"No, love, I didn't mention it. There's no need, yet."

"Philip you must tell him."

Luke sat forwards in his seat. "Tell me what? I pray you, sir tell me everything. I must know."

"Very well, it seems I must," Philip growled. "You said your wife was once abducted by the fourth Lord Fulford?" Luke nodded. "Do you think by any chance said lord was involved in your wife's failure to appear after she deposited the bike?"

"I cannot be certain, but the thought had crossed my mind. Why do you ask?"

"Robyn did some research on the Internet. Do you know what that is?"

Luke nodded in a dazed sort of fashion. "Lydia told me about it."

Philip took a deep breath. "I remembered that in my own time, Fulford Manor was a ruin. It burned down. Luke, we found out that it burned down not so long after the day you left."

"I'm not quite sure where this is leading," Luke said.

"There's something else. Tell him, Philip."

Philip glanced at his wife, coughed, then said, "The body of Lord Fulford was found near the burned out ruins of the house . . . along with that of a young woman. Luke, man, I'm sorry."

"My God." Luke dropped his face into his hands and for a moment thought he might vomit. He found himself gasping for breath and jumped to his feet. "I have to get back! I have to. I beg you, sir, help me. Indeed, I will change history. I shall travel back to when Lydia and I were married. I shall not allow her to go out that day."

"We couldn't find any record of your marriage," Philip said hesitantly.

"Damn that bloody parson. I knew he was well into his cups when he arrived. The bloody fool didn't register the marriage."

"Your whole history is sketchy." Philip paused and glanced at Robyn. "And then the Web site went off line."

"Sometimes fate does strange things," Robyn interjected and glanced back at her husband. "Perhaps we're not supposed to know—not yet at any rate." Both men looked at her. "The Web has never gone down like that before."

"Indeed not, but I had not thought . . . Anyhow, I can do nothing for a few days," Philip said grimly. "And even then I cannot guarantee things will go as we would like. Believe me if there were anything else to be done, I should do it. Oh and, Luke, if you indeed are able to connect with Sir John, you shall have little time to reach Fulford before the fire. "'Twas the fourteenth of December," he added, "and it likely started in the early hours."

"I understand," Luke said miserably. "I appreciate your assistance, and I thank you for your honesty." He addressed his last comment to Robyn.

"Aye, my wife has a penchant for it." Philip got to his feet. "Don't you, my love."

"Is anyone hungry?" Robyn slid her arm around her husband's waist. "You have to eat, Luke. I've a feeling you'll be needing a lot of energy before you're through."

                              *   *   *

The next few days were the longest of Luke's life. When at last the time was imminent, he stood with his hosts in the drawing room.

"We'll come with you to the conservatory, just to make certain you're in the right place." Philip said.

"I know the exact spot," Robyn assured him. Then she laughed. "And I won't be anywhere near it."

They reached the conservatory. "'Tis seven, Luke. Fourteen minutes more." Philip grasped him by the shoulders. "We wish you well, and perhaps we shall come to know of your success. Remember, there is no certainty about this transfer."

"Only time will tell," Luke said in a lighter manner than he felt.

"Indeed. Now remember, give my letter to Sir John; he will understand. There is one thing I ask of you." He glanced at his wife. "Should you arrive prior to Robyn's departure from that time, I beg you stay away until her transfer is complete. And if you and I should meet, I shall not know you of that I am certain, and 'tis better you do not make yourself known to me. The future and the past, though they may intertwine, must be kept separate, for all our sakes."

"I understand." Luke took a deep breath and walked over to the second door of the conservatory. Tentatively he opened it.

"Stand just inside the open doorway," Robyn said. "And perhaps you should move around a little, side to side maybe. It seemed we were always moving when we transferred. I was sort of collapsing inside the doorway. By the way," she added, "I hope you're a better time traveller than I was."

Luke looked mystified but began to turn around and step side to side. He felt rather foolish.

"Don't you think so? Philip?" Robyn nudged her husband. "Philip."

"Philip! Phiiiilip!"

Luke grabbed the side of the doorway, blinded for an instant by an incredibly bright light. The scream had come from somewhere behind him and for a fleeting second he glimpsed the figure of a female, dressed in a luxurious gown, sinking to the ground, and then she was gone. He staggered as wave after wave of nausea overwhelmed him. He recalled what Robyn had told him of her experiences, about how her time travelling had grown more uncomfortable with each transfer, and taking the advice she'd given him, he sucked in a great lungful of air and bent over. Some minutes and several deep breaths later, he stood upright, if a little unsteady, and realised he could hear the sounds of shouting and the clash of metal on metal outdoors, somewhere in the darkness.

Fully aware of the circumstances and having heard the details from Philip's own lips, Luke knew he must not interfere. He waited, fear gripping his heart and disgust rising in his belly at his inability to prevent the attack being perpetrated not a hundred yards away. He remembered Philip's words and tried to content himself in the knowledge that there were happier times ahead for the man outside. He turned, strode quickly through the conservatory, and entered the main house. No one challenged him. His dress wasn't too unusual, a little outdated perhaps, but he still carried himself as a member of the aristocracy, and no servant would dare voice objection to his presence.

"I need a horse, man," he said calling to a footman who raced through the great hall.

"Aye, sir, out in the stable. There be a right goings on," the man gasped breathlessly and continued to run.

Luke carried on walking until he came to the front door. There was no one about, so he stepped out unhindered, into the cold night air. He found the stables—where again no one challenged him, saddled a horse, and rode off down the driveway.

Philip had given him directions to Sir John's home, and Luke rode at a steady rate, knowing Sir John would not be back anytime soon. He would not return until he had recovered Philip's beaten and battered body, half-alive from the mob.

"I am not certain when the master will return," said the elderly man who took Luke's hat and outer garments. "Would you care to step into the drawing room, sir? A drink perhaps?"

"Thank you." Luke followed the man, introducing himself as Sir Luke Waverly.

A commotion outside the door had Luke on his feet. A man in his mid sixties appeared and impatiently waved the servant away. He turned to Luke. "I do not know you, sir, and I have no wish to appear inhospitable, but there is a matter I must attend to forthwith. I know not how long the situation will require my time."

"I understand completely, Sir John." Luke held out a hand. "Luke Waverly, and I shall, with your permission, await your return whenever it may be. My journey here was not undertaken lightly, and I needs must speak with you on a matter of the gravest importance."

Sir John looked at the younger man thoughtfully. "Two hours then we'll speak." With that, he turned and left the room.

Luke sighed and returned to his chair by a welcome fire. He drew the purse from his waistcoat and pulled it open. Inside lay the letter he hoped would convince Sir John to aid him, a letter written by Philip Somersby-Griffith in the twenty-first century. The same Philip Somersby-Griffith who currently lay bloody and battered in some room of this very house.

Sir John Ingleby walked into the drawing room a short while before the appointed two hours, his face drawn and weary. He wasn't a happy man and headed straight for the brandy. Luke waited until the man seated himself before he spoke.

"How is he?"

Sir John looked up sharply. "What mean you?"

"Sir Philip, how fares he?"

"How in the name of hell do you . . . ?" He got to his feet. "No matter, there is little we can do," he said at last. "I fear for his life."

"Please, sir, allow me to explain my reason for being here." Luke took the letter from his purse and held it out. "If you will; it may ease your mind."

"What, what is this? I have no time for foolishness, sir. I hope this is as important as you suggest." He took the letter and sat down. Several times he eyed Luke suspiciously, finally folding the letter in half and placing it on a small table. "You are truly the Lord Beckham he speaks of in this letter?"

"I am, but I should be obliged if you address me without title. 'Tis best I am not known."

"'Tis Philip's hand right enough," Sir John continued. "I never could break him of that habit of curling the ends of his letters. Infuriated me at Oxford he did. And all this . . . ?"

"Aye, all is true. You must believe it. Sir John, I am in dire need of your assistance. Can you help me?"

"Perhaps. 'Tis an amount to digest, but nay, should I be even surprised at this?"

"You should be glad. Indeed, I have not seen a happier man than Sir Philip. His wife is delightful."

"Indeed she is." Sir John's eyes twinkled for a moment. "She once called me a mad old fool. And the children, there were two, they are well?"

"Aye, sir, and now there is another, a young son of some two years. They named him John," Luke said with a slight smile. "After the man who saved his father's life."

Sir John couldn't quite mask the glow of pride he felt and nodded slowly. "I shall help if I can, but I need to thoroughly examine my time charts if we are to be anywhere near accurate."

"I needs must return as soon as is possible. I have to make certain Lydia is not in that house when it burns. The sooner the better, Sir John, I beg of you."

"I understand your need for haste, but we must not allow haste to cause imprecision. 'Twould be folly indeed. Now, you must be exhausted. I know I always was after such journeying. I'll have a room made ready for you."

"Aye, fatigue seems to have overtaken me, and I thank you for your hospitality, sir."

Luke slept far better than he imagined he would and rose after midmorning. Hot water and a comfortable robe had been provided, and he breakfasted alone in his room after being informed that his host would be indisposed for some time.

He sat staring idly out of the window wondering at the fact he was now only a little over fifty years out of his own time, yet still a lifetime away from Lydia. He got to his feet and began to pace the room knowing it to be a useless activity but unable to remain stationary. There had to be something he could do; it seemed not.

Nothing, except wait.

A servant entered the room. "Sir John requests you join him in the library." The man led Luke to where his host stood, leaning over a large desk covered with papers.

"Ah, good morning. I trust you slept well?"

"Thank you, I did indeed, and I breakfasted well." Luke strode without hesitation to where the other man stood. "Do you have anything yet?"

"Slowly, my boy, slowly. It does not do to rush these things. I am also taking time here to discover how I shall send Sir Philip to the future. You understand"—he pushed his spectacles up his nose—"'tis important he leave here very soon. There are too many people interested in the disappearance of his wife."

Luke took a deep breath. His whole future rested on the skill of this man, aye, indeed perhaps Lydia's life may depend on him also. "I do not wish to appear ungrateful for your efforts, sir. I beg pardon if I appear so."

"Nay, you are no less impatient than I would be in your place." He beamed over his eyeglasses. "You have a reason to return, a life to return to, and if all is as you say—a life to protect."

"Aye." Luke bowed his head, unwilling to let the other man see the grief he knew clouded his eyes. He raised his face after a moment and said, "I trust your decisions, sir, believe me."

"I think I may have found something. Come here and look." Sir John pointed to a myriad of circles and graphs, some intersecting, some parallel, others seemingly having little interest in each other at all.

"I fear I do not understand these diagrams," Luke said, helplessly.

"You need not understand, but I wish to give you a brief idea of what will happen, although you have indeed experienced such transport. Here." He prodded a finger at an area on one of the papers. "I have established an occurrence site which I believe I may be able to match with one that will open a way to your time." He tapped his finger on the table then said, "It may not be a pure transfer, and it worries me that you run grave risk of travelling to a place you do not desire to be. Shall you dare it?"

"I will, sir."

"In that case, you will leave the day after tomorrow from a point not five miles east of here, and you should arrive in 1734, on the twelfth day of December, a little after mid-morn. You will be some sixty miles from your desired destination." He looked at Luke. "It gives you but fair time."

"'Twill have to do. A decent horse shouldn't be too difficult to come by."

"We may hope," said Sir John. "You will find yourself near a small hamlet in Nottinghamshire; the site of a civil war incident. There is a slight chance, as I mentioned, of your journey not being accurate. Be aware of the possibility your travel may extend beyond the time distance we desire." He watched Luke's face carefully. "Do you understand what I say?"

"I may find myself farther back in history than I would wish. I understand and I fully intend to pray this night as I have never prayed before. I truly am willing to take the risk."

"Good. There remain a few details to determine. Then we shall be ready, God willing." Luke heaved a sigh of relief. "'Tis a happier man I am than I was one hour ago. May I enquire as to Sir Philip's condition?"

"Considering you know the favourable outcome I should say it is unnecessary for you to ask; however, since you do, he is recovering his senses, though he remains far from whole. Now, if you will excuse me I needs must attend to my charts. Please consider your self at home here, and take rest while you may."

Luke considered the suggestion a reasonable one and spent the best part of his time strolling around the somewhat small but agreeable grounds, lost in thoughts of his anticipated reunion with Lydia—wherever it might be.

THIRTY

Luke stood in a small glade a few miles from Sir John's home, his heart pounding so hard it threatened to leap right out from his chest, and watched as the man at his side made a couple of final calculations.

"I think I have it. Are you ready?" Sir John regarded the younger man gravely.

"I am, sir." He stepped forwards and held out a hand. "And eternally grateful. I wish you well for 'tis doubtful we shall meet again."

"Aye, we are not destined thus." He shook Luke heartily by the hand. "Go now, towards that cluster of trees." He pointed. "And walk slowly. God be with you."

Luke released the man's hand and walked steadily into the trees, suddenly aware of a moist grey fog infiltrating the low branches and swirling around his knees. Was that the sound of his own breathing that pervaded the air around him, that harsh rasping of raggedly drawn breath being expelled in short gasps? He jumped back as a claw-like hand came out of the mists, and grasped at the tops of his boots only to fall away helplessly, and accompanied by an awful groan. Luke stopped moving, horrified at the vision before him and knowing there was little he could do to help the man who lay twisted and torn in the dirt, his face swollen and bloody, his chest and belly opened, his entrails long deathly-pale loops. His legs had been smashed and his feet burned to charred stumps after the fashion of the inquisitors. Luke's hand fumbled for the hilt of his sword, for even as his brain said he should do naught to interfere, he knew he must. The sword left its scabbard hesitantly, and at the same time as a chill wind whipped across the fallen leaves where the man lay, covering him and blotting him from Luke's view. The wind grew to a violent turbulence, and Luke held his sword firmly with both hands ready to do what he knew he must as soon as the wind calmed and he could see his target. He blanched at the thought of killing a man simply because there was naught else to be done. Blinking his eyes rapidly, he attempted to remove the irritating particles of dust that had settled there and steadied himself by planting his feet wide. A wave of nausea overcame him. He bent over and leaned on his sword afraid he was about to retch. Fleeting visions assailed his senses—blood, flames, screaming: the sounds of death were everywhere. Then he was falling, falling into a darkness he was helpless to prevent. His body twisted and tugged, pitched through the air on a seemingly endless descent. The whole world exploded around him like some terrible storm, the like of which he had never known, and Luke felt himself sucked backwards through a blaze of fire and thunder.

*   *   *

He came to his senses with a start and patted the ground with a hand. Snow. Only a ground covering but enough that he was already wet-through from lying in it. He shook his head, and having no idea how long he had lain in his present state crawled to his feet and tried to ascertain the time from the position of the sun where it hung low in the dismal winter sky. It was early morning that much was certain. Seemingly he had arrived earlier than Sir John had predicted. Luke thanked God and sank to his knees his mind a confusion of images. He had seen things he didn't want to remember, things no man should have to see, but seen them he had and remember them he would. He tried to clear his mind of everything except finding Lydia. Crawling to his feet again, he set out across the cold damp expanse of farmland before him, desperately hoping he was in the correct location, indeed that this was even the right year.

A while later he stumbled across a farmhouse, where a woman came forwards to meet him and called for her husband.

"'Tis a wonder you ain't frozen to death, aye a wonder," the woman said, clucking her tongue. "Don' worry, young sir, we'll see you warmed afore you go on your way."

"I have money," Luke rasped and sat down on a low chair. "I need a horse." Then as an afterthought he asked, "What year is it?"

The man and woman looked at each other. The woman shook her head, and the man said, "'Tis the year 1734, the thirteenth day of December."

Luke would have leapt to his feet at the realisation he had lain unconscious for over half a day had he not felt the world spin and his stomach all but rise to the occasion as he lifted his head. It was a frightening thought made only less frightening by the knowledge he had so little time to find Lydia. He cursed. The fire could begin one minute after this very midnight. He almost wept—he wouldn't make it in time.

He accepted the offer of a swift meal of bread and cheese washed down with a mug of hot ale from the farmer's wife then handed over a generous amount of coin for a nag that looked like it may see out the winter at the very most. He rode away at a steady canter, his head throbbing and the desire to throw up ever present.

The horse winded quickly, and he found he had to rest the beast frequently lest it drop dead under him. Frustrating as it was, there was little alternative; he was far from a decent-sized town or any place to trade his horse for a more able one. He rode cross-country hoping soon to make the Great North Road and thus afford himself the possibility of a coaching inn where he could buy another mount. Late morning wore on into afternoon, and Luke rode the horse as hard as he dared, stopping only when it appeared about to collapse.

The skies darkened, and Luke found his progress considerably slower. The appearance of a coach and four, heralding the existence of civilization, did much to boost his spirits. Luke hailed the coach driver who informed him there was an inn some twelve miles hence. He eventually reached the establishment and swung off the horse, not bothering to tether it—the beast didn't have the energy to run off.

"Good evening to you, sir," he called to the proprietor. "I need a fast horse and quickly."

"You ain't likely to get neither," the man drawled. "Last coach through took the only pair. Had two gone lame if you can believe it." He walked over to the fire and began to prod at it with a long poker. "Took the last 'orses, he did."

"You have no horses?" Luke said disbelievingly. It seemed fate was working against him.

"Not until tomorrow."

"You must have a horse, man!" Luke strode forwards and grasped the man by the collar of his frock. "I need a horse!"

The man didn't flinch and said, "Ain't got one. Now if you'll let go of me, sir."

Luke let the man go and sank onto a wooden stool.

"Need to be somewhere in a hurry do you?"

"Aye, a life depends on it," Luke said quietly. "The nag I'm riding will barely go another mile."

The man left the room. Luke rose to his feet and walked to the door of the inn. He could ride the coach he had seen on the road. It would be heading in the right direction but not, he knew, until the next morning.

It would be too late.

The proprietor re-entered. "I took that nag of yours round the back an' set her up with some good feed an' a couple of pints."

"Ale? You gave it ale?"

"Aye, ale 'n' chopped raw meat. Finest remedy for bringing a 'orse back that I knows of." He grinned. "A trick I learned from a gentleman o' the road what 'as been known to stop hereabouts once in a while." He winked and walked past an incredulous Luke. "Be wanting a bevy yourself I should think."

"Jack you old devil," Luke said softly. "Now sir, I thank you for all you are doing. Can you tell me how far I am from Fulford Manor?"

"Not certain. I only 'eard of it. Never been," the man replied and came back across the room with a tankard of ale.

"Which direction then is York?"

"Ah, well, York be north an' to the east."

Luke nodded, pleased at that information. If York were to the northeast, he should pick up the Great North Road sometime soon and make speed towards Fulford. He wished Jack hadn't headed back to London. He could have done with the support.

"How far is York?"

The man scratched his head thoughtfully. "About twenty five . . . thirty miles. I ain't sure. Drink your ale and sit awhile. That mare needs 'bout an hour more afore she sets to work."

Luke blinked wearily and wondered at the real possibility his mare would soon be a new horse. Desperation drove him to believe she would.

*   *   *

He vowed, as he rode, that he would never scorn the power of Jack's remedies again. The horse moved as though infused with the blood of the king's racehorses, and they made good time in reaching the Great North where he put the beast to a gallop. Luke had managed a couple hours of fitful sleep in a chair by the fireside at the inn and had left there at half past seven o' clock. Some hours later, he swung the horse away from the road just before Poachers Hill and smiled to himself at thoughts of Lydia sitting astride Black Bess, holding a coach at bay with a pistol. He pulled out his watch and squinted at it. His smile faded. It was past midnight. The horse was still making ground, but he could feel the slow ebb of power under him. "Give you a few hours," the man had said. Luke understood that. He well remembered his own experience with the herbal brew; it had almost cost him his life.

Familiar landmarks grew in number, the woods west of Beckham and the rise of the hills towards Fulford. The landscape lightened slightly with the appearance of a soft moon but was quickly darkened again by a bank of thick grey cloud. Luke rode cautiously. Unfamiliar as the horse was to him, it would be unwise to push too hard. A fall was the last thing he needed. His eyes soon became accustomed to the gloom as they approached the brow of a hill. In fact, he could make out the shapes of the trees that surrounded Fulford very clearly.

Too clearly.

His heart made an attempt at plunging to his feet, and Luke held a rising fear as he rode nearer the crest of the hill. He knew what he would see on the other side but refused to believe it, not until he saw with his own eyes. The orange glow in the night sky grew brighter and more distinct. Luke gained the top of the hill and for a moment was unable to go on and simply sat atop the horse unmoving, and stared.

Fulford Manor was ablaze.

Throwing caution to the wind, he spurred the horse, which was showing distinct signs of fatigue, down the hill at breakneck speed. They were several hundred yards from the house when the horse faltered and stumbled, catching itself once then tumbling headlong, completely exhausted and drained of its artificial supply of energy. Luke tucked and rolled, coming to his feet several yards away from the animal, which lay prostrate and heaving. He barely gave it a glance and staggering to the nearest tree, he held on to it and vomited the contents of his stomach, deciding at that point that time travel was not something he wished to continue. He wiped his mouth on his sleeve and ran towards the blazing house. The property was an inferno. Every window on the ground floor gleamed red and orange, glass cracked and fragments shattered, exploding like missiles across the courtyard. Luke looked desperately for a way inside. If Lydia were on the upper floors, he could reach her before the flames did, he hoped. He ran back and forth in hopeless realisation that there was no way in, and had started for the back of the house when his ears were assailed by an horrendous scream.

Lydia!

He skidded to a halt and tried to ascertain where it had come from. Barely able to look at the house through the blistering heat that seared his face, he shielded his eyes and cast around in the general direction from which the sound had come. Somewhere by a blazing window, he caught a movement. Straining his eyes, he ran into the furnace. A shadowy figure staggered down the front steps, clothing ablaze, and fell to a blazing heap on the ground. Luke sprinted the last few feet and, scarcely able to tolerate the intensity of the heat, ripped off his surtout and smothered the barely moving form. His eyebrows singed, and he felt his hair do the same. Nevertheless, he grasped handfuls of seared clothing and pulled the figure several yards before carefully lifting his surtout and realising that what he had rescued no longer moved. Melted, charred features and sightless eyes stared at him and he couldn't deny his feelings of horror and revulsion, neither the feeling of sheer gratitude and relief that surged around his heart and soul. He looked a moment more at the smouldering locks of frizzled, once golden, and very long hair, and his senses revelled in the probability that Lydia was still alive. There was record of only one woman's body being found—only one. He thanked God, as he never had. Lydia wasn't at Fulford. She had found her way home. He must get back, to Beckham.

He looked once more at the body of the blonde woman—it was too late for her. His thoughts turned suddenly to the horse; likely it had expired. Fulford's stables. He could capture himself a mount and ride fast to Beckham. Lydia would be there.

He didn't know the layout of Fulford Manor but guessed rightly the direction and was assisted in his search by the screams of terrified horses long before he saw the stables. Mercifully, the building wasn't yet fully alight and although several areas blazed, he was able to pull the doors wide. Soaking his frock skirts in the water trough, he pulled them up over his face and stumbled into the smoke filled interior where six horses plunged and smashed at their half doors in a bid to escape certain death. Avoiding deadly hooves, he ripped open door after door hoping the animals would have the sense to run. Then dropping his coat from his face, he bent low near the ground and took a great breath of air, and grabbing a bridle from a nearby hook, flung it onto a dark horse at the end of the line of stalls. Encouraging the animal, he led it out of the open door and leapt onto its back just as a blazing beam came crashing down across what had been the only means of escape from the building. The horse reared, almost unseating Luke, but he pushed it forwards away from the blazing inferno and towards the relative safety of the trees.

Crack!

A sharp pain tore through Luke's thigh. The ball travelled on and caught his mount on the quarters. The horse screamed and plunged, succeeding in unbalancing its rider as it swung to the right, and unseating him as it hurled itself back to the left.

Luke hit the ground and with a curse was on his feet, thankful all he had sustained was a mild flesh wound. He ripped his sword from his side and stared wildly around for his would be assassin wishing he had a pistol.

A figure stepped out of the dark shadow of a tree.

"Fulford! Curse you." Luke tested the balance of his grip on the sword's hilt.

"Ah, Beckham, come to collect your property I see," the other man sneered. "Too late I'm afraid." He held a pistol. "Pity, she was quite a prize."

With a bellow of pure rage, Luke threw himself forwards, fully expecting a ball in his chest but Fulford hurled the spent weapon aside and drew his own sword. Luke pulled himself up sharply seeing the chance he was now afforded.

"What mean you?" he said, circling Fulford's blade with his own and making a short lunge. "Lydia is at Beckham."

"I fear not," Fulford advised with a malicious laugh. "She's gone, dead. Likely roasted by now."

"You lie, sir. I found the body; 'twas not Lydia's." Only heaven knew how he hated this man.

"You found the body of the countess, no doubt. Ah, such a pity. She was to have fled with me across the borders and eventually to France, but she became greedy. I had to leave her behind. She shot her husband by the way. He found out our plans and tried to interfere; such loyalty to King George." Fulford parried a thrust from Luke's sword and made a futile riposte.

"She was a traitor as are you, and if I don't kill you myself here tonight, I'll make damn certain you are hanged."

"Mayhap." Fulford lunged too far and too wildly, missing his footing and stumbling into a tree.

Luke's blade flicked into the man's arm drawing a scarlet ribbon that glimmered in the glare of the burning ruins behind them.

"Damn you!" The man leapt and came at Luke in a fury, slashing wide and with little accuracy.

Luke ducked, turned and sidestepped, keeping his blade low and ready. His chance came and he was swift, cutting his opponents thigh deeply and coming back to score a hit on his chest. It wasn't a fatal strike, but it unnerved Fulford. Luke knew he had the upper hand; the other man was growing evermore careless and weakened by loss of blood.

"I think I'll cut you up piece by piece." Luke laughed humourlessly, and caught another patch of flesh, this time on Fulford's sword arm. "Unless, of course, you agree to tell me where Lydia really is. I know she's not going to die in this fire," he called confidently and parried another poor attack. "Tell me where she is, and I'll do what I can to save your miserable neck."

"I'll kill you, Beckham," Fulford snarled. "Then you can join your wench—in hell!"

The thrust came fast and hard, straight at Luke's heart. He brought his sword tip under the opposing blade, circled it, and with a harsh slicing sound ran his own blade the length of the other, and sidestepped. He pushed at the first resistance then pushed harder, feeling the bend of steel as his blade was restricted in its advancement. He looked at the man impaled there. With a slight rotation of his wrist, he wrenched the weapon free and watched Fulford crumple to the ground still holding his own sword. Luke knelt by him. The man's eyes were already beginning to glaze.

"Tell me where she is," Luke said quietly. "Do one last thing to save yourself from the pits of hell." He waited for the dying man to answer. "Tell me Fulford, damn you!" He grabbed the man by his coat bringing his face within inches of this own.

Fulford coughed and spat a wad of bloody mucous directly into Luke's face. "You'll . . . never find her." He coughed again but hadn't the energy to spit. "I put her . . . in a . . . passageway . . . not even . . . you can find . . . and"—he attempted to laugh but it came out as a gurgle—"there . . . isn't a way out. No one . . . will ever find her," he gasped and his mouth went slack.

Luke dropped the body to the ground and got to his feet, trembling. So that was why Lydia's body was never found. That was why she had no history. She would die, perhaps slowly if she were not burned, alone and terrified.

"No! Do you hear? No! It cannot be!" He shook his fists at the heavens and his scream, full of anger, fear, and despair rent the cloud-filled skies. He would find her.

He had to.

But where to start? He had no idea where the secret doors and passageways were in this house. He barely knew those in his own. Yet again, Luke wished for Jack Palmer; the man knew his way around most of the houses in the county. He set off, clutching his bleeding thigh, damning Lord Fulford, and damning the horse that had thrown him and galloped off into the night.

By the time Luke reached the back of the house where he thought to try entry, there was no place left to enter. Huge oak beams blazed where they had crashed, stone lintels cracked, and windowpanes shattered, flinging glass though the air. The entire three floors of the house were a crumbling fiery mountain. He couldn't get within a hundred feet of the place.

Had Fulford lied? Luke somehow doubted it. Head bowed, he made his way across the grounds to the front of the house, to where he had left the nag. He little expected the thing would still be alive. Nonetheless, there it stood, head hung low. Luke hadn't the heart to climb on its back and picked up the reins, allowing the horse to simply follow behind him. He left the blazing ruins of Fulford Manor, wishing the whole place to the devil and trudged across the grounds to the back gate, which thankfully was open. He would travel through the woods. It was the quickest way to Beckham on foot. Even as he told himself Fulford had lied and Lydia was alive and well somewhere, he knew in the back of his mind that the man had told the truth. He sensed it. He would bring men from Beckham and as soon as they were able. They would dig through the debris. His heart cried out at the thought of finding his love for it was certain she could not have survived such a blaze, incarcerated or not in a stone tomb.

Luke felt a tug on the reins and turned. The nag stood as still as a rock, refusing to move. He pulled then walked back and slapped the animal on the rump. It ignored him and continued in its defiance, staring at shadows, perhaps at ghosts. Weariness overcame Luke, and he sank to his knees, head bowed as though in prayer—head bowed as though for the executioner. He would welcome the man in the black hood this night if only to ease his pain.

Lifting his head, he stared at the sky where a patch of star-sprinkled darkness, free of cloud, gazed back at him, silent and mocking. Those were the very same stars they had walked under together, the ones beneath which he had loved her one night when she dragged him out of doors with a blanket to a small copse of trees not too far from the house. It had been cold, but neither of them noticed, and were swiftly warmed by the heat of their passions.

A great gulping sob caught in his throat.

"Lydia," he whispered. "Come back to me, Lydia."

THIRTY - ONE

L ydia stumbled along through the complete darkness
of the passageway, sliding her hands firmly along
walls of roughly hewn stone paying no heed to her smashed
nails and bloody fingertips. She had no idea how long she
had been inside the walls of Fulford Manor, except that it was
long enough to necessitate a bladder relieving session, and she
was as thirsty as hell. The heat had begun a short while ago,
accompanied by the most awful creaking and crashing, which
in itself hadn't worried her; it was the faint but unmistakable
smell of smoke that convinced her to find a way out of her
prison and quickly.

Fulford had knocked her unconscious that day in the
woods, which now seemed a hundred years ago, but she
guessed it was likely about two weeks. He had surprised her
as she finished covering the bike with leaves and made it
plain it was no invitation to dinner he was offering. That no
one had come looking for her was alarming, and after the
first week of waiting and worrying, Lydia had begun to plan
her escape. What she wouldn't have given to have Andrew
around somewhere. She supposed him to have returned to his

other duties. It was generally believed that Lord Fulford had
fled north to the Scottish border where, according to Jack,
he would be apprehended by the authorities along with his
accomplices. He had duped them well.

Initially, Lydia's quarters had been a secure but comfortable
bedroom at Fulford Manor, but then she found herself
deposited somewhat unceremoniously inside a hidden
room, with scant supply of bread and water, at the screaming
insistence of the countess.

One thought tormented her. Where was Luke?

She didn't really understand any of it except that Fulford
planned to leave the country with the countess and a great deal
of gold. Having escaped the authorities, the pair had dismissed
the servants and secreted themselves behind the locked doors of
the manor, awaiting their chance to escape. It appeared Lydia
was a security against their capture. Something to be bargained
with until Luke had helped the pair safely out of the country.

Luke never made his appearance, and now she was excess
and unwanted baggage. She had anticipated freedom; after
all she was of no use to Lord Fulford. However, as he had
pointed out, she could still help convict him of high treason.
She would not be released until he and the countess were
away from England.

She had escaped the hidden room by heaving repeatedly
on a wooden panel—rotted over the years by a slight but
incessant trickle of moisture passing across its surface—and
eventually tearing enough of it asunder to crawl through.
Unfortunately her only escape was into the bowels of the
house. And in the darkness, it was impossible to know which
way she was heading. For a day or more she prayed and trudged
on, not caring how many times she slipped and plunged to the
damp earth. She was determined to beat Fulford—damn the
man. Beat Fulford and find Luke. She had to find Luke.

And then she had smelled smoke.

Struggling along the passageway, Lydia cheered slightly
as the ground began to descend and she convinced herself

it was in the same tunnel she had travelled with Andrew. Hope faded as she encountered one dead end and stone barrier after another and she thought of her husband, a terrible dread sowing its seeds in her heart. Luke hadn't come to find her, and she knew nothing would have kept him away. Nothing . . . except inability. She stumbled, grunted, and fell headlong, grazing her temple on a sharp point of rock. Things were not going as well as she would have liked, but she knew that to give in was to give up, and fear would not be her friend. Crawling to her feet she pushed on and almost immediately struck her head again on the abruptly low ceiling. Stunned but on her feet, she felt a surge of hope recalling how Andrew had bade her duck her head as they had gone lower and lower under the house. She was making slow progress without a knowing arm and the light of a candle to guide her, and the air was becoming increasingly oppressive. Smoke in the surrounding cavity increased steadily, and rubbing her eyes on the sleeve of her gown only made them water profusely. She coughed, and wondered vaguely at the fact that smoke was travelling downhill, and concluded that there must be an awful lot of it.

There *was* an awful lot, and it was growing thicker by the minute. Lydia turned at a deep thundering roar behind her and froze at the sight that met her eyes. The roof of the tunnel was ablaze, and a great gaping hole slowly appeared as the timbers of the house collapsed and ignited. Smoke and heat filled the tunnel at an alarming rate.

Smothering a scream, she grasped at the walls and staggered on as fast as she could. She had to get out—and fast. There was no telling which bit might collapse next or how long the oxygen would last.

She began to cough suddenly realising the desperate reality of her situation. She might die in here, and nobody would know.

"Luke." His name rang from her as a lonely forlorn moan. She found herself on her knees not knowing how she got there

and barely able to draw air into her lungs. She sucked air slowly
and crawled along close to the floor; something she had once
seen on an aircraft-safety movie. With each breath, it seemed
her lungs burned and opened about half way then came to
a sudden stop, refusing to fill any more. She tugged at her
petticoats and wished she had the strength to pull them off.
It would certainly be easier to run. Her awareness was fading
fast. She felt light headed and increasingly disoriented. The
one thing clear in Lydia's mind was that if she didn't get out
into fresh air very soon, she most certainly would die.

*   *   *

Luke lifted his head. The crashes and cracks from the fire
had dulled to far off booms and thuds—regular thuds. He
didn't move, there was no point. Everything he'd had in life
was gone. There it was again. *Thud . . . thud . . . thud.* Getting
to his feet, he walked cautiously in the direction of the sounds.
The smell of smoke became all at once stronger and seemed
to emanate from a particular patch of ground. As he watched,
unmistakable wisps of smoke drifted out from between clumps
of grass at his feet. He glanced at the nag; it stood unmoving
and watching the smoke.

Why would there be so much smoke concentrated in one
place? He came closer to the horse, knelt down and listened—
nothing. But then . . . A soft thud sounded, then another.

Was it possible?

He shook his head. Fate was playing the most evil of tricks
upon him. In all likelihood, there was beneath him a cavity,
which had filled with explosive gases and was about ready
to erupt. He jumped to his feet just as another thud echoed
from below.

The nag continued to stare and suddenly it began to paw
the ground.

Unthinkingly, Luke shoved the animal out of the way, got
back down on his knees and listened. He thought he heard

a soft moan and shook his head. It was his imagination; it had to be. But what if . . . ? Without further hesitation, he threw himself to pulling at the sod in a frenzy, which to his astonishment came away easily in large pieces.

"Lydia!" He tore at the grass and dirt until a square wooden trapdoor was almost fully in view. Without waiting to clear it completely, he hefted the thing open. A great gushing furnace of heat and thick black smoke sent him reeling backwards as he struggled to throw the door aside. Regaining his balance, he saw a pale hand clinging grimly to the top rung of a wooden ladder, and two eyes, streaming with tears and reddened by heat and smoke fumes, staring up at him. He grasped the hand just as the bloodied fingers uncurled and began to slip. "I have you! I have you!" he screamed, repeating the words several times to convince himself he really did. He hauled Lydia halfway from the shaft until he was able to grasp her waist, then he pulled her to his chest and dragged her clear.

Tumbling back into the grass, he clutched his wife to him. Lydia gasped most awfully for breath and lifting her up, Luke ran a short distance to where the air was clearer. He knelt down and placed her so she leaned against him. She started to cough and then she started to cry, and turned to bury her face at the side of his neck.

"Oh, Luke, I thought you, I, I . . . ," she sobbed.

"Shh, 'tis over. I have you now," he said, stroking her filthy, tangled hair while trying to keep the trembling from his own voice. "You're safe, my love." He held her, tighter than was comfortable he was sure, but she didn't complain. How many nights over the last weeks had he dreamed of this? How many times had he feared it might never come to pass?

He looked down at the raggedy, dirty female in his arms and stroked the hair from her grimy forehead. She was the most beautiful thing he had ever seen.

"Luke," she whispered finally, "I thought I was going to die in there."

"You were almost baked like a ham," he responded, trying to make light of a grim situation. It was the only way he would prevent the tears in his eyes from coursing down his cheeks.

She looked at him bleakly and nodded, trying her best to force a smile. "Where were you?"

"That, my love, is indeed a tale, and I shall tell you everything once you are bathed and tucked firmly into our bed. Can you stand?"

She nodded. He stood and gently pulled her to her feet, then looked around for the nag, which stood unmoving, just as he had left it. Shaking his head slightly, he wondered that the animal remained on its feet, and thanked God for it.

Lydia looked at the horse, saying nothing as Luke hoisted her into the saddle.

"I fear 'twill be a slow journey home. This beast has done well by me, and I should not care to have it die under us yet. I shall hold you in the saddle as I walk."

Lydia yawned and promptly fell asleep. Her knight in shining armour had turned up—just in the nick of time.

THIRTY-TWO

"**A**re you awake?"
Lydia dared herself to open her eyes, not fully
believing this wasn't all some dream and that she would awake
and find herself back in that smoke-filled tunnel. But she was
clean and bathed, and the naked man lying beside her was no
dream. Neither were the sensations pulsing through her body
as his fingers traced delicate patterns over her flesh, barely
making contact yet undeniable in their presence. Her eyelids
closed unbidden as her husband leaned close and kissed her
lips. "Mmm, but I'll pretend I'm still asleep if you'll continue
doing that," she murmured and opened her eyes briefly to
look into a pair of smiling light blue ones.

"I will, love, and when you're ready to awaken I can
promise you something more." A wicked smile tugged at the
corner of his mouth.

"I might just be almost awake," she whispered and turned
to accept his offer.

*   *   *

Luke dropped back into the pillows, exhausted. "Well, my love, what think you of your husband after these weeks apart?" He groaned and shuffled his arms around her, rolling onto his back and pulling her with him. She had loved him more thoroughly than any man had a right to wish for; returning his passion with like intensity.

"No different to what I thought of him before," she said lightly and kissed him on the nose.

"I see," he said frowning.

Lydia pushed herself up on an elbow. "I love him very much."

"You do? I had begun to wonder," he said with a twinkle in his eye. "Although after the last hour I believe you could convince me."

"Oh, so need convincing, do you?" She slid a hand down over his ribs towards his hips. "Shift over and I'll try to be more persuasive."

Luke laughed and rolled over again. "Don't you want to hear about my travels and your sister?"

"My sister?"

"Aye, was fit to murder me until she realised I hadn't abducted you." He stared down into incredulous brown eyes.

"You . . . met . . . my . . . sister?" She stared back at him.

"Did you not hear any of what I told you last night?"

"I thought it was a dream." She gave him a shove and sat up. "You mean you really went to the future?"

"Aye, and I was somewhat relieved to be back. 'Tis an amazing place but, love, without you—" Briefly he remembered the little matter he must attend to concerning a drunken vicar and some mislaid church records.

"What did my sister say?"

"Many things, all of which I intend to tell you just as soon as you've eaten." He prodded her ribs. "You're a mite on the spare side."

"I am not, but tell me something at least before we have breakfast." She watched his face a moment, wondering at the blueness of his eyes and the emotion she saw there. "Nothing went wrong, did it?"

"Ultimately, no. But there were several strange occurrences."

"Did you meet him . . . you know, Darwin?" she asked suddenly.

"I didn't have that pleasure, but I did try to return the ring, as I assumed you had intended to."

"You *tried* to return it? What do you mean?"

"He didn't want it."

"What!" Lydia sat back in disbelief. "He didn't want it? No, that's impossible. That mercenary bugger would grab it with both hands. Come on, Luke, tell me the truth." She grinned at him. "Truth or I might just have to tickle you."

"In that case . . . I'll tell you. He didn't want it because . . ." He paused. "Lydia, 'tis a fake." He watched her knit her brows. "'Tis a cubic zircon or some such thing."

Lydia felt her mouth drop open. "My God, the cheap bastard!"

Luke burst out laughing. "The exact words used by Sir Philip's wife. Give me time, and I shall tell you their story." He kissed her cheek then swung his legs out of bed.

Lydia watched her naked husband stride across the room and fling wide the drapes to reveal a pale winter sun, low in the sky. She got out of bed, also naked, and went to join him.

"This is the beginning of the rest of our lives," she said quietly, slipping an arm around his waist, and was rewarded by a large strong arm sliding into a similar position upon her own person.

"Aye, love. Just remind me not to let you out of my sight for very long. It seems every time I do, you end up in dire trouble." He gave her a squeeze.

"I do, don't I?" She thought a moment then asked, "What about Lord Fulford?"

"Dead." Luke said without emotion.

"Are you sure? He still scares the you-know-what out of me."

"I'm certain. I killed him."

Lydia looked at him. "You did?"

Luke nodded. "We need speak on this no further. I shall inform the authorities of what transpired in due course."

"Luke"—Lydia moved a little closer to the man at her side—"do you remember telling me about the estates in Ireland?"

"Indeed, love. What of it?"

"I, well, that is, things don't seem as friendly around here as they did. And I've never been to Ireland, and Jack's gone to London. I was wondering . . ."

Luke took her by the shoulders and held her at arm's length. "The estates are in need of my considerable management skills, aye. 'Tis a capital idea. Now kiss me, but quickly now and do not linger. I needs must ring for breakfast, or I'll not have the energy to love you again anytime soon." And he was sure she would want him again before too long. He walked to the bellpull and tugged it.

"You'd better get some clothes on just in case the maid comes in," Lydia suggested. "She'll have a fit if she sees you in the altogether. And besides, I'm a little possessive of my husband. I almost lost him, remember?"

Luke grabbed his robe and picked up Lydia's. He walked to her and slipped it over her arms, drawing it up around her shoulders. His hands slid around her waist, and he groaned when she wiggled her backside against him. She surely would drive him insane, and he would love every minute of it. He foresaw many cold baths in his future.

There was a sharp rapping at the door, and at Luke's bidding it opened. "Breakfast, Your Lordship," a hearty voice called out.

"Jack!" They both turned and spoke in unison.

Jack Palmer strode into the room followed by two men bearing what was obviously breakfast for three. "And, of course, Your Ladyship," he added, encompassing Lydia in a rib-crushing bear hug. He was a little more cautious with Luke and limited his greeting to a handshake and a shoulder slap.

"I wasn't expecting you back, leastways not so soon," Luke laughed. "Good to see you, Jack. Now let's eat."

"I was hoping you'd say that," Jack said pulling a chair to the table. "Now, tell me what's been happening. I heard rumours in London that you were missing, and I made my way north as quickly as I was able. My apologies for not getting here sooner." He looked form one to the other. "Though it appears all is well."

"Fulford is dead, Jack."

"The authorities lost track of him, but dead you say? You know this for certain?"

"I saw to the deed myself." He settled Lydia into her chair. "I suppose I shall have to alert the magistrate to that little matter. Oh, and the countess is dead, and so is her husband."

"What in hell's name have you been about?" Palmer laughed.

"Oh, I had naught to do with that. She killed him before the fire, I assume."

"Fire?"

"Believe me, Jack, there was a fire," Lydia interjected. "I almost died there."

"Fulford Manor is burned to the ground." Luke raised a hand before continuing. I assume Fulford did it, hoping we should think he died there. The body of the countess's husband would likely have been taken for his own. The countess died even as I found her, and I can only suppose that Fulford had intended she perish in the fire also." He stopped speaking for a few seconds, the awful vision of the woman's melted face appearing before his eyes. "I thank God that Lydia was able to make her way through the tunnel."

"I wouldn't have made it out though if you hadn't been there," Lydia said and hugged his arm."

"Well, I have little sympathy for that woman," Jack mumbled. He touched a hand to his face. Now, it seems you have much to tell me, and Luke, man, you have no needs worry about Fulford's demise. 'Tis my belief his majesty will be exceedingly grateful. 'Twill be but another body in the ashes. Now, what other tales have you to entertain me this merry morn?"

Luke glanced at Lydia and said, "Jack, you haven't heard the half of it. Do you have a day or two to spare?"

THIRTY - THREE

A chill wind whipped briskly across rugged cliff tops, bringing with it the damp salty air of the Atlantic Ocean and a promise of new beginnings.

Lydia smiled up into a pair of light blue eyes and felt the two arms around her tighten, pulling her close against her husband's solid form.

"'Tis breezy out today," he observed.

"It's wonderful. I'm so glad we came to Ireland."

"The estate needs some work, but the house—are you happy with the house?"

"Perfectly happy." She stared over his shoulder across the great grey expanse of water. "I wonder if we'll ever see anyone from the future again."

"You're not thinking of trying to go there, are you?" He scowled at her. "Jack put ideas in your head, didn't he?"

She laughed. "No, I've no intention of trying to go there. Everything I want and need is right here, though I'd like to see a few faces when Sir Philip announces the discovery of a letter indicating the whereabouts of an important document at Beckham. You're sure he'll know where to look?"

"I explained fully to him about the panelling and the mechanisms. He'll have no trouble making the discovery, such as it is."

Lydia sighed wistfully. "I'm glad you met my sister. She'll know for certain that I'm okay when she gets my second letter."

"Aye, 'twas a promise I gave her. A way to let her know I had returned and you were safe. Sir Philip assured me he would inform her immediately the package is unearthed."

"When will they look for it?"

"The first week of April when Beckham opens for the season. Sir Philip shall approach the . . . er National Trust with his information, and all will be revealed," he added with a slight grin.

"And the ring?"

"'Twill be found wrapped along with the letter together with a couple of trinkets I thought you might like your sister to have. Sir Philip's name shall be upon it. He assured me he would deliver the package to your sister, unopened."

"Thank you," she whispered.

"'Tis getting colder. What say you we begin our ride home? It may take some time," he added dryly and cast a glance at the two horses grazing nearby. "Your nag has but one speed." He took Lydia's hand and began walking.

"I know," Lydia said and gazed fondly at the animal, "but she brought you to me. And remember how she stood and pawed at that trapdoor? A nag she may be, but she's safe and secure, and she didn't run off after you'd nearly ridden her to death."

"She wasn't able," Luke remarked with a wry smile.

Lydia punched him on the arm. "That's not nice, and you said yourself if it hadn't been for her you probably wouldn't have found me." She squeaked as her husband pulled her against him.

"How my life turned around when you came into it I can barely comprehend." He looked into her dark eyes and kissed her once on the lips. "Come, I'll assist you to mount." Lydia grinned and threw her right leg gracefully over the cantle as he booted her up. He glanced at his wife sitting astride the nag in her breeches and jacket. "You're dressed as though to ride fast," he commented.

"Don't you say one more word about my riding speed, and anyway, I should get used to riding a little slower, given my present condition." She tipped her chin in the air and set her horse at a slow trot.

Luke nodded and picked up the reins of his own very black, very large animal. "What did you say?" The realisation of her words suddenly hit him, and he flung himself into the saddle. As though deliberately lighting their way, an almost spherical moon pondered its ascent over the hills, casting long shadows behind Lydia's mount as Luke came alongside. Unable to prevent a grin widening his mouth, he studied her face a moment. "My love? Your condition?" His gaze slid to her belly.

"You sound surprised, Your Lordship," she said haughtily. "Surely you don't need a lesson about the birds and the bees."

Luke said nothing more and allowed his horse to take the lead. He turned to watch the moonlight play on Lydia's features and noted the smug smile she wore—as she jogged along riding the slowest and dearest nag in the world.

Author's note: Richard (Dick) Turpin, alias Jack Palmer, was hanged at York tyburn April 7th 1739. However, true to his word, he was not "dropped"—he jumped.